THE
CAIRO
AFFAIR

ALSO BY OLEN STEINHAUER

An American Spy
The Nearest Exit
The Tourist

Victory Square
Liberation Movements
36 Yalta Boulevard
The Confession
The Bridge of Sighs

THE
CAIRO
AFFAIR

OLEN
STEINHAUER

CORVUS

First published in the United States in 2014 by Minotaur Books,
an imprint of St. Martin's Press.

First published in trade paperback in Great Britain in 2014 by Corvus,
an imprint of Atlantic Books Ltd.

This paperback edition published in Great Britain in 2015 by Corvus,
an imprint of Atlantic Books Ltd.

10 9 8 7 6 5 4 3 2 1

A CIP catalogue record for this book is available from the British Library.

Paperback ISBN: 978 1 78239 270 5
OME ISBN: 978 1 78239 388 7
E-book ISBN: 978 1 78239 269 9

Printed and bound by Novoprint S.A, Barcelona

Corvus
An imprint of Atlantic Books Ltd
Ormond House
26–27 Boswell Street
London
WC1N 3JZ

www.corvus-books.co.uk

For
JN & EP,
whose friendship
helps keep us sane

Acknowledgments

Thanks to Mark Milstein, who was there, for revisiting his memories of the road from Novi Sad to Vukovar for me.

COLLECTION
STRATEGIES

On February 19, 2011, two days after the Day of Revolt, the first kidnapping occurred in London, and over the following seventy-two hours similar scenes occurred in Brussels, Paris, and New York. In only three days, five politically active Libyan exiles vanished from the face of the earth: Yousef al-Juwali, Abdurrahim Zargoun, Waled Belhadj, Abdel Jalil, and Mohammed el-Keib.

Word of these abductions reached Langley along the usual paths—updates from the cousins, intercepted e-mails, news feeds, and worried reports from friends and colleagues—yet the computer algorithms somehow missed the possibility that they were part of a single event. It took a researcher in the Office of Collection Strategies and Analysis, Jibril Aziz, to see the connection. As a native Libyan who had been reared on the anxieties of his family's political exile, he was primed to find connections where others wouldn't be looking, and his enthusiasm sometimes meant that he found connections where they didn't actually exist.

Jibril worked in the Original Headquarters Building in an office the size of three, for in 1991 a contractor had altered the penitentiary-like 1950s design by bringing down two walls, finally connecting all the members of the North Africa section of Collection Strategies.

Jibril was one of fifteen analysts in that long room, each half-hidden behind cubicle walls, and occasionally they coalesced at one end to puzzle over the decade-old coffeemaker and joke about their view, which was largely obscured by sculpted rhododendron bushes, though if they stood on tiptoe they could catch sight of the busy parking lot. At thirty-three, Jibril was the youngest analyst in Collection Strategies.

Before coming across the disappearances on Tuesday, February 22, Jibril had spent his lunch break eating a meal packed by his wife, Inaya, and verifying the translation of a just-broadcast speech by Muammar Gadhafi, who had rambled for more than an hour in a diatribe against "rats and agents" and "rats and cats" and "those rats who've taken the tablets."

If they're not following Gadhafi, who would they follow? Somebody with a beard? Impossible. The people are with us, supporting us, these are our people. I've brought them up. Everywhere they are shouting slogans in support of Muammar Gadhafi.

After this depressing chore, he tried to divert himself with the Libya-related reports that had come in over the transom, searching for something—anything—to buoy his spirits. This was how he came across the disappearances, and when he read of them he felt as if a light had been turned on. Finally, something palpably real after the fantasy mutterings of a dictator. He was excited in the aesthetic way that all researchers are when they've discovered connections where previously nothing existed.

Yet there was more: There was Stumbler.

To reach his direct supervisor, Jibril had to walk down the corridor, steeling himself against the sharp aroma of disinfectant, and climb a set of noisy stairs, then wait in Jake Copeland's anteroom, often chatting with researchers from the Europe and South America sections as they all waited for a word with the boss. Because of the state of the world, the Asia section had recently begun reporting directly to Copeland's superior, so, beyond the weekly reports and biweekly meetings that brought the whole world together, no one really knew what was happening in that part of the globe.

"They're doing it," Jibril said once he'd gained access. He spread five pages across Copeland's desk, each with a photo, ten lines of bio, and the circumstances of the man's disappearance.

"It?"

"Stumbler, Jake. It's *on*."

"Slow down. Take a breath."

Jibril finally took a chair, leaned forward, and used a long brown finger to point at each of the faces. "One, two, three, four, five. All gone, just as the plan says. That's step one, by the book."

Copeland frowned, rubbing an eye with the heel of his hand.

"Check your in-box," Jibril commanded. "I sent you the memo."

Copeland pulled up his e-mail. He scrolled through Jibril's report. "Wordy, isn't it?"

"I'll wait."

Copeland sighed and began to read.

22 February 2011

MEMORANDUM
SUBJECT: Unexpected Developments in Exile Behavior, Libyan

LONDON:

On the afternoon of 19 February, after a lunch with other members of the Association of the Democratic Libyan Front (ADLF) at Momo (Heddon Street), Yousef al-Juwali took the Picadilly Line south, presumably toward his home in Clapham. According to intelligence shared by MI-5, cameras recorded that al-Juwali was approached on the train by a man in a heavy padded coat, appx 6 feet tall. Arabic features, nationality undetermined. After a brief conversation, both men disembarked at Waterloo Station and proceeded on foot to York Road, where a black Ford Explorer pulled up. Aboveground cameras noted al-Juwali's hesitation—the Explorer, it is assumed, was unexpected—but after another moment's conversation both men got into the car. Yousef al-Juwali has not been heard from since. Inquiries showed that the Explorer had been stolen the previous evening. It was recovered two days later in South Croydon, abandoned and wiped clean.

BRUSSELS:

In a similar scene, Abdurrahim Zargoun of Libyans United (LU) boarded a bus in Place du Petit Sablon with a smaller, dark-skinned man on 20 February. Zargoun, too, is now missing.

PARIS:

Waled Belhadj, an ex-founding member of the ADLF who was rumored to be building an as-yet-unnamed exile network, simply vanished on 20 February. There is no record of the circumstances leading to his disappearance.

MANHATTAN:

Yesterday (21 February), two men—Abdel Jalil and Mohammed el-Keib of the Free Libya Organization (FLO)—were seen at a wedding party on Long Island. Together, they returned by train to Manhattan, where they continued to el-Keib's apartment on the corner of Lexington and 89th. When they left an hour later they were in the company of a man whose size suggests he is the same one who approached Yousef al-Juwali in London. Appx 6 feet with North African features, dressed in an overcoat. Together, they took the subway north to the Bronx, then boarded the BX32 bus to Kingsbridge Heights. They presumably got off at one of four unobserved stops before the bus reached its terminus. They have been missing for sixteen hours.

ASSESSMENT:

To place these items in perspective, one should note that the uprising in Libya is at one of its (presumably) many peaks. Forty-eight hours before the first disappearance, in Benghazi, Libyans stepped into the streets for a "day of revolt" to voice contempt for Muammar Gadhafi's regime. The Libyan government's reaction has been to strike back in a violent crackdown. The Libyan exile community (of which I am a member) lives in a state of anxiety as the news trickles out of North Africa.

The men listed above comprise the backbone of the international anti-Gadhafi movement. Indeed, they are each named in the 2009 draft proposal for regime change composed by myself (AE/STUMBLER). If these five men are on the move, then something large is in the works.

Given the sparse evidence above, there are two possibilities:

a. Agreements. An under-the-table agreement has been reached between the various exile groups (FLO, ADLF, LU), and they are either mobilizing for a united public relations front or are preparing to enter Libya itself.

b. Agency Presence. While Stumbler was officially rejected in 2009, there remains the possibility that our own agency, or a section working independently, has decided that with the emergence of a viable active opposition within Libya the time is right to put the plan into action, beginning with the covert assembly of these primary exile figures.

Given the historic animosity between the groups mentioned above, "Agreements" is unlikely. While all three organizations share a desire for the end of Gadhafi's rule, their visions of a post-Gadhafi Libya keep them at odds, split apart by ideological rifts. Yet this would be the preferred scenario.

"Agency Presence," while potentially more likely, would be disastrous in this analyst's opinion. Stumbler began life in this office, but it was a product of a particular time, and with the emergence of an Arab Spring that time has passed. The practical objections brought up to the original plan remain, and now, with reports of Libyans dying in Benghazi in order to oust their dictator, any incursion by the United States (either by American soldiers or leaders handpicked by the U.S. from the exile population) would be rightly viewed as a hijacking of Libya's revolution, giving increased credibility to the Gadhafi regime and delegitimizing any pro-West government that would follow.

Jibril Aziz
OCSA

Jake Copeland leaned back, hoping to relieve a backache that had been troubling him for nearly a week. Backaches and hemorrhoids—that was how he described his job at parties when his friends asked with arched brows what life in intelligence was like. He'd sat at this desk for two years, riding in with the new administration, and had during that time watched many researchers run into his office with wild, unsubstantiated theories. Jibril was no more levelheaded than any of them, but he was smart and committed, and unlike most OCSA researchers he had Agency field experience. Yet as the child of Libyan exiles Jibril also had a personal stake in the region and sometimes couldn't see past his emotions. And now this. "Stumbler, huh?"

"What have I been saying? They're putting Stumbler into motion."

"And when you say *they*—"

"I mean *we*. And it's morally abhorrent."

"It was your plan, Jibril."

"And two years ago it would have been the right thing to do. Not now. Not anymore."

Copeland liked Jibril. The man was obsessed; he was short-sighted. Yet his plans and schemes usually contained a nugget of glory, and it was Copeland's job to dig it out. Working with Jibril Aziz was seldom boring.

"If, as you suggest, we *are* behind this, then why are you bringing it to me?"

"So you can stop them. Stop us."

"You really think I have that kind of pull?"

The younger man hesitated. "Then send me in."

"Into Libya? No way. No war zones for you."

Jibril was rash, but he wasn't stupid. "You're right, Jake. I don't have anything here. Nothing solid. But there's *something*. You agree?"

"Certainly there's something. I'm not saying there isn't. But if—"

"So I need to look into it."

Copeland chewed his lower lip, shifting to relieve his back of a sudden shooting pain. "Go on."

"I'll need authorization to travel."

"You're not flying into Tripoli."

"Budapest."

"Budapest?"

Jibril nodded. "Just an interview. A quick talk, and then I'll tell you one way or the other."

"Can I ask who you're interviewing?"

"Our deputy consul, Emmett Kohl."

"I'm afraid to ask how he connects to this."

"Don't you trust me, Jake?"

Copeland trusted Jibril, but he also knew when his employees were trying to manipulate him. So he listened with a wary ear as Jibril stepped back into time, bringing them back to Stumbler and the route it had taken through embassies and government offices before being returned to them, rejected. Jibril was stretching to find connections, but he was doing it for Copeland's benefit, to make his acquiescence more bureaucratically defensible. It was, as Jibril put it more than once, just another research trip. Jake approved those on a daily basis. Finally, Copeland said, "Okay. I'll write out an authorization and ask Travel for a ticket."

"I'd rather take care of that myself."

"Don't trust Travel?"

Jibril scratched at the side of his nose. "Travel will put it in my file. There's no reason for that, not at this point. I'd like a week off. Maybe more, depending on what I find."

"You're paying for this out of your own pocket?"

"I'll save my receipts. Research can reimburse me later."

"If you're lucky," Copeland said as it occurred to him that this wasn't merely a way to keep his trip secret; it was yet another way to make his deal entirely acceptable. If Jibril caused trouble, he was just a wayward employee on vacation. Copeland remained blameless.

So he agreed to the time off, beginning in two days, and wrote out a memo to this effect for Jibril to pass on to his secretary. "Thank you, sir," Jibril said, and Copeland wondered when he'd last heard "sir" from this man's lips. Ever?

He saw Jibril again that afternoon, the young man's coat folded over a forearm as he headed out to the parking lot. They nodded at each other, just a nod, but he could see that Jibril was walking on air. He was on the move again. Not all researchers felt this way, but Jibril had once known the dirt and grime of fieldwork; unlike many of his colleagues, he'd cut his teeth by seducing foreign nationals into betraying their own countries. Once you've learned how to do that to people, you develop a taste for deception, and drab office walls, carpeted cubicle dividers, and pulsing computer monitors feel like a poor substitute for living. So does honesty.

PART I

A DISLOYAL WIFE

Sophie

———

1

Twenty years ago, before their trips became political, Sophie and Emmett honeymooned in Eastern Europe. Their parents questioned this choice, but Harvard had taught them to care about what happened on the other side of the planet, and from the TV rooms in their dorms they'd watched the crumbling of the USSR with the kind of excitement that hadn't really been their due. They had watched with the erroneous feeling that they, along with Ronald Reagan, had chipped away at the foundations of the corrupt Soviet monolith. By the time they married in 1991, both only twenty-two, it felt like time for a victory lap.

Unlike Emmett, Sophie had never been to Europe, and she'd longed to see those Left Bank Paris cafés she'd read so much about. "But *this* is where history's happening," Emmett told her. "It's the less traveled road." From early on in their relationship, Sophie had learned that life was more interesting when she took on Emmett's enthusiasms, so she didn't bother resisting.

They waited until September to avoid the August tourist crush, gingerly beginning their trip with four days in Vienna, that arid city of wedding-cake buildings and museums. Cool but polite Austrians filled the streets, heading down broad avenues and cobblestone walkways, all preoccupied by things more important than gawking American tourists. Dutifully, Sophie lugged her *Lonely Planet* as they visited the Stephansdom and Hofburg, the Kunsthalle, and the cafés Central and Sacher, Emmett talking of Graham Greene and the filming of *The Third Man,* which he'd apparently researched just before their trip. "Can you imagine how this place looked just after the war?" he asked at the Sacher on their final Viennese afternoon. He was clutching a foot-tall beer, gazing out the café window. "They were decimated. Living like rats. Disease and starvation."

As she looked out at shining BMWs and Mercedeses crawling past the imposing rear of the State Opera House, she couldn't imagine this at all, and she wondered—not for the first time—if she was lacking in the kind of imagination that her husband took for granted. Enthusiasm and imagination. She measured him with a long look. Boyish face and round, hazel eyes. A lock of hair splashed across his forehead. *Beautiful,* she thought as she fingered her still unfamiliar wedding band. This was the man she was going to spend the rest of her life with.

He turned from the window, shaking his head, then caught sight of her face. "Hey. What's wrong?"

She wiped away tears, smiling, then gripped his fingers so tightly that her wedding ring pinched the soft skin of her finger. She pulled him closer and whispered, "Let's go back to the room."

He paid the bill, fumbling with Austrian marks. *Enthusiasm, imagination, and commitment*—these were the qualities she most loved in Emmett Kohl, because they were the very things she felt she lacked. Harvard had taught her to question everything, and she had taken up that challenge, growing aptly disillusioned by both left and right, so uncommitted to either that when Emmett began his mini-lectures on history or foreign relations, she just sat and listened, less in awe of his facts than in awe of his belief. It struck her that this was what adulthood was about—belief. What did Sophie believe in? She wasn't sure. Compared to him, she was only half an adult. With him, she hoped, she might grow into something better.

While among historical artifacts and exotic languages she always felt inferior to her new husband, in bed their roles were reversed, so whenever the insecurity overcame her she would draw him there. Emmett, delighted to be used this way, never thought to wonder at the timing of her sexual urges. He was beautiful and smart but woe-fully inexperienced, whereas she had learned the etiquette of the sheets from a drummer in a punk band, a French history teacher's assistant, and, over the space of a single experimental weekend, a girl-friend from Virginia who had come to visit her in Boston.

So when they returned to their hotel room, hand in hand, and she helped him out of his clothes and let him watch, fingertips rattling against the bedspread, as she stripped, she felt whole again. She was the girl who believed in nothing, giving a little show for the boy who believed in everything. Yet by the time they were tangled together beneath the sheets, flesh against flesh, she realized that she was wrong. She did believe in something. She believed in Emmett Kohl.

The next morning they boarded the train to Prague, and not even the filthy car with the broken, stinking toilet deterred her. Instead, it filled her with the illusion that they were engaged in *real* travel, cutting-edge travel. "This is what the rest of the world looks like," Emmett said with a smile as he surveyed the morose, nervous Czechs clutching bags stuffed with contraband cigarettes, alcohol, and other luxuries marked for resale back home. When, at the border, the guards removed an old woman and two young men who quietly watched the train leave them behind, Sophie was filled with feelings of authenticity.

She told herself to keep her eyes and ears open. She told herself to absorb it all.

The dilapidated fairy-tale architecture of Prague buoyed them, and they drank fifty-cent beers in underground taverns lit with candles. Sophie tried to put words to her excitement, the magnitude of a small-town girl ending up here, of all places. She was the child of a Virginia lumber merchant, her travels limited to the height and breadth of the East Coast, and now she was an educated woman, married, wandering the Eastern Bloc. This dislocation stunned her when she thought about it, yet when she tried to explain it to her husband her words felt inadequate. Emmett had always been the verbal one, and when he smiled and held her hand and told her he understood she wondered if he was patronizing her. "Stick with me, kid," he said in his best Bogart.

On their third day, he bought her a miniature bust of Lenin, and they laughed about it as they walked the crowded Charles Bridge between statues of Czech kings looking down on them in the stagnant summer heat. They were a little drunk, giggling about the Lenin in her hand. She rocked it back and forth and used it the way a ventriloquist would. Emmett's face got very pink under the sun—years later, she would remember that.

Then there was the boy.

He appeared out of nowhere, seven or eight years old, emerging from between all the other anonymous tourists, silent at Sophie's elbow. Suddenly, he had her Lenin in his hands. He was so quick. He bolted around legs and past an artist dabbing at an easel to the edge of the bridge, and Sophie feared he was going to leap over. Emmett started moving toward the boy, and then they saw the bust again, over the boy's head. He hurtled it into the air—it rose and fell.

"Little *shit*," Emmett muttered, and when Sophie caught up to him and looked down at the river, there was no sign of her little Lenin. The boy was gone. Afterward, on the walk back to the hotel, she was overcome by the feeling that she and Emmett were being made fools of. It followed her the rest of the trip, on to Budapest and during their unexpected excursion to Yugoslavia, and even after they returned to Boston. Twenty years later, she still hadn't been able to shake that feeling.

2

Her first thought upon arriving at Chez Daniel on the evening of March 2, 2011, was that her husband was looking very good. She didn't have this thought often, but it was less an insult to Emmett than an indictment against herself, and the ways in which twenty years of marriage can blind you to your partner's virtues. She suspected that he saw her the same way, but she hoped he at least had moments like this, where warmth and pleasure filled her at the sight of his eternally youthful face and the thought that, *Yes, this one's mine.* It didn't matter how brief they were, or how they might be followed by something terrible—those bursts of attraction could sustain her for months.

Chez Daniel, like most decent French restaurants—even French restaurants in Hungary—was cramped, casual, and a bit frantic. Simple tablecloths, excellent food. She joined him at a table by the beige wall beneath framed sepia scenes of the dirty and cracked Budapest streets that made for hard walking but wonderfully moody pictures. As they waited for the wine, Emmett straightened the utensils on either side of his plate and asked how her day had been.

"Glenda," she said. "Four hours with Glenda at the Gellért Baths. Steam, massages, and too many Cosmopolitans. What do you think?"

He'd heard often enough about the Wednesday routine she'd been roped into by the wife of his boss, Consul General Raymond Bennett.

Always the Gellért Hotel, where Sophie and Emmett had spent part of their honeymoon, back when even students could afford its Habsburg elegance. Emmett said, "Anything exciting in her life?"

"Problems with Hungarians, naturally."

"Naturally."

"I tell her to ask Ray to put in for a transfer, but she pretends it's beyond her means."

"How about you?" he asked.

"Am I anti-Hungarian, too?"

"How are you doing here?"

Sophie leaned closer, as if she hadn't heard. It wasn't a question she posed to herself often, so she had to take a moment. They'd lived for six months in Budapest, where Emmett was a deputy consul. Last year, their home had been Cairo—Hosni Mubarak's Cairo. Two years before that, it had been Paris. In some ways, the cities blended in her memory—each was a blur of social functions and brief friendships and obscure rituals to be learned and then forgotten, each accompanied by its own menagerie of problems. Paris had been fun, but Cairo had not.

In Cairo, Emmett had been irritable and on edge—a backfiring car would make him stumble—and he would return from the office itching for a fight. Sophie—maybe in reaction, maybe not—had built a new life for herself, constructed of lies.

The good news was that Cairo had turned out to be a phase, for once they arrived in Hungary the air cleared. Emmett reverted to the man she had decided to spend her life with twenty years ago, and she let go of the puerile intoxication of deceit, her secrets still safely kept. In Budapest, they were adults again.

Emmett was waiting for an answer. She shrugged. "How can I not be happy? A lady of leisure. I'm living the dream."

He nodded, as if it were the answer he'd expected—as if he'd known she would lie. Because the irony was that, of the three cities they had called home, Cairo was the only one she would have returned to in a second, if given the chance. There, she had found something liberating in the streets, the noise and traffic jams and odors.

She had learned how to move with a little more grace, to find joy in decorating the apartment with star clusters and flowers of the blue Egyptian water lily; she took delight in the particular melody of Arabic, the predictability of daily prayers, and the investigation of strange, new foods. She also discovered an unexpected pleasure in the act of betrayal itself.

But was it really a lie? Was she unhappy in Budapest?

No. She was forty-two years old, which was old enough to know good fortune when it looked her in the eye. With the help of L'Oréal, she'd held on to her looks, and a bout of high blood pressure a few years ago had been tempered by a remarkable French diet. They were not poor; they traveled extensively. While there were moments when she regretted the path her life had taken—at Harvard, she had aspired to academia or policy planning, and one winter day in Paris a French doctor had explained after her second miscarriage that children would not be part of her future—she always stepped back to scold herself. She might be sometimes bored, but adulthood, when well maintained, was supposed to be dull. Regretting a life of leisure was childishness.

Yet at nights she still lay awake in the gloom of their bedroom, wondering if anyone would notice if she hopped a plane back to Egypt and just disappeared, before remembering that her Cairo, the one she loved, no longer existed.

She and Emmett had been in Hungary five months when, in January, Egyptian activists had called for protests against poverty, unemployment, and corruption, and by the end of the month, on January 25, they'd had a "day of rage" that grew until the whole city had become one enormous demonstration with its epicenter in Tahrir Square, where Sophie would once go to drink tea.

On February 11, less than a month before their dinner at Chez Daniel, Hosni Mubarak had stepped down after thirty years in power. He wasn't alone. A month before that, Tunisia's autocrat had fled, and as Sophie and Emmett waited for their wine a full-scale civil war was spreading through Libya, westward from Benghazi toward Tripoli. The pundits were calling it the Arab Spring. She had health, wealth, and a measure of beauty, as well as interesting times to live in.

"Any fresh news from Libya?" she asked.

He leaned back, hands opening, for this was their perpetual subject. Emmett had spent an enormous amount of time watching CNN and shouting at the screen for the Libyan revolutionaries to advance on Tripoli, as if he were watching a football game, as if he were a much younger man who hadn't already witnessed civil war. "Well, we're expecting word soon from the Libyan Transitional Council—they'll be declaring themselves Libya's official representative. We've had a few days of EU sanctions against Gadhafi, but it'll be a while before they have any effect. The rebels are doing well—they're holding onto Zawiyah, just west of the capital." He shrugged. "The question is, when are we going to get off our asses and drop a few bombs on Tripoli?"

"Soon," she said hopefully. He had brought her over to the opinion that with a few bombs Muammar Gadhafi and his legions would fold within days, and that there would be no need for foreign troops to step in and, as Emmett put it, *soil their revolution.* "Is that it?" she asked.

"All we've heard."

"I mean you. How was your day?"

The wine arrived, and the waiter poured a little into Emmett's glass for approval. Sophie ordered fresh tagliatelle with porcini mushrooms, while Emmett asked for a steak, well done. Once the waiter was gone, she said, "Well?"

"Well, what?"

"Your day."

"Right," he said, as if he'd forgotten. "Not as exciting as yours. Work-wise, at least."

"And otherwise?"

"I got a call from Cairo."

It was a significant statement—at least, Emmett had meant it to be—but Sophie felt lost. "Someone we know?"

"Stan Bertolli."

She heard herself inhale through her nose and wondered if he had heard it, too. "How's Stan?"

"Not well, apparently."

"What's wrong?"

Emmett took his glass by the stem and regarded the wine carefully. "He tells me he's in love."

"Good for him."

"Apparently not. Apparently, the woman he's in love with is married."

"You're right," she said, forcing her voice to flatline. The air seemed to go out of the room. Was this really happening? She'd imagined it before, of course, but never in a French restaurant. She said, "That's not good."

He took a breath, sipped his wine, then set it on the table. The whole time, his eyes remained fixed on the deep red inside the glass. Finally, quietly, he said, "Were you ever going to tell me?"

This, too, was not how she'd imagined it. She floundered for an answer, and her first thought was a lie: *Of course I was.* Before transforming the thought into speech, though, she realized that she wouldn't have told him, not ever.

She considered going on the defensive and reminding him of how he had been in Cairo, how he had treated her as if she had been a perpetual obstacle. How he had pushed her away until, looking for something, anything, to complement her feelings of liberation she finally gave in to Stan's approaches. Only partly true, but it might have been enough to satisfy him.

She said, "Of course I was going to tell you."

"When?"

"When I got up the courage. When enough time had passed."

"So we're talking about years."

"Probably."

Chewing the inside of his cheek, Emmett looked past her at other tables, perhaps worried that they all knew he was a cuckold, and the corners of his eyes crinkled in thought.

What was there to think about? He'd had all day, but he still hadn't decided, for this wasn't only about an affair—it was about Emmett Kohl, and what kind of man he wanted to be. She knew him all too well.

One kind of man would kick her out of his life, would rage and throw his glass at her. But that wasn't him. He would have had his "little shit" moment as soon as he hung up the telephone; his day of rage was over. He needed something that could show off his anger without forcing him to break character or descend into cliché—it was a tricky assignment.

She said, "It's over. If that helps."

"Not really."

"Do you remember how you were in Cairo?"

His damp eyes were back on her, brow twitching. "You're not going to twist this into my fault, are you?"

She looked down at her glass, which she still hadn't touched. He knew very well how he had been in Cairo, but he wasn't interested in drawing a connection between that and her infidelity. Were she him, she would have felt the same way.

He said, "Do you love him?"

"No."

"Did you love him?"

"For a week I thought I might, but I was wrong."

"Were you thinking about a divorce?"

She frowned, almost shocked by the use of a word that she had never considered. "God. No. Never. You're . . ." She hesitated, then lowered her voice, pushing a hand across the table in his direction. "You're the best thing that ever happened to me, Emmett."

He didn't even acknowledge her hand. "Then . . . *why?*"

Anyone who's committed adultery envisions this moment, plots it out and works up a rough draft of a speech that, she imagined, will cut through the fog with some ironclad defense of the indefensible. Sitting there, though, staring at his wounded face, she couldn't remember any of it, and she found herself grasping for words. Yet all that came to her was hackneyed lines, as if she were reading from a script. But they were both doing that, weren't they? "I was lonely, Emmett. Simple as that."

"Who else knew?"

"What?"

"Who else knew about this?"

She pulled back her untouched hand. He was being petty now, as if it truly mattered whether or not someone knew of his bruised pride. But she could give him that. "No one," she lied.

He nodded, but didn't look relieved.

The food came, giving them time to regroup, and as she ate, cheeks hot and hand trembling, she reflected on how betrayed he had to feel. Hadn't she known from the beginning that she would do this to him? Hadn't she seen all this coming? Not really, for in Cairo she'd gone with the moment. In Cairo she'd been stupid.

Daniel had done an excellent job with her tagliatelle, perfectly tender, and there was a pepper sauce on Emmett's steak that smelled divine. Emmett began to stab halfheartedly at his meat. The sight made her want to cry. She said, "What was it? In Cairo."

He looked up—no exasperation, just simple confusion.

"You were a mess there. Me, too, I know, but you . . . well, you were impossible to live with. Paris was fine, and here. But in Cairo you were a different man."

"So you *are* trying to blame me," he said. Coldly.

"I just want to know what was on your back in Cairo."

"It doesn't matter," he said as he lifted a bite to his mouth. He delivered it. It was like a punctuation mark, that move.

"Cairo was bad from the start," she went on, forcing the words out. "Not for me. No—I loved it. But you changed there, and you never told me anything."

"So you fucked Stan."

"Yes, I fucked Stan. But that doesn't change the fact that you became someone else there, and once we left Cairo you returned to your old self."

He chewed, staring through her.

"I'm not trying to start a fight, Emmett. I *like* the man you are now. I love him. I didn't like the man you were there. So let's get it out in the open. What was going on in Cairo?"

As he took another bite, still staring, something occurred to her.

"Were *you* having an affair?"

He sighed, disappointed by her stupidity.

"Then what was it?"

He still watched so coldly, but she could see his barriers breaking down. It was in the rhythm of his chewing, the way it slowed.

"Come on, Emmett. You can't keep it a secret forever."

He swallowed, his wrist on the edge of the table, his fork holding a fresh triangle of beef a few inches above his plate. He said, "Remember Novi Sad?"

There it was. Yugoslavia, twenty years ago. *I saved you, Sophie. This is how you pay me back?* She nodded.

"Zora?" he asked.

"Zora Balašević," she said, her throat now dry.

"Zora was in Cairo."

She knew this, of course, but said, "Cairo?"

"Working at the Serbian embassy. BIA—one of their spies. Not long after we arrived, she got in touch. Ran into me on the street." He paused, finally putting down his fork. "I was pleased to see her. You remember—despite everything, we got along well in the end. We went to a café, reminiscing about the good stuff, careful to avoid the rest, and then it came. She wanted me to give her information."

To breathe properly, Sophie had to leave her mouth open. This wasn't what she'd expected him to say. Her sinuses were closing up. She said, "Well, that's forward."

"Isn't it?" he said, smiling, not noticing anything. Briefly, he was in his story, looking just like her old husband. "I said no, so she put her cards on the table. She blackmailed me."

She didn't have to ask what Zora had blackmailed him with, and at that moment she had a flash of it: A filthy leg in a black army boot, spastic, kicking at the dirt of a basement. "The bitch," she snapped, but she could feel herself reddening. It was so hot.

"You know what would happen if that came out. I'd never work in the diplomatic corps again. Ever. But I still said no."

She was burning up. She grabbed the collar of her blouse and fanned it, drawing cool air down her shoulders. "Good for you," she managed.

He shrugged, modest. "My mistake was that I didn't report it."

She tried to empty herself of all the heat in a long exhale. "You could have. You could've told Harry, or even Stan."

"Sure, but I didn't know that then. I'd been at the embassy less than a week. I didn't know anything about those guys. Neither of us did. By the time I realized my mistake, it was too late. It would've looked like I'd been covering it up."

He wanted affirmation, so she said, "I suppose you're right."

"Living under that cloud certainly didn't help my mood. But that didn't compare to later, when the whole thing came back to bite me."

She waited.

"About a year ago, last March, Stan started asking questions. Not very subtle, your Stan." A faint smile. "It turned out that loose information had been floating around, intel that originated in Cairo— intel I'd had access to. I was under investigation for most of last year."

She moved back in time, remembering the fights, the moods, the drinking, the anger. It all played differently now. "Why didn't you tell me?"

That faint smile returned. "I didn't want to burden you," he said. "You were having such a good time. Of course, I didn't know *why* you were so happy, but . . ." A shrug.

She didn't know how he could have said that without hatred, but he had. She felt a hard knot in her chest.

He said, "It turned out that Stan already knew about Zora. His guys had been watching me when we first got there—normal vetting procedure. He'd seen me with her, and when the compromised intel came to his attention he followed up on it. So I told him what happened. I told him what she tried to do, and I told him that I refused."

"Did you tell him about . . . ?"

"I left the blackmail a mystery, and he finally let that go. He never asked you?"

She shook her head, but she wasn't sure. Maybe he had.

"Anyway, I told him that Zora hadn't tried again. I never even saw her after that. But he didn't believe me. He sat me down for more talks, trying to trip me up on my story. Eventually, he brought Harry into it. Stan showed him his evidence, but no one ever showed it to me. I was lucky—Harry wanted to believe me. Still, he couldn't afford to have me around anymore, so he suggested I put in for a transfer. Make me someone else's problem, I suppose."

"Stan never told me any of this," she said, but it was getting harder to find air, and the last word barely made it out.

"Secrets are his game, aren't they?"

Silence fell between them, and Emmett returned to his steak.

People talk of conflicting emotions as if they're a daily occurrence, but at that moment Sophie felt as if it were the first time she'd experienced them. Honesty pulled from one side, while the other side, the one that was motivated by self-preservation, held a tighter grip. She stared at her pasta, knowing she wouldn't be able to taste it anymore, maybe not even be able to keep it down, and it occurred to her that maybe her husband deserved to know. To *really* know. Exactly what kind of a woman he was married to. It would be the end, of course. The end of everything. Yet when she thought back to their honeymoon, it was obvious that he was the one person on the planet who deserved to know it all. He was probably the only person who could understand.

She was still trying to decide when the restaurant was filled with a woman's scream. It came from the table behind her. She began to turn to get a look at the woman, but instead saw what the scream had been about. It was at their table, where their waiter should have been standing, a large man—bald, sweating, in a long, cheap overcoat. Upon looking at him, she understood why their neighbor had screamed, for she had the same impulse herself. He was all muscle—not tall but wide—with muddy blue prison tattoos creeping out from under his collar. A man of absolute violence, like those tracksuited Balkan mafiosi she occasionally saw in overpriced bars. He wasn't looking at her, though, but at Emmett, and he was holding a pistol in his hairy hand.

It was the first time she'd ever seen a gun in a restaurant. She'd seen hunting rifles disassembled in her childhood living room, then put to use outdoors when her father went hunting for red stag deer in West Virginia. She once saw a pistol hanging from inside a jacket in their Cairo kitchen when an agent of one of the security services had come to have a talk with Emmett. In Yugoslavia, they had been on soldiers and militiamen and in one grimy kitchen that still sometimes appeared in her dreams, but she had never seen one in a restaurant. Now she had, and the pistol—a modern-looking one, slide-action— was pointed directly at her husband.

"Emmett Kohl," the man said with a strong accent, but it wasn't a Hungarian accent. It was something Sophie couldn't place.

Emmett just stared at him, hands flat on either side of his plate. She couldn't tell if he recognized the man, so before she had a chance to think through the stupidity of her actions she said, "Who are you?"

The man turned to her, though his pistol remained on Emmett. He frowned, as if she were an unexpected variable in an equation he'd spent weeks calculating. Then he turned back to Emmett and said, "I here for you."

Mute, Emmett shook his head.

Behind the man, the restaurant was clearing out. It was surprising how quietly so many people could retreat, the only sound a low *rhubarb-rhubarb* rumbling through the place. Men were snatching phones from their tables and holding women by the elbows, heading toward the door. They crouched as they walked. She hoped that at least one of them was calling the police. A waitress stood by the wall, tray against her hip, confused.

Sophie said, "Why are you here?"

Again, the look, and this time she could read irritation in his features. Instead of answering, he glanced at the gold wristwatch on his free hand and muttered something in a language she didn't recognize. Something sharp, like a curse. He looked back at Emmett and, his arm stiffening, pulled the trigger.

Later, she would hate herself for staring at the gunman rather than at her husband. She should have been looking at Emmett, giving him a final moment of commiseration, of tenderness, of love. But she hadn't been, because she hadn't expected this. Despite all the evidence to the contrary, she hadn't actually expected the man to shoot

Emmett twice, once in the chest and, after a step forward, once through the nose, the explosion of each shot cracking her ears. She supposed it was because she was still dealing with the shock of Zora Balašević, of Stan, and the novelty of a gun in a restaurant. It was so much to deal with that she couldn't have expected more novelty to come so quickly. Not that night.

Yet there it was. She turned to see Emmett leaned back against the wall, his hazel, bloodshot eyes open but unfocused, sliding out of his chair, his face unrecognizable, blood and organic matter splashed across the wall and a sepia city scene. Screams made the restaurant noisy again, but she didn't look around. She just stared at Emmett as his body slid down, disappearing gradually behind the table and his plate of half-eaten steak. She didn't even notice that the gunman had jogged out of the restaurant, pushing past the remaining witnesses— this was something she would be told later.

For the moment, it was just Sophie, the table with their wine and blood-spattered food, and Emmett slipping away. His chest disappeared, then his shoulders, his chin pressed down against the knot of his tie, then his face. The gory face that was missing the short, almost pug nose that, more than his hair or his clothes, always defined her husband's look. The table rocked as he fell off the chair, leaving a mess on the wall. She didn't hear him hit because her ears were ringing from the gunshots, and she felt as if she were going to vomit. There was more screaming and the distant sound of weeping, but she soon learned that all of it was coming from herself.

3

———◆———

She had never imagined that it would be like this. Not that she'd
ever imagined *this*, but whenever she'd imagined something terrible happening before her eyes, her imagination would take in the
event itself, that first taste of horror, and then ... *cut*: to the next
day, or the next week. Her brain worked like a film editor, even dic-
ing up actual memories, jump-cutting over hours, balking at the
grimy minutes and hours that stretched between the initial shock and
the final passing out, when a night's sleep would come along to wash
away a little of the metallic taste of disaster.

Yet it became abundantly clear that this in-between time *was* the
event. The adrenaline and the endless replay of her husband's pink
bits splattering across the wallpaper, the contradictory calm voice of
some restaurant customer, an American who thought she could re-
late to Sophie, the barely intelligible grunts of Hungarian policemen
who seemed, more than anything else, baffled by what their role was
supposed to be, and then the trained, cool, faux-comforting voice of
a skinny, pink-cheeked young man from the embassy who arrived
with a doctor and introduced himself as Gerry Davis. Gerry Davis
told her that the doctor was going to take a look at her—nothing to
worry about—and maybe give her a little something to take the edge
off. They brought her to an empty table in another room so she
wouldn't have to see her husband anymore. Someone gave her a real

silk handkerchief that smelled faintly of vinegar. She focused for a long time on a cigarette burn in the tablecloth. This was *all* the event.

Gerry Davis said, "Do you have a phone?"

"Excuse me?"

"A cell phone. If you do, you might want to turn it off."

She took out her iPhone and stared at it, unsure of what to do. Gerry Davis took it from her, powered it down, and handed it back. "It's better that way. For the moment, at least."

When Gerry Davis explained that he was going to take her back to her apartment, where there would be someone else from the embassy to stay the night with her, she realized that he was smart, this Gerry Davis. Though he knew her future had just evaporated, he was giving her precise, manageable plans to carry her forward. Until the next day, at least.

Later, she would ask herself how she could make such judgments—that Gerry Davis was smart, that the policemen didn't know what to do with themselves, and that she'd misjudged the parameters of a tragic event. After what she'd been through, she shouldn't have been able to see past her own fingertips, but she could see clearly to the end of the room where Daniel himself, in a smeared apron, was giving a statement to a uniformed cop. Why were her eyes so clear and her senses still acute?

One of the policemen, an older Hungarian in civilian clothes, introduced himself as Andras Something and squatted in front of her chair. In a heavy accent, he asked a few questions: Did she recognize the killer? Had he said anything that might explain why he had come tonight? She tried to give him useful answers, but in the midst of her words she began to spill too much information; she couldn't help herself. "Beforehand, we were talking, Emmett and me. About the affair I had. He was hurt, really hurt. I don't know—maybe this had something to do with it . . . do you think? I mean, it lasted so long, right under his nose. Do you think that maybe—"

She felt a hand on her shoulder. Gerry Davis said, "I think that's enough for now."

Andras Something climbed to his feet, knees cracking like a log fire, and thanked her for her help. Then Gerry Davis drove her home, across the Chain Bridge, away from the clotted cityscape of Pest into the greener Buda hills, keeping his Ford full of chatter about what to expect, what the name of her babysitter would be, and who she should expect to hear from tomorrow. Anything and everything to keep from touching on an hour ago. As he spoke, though, she heard the killer's voice: *I here for you.*

Fiona Vale was already in the apartment when they arrived. She was in her fifties, from Nebraska, and told Sophie that she knew Emmett well. She knew better than to start offering assessments of her husband—no "a lovely man" or "he will be missed." Just the fact that she knew him, brief condolences, and a plate of chicken breast, potatoes, and grilled asparagus that she had picked up on her way over. Sophie was famished, but she didn't touch the food at first. She headed toward the liquor cabinet. Predicting everything, Fiona cut her off and asked what she wanted to drink. "Take a load off. I've got this."

Gerry Davis had left by then, and soon they were settled in the quiet living room with glasses of Emmett's Jim Beam. Before they could speak again, the kitchen phone rang, and Fiona went to get it. She reappeared after a moment. "It's Glenda Bennett—you up to talking?"

Sophie heard: *Rhubarb-rhubarb.*

"Sure," she told Fiona Vale.

She heard: *Bang!* Then: *Bang!* A wet sound.

"Oh my God, Sophie. Oh my God. Ray just told me."

She soon found herself trying to calm Glenda; her friend was hysterical.

"I'm coming over, Sophie. I'm calling the taxi right now."

"No, Glen. Don't. I've got someone looking after me, and I just want to sleep now. Really."

"But it's not right. I just. *Sophie.*"

"Tomorrow. Tomorrow you'll come over and spend a couple hours listening to me, okay? Right now, I'm exhausted."

"Well, let me do *something*," Glenda said, and from the background came her husband's voice.

"Let me get to sleep."

"Okay," she said, then: "Just a sec. Ray wants the phone."

Raymond Bennett, consul general, came on. "Sophie, I know you want to get some rest. I only want you to know how shocked we are by this, and that we're here for you. Anything you need."

"Thank you, Ray."

"This is being investigated from the top. We're going to have answers soon. Who's there with you?"

"Fiona Vale."

"Fee's great. Ask her for anything you need, and if there's something she can't take care of don't hesitate to call."

"Thanks, Ray. I should probably just go to sleep."

"Absolutely. Good night, then."

But even after the whisky, a few bites of the chicken and vegetables, another whisky with Fiona, and a hot shower followed by Fiona tucking her into bed at one in the morning—even after all that, she lay in the darkness, staring. She saw it again, the endless loop of *I here for you, rhubarb-rhubarb,* and *bang!* She also heard every early morning noise: cars passing on the street, a dog in pain somewhere, people laughing on their way home from bars, and the fan of Emmett's laptop on his side of her now-enormous bed—that last sound was the worst.

She got up and closed the computer, waiting the extra minute until the fan shut off, then heard more street noises—but they were in her head. They were Cairo voices, the jumble of melodic arguments and the muezzins' calls to prayer that she remembered from that dusty hotel room in Dokki where she and Stan, after their groping, lay sweaty and exhausted. She, outlining her plans for the rest of the day. He, listening with odd satisfaction to the unimaginative details of her life, for she never shared the imaginative ones.

Then it came. It wasn't unexpected, but it still took her off guard, the cold shiver running from head to heel, the twist in her stomach, and then the weeping. It leapt upon her, loud and wet and very messy. It was real, and for a moment she believed it was the most real thing she had done in her life.

She would never see him again. She would never sit across from him at dinner, never touch him or worry over his inability to match his own clothes. She would never listen to his soft snores, and she would never feel the length and weight of his body on hers. They had tapered off over the last years, sex coming along rarely, but she'd always thought that they were going through a phase from which they would inevitably emerge, just as they had emerged from Cairo intact—or mostly intact. There would be no more phases, no more of the rhythms of living with a man who, for twenty years, had been the central figure in her life.

There was a hole in her stomach and an empty space in her skull that nothing and no one, certainly not Stan, would ever be able to fill. And guilt. So much damned guilt.

She wasn't sure how long this went on. As she gradually recovered she realized that her pillow was soaking wet, so she took Emmett's pillow, and that brought on fresh tears. Eventually, she went to the bathroom for tissues and stared into the mirror, wiping at her splotchy face. She hardly even saw herself, but the reflection helped. The tears began to dry. She took a breath.

He's dead.

It's your fault.

It's Stan's fault.

In that moment this seemed reasonable—that her yearlong affair had pulled that trigger—though she knew it wasn't true. Her affair only ensured that Emmett's final moments would be miserable.

Stan had called Emmett. Actually called him, months afterward, to announce his love for her. Stan had always been old-fashioned, but Jesus.

She returned to the bedroom, flipped on the bedside lamp, and took out her phone. She turned it on, watching the start-up screen until it lit up with messages: six missed calls, two from Glenda, one from Ray, and one each from other friends, Mary, Tracey, and Anita. She ignored the voice mails and went through her contacts until she found Stan. Two rings and, as always, he was a man who answered with identification, even at three in the morning: "Stan Bertolli." Voice achingly familiar.

"Sophie Kohl," she said, then listened to his breathing.

Finally, he said, "Wow. Sophie. It's good to hear your voice."

"You talked to Emmett today."

"No."

The outright *no* threw her. "When did you last talk to Emmett?"

"Never—I mean, not since you left. Are you all right?"

"Shouldn't I be? Yes, I . . . well, no. Not right now. But I was angry."

"Angry?"

"I was, but not now. Emmett's dead."

"Emmett's . . . *what*?"

"We were having dinner and a man walked into the restaurant and shot him in the head and the chest."

"Oh, God. Sophie. I'm sorry, I—" He paused. "What can I do?"

"There's nothing you can do. I just had to talk to you."

"Right. Of course."

"They gave me a babysitter."

"They do that."

"She fed me and put me to bed, but I can't do this."

"I'm coming. Next flight out."

"No, Stan. I'm not calling for that."

"Of course I will. Anything you need. You know that."

"Just tell me why you told him. Now, of all times."

He paused again. "Told him what?"

He was being coy, she thought. Diplomatic. But he was a spook, not a diplomat, so perhaps it was better to call it lying. "About us. You told him about us, and you said you were in love."

His silence this time was longer, and it was a silence she recognized. The gears were moving in his head. He said, "Sophie, I didn't tell him anything about us. You know I wouldn't do that."

"Then why did he tell me otherwise?"

"I don't know. Maybe . . . I don't know. He *told* you that I told him?"

"One of the last things he said."

An intake of breath. "Maybe he was just fishing. Maybe he heard it somewhere else. He certainly didn't hear it from me."

She wasn't sure she believed him, then she wasn't sure she wanted to believe him. If Emmett had heard this from someone else, it would have been a simple thing for her to deny it into the ground. Emmett would have been relieved, and she would have been free of at least some of this crushing guilt. She said, "He sounded convincing."

"I don't know what to tell you, Sophie. I haven't talked to him since your going-away party."

She digested this slowly, finally saying, "Okay. I believe you."

"I hope so. Now, do you want me to come? It's no problem at all."

"No, Stan. Really. Thanks, though. I just need to sleep."

"Can I call you tomorrow?"

"Sure."

She hung up and, after considering it a moment, dialed the other number, the one she still knew by heart, though her heart was in her throat when she pressed the buttons. A single ring, then a recorded voice told her something in Arabic. Sophie didn't know the language but she knew the tone—the number had been disconnected. Of course. She hung up and turned off the phone again. Yet even with that done, she still couldn't sleep.

4

—◆—

1991

After Prague they moved on to Budapest and the drearily aristo-cratic Gellért Hotel. With the memory of that Czech boy and her stolen Lenin still fresh, Sophie shied away from tourist spots, pre-ferring to sit with Emmett in dusty Hungarian cafés on streets called Vaci and Andrassy, reading the *Herald Tribune* and pretending to be locals. It didn't work, for their clothes gave them away, and as soon as they opened their mouths they received shocked stares, but it did give them time to read and learn about the war bubbling just to the south, in Yugoslavia.

In late June, Croatia and Slovenia had declared their indepen-dence from the Socialist Federal Republic of Yugoslavia, and after a brief ten-day war Slovenia had become sovereign. By September, as they huddled over their newspapers, the young Croatian republic had been fighting for its existence for two months.

"It's the biggest news since the Berlin Wall," Emmett told her in their hotel room as they watched grainy television images of bombs and talking heads. "And we're right here, one country away." She could feel his excitement.

During breakfast, their waitress told them in spotty English that Budapest was swelling from an influx of Yugoslavs—mostly Serbs—

fleeing military conscription, smuggling goods across the loose borders, and escaping the prospect of an unknown future. "Criminals," she said with undisguised contempt, but this only added to their vision of themselves as explorers into the unknown. At a bar in Liszt Ferenc Square they listened to a drunk young Serbian man ranting in English to a table of Hungarians about how Slobodan Milošević and Franjo Tuđman were preparing to "set fire to the Balkans, you mark my words."

The tension in the air, whether real or imagined, added a new dimension to their honeymoon, and on the white Gellért sheets they tangled and fought as if their room had caught fire and this was their last chance for connection. Sophie lost track of herself during sex; this kind of exhilaration was new to her. While a part of her was terrified by the loss of control, when she saw the look of pure satisfaction on Emmett's face her fear faded away.

On September 18, two days before their scheduled return to Boston, Emmett suggested they travel south. "We missed the Wall, Sophie. You really want to miss this?"

She didn't know. They were at breakfast again in the Gellért dining room, and she was tired. A part of her longed to get back to their friends in Boston, where they could understand the language again and spread tall tales of their adventures; another part was enchanted by the idea, recently hatched, that this honeymoon could be the first step of a journey that would take them around the world.

"We can go down to Novi Sad," Emmett said as he pulled out the regional map they'd only used a couple of times. Now, she saw, there were pencil circles around cities, and she realized that he'd gotten up sometime during the night to scribble on it. Where had he worked? The bathroom, or had he snuck down to the hotel bar?

Novi Sad, she saw, was a town in the north of Yugoslavia, on the banks of the Danube, not so far from the Hungarian border. To the west, he'd circled another town, also along the Danube, called Vukovar, just inside Croatia, though on their map Croatia did not exist. He pointed at it. "There's fighting right there."

Sophie knew the name. For nearly a month, Vukovar had suffered under a continuous rain of artillery by the JNA, the Jugoslav National Army. "It's not too close?" she asked.

"I'm not suggesting we go *to* the fighting, Sophie. We get to Novi Sad, and we settle in for a week. We keep our ears open; we see what we can see."

"To what end?"

He stared at her a moment, as if he only now realized that he'd married an imbecile. Or maybe he was asking himself the same question. He smiled and opened his hands. "To go. To see. To experience."

They were only twenty-two.

It was a straightforward enough proposition, but Sophie saw it as a life-changing decision. She was right to think of it like that, for in a way the decision redirected their shared life. At the time, though, she couldn't predict any of this. It was simply the first test of their marriage. Either she would encourage her husband's sense of adventure, or she would take the initial steps toward clipping his wings. She was already thinking more like a wife than the independent woman she'd always told herself she was.

She was also thinking of that boy in Prague. She was no wiser a week later, but her eyes were a little more open, and she was beginning to understand how ridiculous she had looked among those gray, historically miserable people with her dollars and her American smile and her little trinket of communist kitsch. She didn't want to be like that anymore. She, like Emmett, wanted to be someone who'd *seen* things, and not just on television. She was beginning to think of her friends in Boston as cloistered, just as she had been. While her courage faltered occasionally, she knew that she wanted to be different from them. She wanted to be authentic. She wanted to *know*. She said, "Sure, hon. Let's go look at a war."

5

———

Thursday was full of visitors. Fiona was ready with coffee and eggs when Sophie rose around noon, and soon afterward Mary Saunders, the ambassador, called to tell her that everything was being done to track down the cretin who had shot Emmett. "Like what?" Sophie asked.

Perhaps noting the tone in her voice, the ambassador hesitated. Or maybe this was just Sophie's imagination, for she felt as if she'd woken a different woman from the night before. The grief and guilt remained, but she'd woken angry—angry that some thick-necked bastard had been able to walk into a restaurant and end life as she'd known it. She was angry for Emmett, because he hadn't had the chance for his "little shit" moment, and that was something he had deserved. She was angry with Stan, because she wasn't sure she believed him, and she was livid with Zora Balašević, who had destroyed her marriage long before that gunman had destroyed Emmett. Most of all, she was angry with herself for being so much less than she could have been.

Mary Saunders listed the law enforcement and security agencies who were "on top of this" and told her that she should expect to have to answer some questions for them. "Of course," Sophie said, "but is this a two-way street?"

"Excuse me?"

"Are they going to answer my questions?"

"I'm sure they'll be as helpful as they can be, Sophie."

Afterward, she received a call from Harry Wolcott—a colleague of Emmett's in Cairo, and Stan's Agency boss. He offered breathy, muddled condolences. Sophie appreciated that the man was emotional and confused, but that wasn't much use to her now. She wanted answers—and if not answers, then at least the feeling that people she trusted knew what was going on. She'd lived in the diplomatic corps long enough to know that just because people act as if they understand the world, it doesn't mean they know it any better than you do.

After she hung up, Glenda appeared at the front door, her dark, wiry hair out of sorts, claiming to have been accosted by a journalist, though when they looked out the window there was no sign of paparazzi. "But it has made the news," she told them as she crouched in her short skirt, long-legged on insecure heels, and turned on CNN, where they saw a picture of Emmett from when he first arrived in Budapest. A newscaster mentioned "sketchy details" and a "Hungarian restaurant" and an "unknown assailant." A talking head gave some noncommittal words on what this could mean for American-Hungarian relations ("Nothing," he finally admitted). There was no mention of Sophie, just the banner headline MURDER IN BUDAPEST. The embassy, Fiona Vale guessed aloud, was working overtime to keep her out of the news cycle.

Glenda held her hand and whispered lovingly that she was going to take care of her. Fiona disappeared to make calls—babysitting, Sophie suspected, wasn't her actual job, and her work was probably piling up. Then Gerry Davis, pink and clean in a perfectly pressed greatcoat, arrived to take her through more of his vision of the future. She couldn't help but admire the way he was able to act as tragedy's soothsayer.

There were funeral arrangements to be made, but she wasn't to worry—the embassy was taking care of the details. After an inquest ("Sorry, this is required, but we'll deal with it"), Emmett's body would be sent back to Massachusetts and the family plot near Amherst. Would she like to fly back with him? "Of course," she answered without even considering the question. Twenty minutes later, Gerry Davis told her that there was a first-class reservation for tomorrow, Air France to Boston via Paris, with her name on it.

The Hungarian police were scheduled to visit at four, but beforehand, Gerry Davis said, some folks from the embassy wanted to have a word with her. It turned out they were already in the apartment, drinking coffee in the kitchen with Fiona. Two tall men wandered in, smiling stiffly, and asked Glenda if she would please step out for a little while. (Glenda's *Hell no* caught in her throat once she realized they were spies.) They introduced themselves, but their given names passed Sophie by. She referred to them by their surnames: Reardon and Strauss.

Reardon took the lead. He was bald on top, cropped short on the sides, and blushed whenever the subject made a turn toward the personal. Strauss was younger, early thirties, and more dark than his name would have suggested. He used both thumbs to type notes into his BlackBerry.

Reardon said, "Did your husband share information about his work?"

"Not usually, no."

"But you know what he did?"

"He was a deputy consul," she said. "He worked under Ray—Raymond Bennett, the consul—sometimes taking over his schedule, meeting with Hungarian officials and businessmen. That sort of thing."

Reardon nodded—he knew this already. Of course he knew this. "We're looking into it now—whether some part of his job led to this incident. If, however, the cause is rooted in something else, something more personal, then perhaps you would know about it." He was already blushing.

Yugoslavia, 1991.

Zora Balašević.

A disloyal wife.

But all she said was "I have no idea."

There were more questions—Emmett's friends, his extracurricular activities, his business interests—but they were softball compared to the lie she'd begun the conversation with: She had plenty of ideas, too many ideas.

Reardon and Strauss were attentive, but not suspicious, and as they talked Sophie began to relax, describing her and Emmett's shared life to them. It was almost comforting speaking these things aloud, and by the time they stood and handed her their cards she was feeling a warm wave of nostalgia. The anger had slipped away, and she only wanted Emmett back. She gave them thankful smiles, but Glenda gave them another face, for she was in hysterics again, furious that they'd kept her away from Sophie for a full forty minutes.

Fiona was manning the phone in the kitchen, which was by then ringing off the hook. Journalists. Each time, Sophie heard a single ring, then Fiona's cold voice saying, "Kohl residence," and then lowering to a whisper as she got rid of them. Around two, though, she came in and announced that Emmett's parents were on the line.

Why hadn't she thought to call them?

Though his mother cried nonstop, neither of them blamed her. They believed that they understood what Sophie was going through, and they simply wanted to know how she was holding up. They were good people, she realized, as if she had never truly known it before. Once she was finished with them, she called her own parents. They were at the cabin in West Virginia and had no access to the news. After the shock, they were much the same as Emmett's parents, but without so many tears. They were just happy that she was the one still breathing. "Come home," her father told her, and she said that she would see them soon.

As she hung up, it occurred to her that her father had been suggesting this ever since she was a child: *Come home.* He'd treated her scholarship to Harvard as an inconvenience that would likely damage his frail daughter, and when she thrived in Boston he tried to lure her back to Virginia with health problems—he was suddenly diagnosed with arteriosclerosis, celiac disease, and depression. She'd resisted the pull, but during much of her college career she'd lived with the fear that her mother would call with the news that he was dead. Over time, of course, he'd emerged from his ailments stronger than ever, finally aiming his daggers at Emmett: *What kind of life is all this moving around? It's no good for Sophie—can't you see that? What about roots?* Emmett had shrugged it off better than she, cruelly referring to her father as "euthanasia's poster child."

She found Glenda napping on the sofa, television off. Fiona pointed at the Jim Beam; apparently, Glenda had been sipping at it from the moment she showed up. Gerry Davis reappeared—from where?—and announced that the Hungarian police had arrived.

To avoid waking Glenda, she met with them in the dining room, but it was only one man—the same older man from the night before, Andras Something. Andras Kiraly—*key-rye*, with a rolled *r*—which she knew meant King. He had the slow-moving, depressive presence of popular television detectives, and she realized that she was more comfortable with him than with any of the people she'd met that day. He smiled only now and then, always in embarrassment, and she found this charming. Gerry Davis hovered protectively behind her, occasionally asking if she was too tired to do this, but she locked eyes with Andras Kiraly and said that she was happy to help the Hungarian police with their investigation.

"I should be up-front, Mrs. Kohl," Kiraly told her softly. "I'm not actually police—I'm from the *Alkotmányvédelmi Hivatal*, the Constitution Protection Office."

She knew of this office—until the previous year, it had been called the Office of National Security, the *Nemzetbiztonsági Hivatal*. He, like Reardon and Strauss, and like Stan, was a spy. When they came out, they came out like hives.

He asked the same questions as her CIA visitors, but she found herself elaborating a bit more, perhaps from practice. This time, she didn't dwell on her infidelity. He said, "Do you mind if I show you a few photographs?"

Behind her, Gerry Davis cleared his throat. Kiraly looked up, but Sophie couldn't see what Gerry Davis was trying to communicate to him. Whatever it was, the Hungarian didn't seem interested in playing ball. "It's up to Mrs. Kohl," he said.

She said, "Please. Show me your photographs."

Gerry Davis pulled out the chair beside her and sat close. Despite how scrubbed he looked, he smelled of sweat. "There may be security issues here, Sophie. That's my only concern." To Kiraly, he said, "May I see the pictures first?"

A laconic shrug, and the Hungarian reached into his jacket and took out some passport-sized snapshots that he passed on to Gerry Davis, who held them up like a hand of tiny cards to examine. There were four in all, she saw, and on one he paused. He took it out and placed it facedown on the table. He pushed it over to Kiraly. "The rest are fine, just not that one."

Kiraly lifted the photo, glanced at it, and slipped it into his pocket. "Please," he said. "Let Mrs. Kohl see the others."

Reluctantly, Gerry Davis gave her the three remaining photos, and she saw two men in their late thirties or early forties and a much older man, nearly sixty. She didn't recognize any of the faces, but what struck her was the color of their skin. "I don't understand," she said aloud.

"Yes?" asked Kiraly.

"These men—they're not Hungarian, are they? I mean, unless they're Roma."

He shook his head. "No, they are not."

"Where are they from?"

"Do you recognize them?"

She gave them another look. Not only different ages, but different forms of dark-skinned masculinity. Middle Eastern or North African. The overweight one who looked addicted to smiles. The thick-necked thug—a darker model of the one who killed Emmett. The older one in glasses, maybe their leader, or maybe just nearsighted. "No," she said. "I've never seen them before. What about the other?"

"They're from different places," Kiraly said, ignoring her question by answering her previous one. "Turkey, Egypt, Bosnia."

"And what do they have to do with Emmett?"

Kiraly pursed his lips, then reached out to accept the photographs. "Nothing, perhaps. But we sometimes follow many different cases,

and if incidents occur around the same time, then it's a good idea to
see if they are connected."

"These aren't?"

More of the lips, then he shrugged.

"I think Mrs. Kohl has answered enough. She's tired."

"I'm not tired," she said, tired only of Gerry Davis's shepherding.
"And I'd like to know who you're hiding in your jacket pocket."

Kiraly looked as if he might bow to her demand, but instead he de-
ferred to Gerry Davis, who just gave back a cool stare. Sophie turned
on him.

"Why not, Gerry?"

He inhaled, finally giving her his full attention. "National security, Sophie. And if those other men aren't connected to Emmett,
then this one won't be, either."

"But I'd like to see the picture."

Kiraly said in a tired voice, "Gerry, it's just a face."

Gerry Davis turned to the Hungarian, maybe angry, and after a
full four seconds dredged up a smile. "Well, okay. If it'll make you
feel better. Go ahead, Andras."

Kiraly reached into his jacket and handed over the final photograph. It wasn't, despite what she was beginning to suspect, the gunman, nor was it Zora Balašević. Instead, it was another swarthy man
in his thirties, a shadow of a smile on his face. Clean cheeks, dark
eyes. He seemed different from the others, though she couldn't place
how. Healthier, maybe. Less a victim of a hard life.

She looked up at Kiraly. "Egyptian?"

He shook his head and began to speak, but Gerry Davis cut him
off: "You don't recognize him?"

She didn't, and she admitted as much.

Like the CIA men, Kiraly gave her his business card and asked
her to call if anything occurred to her. Perhaps sensing that Sophie
was angry with him, Gerry Davis left with Kiraly, promising to remain in touch.

Then it was a home of women. Glenda had recovered and was in
the kitchen cooking something with an entire chicken and a bottle

of wine in a large pot. Fiona was flitting between CNN and her cell phone. She smiled when Sophie came in, then patted the sofa cushion next to her. "How you doin'?" she asked as Sophie sat.

"What's the deal with Gerry Davis?"

"Gerry?" Fiona considered the question. "He's very good at his job."

"What's his job?"

"Some kind of liaison. Quite fluent in Hungarian."

"Is he a spook, too?"

A high-pitched laugh. "Gerry? He's more of an errand boy."

"What does that mean?"

She shrugged. "It's how he was described to me."

Together, they watched footage from Libya, young rebels in need of razors looking sweaty but optimistic on the desert roads, carrying rifles they sometimes waved over their heads. She could imagine the men from Kiraly's photographs in these newsreels.

Smelling something burning, Sophie went to check on Glenda, who shooed her from the kitchen and told her to take a rest, but then opened a bottle of Emmett's Chilean red and insisted she take a glass. Sophie lingered, and as they drank Glenda asked about Kiraly, whom she had seen leaving. "He didn't look like a cop to me."

"He isn't. He's a spy."

She grinned. "Well. Isn't *that* something?"

Sophie took her wine upstairs and sat on the bed but didn't lie down. She was unsure what to do with herself. The food was being taken care of, and Fiona had spent much of her time tidying up the place. She remembered that there was a load of shirts in the dryer, but it seemed ridiculous to deal with that.

Yet as the minutes of her doing *nothing* ebbed past, she began to feel the pressure in her intestines, the discomfort, the hole.

She took the business cards out of the pocket of her slacks and looked at them. It was as if she'd been to one of Emmett's parties, where each handshake came with one of these, everyone ready to hand out their personal details to anyone who might do their career some good. But she couldn't do any of these people any good, not really. Not if she wanted to remain a free woman.

Is that what I am now?

The truth was that, even taking her own crimes into account, she knew nothing about what had happened to Emmett; she knew less than nothing. And if she had shared everything with the people behind these business cards, would it really have accomplished anything?

Like Gerry Davis, she was suddenly able to see the future. Rather, she saw multiple futures, and they all began with a simple decision—whether or not she would choose ignorance. All she had to do was stop asking why Emmett's life had ended like that. Of course, she wanted to know, but how *strongly* did she want to know? Did she want to know so badly that she would be willing to give up everything else? Or was it better to keep her eyes closed, to let it go and return to Boston with her husband's corpse? Let the machine of law enforcement take over. After the funeral she could change her life, maybe even for the better. Go back to school—teaching wasn't out of the question. They had a sizable savings account, and there was another, very private account in Zurich, which she had never touched. There wasn't much she *couldn't* do. Or—and this thought came quickly—she could eventually return to Cairo and try to rekindle that joy she once felt. Not with Stan—no—but with the city itself.

Was that even possible now?

The cheapest of the business cards, laser-printed on low-quality stock, was Andras Kiraly's. King. She wiped her eyes dry and picked up the bedroom extension and dialed. He answered after two rings like Stan—"Kiraly Andras"—reversed because Hungarians begin with their surnames.

"Mr. Kiraly, it's Sophie Kohl."

"Mrs. Kohl. Hello. How may I help you?"

How could he help her? It was an excellent question. But of all her visitors, she thought that he was probably her favorite. "I got the feeling," she began, then, "I sensed during our talk that you wanted to tell me something more, and so I'm calling."

She waited for him to speak. She didn't know exactly how he had felt about Gerry Davis's meddling, but she couldn't imagine that he had liked it. Finally, he said, "Perhaps you would be interested in asking a precise question, so that I may better help you."

There was a difference, in his mind at least, between answering questions and offering unsolicited information. So she gave it a try. "That last photograph, the one Mr. Davis didn't want me to see. Who is he?"

By his longer pause, she guessed—and this filled her with a tingle of pleasure, her first of the day—that she'd asked something crucial. Then the silence went on, and she wondered if he'd walked away from the phone.

"Mr. Kiraly?"

"I'm here."

"Maybe you can just tell me what his nationality is."

"He's American, Mrs. Kohl. I'm just looking through my papers for his information."

American?

"Here it is. Jibril Aziz. Would you like me to spell it?"

"Please," she said. *American?*

He spelled it, and she wrote in clear block capitals on the Post-it pad Emmett had always kept beside the phone.

"What does he have to do with my husband?"

"That's unclear. Mr. Aziz was in Budapest last week, and he met twice with your husband. He came in without any diplomatic visa, or any official standing. But we were curious."

"Why?"

"He's an employee of the Central Intelligence Agency."

"He's . . ." There was no point repeating it. Later, she would think that this was not so strange—as deputy consul Emmett met with CIA now and then; Sophie herself had gone to bed with CIA—but at that moment it floored her. "How about the other men?"

He sighed loudly into the phone. "I could tell you their names, but none of those names are real. Their nationalities are also suspect. In fact, we know nothing about them, only that they came to Budapest around the same time as Mr. Aziz and, early last week, met with him in a bar. Your husband was not in attendance. We do not know what they talked about, or why."

"But you have suspicions."

An amused grunt. "Mrs. Kohl, when a group of Arab-looking men, most with false passports, meet in secret, I think you know what we suspect. But we've found nothing to connect them to terroristic activities."

"Does the embassy know about this?"

"I don't know," he said, which Sophie took to mean that he hadn't been sharing his information with the American embassy. He was telling her, though.

She tried to take all this in, not even sure what she was ingesting. These were not the answers she'd been looking for. In fact, they didn't look like answers at all. She had a name, though, and that was more than she'd had before. She said, "Where is he now? Where is Jibril Aziz?"

"I don't know, Mrs. Kohl. The last we heard was that he flew to Cairo from here, but that was nearly a week ago. He could be anywhere."

Cairo. "Is there anything else you wanted to tell me?"

"I was hoping you might have something to share," he said, quite reasonably.

But he didn't know who he was dealing with. "I wish I did," she said. "Emmett was very quiet about his work."

"If you do think of something . . ."

"Of course, Mr. Kiraly. I won't hesitate to call you. I appreciate what you've already done."

"I've done nothing, Mrs. Kohl."

"But you—"

"*I* have done nothing for you. You understand?"

The slow-witted widow suddenly understood. "I'm sorry you couldn't help me."

"As am I, Mrs. Kohl. Have a pleasant evening."

6

It turned out that Fiona Vale had no plans to leave her alone, and when, at six, Ray showed up to give more condolences, Fiona served the meal Glenda had spent the day cooking: coq au vin with herbed rice and grilled zucchini. Sophie had never imagined that Glenda knew her way around a kitchen, but it turned out that she was an excellent cook.

What Sophie wanted was to ask Ray about Jibril Aziz and his connection to Emmett. Presumably, Emmett had been meeting Aziz on consul business. Yet all through dinner she couldn't think of a way to ask without betraying Andras Kiraly, who had stuck his neck out for her.

What to do with this information? She tried sidewinding queries. "Ray, was Emmett meeting with anyone out of the ordinary recently?" *No, Sophie. Why do you ask?* "Ray, did Emmett share any personal worries with you, like—I don't know—about debts he might not have mentioned to me?" *Emmett was the most fiscally sound man I've ever known.* "To tell the truth," she lied, "I thought that maybe he had gotten tangled up in something. I don't know—something illicit?" A surprised look, then a slow shake of the head. *Forget it, Sophie. Emmett was clean, absolutely upstanding. And unlike a lot of the guys we work with, he never even looked at another woman.* That one hurt.

Finally, she excused herself and ran upstairs to find the slip of paper where she'd written Jibril Aziz's name in capitals. It wasn't the way she usually wrote, for she had wanted it to be perfectly legible. She took the paper downstairs and, as Glenda and Fiona watched in silence, handed it to Ray. He took it, read it, and looked up at her blankly. She said, "I found this in Emmett's things. In one of his jackets," the lie becoming more specific as the words came out. "The gray one. Why does Emmett have an Arab's name in his jacket?"

"Gosh, Sophie. I don't know." He actually said *gosh.* "But it could be anything, couldn't it? Maybe he's a friend."

She wanted to say, *He's an American spy, you condescending shit,* but said, "Do you know the name?"

When he shook his head, she realized that she didn't really know Raymond Bennett. She knew Glenda's perception of him—sturdy but weak-willed, an easy man to cheat on—but she didn't know *him.* It was easy to forget that he was a consul, an important man. It was easy to forget what that job might entail. It was easy to underestimate him. Then she wondered if he was someone she should fear. She'd been frightened by very few people in her life; since Yugoslavia, most people hadn't measured up. Maybe this was someone who could measure up.

It wasn't until after dinner, once she had convinced Glenda to go home with her husband and Fiona had finally headed off to sleep, that she had a chance to be alone with the threads weaving through her head.

What did she have?

She had men who looked like terrorists but might not be. One of them was a CIA agent who met with Emmett, twice.

She had Emmett, who had been too strong and too good to be blackmailed by Zora Balašević. She'd had no idea he could be such a hero. She certainly was not.

She had American spies who smiled diplomats' smiles and a kind-faced Hungarian spy who knew she had information and hoped that she would eventually share it.

What she had—all she *really* had—was a name, Jibril Aziz, and like the rest of the world she went to Google to assist her investigations. She would have used Emmett's laptop, but it was no longer by the bed; she had no idea where it was. She turned on her iPad and began typing on its smooth screen.

There were many Jibril Azizes, she learned. They were on Facebook, on dating and gaming sites, and they had their own LinkedIn pages. But none of these looked right. They were young men, comfortable with sharing their lives online. No, Emmett's Jibril Aziz would have been elsewhere—or, more likely, nowhere.

Almost nowhere.

For when she added "CIA" to the search, on the third page of results she came across something that made her throat choke up. A Dutch hacker had set up an automated blog to index and tag all the material contained in WikiLeaks, the infamous organization that had, over the previous year or so, leaked hundreds of thousands of classified cables and e-mails to the world at large. In the automated list, Jibril Aziz appeared on one entry among a thousand others:

AMEMBASSY CAIRO to SECSTATE WASHDC: FALSE PREDICTIONS RE: STUMBLER. (link) TAGS: AE/STUMBLER, Africa, ALF, American, Arab, China, CNPC, Frank Ingersoll, Geneva, IFG, Jabal al Akhdar, Jibril Aziz, Libya, London, Muammar Gadhafi, Muslim, Paris, Revolutionary Guard, Rome, Washington, WRAL

She followed the link and was rerouted to WikiLeaks.org, where she found herself in a section called "Cablegate: 250,000 US Embassy Diplomatic Cables," faced with a communiqué from December 2009, more than a year ago. It was the first of three cables dealing with something called Stumbler, but a search proved that the other two cables were not available.

She read it once, then sent it to the wireless laser printer in the closet and read it again. December 2009: She and Emmett had been in Cairo when the embassy worked on Stumbler—an operation, it seemed, that had originated with one Jibril Aziz. Which meant, she supposed, that Emmett had been working on it as well.

She took the printout to the kitchen and poured herself a glass of rosé from a half-sized Napa Valley bottle. As she was reading it a third time a voice said, "What's that?"

She nearly dropped her glass.

Fiona grinned. "Sorry. Just saw the light."

Instinctively, she folded the paper and slipped it into the pocket of her robe. "Old stuff. Memories."

Fiona nodded mournfully. "I can't imagine."

"Maybe not," Sophie said, "but thanks." Then, "By the way, have you seen Emmett's computer? It was in the bedroom."

"I meant to tell you. Mr. Strauss took it. For the investigation. I've got a receipt around here somewhere."

"I see," she said, but she wasn't thinking of the laptop. She was thinking of tomorrow, for while reading the secret cable it had dawned on her that she wasn't going with Emmett back to Boston. She wasn't going to sit around dealing with Glenda. She wasn't going to do anything that she'd done before in her life. Emmett had been too good and too strong, and so she would try to at least be something better than what she had been.

She returned to bed and picked up her cell phone, again turning it on. It was three thirty in the morning, and there were twenty-eight missed calls. Mother, father, friends, unknown numbers, and, twice, Stan Bertolli. Dependable Stan. She pressed the green button to call her old lover in Cairo.

7

Not surprisingly, Glenda was amenable to morning drinks, though when Sophie told her where they were going she paused, silence over the line, wondering if grief had driven her friend mad. "But it's full of *Hungarians*," she whispered.

"It's full of people who don't know me."

"Ahh . . ."

It was a real fear, but not for the reason Glenda suspected.

When she told Fiona that she was going out with Glenda, her babysitter frowned. "You think that's a good idea?"

"I think it's an excellent idea. For the next week I'm not going to be able to get away from anyone—family, press, police—and right now, while it's still calm, I'm going to have a drink and a chat with my best friend."

"Your plane's at three forty-five."

"And everything's packed. I'll come back a little tipsy, and you'll guide me into the taxi. Really, Fee. Don't worry."

Eventually, she nodded her acquiescence, as if with Emmett's murder she had become Sophie's mother. "Shall I come along?"

"I'm a big girl."

"At least tell me where you'll be, in case there's some emergency."

"Menza, in Liszt Ferenc," she said, her fifth or sixth lie of the day. The paparazzi had finally arrived, but it was a small contingent—

two photographers lounging with cigarettes in the sharp cold just outside the gate to the apartment building. When she came out to climb into Glenda's car, they snapped photos, and she wondered if later those photos would be requisitioned by the authorities, the last record of Sophie Kohl before she disappeared. Of course, the Budapest airport was full of cameras, and so was Cairo, but these clear, professional shots would be far more useful for the newspapers or some missing persons circular.

She slammed the passenger door behind herself. Glenda, behind the wheel, said, "Well, aren't *you* all dolled up?"

"You want to drive?"

Glenda put the car in gear, and they began to move, leaving the photographers behind. "You're not thinking of throwing yourself at some Magyar, are you? Because it's a losing proposition."

She went on, but Sophie was hardly hearing her. Instead, she was inventorying what she'd stuffed into her shoulder bag. Passport, credit cards, euros and forints, phone, iPad, address book, four pairs of clean panties, tissues, antibacterial lotion, aspirin, perfume, and the burgundy lipstick that Stan once said he loved. And, folded into quarters, the WikiLeaks cable: Aziz and Stumbler. She was thinking of chronology—the flight she'd reserved online early that morning left at three thirty-five, only ten minutes before the Boston flight, but she couldn't risk Fiona staying with her at the airport. She could only hope that of all the places Fiona Vale would think to look for her, the airport would be her last choice.

She was thinking of logistics. She wasn't thinking of Zora Balašević, Jibril Aziz, or even poor Emmett. She was trying not to think of Stan, but was only partly successful, for when she had called him at three thirty that morning she'd noted the doubt in his voice. Would he be there, and if so would he be alone? She kept flashing back on their hotel room, and the particular nuances of his bed etiquette. Stan, unlike Emmett, was extremely oral.

With shocking appropriateness, Glenda's voice broke through. "And they're a *mess* when it comes to cunnilingus. I don't know what it is, maybe all that paprika they eat."

"You're unfair, Glen."

She gave Sophie a sidelong glance as she took a turn, but didn't bother replying.

Bitch Lounge was on Üllői Avenue, Budapest's longest street, which headed straight out to the airport down a corridor of sooty Habsburg buildings. The front door was half buried in the sidewalk, with a small, unassuming banner beside it. Glenda was right—though an influx of gay-scene foreigners attracted by the lounge atmosphere and drag shows had been changing the place, it was still largely Hungarian. And at that time, eleven thirty in the morning, it was mostly empty.

The bartender was a prim young man who spoke spotty English. He brought their Cosmos to a zebra-print sofa along the brick wall. Over the speakers Édith Piaf sang "Non, je ne regrette rien."

"What time's your flight?" Glenda asked, momentarily throwing her, but she meant the one Sophie wouldn't be on.

"Three forty-five."

"I'll lay odds I can manage a ticket. Consul's wife and all that. We can cause a drunken ruckus."

Sophie grinned. "No. Please. I'm hoping to catch up on sleep."

"Thatta girl."

"But right now," she said, "I'd like you to open up to me."

Glenda arched a brow—only she could arch one that way. "I thought we were drinking."

Sophie leaned close and rubbed Glenda's knee through her slacks. "Tell me what Ray's been saying."

"About what?"

"About what do you think?"

The brow relaxed and Glenda shifted, her knee slipping out from under Sophie's hand. "Well, first of all, he's devastated. You know how crazy he was about Emmett."

"Yes, of course he is, Glenda. That's not what I'm talking about."

"What *are* you talking about?"

She was talking about CIA agents; she was talking about terrorists; she was talking about an operation called Stumbler. She said, "I'm talking about the investigation."

"Oh, *that*," Glenda said. She took a sip of her drink, looked at it, then took another sip before setting it on the table. "Well, you didn't hear it from me, okay?"

Sophie waited.

"They found him."

"Who?"

"The man." She held Sophie's gaze. "The killer."

Her vision went a little fuzzy. "When?"

"Yesterday. Morning, I think. They don't *have* him, not in custody, but they got his picture on CCTV at Keleti Station—he took the Munich train."

Sophie blinked, trying to clear her sight, but it was hard. She felt a lump in her throat. "All yesterday you were with me. Ray came for dinner."

"It's hush-*hush,* Sophie. I shouldn't even be telling you now."

"But you knew?"

"Not until we got home. Ray told me."

"Who is he?"

A shrug, then Glenda reached for her Cosmo again. "I don't know. Albanian, though. Some Albanian prick."

"And?"

"And nothing. That's all Ray would give me. Maybe he knows more, maybe they're just kicking around in the dark, but that's all I know."

Sophie closed her eyes, blocking out everything, then opened them again, but it was all the same. That zebra print, Glenda with her drink, and, in the distance, one of the tinted windows just above the sidewalk, where high heels and cheap casuals hurried by. She felt the same way she had felt twenty years before on the Charles Bridge, mourning the loss of her Lenin—ignorant, an outsider, an object of scorn.

"I need to make a call," she said, taking her shoulder bag as she stood.

Glenda made a worried expression. "Not angry?"

She shook her head.

"Sisters?"

Sophie gave her a smile that felt entirely false. "Sisters, Glen. I'll be right back."

She climbed to the front door, stepped outside, the cold descending on her, and continued up to the sidewalk. There were two City Taxis coming up Üllői, and she waved at them. The second stopped. She climbed inside and said, "Ferihegy." As they moved, she took out her phone and dialed Andras Kiraly's number.

"Kiraly Andras."

"Sophie Kohl."

He took a breath. "Mrs. Kohl, how may I help you?"

"I'd like the name of the man who killed my husband."

Another breath, a cough. "You haven't been told this?"

"I suppose my friends forgot to mention it."

He waited, as if his patience would convince her to hang up. It wouldn't. She watched the dirty buildings pass by, shadows of a grander age. She had all the time in the world.

Finally, he said, "He has a Hungarian passport under the name Lajos Varga. However, his real name is Gjergj Ahmeti, and he is Albanian by birth. He is a known criminal, usually hired to kill people."

"An assassin?" she said, but kept her voice low so that the driver wouldn't hear.

"Yes."

"Does he work for the Serbs?" she asked without thinking through the question.

"Why would you ask that, Mrs. Kohl?"

"I . . ." She wasn't ready to share with him what she hadn't shared with the embassy—or anyone, for that matter. She wasn't ready to trust Andras Kiraly. "Sorry, I have to go now." She hung up. Immediately, the phone began to ring. It was Glenda. She disconnected her friend, then turned off the phone.

SOURCE: WikiLeaks.org
"Cablegate: 250,000 US Embassy Diplomatic Cables"
AUTHOR: Harold Wolcott
9 December 2009

O 261214Z DEC 09
FM AMEMBASSY CAIRO
TO SECSTATE WASHDC IMMEDIATE 1752
INFO NSC WASHDC IMMEDIATE

S E C R E T SECTION 01 OF 03 CAIRO 001403
STATE FOR F
AID FOR AME
STATE ALSO FOR NEA/ELA

E.O. 18239: DECL: 12/09/2019
SUBJECT: FALSE PREDICTIONS RE: STUMBLER

Classified by DCM Frank Ingersoll for reasons 1.4 (c) and (d).

¶1. (C) Summary and Key points: This is an analysis of the May 2009
draft proposal, AE/STUMBLER. Based on present assessments of the
regime in Tripoli, the primary assumptions behind STUMBLER are in
doubt. It is the belief of this embassy that the operation should be
abandoned in favor of more assured goals.

_____

ASSUMPTIONS
_____

¶2. (C) Signs that the assumptions of instability, outlined in the May
2009 proposal by Jibril Aziz (CIA), are mistaken include:

--The failed September 2009 protests in al Jabal al Akhdar
Governorate, dealt with by government forces in less than 24 hours.

--A November 2009 increase in salary to the Revolutionary Guard,
which reports say have solidified the regime's control.

--Most importantly, the recently signed oil contracts between the regime and China's CNPC, which has made the regime more flush with cash than in recent years, and would facilitate the easy purchase of mercenary support from throughout Africa.

NEXT STEPS

¶3. (C) Given the low probability of success with STUMBLER, this office suggests the following course of action:

--Continued support of underground resistance groups within the country, including the ALF and the WRAL.

--Support for the IFG, which, despite central policies that contradict our own, could be moved into our sphere of influence. They have on numerous occasions attempted Muammar Gadhafi's assassination.

--Support to a variety of exile groups in order to pave the way for a post-Gadhafi regime educated in the methods and practice of democracy. See the list included in section 3.

CONCLUSION

¶4. (C) With all that has been stated above, and will be detailed in section 2, the prospect for STUMBLER's success is, in all likelihood, doomed to failure. To go forward would cost not only money and lives but American influence within the Arab and Muslim worlds, as Gadhafi would certainly use a failure to maximum propaganda effect. Instead, this office proposes a continuation of support for democracy groups within Libya, and the rise in funding of exile groups based in Washington, London, Rome, Geneva, and Paris.

WOLCOTT

PART II

WE SHOULD LOOK
AT OURSELVES

Stan

1

He first discovered Emmett's treachery in March 2010, though he had been following clues for at least a month. In early February Langley had sent a classified directive via one pale, sweating official from Internal Affairs who waited at Stan's apartment, holding a file flown over in the diplomatic pouch. He sat in the kitchen while Stan called Virginia for verification, then in the living room he opened the file and laid out four pieces of intercepted communications from three Washington embassies, with the simple explanation, "The Bureau passed this on to us." Syria, Libya, and Pakistan had been using material from top-secret communications that had originated in Harry's office, material that covered aspects of trade, military analyses, and in two cases undercover operations. One was still in play, while the other—an exfiltration from Libya a month ago—had ended when the operative's body was discovered, cut into pieces, in the desert outside Homs.

"Christ," Stan said as he went through the papers. He had personally known the dead undercover agent, whose names—both his birth name and the one on his documents—were right there in capital letters. Yet the emissary was treating this like business as usual. "Who's selling us out?"

The emissary shrugged. "That's why we've come to you."

"I'm that squeaky clean?"

"The easiest. We don't have the manpower to send over a team at this point, so we decided to clear one of you and have you continue the investigation."

Stan knew what he meant by "easiest"—his father, Paolo Bertolli, was a legend in Langley circles, and the Bertolli name still carried weight eight years after his death. Stan said, "You want me to do this on my own?"

The emissary smiled. "Is it really true your father spent six years undercover in the Brigate Rosse?"

"What do the files say?"

"Six years, entirely on his own."

Stan scratched at his nose. "Is this what the office told you to say? In case I resisted?"

The emissary shrugged. Of course it was.

He and Sophie had been involved for three months by then, meeting twice a week in their Dokki hotel, and for this reason it didn't occur to him to focus on Emmett. He was already cuckolding the man; he felt no desire to ruin him completely.

He first examined members of the U.S. & Foreign Commercial Section, in particular his boss, Harold Wolcott, and the other submanagers—Jennifer Cary, Dennis Schwarzkopf, and Terry Alderman. This took longer than expected, and while no amount of vetting could clear an individual with absolute certainty he decided eventually to move on. He expanded his search to include embassy staff who'd had access to the compromised trade, military, and undercover materials. Emmett made that list, but so did eighteen others from various embassy departments. He eventually discovered, from one year earlier, the surveillance photos taken by Terry's men of Emmett meeting with an unidentified woman in a restaurant soon after his arrival in Cairo. No one had followed up on her identity— a note with the photo suggested it was a business associate, or a friend—so Stan sent Langley two shots of her face, with Emmett cropped out, and asked for an ID. Three days later he received the reply: Zora Balašević, suspected employee of the *Bezbednosno- informativna agencija*—the BIA, Serbia's intelligence agency, which was run out of their Cairo embassy by a clever old man named Dragan Milić.

Was it really possible that Emmett Kohl was selling them out to the Serbs? Even then he doubted it, for everything he knew about Kohl suggested otherwise. But Stan had come up empty on everyone else; he had no choice but to push on.

After verifying that Emmett had had access to all four pieces of wandering intelligence, he spent another week following him through endless meetings and scouring his cell phone records. In their shared hotel bed, he asked Sophie about their past. He knew that she and Emmett had spent a week or two in Yugoslavia at the beginning of its long civil war, so he asked about their connections. She shrugged and told him that their Serbian relationships had faded soon after they returned to the States. "When you leave you're convinced you'll see your new friends again, but absence doesn't really make the heart grow fonder, does it? It makes it colder."

She also told him that on the morning of March 29, the following Tuesday, she and Emmett would be joining the consul general at the Sayed Darwish Theater for a performance of *The Nutcracker* by the Moscow Stars on Ice, followed by a reception at the Russian embassy. So that Tuesday morning he arrived at their apartment a little after eleven, typed in their alarm code, and went inside. He tethered his computer to Emmett's laptop with a FireWire cable and began to copy his hard drive. Though he didn't imagine that Emmett would have kept evidence of treachery lying around, he searched the apartment anyway, finding things he shouldn't have looked at—old love letters between Emmett and Sophie that she had dutifully kept in a shoe box, faded photos of the two of them when they were much younger and, it seemed, much happier, and, in a secret box behind Emmett's underwear, naked shots of Sophie in bed, smiling. As soon as the copying was finished, he disconnected the cable, reset the alarm, and left.

Emmett was a diplomat, not a spy—he had no idea how to cover his tracks. While deleting a file was enough to deny Stan access to the file itself, he was still able to find the record of its existence, and

Emmett had never thought to rename anything. So among the deleted items he found W090218SQR and W090903SQB and W090729SQL—three top-secret documents that Langley believed had been the source of the compromised intelligence, items that were forbidden outside embassy walls.

The evidence was damning, yet it still took him two more days to accept the obvious. While "love" was a word he still struggled to use, he soon realized that his unspoken feelings for Sophie had been clouding his judgement. The facts couldn't be ignored: His lover's husband was a traitor. He thought of that undercover agent whose mutilated body had festered under the desert sun. How many other agents had been killed or kidnapped because of Emmett's misdeeds? Stan's own mideeds paled to insignificance, and he lost all sympathy for Emmett Kohl. He even allowed himself to hate.

He waited for Emmett on a street near the embassy. It was a warm day, and Sophie's husband looked harried. Stan asked about *The Nutcracker,* and Emmett gave a noncommittal shrug. "Take a walk with me, will you?" Stan asked as he led him down a sweltering Cairo alley he had scouted beforehand, to a little courtyard café with yellow paint peeling off of old stone walls. Emmett had grown anxious by then, but Stan reassured him with aimless talk about personal problems he desperately needed help with until, finally, they were sitting across from each other at one of the plastic tables.

Neither of them had a lot of time—end-of-the-month meetings were filling both of their schedules—so Stan didn't bother easing into it. He showed Emmett the photographs of his meeting with Balašević and a CD-ROM that he assured him proved that Emmett had been loading secret files onto his laptop. "Jesus," Emmett said, seeming to shrink before Stan's eyes.

"This is about as serious as it gets," Stan told him.

Emmett looked like a little boy who was going to be sick, his round, smooth face preternaturally young. Hiding his contempt, Stan reached across the table and patted Emmett's hand.

"Just consider yourself lucky that I'm the one who discovered it."

Emmett couldn't manage an answer.

"Let's start with who this woman is."

He gave Stan the name he already knew, Zora Balašević, then the name of her employer: BIA, the Security Information Agency.

"You want to tell me what she has on you?"

A firm shake of the head. For the moment, it didn't matter. "But I refused," Emmett said.

Despite himself, Stan let a smile slip into his face. "You don't expect me to believe that, do you?"

"It's the truth."

"Listen, Emmett. I don't need to come to you with this. The information you gave her didn't sit around in the Serbian embassy—it *traveled*. The Serbs sold it on to at least three different governments. By now it's common knowledge. With what I've got, Harry can send you home in shackles."

His eyes had grown into saucers. "I'm telling you, Stan. I didn't give her anything. She asked—*threatened*, really—but I refused."

People lie. During his ten years with the Agency Stan had listened to more lies than he could count, and he'd lied at least the same number of times. Being his father's son, he was pretty good at it, but in his experience diplomatic staff were among the most skillful liars around. So it was no surprise that Emmett told him these things with a straight face. He went on to say that, yes, he'd brought home his work, even brought home material that wasn't supposed to leave the embassy. "I'm loose with the rules. I'll admit to that. But I'm *not* a traitor."

"What does Balašević have on you?"

"It doesn't matter, Stan. That was a *year* ago. She asked, I said no—end of story."

"Then why didn't you report it?"

"Because I didn't know you. I didn't know Harry. I was worried about my job."

Stan gave him a good long stare to show that he wasn't buying any of this. He said, "You're going to close it down. Tell her the truth—you were uncovered, and now it's all over."

"It never started."

"I'm trying to close a leak, Emmett. I'm not here to abuse you. I'm not even going to make you feed them disinformation—the Serbs aren't worth it. But you have to be open with me. What you need to do now is admit it to me." He opened his hands. "I'm not carrying a wire, I swear. You and I just need to come to an understanding. You admit what you've done, and I promise to control the fallout. But I'll only do that if I know it's over. Right here and now. Am I making myself clear?"

It was Emmett's turn to stare, turning over his options, examining them from different angles. He gave a long exhale and said, "I don't know how many ways I can say this. I gave away nothing."

"This isn't a game, Emmett. One of our men was *killed* because of what you did. Understand? If you don't give me what I need, then I'm taking this to Harry. Got it?"

Emmett understood perfectly. He chewed the inside of his cheek, leaned back, and, frowning, finally said what Stan had never thought he would have the courage to say: "Why *haven't* you gone to Harry about this? If it's so goddamned serious, then why are we having coffee and a chat? I mean, look. Maybe I'm not the brightest bulb in the store, but I'm wondering why I'm not on a plane back to D.C. If your evidence is so damned ironclad." When Stan didn't answer immediately, he leaned closer. "You don't *want* to bring this to Harry. Why?"

Because I'm sleeping with your wife! he wanted to scream. He didn't give a rat's ass about Emmett Kohl, but if Emmett was sent home his wife would follow him back to the States—he feared that even more than a leak in the embassy. Instead, he controlled himself. He answered Emmett's lies with his own.

"Emmett, you and I are friends. I happen to place some importance on such things, so don't try to take advantage of me. Right now you have two options. You can do as I ask and return to your life. Don't worry about Balašević. If she knows you're blown, she won't use whatever she has on you—she'll step back. Or you can go on with what you're doing, and we can both find out how many days it takes for me to drop friendship in favor of duty."

Emmett spent another minute thinking about this, his expression drifting between moods that Stan could not interpret. Then he raised his head and looked squarely at his accuser. He smiled, nodded, and stood up. "Thanks for the coffee," Emmett said before walking away.

At three in the morning one year later, still sticky with sleep, Stan listened to Sophie: "We were having dinner and a man walked into the restaurant and shot him in the head and the chest." Then the conversation was over, and he poured himself a drink—the first sip was a toast to Emmett Kohl, but the second became a toast to Emmett Kohl's passing, and it took a while to shake the terrible pleasure this news had given him.

When it finally did leave him, he called Harry Wolcott to pass on the news. Though Harry had also been asleep, he sounded sharp, asking why Sophie had thought to call him of all people at that hour.

"She scrolled through her phone, and my name was the first she came across," Stan lied—smoothly and without self-consciousness, the way his father would have.

"The mind of a woman is an unfathomable thing," Harry told him, as if that could explain a lifetime of confusion regarding the opposite sex. "Let me make the announcement, all right? I'll call Budapest for details and share everything in the morning."

"Sure."

"Did she say who was investigating it?"

"I didn't think to ask."

Harry grunted. "Next time, think."

2

Stan didn't need to tell anyone about the murder, for when he arrived at the embassy it was already on everyone's lips, having been an easy splash in the twenty-four-hour news cycle. It was the only subject his five agents—Ricky, Tim, Klaus, Mike, and Paul—wanted to discuss. He allowed them a few minutes of conjecture before steering them back to the agenda they were obliged to deal with during their Thursday morning meetings: their sources, and how to handle them. Paul was having trouble with his primary source in Egyptian intelligence, RAINMAN, who had recently dropped off the radar and wasn't answering his requests to meet.

They had various explanations for this—Ricky thought he was trying to prove his worth before hitting them up for a better deal; Tim was more generous, believing that since Mubarak's fall RAINMAN's position was less secure, so he was simply watching out for himself. Ricky's cynical take was unlikely, for RAINMAN had come to them last year—not the other way around—and they had accommodated most of his requests for help getting business associates into the American markets. Tim's felt more likely, as the end of Mubarak's reign had thrown everything into disarray. While the military leadership running the country wasn't interested in overturning the entire security apparatus, everyone knew that once the elections came around all bets were off.

"Maybe his superiors discovered he's our friend," said Klaus.

Stan shook his head. "If Ali Busiri knew, then RAINMAN would be locked up or dead. Yet we see him in all the usual places."

"Send John" was Ricky's suggestion. "Scare him into shape."

That earned a few laughs. John Calhoun was their sole contractor, a huge Global Security tough who'd been around since late November. He wasn't around today, though. Harry had borrowed him for a job. "Where *is* the dark knight?" asked Klaus.

"Boss isn't sharing," Stan told him.

Nancy, the pool secretary, tapped on the door and summoned everyone to Harry's office.

They piled in, joining the embassy's entire Agency presence—twenty-five or so people—and Nancy closed them inside. Harry stood behind his desk, white hair brushed so meticulously that it looked like a rug, hands deep in his jacket pockets. Though he had a great view that included a small slice of the Nile between other Garden City buildings, Harry kept his venetian blinds closed. He was chewing on gum when he said, "Folks, I've got some bad news."

He told it in his measured, heavy voice, the one reserved for Statements of Importance, and Stan learned that by the time Sophie had called him the list of suspects had already been narrowed down to a single individual: Gjergj Ahmeti—a.k.a. Dumitru Cozma, Lajos Varga, and Andrzej Wójcik. Jennifer Cary asked the obvious question: "Sir, how did we verify this guy?"

"Hungarian police cameras. One down the street from the restaurant ID'd his car, which he left in a train station lot, then cameras inside the station saw him catch a EuroNight to Munich. One of our guys in Budapest, George Reardon, tells me that by the time they stopped the train to search it, just inside the Hungarian border, he was gone."

That earned a collective sigh.

Harry shared an enormous rap sheet on Gjergj Ahmeti that included, among other things, two bank robberies in his native Albania, time in a Belgrade prison for multiple homicide, connections to two murders in Marseilles, and star billing on two "persons of interest" lists, in Yemen and Brazil. The man got around.

"But who does he work for?" asked Dennis Schwarzkopf.

With his index finger, Harry drew a question mark in the air. "Interpol's spent a lot of time on his case, and there's a file a few inches thick, but no one even knows for sure if he's freelance. Looking at his sheet, though, I think he must be. There's no single organization we know of that could account for the variety of places he's worked."

"Except us," said Jerry, one of Jennifer's agents. A couple of polite chuckles, until they saw the look on Harry's face.

"Jerry," he said, "I don't want to ever hear that joke again."

Jerry nodded, flushing immediately.

To the rest of them, Harry said, "Many of you knew Emmett. He was a good man, as well as a friend. I want everyone beating the bushes. If his murder has anything at all to do with Cairo, then that information belongs on my desk immediately. Any questions?"

As they were clearing out, Harry asked Stan to stay behind, and once they were alone Stan closed the door. Harry settled in his chair, popping a fresh ribbon of gum into his mouth. "So what do you think, Stan?"

"I don't know what to think."

Harry waved a hand, irritated. "You know what I'm talking about."

Stan approached the desk, considering it. "As far as I know, he had no contact with Balašević after I brought my case to you. So it doesn't make sense. Why would the Serbs wait a year and then get rid of him in another country?"

Harry rocked back in his swivel chair. Behind him was a portrait of the president, smiling. He said, "Maybe they tried to recruit him again."

"They had to know he was already blown. It would be shockingly amateur."

Harry nodded at that, as if the possibility of an intelligence agency acting stupidly weren't commonplace, then said, "Just check on what you can, but keep it quiet. I'm not interested in slandering a dead man."

"He was a traitor."

A look crossed Harry's face, a flicker of anger. "You never proved it. Not conclusively."

"How often are we able to prove anything conclusively?"

"Often enough that I wasn't going to ruin a man's life. Often enough that we're not going to smear a dead man's name."

Though they rarely brought it up, the disagreement had colored their relationship, lurking beneath the surface of all their conversations for the past year. Stan wondered—not for the first time—if Harry already knew about Sophie, and if he had suspected ulterior motives when Stan had demanded that Emmett be taken into custody. Whatever Harry knew or suspected, right now he just opened his laptop and said, "Go get me some results, all right?"

He collected his agents again. RAINMAN was on the back burner, and Stan was finally free to discuss what had been on his mind since three in the morning.

They ran through their contacts, finding seven who'd had even a distant connection to the business affairs that Emmett had spent most of his time dealing with in Cairo. Each agent received his assignments and headed out to make calls and schedule meets. Once they were gone, Stan called the Serbian embassy and asked to speak with Dragan Milić.

Stan and Dragan had had plenty of informal conversations, that tit-for-tat between agencies that keeps intelligence in motion, and so he took the call quickly. When asked if he'd heard about Emmett Kohl, Dragan gave an exaggerated sigh. "My condolences, Stan. Yes, of course I heard about that."

"Are you free for lunch?"

"For you?"

"Yes, Dragan."

"Of course, my friend."

They met halfway between their embassies, Stan walking to clear his head, and it took a half hour to weave through the crowds to-ward the 15th of May Bridge, where he crossed to Gezira Island and finally reached La Bodega Bistro on the 26th of July, in the old Baehler's Mansions Building. It was a good walk, refreshing despite the stink of the Nile and the traffic backed up along the Corniche El Nil, and he took in the hijabbed women walking in pairs and trios, the gaunt men in sweat-dyed shirts, smoking. Arabic pop music, as ubiquitous as prayers, blared from cars, drowned out at times by the buzzing of mopeds and the choking roar of old, barely functioning pickups. At one point just before the bridge, he saw two men taking off their shoes and laying towels on the ground in preparation for midday Dhuhr prayers.

He had a brief flashback of late January, when the bridges had been stages for armies of black-clad men in riot gear facing off with angry crowds trying to break through government lines to reach Tahrir. He'd mostly kept out of it, slipping out of the embassy only a few times to get a better look at the conflict. Early on, he found himself standing off to the side among government forces. Later, standing at the same corners, he found himself among the weeping, jubilant Egyptian masses as the Central Security Forces were pushed back and then scattered, running for their lives, stripping off their black uniforms. Now those same revolutionaries were walking the bridge, loitering and laughing, occupied again by the little dramas of work, life, and love. They were relentless, he thought. After millennia suffering under the heels of autocrats, from the pharaohs to the meager dictators propped up by Western investments, they were still standing, laughing and holding on to their faith. Up ahead, a line of twelve shoeless men were on their knees, facing Mecca.

He took out his phone and called Sophie but got her voice mail. He didn't leave a message.

La Bodega was busy, but Dragan had used his considerable influ-ence to get a secluded table in the rear booth. Yellow fin-de-siècle lighting and art nouveau furnishings enhanced the ambience, which only made Dragan Milić look more out of place. He was not the kind of man who appeared comfortable in a suit; to Stan, Dragan always looked as if he should be wearing bikini briefs and lounging beside a concrete pool in some cheap Adriatic resort, his flabby torso burned pink and his wiry gray hair bleached yellow. He smiled a lot and gestured to the world with fat fingers that ended in gnawed nails, all his words effusive. He'd known Emmett, he told Stan. Not well, "but how well do any of us know each other?" By the time the platters arrived—sea bass for him, scallops for Stan—he was on to other topics, and Stan let him go on with his complaints about the new Egyptian security services. "They're not gentlemen anymore, Stan. You understand me?"

Dragan had obviously run into a particularly troublesome bureaucrat that morning, for most of Egypt's security infrastructure was still intact, with the same old hands at the wheel. Yet Stan said, "I understand perfectly."

Dragan clapped his hands together. "Say what you like about the old boys, but they knew how to wine and dine. That's how you get things done."

"Like what I'm doing to you right now."

"Exactly," he said without hesitation. "You bring me to an excellent restaurant, you let me order what I like, and you soften me with compliments, perhaps a little inside information. Only *then* do you place your cards on the table. These new guys . . ." He shook his head, lost for words.

"It's time," Stan told him.

Dragan patted his lips with a napkin. "Time?"

"My cards."

"Of course, of course. Tell me, my friend."

Though they had talked around the subject before, they had never broached it directly. With Emmett's murder, there seemed to be no choice. He said, "Is Zora Balašević still in your shop?"

Eyebrows rose. "Balašević? Do I know her?"

"Look at the label on that wine, Dragan. That's a chunk of the national budget right there."

A grin. "Oh, Zora *Balašević*! Like the great singer. I know of this woman, yes, but she's not part of my shop, as you say."

The lack of sleep and a gin-heavy Negroni before the meal were catching up to Stan. He rubbed his eyes. "Please, Dragan. This is about a murdered diplomat. I need a little perestroika here."

"Why does everyone think that Russian words will get you anywhere with a Serb? I hate those bastards."

"Zora Balašević."

He sniffed and sipped at his glass of Clos des Papes Rhone, then spoke very seriously and quietly. "If Zora Balašević has come to you, I firmly suggest you give it a second thought. She's connected to criminal gangs in Belgrade, probably trading in little girls. You don't want someone like that on your team."

"She was on your team, though. Wasn't she?"

"Once," said Dragan. He frowned and seesawed his right hand. "Briefly, Stan. Then we kicked her onto the street. Seriously."

"But you ran her when Emmett was in town."

"When did Emmett come to town?"

"February of 2009."

"That's when we got *rid* of her, Stan. February—no: March of 2009."

There was something convincing about Dragan's manner, and if he *was* being honest, then the events of last summer had been something entirely different than he had imagined. Stan leaned close, his voice serious and low. "Let me tell you a story, and maybe you can help me explain it."

Dragan waited.

"This woman, Balašević, came to Emmett. This would be February of 2009. They knew each other back in the nineties, but times had changed since then. Emmett was now a diplomat, and she, she claimed, was one of your people. She used blackmail. She told Emmett that she would publicize some nasty secrets from his past if he didn't give her classified embassy intelligence. For at least a year this went on." He paused, staring hard, but Dragan wasn't saying anything. "Look, if she *was* one of your people during that year, then I might become angry. I might even call you names. But I'll soon get over it, and next year you'll have some similar complaint about me.

If, however, she *isn't* one of your people, then I'm not only going to become angry, I'll become destructive. I'll start digging into her life, and into yours, until I find out who stole our information. You understand my position?"

Dragan held his gaze for ten full seconds before saying, "Perfectly." Then: "I'm sorry to say that Zora Balašević never passed intelligence from Emmett Kohl to my office. More's the pity."

"Why did you get rid of her?"

He glanced over Stan's shoulder at the restaurant. "She was *moon*lighting—that's the correct word? We discovered, with the greatest sadness, that we were not the only client for her intelligence. I wanted to have her sent home missing some body parts, but it turns out that she has friends in Belgrade, friends who owe her. So I was told to keep my hands to myself."

"Who was she moonlighting for?"

"Our hosts, the Egyptians." He shook his head. "She is like Hosni."

Stan frowned, not understanding.

Dragan smiled. "Remember what that Iraqi corpse, Saddam Hussein, used to say of Mubarak? That he was like a pay phone. *You deposit your money, and you get what you want in return.* Zora Balašević is the same. She will take a coin from anyone."

Stan considered this. "She continued working for them?"

"I don't know."

"Where is she now?"

"I will look into it." He took another sip of his wine, then set it down. "This is what I do know: She's from Novi Sad. During the Bosnian War she supported Republika Srpska, which was how she made her influential friends. She's in her early fifties, and she used to own a small place on Al-Muizz Street, in Islamic Cairo. And for a brief, wondrous period she held a respectable job in my office before she threw it away. That's the extent of my knowledge."

"So she's a mystery."

Dragan nodded, leaned back, and, proving he was as well connected as he had ever been, said, "Just like that Albanian thug who killed Mr. Kohl."

3

Zora Balašević had left Cairo less than a week after Emmett and Sophie moved to Budapest, a fact that Stan had taken as further evidence of Emmett's guilt. With her star source gone, why would she stay? Still tipsy from lunch, he returned to her file, tracking down the flight plan that had taken her back to Serbia. According to airline records, she had boarded a plane for Frankfurt and transferred to a Jat flight to Belgrade six hours later—an odd route. Direct flights from Cairo to Belgrade existed, yet she had chosen to spend six whole hours in Frankfurt's dour international hub. An arranged meet? He thought a moment, then texted Saul, an old friend at Langley who had been part of the communiqués involving the leaked materials last year, asking how long Frankfurt International held on to security footage.

As for her criminal connections, there was little to go on. She was on a list of suspected members of the Zemun clan, which specialized in the transport of drugs, contract murder, and kidnappings. What was her connection? Association, and not much more: She'd been seen in the company of ranking Zemun members. Her criminal record was more than a decade old, from when she had run guns into Republika Srpska, that little mountainous region of Serb nationalism within the borders of Bosnia-Herzegovina. Zealot or opportunist? As he stared at her file photo Stan suspected the former, but he was only guessing. She looked, with her dark eyes and black hair, as if she had been attractive in a slow-burn sort of way when she was younger, but that beauty had since been marred by hard living: eyes hollow and cheeks loose from a lifetime of heavy smoking. She had the face of someone with a whole world of tragedy behind her; she had a refugee's face.

Though Dragan had been convincing, Stan wasn't ready to accept his claims to innocence. Balašević could easily have been part of his crew, brought in temporarily because of her connection to Emmett, and in the face of Stan's accusations Dragan's only move would have been to wash his hands of her. But Stan thought he had a pretty good fix on Dragan Milić. The Serb was enough of a pro, and enough of an engaged station manager, to know that Stan wouldn't attempt retaliation for what had been, in essence, a beautifully run operation to collect intelligence from the American embassy. In fact, had Dragan admitted to it, Stan would only have admired him more—his panache as well as his honesty. Stan, in turn, would have felt encouraged to act similarly. Despite the proliferation of satellites and networked databases and laser-guided drones, espionage was still a very personal business.

Were the rest of Dragan's claims true? *Had* Balašević worked for the Egyptians? If so, then it was the Egyptians who had sold the intel on to Syria, Libya, and Pakistan. It was possible. Was it likely? He couldn't be sure.

By close of business, Ricky and Klaus had heard back from two contacts but come up empty. These two Egyptians had known Emmett only distantly, having met him at embassy get-togethers in order to ask for ridiculous trade concessions that Emmett hadn't even been in a position to consider. Stan gave Harry an update before leaving, and the station chief sat glumly behind his desk, listening distantly to their failures. Dragan Milić's claims to innocence didn't seem to surprise him, nor did the possibility of Egypt receiving Balašević's intel.

Eventually, Harry said, "You know, Stan, it may have nothing to do with Cairo. Maybe Emmett made the mistake of sleeping with the wrong Hungarian girl."

"Whose boyfriend just happened to be an international hit man?"

"I've seen worse luck in my time."

"I haven't," Stan said.

"Then you need to get out more."

Stan didn't live far from the embassy, so he walked home in the growing darkness along Garden City's elegantly curved, tree-lined streets, which had been built by the British at the start of the twentieth century to surround their embassy. On an empty block of colonial villas he gave Sophie another try. No answer, and no voice mail, either—he guessed it was full.

What was Sophie's life like now? Had she found someone else in Budapest, some Stan-replacement to make up for her wreck of a husband? And who had told Emmett about them—who else knew? He had told no one, so there were two possibilities. First, that Sophie had trusted the wrong person with her secret. Though generally tight-lipped, Sophie Kohl had a tendency to wander when she became comfortable, heading down trails of association, and it didn't seem improbable that, maybe after a few drinks in some Budapest bar, she'd let their secret slip to the wrong person. That, at least, was preferable to the second possibility, which was that their affair had not been as much of a secret as he'd thought. Had someone in the office decided to expose him to Emmett? To what end? He thought through his colleagues in the embassy—who among them was jockeying for power? All of them, really, but there were easier ways to unseat Stan than throwing mud at his sexual life.

Maybe it wasn't anyone in the embassy, but a representative of another government. The Egyptians, the Serbs, or even, for all he knew, the Hungarians. But why? The affair had been over for half a year—what would the embarrassment serve at this point?

He scratched at the side of his nose, remembering Sophie's burgundy lipstick, the arch of her calf, the cinnamon tint of her perfume. Stan wasn't a man of great experience; at thirty-seven, he could count all his lovers on a single hand, and perhaps for that reason it still hurt to remember the end of his relationship with Sophie Kohl.

It had been sudden, so abrupt that they hadn't even had time for a final teary fight. Her husband announced that they were moving on to Budapest, and then she stopped answering his calls. Just like that. Had she known that their flight from Cairo was a direct result of his investigations? He didn't think so, but he had suddenly become her husband's co-worker again, and nothing he whispered during their brief moments in the same room did anything to change that. Her excuse, muttered under her breath, was that they'd both known this time would come, and ending it quickly was the best course. She hadn't been cold about it; she'd just been incomprehensibly rational. Stan, on the other hand, had not been. He began drinking too much, slipping up at work, and it took many weeks before he was able to climb out of his hole again. Then, six months later, at three in the morning, she was calling him. How could he not be surprised?

You told him about us, and you said you were in love.

He had not told Emmett any such thing, but he easily could have.

"Mr. Bertolli?"

He was at his corner, and the voice belonged to one of two men with dark hair and severe smiles. He'd been too distracted to notice them approaching.

"Mr. Bertolli, right this way."

Polite but firm. Late twenties, Slavic accents, and tight-fitting suits. No guns, but their manner suggested they didn't really need them. So he followed them to a black Audi parked on the other side of the street, in front of his building. One of them opened a rear door, and, before getting in, Stan peered inside to verify his suspicion: It was Dragan. He was sitting back against the opposite door, an arm across one headrest, his free hand holding a highball glass with an inch of something strong in it, an old man at rest. He was smiling, winking.

"Come, Stan. A quick word."

He slid in; the young man behind him closed the door.

"Drink?"

Stan shook his head, for all he really wanted was sleep.

Dragan looked into his glass. "*Vinjak,* a lovely brandy from home."

"I'm sure it's lovely, but no thanks."

A shrug, and he took a swig. "That woman, Zora Balašević. You are still interested?"

"Absolutely."

He nodded, closing his eyes briefly, then said, "I was not giving you the runaround earlier—I told you what I knew. But I made some calls. She's in Novi Sad right now. She came into some money last year—Egyptian, no doubt—and now she's living in an enormous house on the Danube. Amazing security system on this place, they tell me. If you like, we can pick her up and have a word with her." He waited, and when Stan didn't answer he said, "All you have to do is tell me what questions to ask."

On the surface, it was an excellent offer, but Stan hesitated. All Dragan wanted in return was to know everything that he knew—or to know what he *didn't* know, which in the intelligence game was the same thing. What Dragan didn't realize was that Stan didn't know anything yet. "I just want to know who she works for—or who she worked for when she was in Cairo."

"Nothing more?" Dragan asked, but the answer hadn't disappointed him at all, and that was when it happened: Stan became his father. Such moments were rare, but when they occurred they often saved him. He felt it in his thighs, a weight that mocked Paolo Bertolli's fat legs, and his thoughts turned labyrinthine, motivations twisting upon themselves until, in a sudden burst of clarity, a simple truth presented itself. In that warm Audi, he realized that his questions for Zora Balašević were entirely beside the point. Dragan simply wanted to bring in a woman who he now knew had had access to reams of classified American material—*that* was his real interest.

Stan imagined the hours since their lunch: Dragan's piqued interest, looking into Balašević, then the disappointment that he hadn't actually extorted Emmett himself. Dragan would have wondered how to make up for his shortcomings. Maybe he had called home and learned that, given Balašević's connections, simply picking her up was out of the question. Therefore, he wanted to come with a different story: *Brothers, this is a request from the Americans. We do this, and we get a new level of cooperation.* They would bring her in, and Dragan would fly back to sit with her in a barren room in the countryside, with easy access to all the American secrets in her head.

It wasn't worth it, not yet at least. "Leave her alone," he said. "Maybe later I'll come to you, hat in hand, asking for this. But it's too early."

"I can't promise that I'll know where she is later."

Stan gave him a smile. "I have faith in you."

Dragan smiled then, too. The Paolo Bertolli in Stan knew that Dragan had suspected this outcome from the start, and if he'd gone along with the plan Dragan probably would've been disappointed in him. Instead, he'd earned a little respect from the old spy. Perhaps it was that respect that led Dragan to pat Stan's knee lightly and say, "There is one more thing, my friend. While I might enjoy watching you chase your tail, I will admit that I did know about that meeting between Zora Balašević and Emmett Kohl. This is why she came to Cairo. She claimed she had an old friend in the American embassy she could extort. A very forthright woman, Zora. She convinced Belgrade, and Belgrade sent her here. She approached Emmett and made her case to him. According to her, he refused. A patriot, she called Emmett. Soon afterward, she was no longer working for us, because we had discovered her connection to the Egyptians."

Stan felt as if Dragan had tossed him a live grenade, shattering his entire vision of the last year. If Emmett hadn't been leaking to Balašević, then it meant that he'd been wrong from the start. Did that mean that someone else in the embassy had been selling information? If so, Emmett and Sophie never would have had to leave town. He and Sophie could have remained together. Emmett, perhaps, would still be alive. Stan squeezed his forehead. "Did you believe her?"

"I did," Dragan said, musing over this. "Until, that is, we realized she had those new employers. I thought to myself, *Why would the Egyptians want an old bitch like that?*"

"Because she really did have Emmett."

Dragan shrugged, smiling.

"What did she have on him?"

"On Emmett?"

Stan released his forehead and nodded at him. "What was she blackmailing him with?"

Dragan shrugged. "I have no idea. She wouldn't share with me, and when I insisted she referred me to those offices in Belgrade, where her protectors work. I'm just a station chief, Stan. I don't have any actual authority."

"Do you know who she reported to in the Egyptian service?"

Dragan considered this a moment, wondering how much to share, then shrugged. He'd already shared more than Stan would have, but tonight he was feeling generous. "Two meetings in public parks with someone from Ali Busiri's office. You know Busiri, of course."

Of course. Ali Busiri: a tough nut who ran his own section in *Al-Amn al-Markazī,* the Central Security Forces, where Paul's source RAINMAN worked. Occasionally, Busiri butted heads with embassies, for while part of Central Security's mandate was to protect foreign missions, Busiri's office often used that access to turn embassy staff into sources. He'd apparently done that with Zora Balašević. He was very good at the game, but he was also an old hand—someone who, like Dragan, Stan could probably talk to.

As if reading his mind, Dragan said, "I'm not sure he'll be very forthcoming. I tried to have Zora kicked out of Egypt, and he bought me lunch in order to threaten me."

"Did he?"

"Ali Busiri is a man who knows the value of brute force. Still, he's one of the old ones, and I can't help but respect his muscle."

"Thank you, Dragan."

The Serb raised his glass. "You enjoy your evening, my friend."

Stan pulled the latch and opened the door, then climbed out. Dragan's two assistants, waiting on the curb, climbed into the front seats. The Audi drove off as, from over the rooftops, Stan heard a crackly speaker call the faithful of Cairo to Maghrib prayers.

That haunting sound came back to him later, in his dreams, lingering when, at three thirty, Sophie woke him to say that she would be arriving the next evening on EgyptAir 552, landing at seven. "Can you keep it quiet?" she asked.

"Why?"

"Because I don't want anyone to try to stop me."

Amen, he thought as a thrill rippled through his body. It felt a lot like hunger.

4

In the office, he barely held on, waiting for seven o'clock. Questions plagued him. Was Sophie running from the mess her life had become, or was she running toward him? He wasn't sure how he felt about either of these possibilities. Should he tell Harry about her imminent arrival? She wanted to come in quietly, and the fact was that Stan wanted this, too. Harry would eventually learn she was in town, but first he wanted her all to himself. And finally, who told Emmett about the two of them? As he watched faces pass by the window of his office, their features tightened by the tension in the building, he speculated one by one on who might want to stab him in the back.

Enough.

He straightened himself and logged into one of five anonymous e-mail accounts he used for signaling contacts, then cut-and-pasted a short note in Arabic to Ali Busiri. It was a bit of spam, boasting investment opportunities in Southeast Asia, but the content wasn't important. All Busiri needed to see was the from-address, and he would know that Stan Bertolli from the U.S. embassy wanted to have a chat with him as soon as possible. If RAINMAN, their source in his office, wasn't returning their calls, then he would go straight to the boss.

He looked up to see the whole floor walking past his door, in the direction of Harry's office. Jennifer Cary waved for him to follow.

Cramped tight in that room, they listened to the dismal news of potential leads that had led nowhere. Terry Alderman's people had uncovered odd wires to Emmett's Bank of America account, but those turned out to be for speaking engagements he'd done the previous year. Dennis Schwarzkopf's agents were at first excited by the news that one of Emmett's Egyptian associates, a real estate developer, had begun investing in Budapest a couple of months after Emmett relocated, but more probing revealed that the developer, after a month of fruitless negotiations, had thrown up his hands and abandoned the country entirely. That had been in December, and Emmett had had no connection to the failed dealings. Jennifer Cary's people, like Stan's, had nothing to offer the group, and Harry told them to get off their asses and back to work, as if he were speaking to a room full of auto workers. Then he took a breath, sat down, and waved his hands in the air. "Okay, okay. If there's no connection to us, then there's no connection. But *try*, all right? I'm not just asking for personal reasons. If we don't find a local connection, but next week the Hungarians or the Egyptians do, then you know how that's going to make us look."

The office door opened, and Nancy looked in, aiming a long, painted fingernail. "Stan, line two."

Everyone was watching, and he felt damp with sudden perspiration, fearing that it was Sophie. "Can you take a message?"

"It's Paul. He says you'll want to take this."

He hurried to his office. Paul's voice came in clearly despite traffic noises in the background. "Sorry for dropping out on you, but it was a last-minute meet."

"You should've checked in."

"It was RAINMAN."

"RAINMAN?" Stan asked, the coincidence making him briefly stupid. "Anything interesting?"

"I'll tell you in a few minutes."

A quarter hour later, Paul was sitting in his office. A blond Pennsylvanian with a farm childhood and a Princeton education, he looked like he had just gotten out of bed, which was apparently where he had been when RAINMAN called. "He got my message about Kohl."

Civil servants come and go, but RAINMAN, or Omar Halawi, had been around for decades and, based on his position in the Central Security Services, just under Ali Busiri, knew a lot about a lot of people. For a while he had been willing to share that knowledge. Sometimes the Agency paid for information with trade concessions for him and his friends. His original contact had been Amir Najafi, John Calhoun's Global Security predecessor, but he'd been killed in a five-car pileup on the Ring Road around Cairo. So Paul had taken over the role.

"He tells me one thing, just one thing. But he wants to tell it face-to-face. He tells me that if we want to find Emmett's murderer, we need to look at ourselves."

Stan frowned. "Does that mean what I think it means?"

Paul leaned back, opening his hands. "I asked the same thing, and apparently it does. I asked him *why* we would want to get rid of one of our own consuls. What do you think he said?"

"I don't know, Paul."

"To keep him quiet."

"About?"

Paul shrugged. "He wasn't going to say. But he told me to tell you—he mentioned you by name—that you should watch your back."

"Sounds like he's trying to scare me."

Another shrug. "I'm just the messenger."

Stan nodded, taking this in.

"Well? It's something, no?"

"It's certainly that," Stan said, then shook his head. "Or it's nothing. He drops contact for a few weeks and suddenly pops up with this? Halawi's an old pro—he could even be passing on a message from Busiri. I wouldn't take anything either of them says at face value. Not yet."

"Want me to send a reply?"

"Let me talk to Busiri first, establish some parameters, then we'll have better questions for Halawi. And keep this under your hat. If we bring in something like this and it fizzles out, Harry's going to have a coronary."

After Paul left, Stan puzzled over the accusation. The Agency had a checkered history, but when it wanted to keep fellow Americans quiet, it smeared their names in the newspapers and slapped them with lawsuits. It seldom had reason to reach for a gun.

His phone rang. Nancy said, "I've got John Calhoun. He wants the boss, but Harry's out for a cigarette."

"Patch him through." Once the familiar sequence of clicks ended, he said, "John, you back already?"

He hadn't seen John in a couple of days—Harry had taken his contractor away for some unknown job. But instead of giving Stan a clue John only muttered, "Yeah."

"We'll see you today?"

"No."

Like many big men, John used silence to his advantage, and that morning he was master of the monosyllable. "So you're just checking in?"

"That's right."

"Everything okay?"

"No," John said, then paused, preparing himself for more words than he'd planned to use. "But I'll need to sleep it off. Just tell Harry that it didn't work." As an afterthought, he added, "Please."

"It . . ." Stan said, waiting for him to fill in something, anything.

"I'll file my report for him Monday. If he wants it sooner, I can come in tomorrow."

"I'll let him know, but he's a little backed up today. We got some shit news from Budapest."

"Budapest?"

Stan told him about Emmett, and he said, "My condolences," as if he gave a damn. Stan doubted he did.

When Harry returned from his cigarette break, Stan knocked on his door and found him immersed in his laptop, which he closed. The room smelled of cigarette ash. "Anything?" he asked by way of greeting.

"I'll let you know later," Stan said. "John called in and said something about *it* not working. He's going to sleep but will report on Monday. Unless you want him to come in tomorrow."

The sign was unmistakable. Harry's forehead crinkled, as if it had been slapped. "That's all he said?"

Stan nodded. "What does *it* mean?"

Harry exhaled through his nose. After a pause, he said, "It means Langley is going to be even more irritated with us than it usually is."

Stan waited for more, but Harry was already reopening his laptop. On the way back to his desk, the BlackBerry in his pocket vibrated a message from his friend at Langley, Saul.

> FRA holds footage indef. In practice about 5 yrs. What are you
> looking for? I'll make some calls.

Stan switched to email to thank Saul and send the details: September 4, 2010, Zora Balašević, Lufthansa 585 from Cairo to Frankfurt, and Jat 351 to Belgrade.

Then his mind was drawn inevitably back to Omar Halawi's warning. *Look at yourselves.* He hesitated a full five seconds before clicking SEND.

5

He was at the airport a half hour early because he couldn't think of what to do with himself, and he wandered among the listless crowds and armed security, wondering how his father would have approached the questions before him. Paolo Bertolli would have taken it easy. He had been a doyen of the long-term operation, an agent with immeasurable patience—it was the only way he could have survived for so long within the Red Brigades, while around him young Marxist-Leninist Italians ate themselves up with paranoia. Stan had never had that kind of patience, nor that kind of bravery.

Sophie Kohl, he believed when he first laid eyes on her trailing the other passengers out of Arrivals, wouldn't be any help. She looked overused, slumped under the weight of her bulky shoulder bag, which was apparently her only luggage. Even broken, though, she had taken the time to apply the burgundy lipstick he remembered so well. He took the heavy bag from her, gave her a hug and a kiss on the cheek, and thought, *Christ you're beautiful,* though he didn't say it aloud. He noticed how easily she still fit in his arms, and how holding her brought on a carnivorous instinct, the desire to consume her whole. It was a strong desire, and six months hadn't done a thing to lessen it. Without her, he had been able to convince himself that he was fine being alone, but in her presence the whole illusion was shattered, and he was just as stunned as he had been the previous year.

Besides the how-are-yous and let-me-help-yous they didn't speak in the airport, and on the way to the parking lot she only said, "It's warm here."

"I suppose it is."

"I'd forgotten."

It wasn't until they were in the car, heading out of the airport and onto the long, well-lit El-Orouba Road into town, that he said, "Tell me about it, Sophie."

"Do I have to?"

"You don't have to do anything. But maybe you'd like to tell me why you're in Cairo. I thought you'd be heading home."

He got silence for his efforts, and when he looked over her face was twisted in an expression he recognized: eyes sad and the left corner of her lips sucked in, held tight between her teeth. It was a look of guilt—she had sometimes worn the same expression after their trysts.

"You're here for a reason."

Gazing at the passing streetlamps, she said, "It just seemed like the place to be. He—Emmett—was talking about Cairo before. It. Happened."

"What about Cairo?"

"About a woman we knew a long time ago. Serbian. She was in Cairo, too."

Stan had to concentrate on his hands to make sure he didn't jerk the car off the road. Who else could she have been talking about? "Does she have a name?"

"Zora Balašević."

He breathed through his nose, waiting, but she said nothing. "How did you know her?"

"Honeymoon. Back in '91. We went to Novi Sad. I didn't tell you?"

"Only that you'd been there."

"The war was getting started," she said, but didn't continue.

"So he was talking about an old friend of yours."

"Sort of. But we hadn't seen her in twenty years, then she popped up in Cairo. They had lunch."

"Why did he tell you about lunch with this Serb woman?" he asked. Maybe he'd been wrong—maybe she did hold answers.

"It was a story. It was on his mind."

"What's the connection?"

"Excuse me?"

"He talks about her just beforehand," he said, sharing her unwillingness to say "murder" aloud, "and now you're here. Do you think there's some connection?"

"Maybe." He couldn't see her face; he was focused on a weaving truck up ahead. "Maybe I can find her and see if she knows something. I don't know." She shrugged. "I'm just so tired, Stan. Can I sleep at your place?"

"I wouldn't let you sleep anywhere else."

Hiding what he'd known about Balašević hadn't been his plan. In fact, he'd had no plan before collecting her from the airport. But she'd come out with the name so quickly that he didn't have a chance to reflect; the concealment began on its own. Then he was trapped in a deception that he would have to carry on all night, at least. How easily these things could happen. At moments like this, he was in awe of his father.

Tomorrow, he thought as he focused on his driving, he could pretend to discover the name. But for that night deception would define their relationship. He hadn't wanted that.

Perhaps because of this, there was a definite awkwardness between them when they got to Stan's apartment. He made dinner— frozen tilapia filets and garlic simmered in olive oil—and they drank an Australian Riesling, but even with the alcohol in them the overwhelming feeling that they were strangers stuck in the same room never quite left. Yet she was here, actually *here*, and he remembered the feel of her skin, its texture and pliability and scent. It was all he could do to resist hauling her to the bedroom.

He squeezed his eyes shut.

After dinner, they moved out to the terrace, and he brought out some throw blankets to fight the mild chill. His apartment was just high enough that, when you stood, you could see over rooftops and straight across the Nile to the concrete cacophony of Giza and, beyond, the pyramids Khufu, Khafre, and Menkaure, lit up for the evening's Sound and Light Show. He paid a lot for that partial view, but Sophie only gave the monumental structures a glance before settling down on one of his wooden chairs and losing sight of them entirely. She talked a while, telling him about the idiosyncrasies of her life in Budapest, her "quite crazy" friend Glenda, and how much she missed Cairo (Cairo, she said, not him). Then she asked, "What do you know about Jibril Aziz?"

He repeated the name back to her, and she nodded. "Nothing," he said. "Who is he?"

"He's American. I think he's CIA."

"Why do you think that?"

"Because the Hungarians know that he is."

Stan had no idea who Jibril Aziz was. "I'll look into it," he said.

"I'd appreciate that. And now that I'm here, I want to talk to Harry."

This gave him pause. He thought of how it would look, Sophie staying in his place just after her husband had been killed. Would Harry connect that to Stan's attempts to throw Emmett to the wolves at Langley? Of course he would. Harry was as suspicious as anyone in the department. "Wait," he told her. "I can get more out of him than you can."

She frowned, not liking this, so he explained himself:

"You're going to come in, and he's going to handle you. He'll sweet-talk you and give you the illusion that he's sharing everything—but you're not cleared for things, and it doesn't help that you're a grieving widow. He won't really tell you a thing. You can talk to him, of course, but wait. Let me get in there first."

"You'll ask about Jibril Aziz?"

"I will. Just tell me how he connects to Emmett."

She sighed, a touch of irritation, as if the connection were obvious, and he noticed the mellow glow of sweat on her upper lip. She said, "He was in Budapest; he met with Emmett. Twice. He also met with some people the Hungarians think might be terrorists."

Stan rubbed his face, wondering how to connect this to Zora Balašević. He had no idea. Maybe to avoid the increasing confusion, his thoughts began to grow carnal again. He could feel it in his legs, different from the weighty feeling of his father coming to him, for this tingling rose higher. The same desire he'd felt in the airport, to crawl across the terrace and pull her down off her chair, wrap himself around her, lick the sweat off of her lip, and slowly, meticulously, devour her. He pressed his eyes with his fingertips and tried to focus.

"I'll do everything I can. You know that. But it sounds to me like this is all connecting to Budapest, not Cairo."

She smiled suddenly, and it was then that he realized she hadn't really smiled, not a real smile, since she arrived. Her eyes were wet. "You don't understand, do you?"

He apparently didn't.

She leaned forward and took the hand he had left on his knee, squeezing. "I know you'll help me, Stan. That's why I'm here. *You're* why I'm here."

Just like that, he was in love all over again.

Then the moment was gone, and she was looking out, as if through the villa across the street she could see the pyramids. She stood slowly to her full height and squinted at the distant glow. She exhaled. "They're so damned beautiful, aren't they?"

"Yes," he said, but he had no need to stand. Now that she was here, he felt little need for anything.

John

1

WELCOME TO THE NEW LIBYA, read the spray-painted greeting, for the border guards had fled the night before. Creeping in his direction along the desert road, loaded-down cars and handcarts and burdened refugees on foot made their painful way toward Egypt. John wondered how they could stand so many miles under this sun, fingers burned yet chapped by the desert winds, straining under the weight of woven luggage and plastic bags, duct-taped boxes and suitcases, hauling clothes, food, and babies. The Mediterranean wasn't far away but the landscape gave no sign of this. Each time he heard an infant scream his heart jumped into his throat.

How did they keep moving? It was instinct, he supposed. They were just motivated by the human urge to run from danger, and that was explanation enough.

Danisha had once told him that the instinct for flight was natural—it was a sign of health. The inverse was a symptom of sickness. It wasn't the reason for the divorce, but it certainly hadn't helped, and it was impossible not to think of her as he leaned against the dirty hood of the Peugeot, preparing to move against the tide of healthy people fleeing a civil war.

Still, it was a giddy time. In Cairo, he'd seen young faces rapturous with the wild-eyed jubilation of the Apocalypse. The world had changed so quickly. A couple of months ago, people on the streets of

North Africa wouldn't have thought to raise their voices at all, but in Tunisia one Friday morning in December a produce seller named Mohamed Bouazizi, driven to the edge by corrupt police and a senseless bureaucracy, soaked himself in paint thinner and set himself on fire. Protests had grown until President Ben Ali, after twenty-three years of power, fled the country. Algeria came next, protesting and rioting, followed soon by Lebanon.

John had been on hand to watch Egypt rise up, and Libyans had been watching it, too. Four days after Hosni Mubarak stepped down, unrest rolled through Benghazi, Libya's second city. Protesters had been shot and kidnapped from the sidewalks, yet it went on. The protesters raided government weapon depots and went to war. Blood on the pavement, it turned out, wasn't enough to stop history.

More fires were raging elsewhere: Jordan, Mauritania, Sudan, Oman, Yemen, and Saudi Arabia. Syria, Djibouti, Morocco, Bahrain, Iran, Kuwait, and the perpetual fire of Iraq. It was, John had been told by enthusiasts, a remarkable time to be alive.

Even the Bedouins guarding the Egyptian side of the border had seemed lighthearted as they checked their passports and waved them through. "Journalists? Yes? Go, go!" Though the guards were overwhelmed by the flow of refugees and Egyptian workers returning home, their steps were buoyant. *Hold on to that feeling,* John wanted to tell them. *Next week you'll be dreaming about it.*

By that day, March 3, one day after the murder of an American diplomat in Budapest and two weeks after the Day of Revolt, the Libyan body count—estimated from panicked reports, anecdotes, and unreliable official statements from Tripoli—had passed a thousand. The east was in rebel hands, based in Benghazi, where revolutionary councils were optimistically setting up new local governments, while Tripoli and most of the west were still held by Muammar Gadhafi's loyalists, who showed their allegiance by wearing green shirts and scarves. Green was Gadhafi's color.

Somewhere, another baby was screaming. He couldn't find it in the crowd.

He smelled smoke on the cool desert wind as he adjusted the

wide-brimmed safari hat he'd picked up that morning in Marsa Matrouh, then examined the loose groups of men in soiled jackets and
clean shirts, in robes and local headdress, talking. Families squatted
in protective circles on the sand, others joining a long line heading to
the Egyptian border post. There were cars parked here and there,
dusty Western makes cooling off around a makeshift refreshment
stand stocking warm bottled drinks and hot tea. A few yards from
the stand, Jibril Aziz was talking in Arabic to three men who had
come from Benghazi.

He had picked up Jibril from the Semiramis InterContinental
before dawn, as Cairo was just starting to wake up. They hadn't
met before, but the man from Langley had been interested in only
the briefest of introductions. John was just a driver, after all. Jibril
had sniffed at their late-nineties Peugeot before climbing in, and as
they took the long coastal road, fighting heavy traffic along the way,
Jibril had spent a lot of time on his smartphone, checking maps, news
reports, and weather forecasts, and occasionally holding conversations in Arabic. Did he know that his driver only understood enough
of the language to order a meal? John had no idea.

It had been a long drive from Cairo. They had refueled and bought
grilled lamb from a street vendor in Marsa Matrouh, where Jibril
met with a short man in a red-checked ghutra for a quick coffee at an
outdoor café while John bought his hat. Once the meeting was over,
Jibril laid down some coins, shook the man's hand, and nodded at
John to meet him back at the car. They drove on in silence. John
wanted to ask questions, but he knew his place. His only responsibility was to get this man safely to Ajdabiya, on the Gulf of Sidra.
From there, a contact would take him farther, to Brega, where fighting was going on—he'd told John that much. Afterward (John guessed
from the occasional proper nouns amid the Arabic), Jibril was heading toward Tripoli.

Once inside Libya, John's plan had been to stick to the northern
coastal highway that arced westward from Tubruq, through the
green cities of Derna and, inland, Al Bayda, before heading south
through Benghazi to Ajdabiya. In case of trouble, they could find

help. Jibril, though, was in a hurry and insisted that they take the direct but unpredictable desert road from Tubruq down to Al`Adam, then straight on to Ajdabiya, through 250 miles of desert, much of it, he guessed, with no phone reception. It had been their single subject of conversation, and the one thing they couldn't agree on.

When Jibril finally returned to the car, he was carrying a dirty Kalashnikov. His white shirt was clean and dry, but he had a few days' growth on his cheeks; with another day and a change of clothes, he would be indistinguishable from these refugees. "We're skipping the coastal road," he told John.

"Don't say that."

"After Tubruq it's a mess. We'll never get through in time."

In time for what? John wanted to ask, but there was nothing to say. The decision had been made. So John nodded at the Kalashnikov. "How much did that cost?"

Jibril raised the weapon, turning it over in his hands. "Hundred fifty."

"Dollars?"

"Euros."

"How many rounds?"

"Twenty-eight."

"Does it even work?"

Jibril looked down at the weapon and, with a flash of embarrassment, said, "That's an excellent question."

John tried to hide the judgment in his face as he walked around the Peugeot and took the rifle from him, then carried it out past the road, past the groups of huddled smoking men, and into the cracked desert. Jibril followed from a distance and watched as he cleared the breech, then pulled out the banana clip and checked the cartridges. This, at least, was an area in which John had some authority. He got down into a kneeling position and adjusted the rear iron sight, raised the gun to his shoulder, and aimed into the desert at a small boulder about a hundred yards away. He fired a single shot. A couple of yards to the right of the rock, sand exploded. He adjusted the front sight, then fired again. Another burst of sand. He adjusted once more, and this time the rock went up in a burst of cloud. He carried the rifle back, noting all the stares as he approached Jibril and handed it over. "Looks all right."

"I could've done that."

"What if it had blown up in your face?"

"Doubtful."

"I'm supposed to keep you safe. If you do get killed, it better not be for something as stupid as this."

During the drive toward Tubruq, weaving occasionally around stalled cars and children and goats that had broken loose, John said, "How long has it been?"

"What, been?"

"Since you were last here." When he didn't receive an answer, John said, "Langley isn't sending in someone cold to chat with the opposition." He hadn't been told why Jibril was going into Libya, but with Libyan affairs the way they were, it didn't take a foreign relations expert to figure it out.

Jibril thought a moment, maybe considering evasions, but said, "Six years."

"Your contacts are still there?"

"Some, maybe."

"Maybe? You're taking one hell of a risk."

Jibril sucked at his lower lip. "You're with Global Security, right?" John nodded.

"You get sent somewhere for a few weeks, maybe a year, and then you go home."

"If I'm lucky."

"But you're never permanent."

"I'm a temp. Sure."

"Then you don't know what it's like to find a group of people and develop them and convince them, over years, to risk their lives simply so that you can get some information."

As a contractor, John had spent a lot of his time being told by Agency employees what he couldn't understand. "I do have imagination, Jibril. Why don't you tell me what it's like?"

"It wouldn't make sense to you."

"You owe them. Is that what you're trying to tell me?"

"Yeah, John. I suppose that's what I'm trying to tell you."

"And Langley agreed to this?"

There was no reply at first, and John looked to see his passenger lost in thought, one hand gently stroking the barrel of the Kalashnikov. Finally Jibril said, "I think they trust me to make my own decisions."

"That's what they'll say if it goes south. That you were making your own decisions."

Jibril squinted ahead into the sinking sun. "Well, when you owe someone, you owe them. There's no getting out of it. Not for me, at least."

"Sounds like a quick way to get yourself killed."

There were about four seconds of silence before Jibril snapped. "Fucking cynics like you ruin everything. It's always easier to tear down than to build up, isn't it?"

"Is it?" John asked, cynically.

"Try being constructive for once. You might break a sweat."

There was no point answering that one, or answering anything. Harry Wolcott, the station chief, had made the assignment clear: *Just get him to Ajdabiya. Alive. And keep your trap shut about it.*

In silence, they passed a sign in Arabic that had been spray-painted over with WELCOME TO FREE LIBYA. Neither of them wondered aloud why it was written in English, but John believed they were both thinking it. He knew he was.

2

They took a turnoff before Tubruq, escaping the traffic and the Mediterranean and saying good-bye to the green of coastal foliage. The low, pale hills and long flat stretches were hypnotic and at times breathtaking. Occasionally cars blew past in the opposite direction, usually stuffed with men, one full of Bedouins with rifles. Some honked loud greetings. John kept the speedometer at about 70 miles per hour, watching out for boulders that might have rolled onto the road, or been pushed, and IEDs.

"Do you know what you're doing once you get there?" he asked after the silence had grown tedious.

"I know who to look for," Jibril said. "Some will still be around."

"And you'll be America's ears in the heart of the revolution."

"Hardly." Jibril scratched his long nose. "This is bigger than me, John. It's bigger than the Agency, no matter what Langley thinks. The Agency has a bad habit of doing the right thing at the wrong time, and that won't happen here."

"What *does* Langley think?"

There was a pause, and again John turned to look at Jibril, but his passenger was staring out the window at the desert creeping by. He heard Jibril say, "What Langley thinks is a drop in the ocean of history."

John didn't bother asking for an explanation.

Jibril finally turned back, his expression changed. "It's all new. Geopolitics will never be the same. Remember the Green Revolution in Iran? The Arab Spring is Green two-point-oh, and this time they're getting it right."

Green, John thought.

"And until they invite us in," Jibril continued, "we've got no business being here at all."

"So why are you risking your life?"

He pinched his nose. "The point, John, is intelligence. Everything starts with a conversation. That's how you show respect."

He'd said that with an edge of disdain, but John was used to it. He'd been around long enough to know that most of the Agency viewed contractors as backwoods militia nuts, weekend soldiers disappointed by the drudgery of real life, by failed marriages and failed lives. Not that they were *entirely* wrong—it was just a point of prejudice with them. But Jibril Aziz was being opaque and contradictory. He certainly wasn't the first Agency representative heading in to have a chat with the Libyan opposition—so what, really, was he going on about? He was acting as if he were the linchpin that would decide the fate of the entire nation.

"You get me there," Jibril said. "That's all you've got to worry about."

"No, it isn't. I've got to get out again."

After passing a few tin buildings, they reached Al `Adam, a desert town on a limestone plateau. Had they continued to the southern end of town, they would have reached Gamal Abdul El Nasser Air Base, which had once launched Allied planes against the Nazis. But Jibril wasn't interested in planes. He directed John to a small, dusty gas station—generic, no oil company logo on its sign—where they went inside and leaned against a counter, and Jibril held a conversation with the station manager. He ordered two Nescafés. As they were drinking, a tall, very dark Bedouin wearing sand-colored robes and an old pistol in his belt wandered into the station. John tensed. They'd left the Kalashnikov in the car. But Jibril stood, crying, "Salaam," and the Bedouin strode briskly over. The two men embraced, even touching noses—they were old friends. The Bedouin broke out a huge smile, exposing a lost front tooth, and they walked outside, leaving John to the bad coffee. As he waited, gazing out the dirty windows at two children, no older than five, on the other side of the dusty road teasing a dog, the station manager returned to eyeball him, so John used hand signals to order some stale butter cookies with almonds the manager called *ghrayba*.

Jibril returned on his own, carrying a leather-bound book about a foot tall, then paid for the coffee, cookies, and gas. In the car, he put the book into the glove compartment, and they headed west into the chilly, open desert, the only landmark a long ridge of dunes in the distance. To reach Ajdabiya on the gulf, they were looking at three hours, minimum, along a road that was sometimes hidden by drifts of sand, but John at least understood why they were taking it. Jibril hadn't been concerned about traffic along the coast; he'd just wanted to meet his contact in Al ʿAdam.

After a while John noticed the engine temperature rising, so he turned on the heater, which seemed to help. Jibril opened the glove compartment and took out the Bedouin's book. It was a journal, primitive-looking with hand-sewn binding. "Can you do something for me, John?" The judgement was gone from his voice.

"Shoot."

Jibril tapped the book with an index finger. "If I die, I'd like you to destroy this."

"If you die, I'll give that to the embassy."

"No. I need a promise from you, or you can drop me off right here. If I die, then you will take this out into the desert and burn it."

John gave him a look. He was serious. "What is it?"

"Just names. But if this gets into the wrong hands, all of these people are dead."

"What's the wrong hands?"

"Anybody's except mine."

"Including the Agency's?"

"Just burn the papers and pretend you never saw them. Can you promise?"

There seemed no point denying him this, so John made the promise. If Jibril died, then it was a dying man's final wish. If he survived, then John could console himself with the knowledge that he'd lied. If they both died, then it wouldn't matter.

"On your mother's life," Jibril said.

"My mother's dead."

A pause. "On your children's lives. You have children?"

"I've promised, Jibril. That's enough."

Jibril he waited a moment before nodding and putting the book back into the glove compartment. "It's not just intelligence," he said.

"Of course it isn't," John agreed, though once again he wasn't entirely sure what the man was talking about.

Jibril said, "In 1993, my father was part of an attempted coup by the Libyan army. Beforehand, he sent me, my sister, and our mother to Florida to stay with relatives. Next time we heard from him, it was by phone, and he told us the Revolutionary Guard was at the door. He wasn't striking some metaphor—we *heard* them banging against his office door as he screamed good-bye to us down the line. I was fifteen. With outside assistance, that coup might have succeeded, but it didn't, and the outcome was that my father was tortured and beheaded in a basement in Tripoli. We know this because an agent of the Libyan Intelligence Service showed up in Florida to share photographs of my father—before, during, and after the beheading."

There wasn't anything to say to that, so John only watched the unchanging landscape.

"In that situation," Jibil said, "we might have been able to do some good, because the coup was doomed to failure. Every year since then, the Agency could have helped the opposition topple Gadhafi. But this year the situation is different. This year, the people are rising en masse. Nothing can stop them. We can supply them with weapons; we can send in food. But this year the revolution is theirs, and theirs alone. They deserve it."

"Sounds like you're splitting hairs," John said before realizing that Jibril wasn't interested in his opinion. This was a lecture, not a conversation. A hard silence followed, and when he finally glanced over, he saw the back of Jibril's head as he stared out his dirty window. He said something John couldn't hear. "What?"

Jibril turned back, but there was no anger in his face. "I told you it'd been six years since I was here. It didn't end well. I was blown, and some of the people in this book ended up as dead as my father. I made mistakes, and those mistakes killed good people. I don't want that to happen again." He paused. "You'll burn it, right?"

"I said I would."

"Good." Jibril blinked and rubbed his face with the palms of his hands. Anxiety, or frustration. After another moment, Jibril said, "Sorry. You didn't need to hear all that."

"No problem."

"It was lousy security."

It had been, but so had most of this trip. Case in point: He hadn't needed to know Aziz's real name. Harry had only given him a description and pass-phrase, but Jibril, perhaps taken by the excitement of the road, had handed over his name the moment they shook hands outside his hotel. At the border, as if remembering something of his long-ago field training, Aziz had demanded that John give him his passport so that he could deal with the border guards, and when they were handed back John saw that Aziz had used a Libyan passport. John didn't know Aziz's cover name, but if he was captured on the way back from Ajdabiya that would be small consolation. John said, "Look. By tomorrow I'll be back in Cairo. I'll be busy forgetting this entire conversation. I'll be busy forgetting you."

Jibril smiled. "Good man." Then, despite the apology, he opened up further, but not about the mystery of his trek into the desert. He asked about John's family, and once he'd heard a few sketchy details that did not include the divorce, Jibril talked mistily about his wife, Inaya, whom he'd met in Baltimore. Her family had been Berbers, he told John, "a hard people." She was seven months pregnant with their first child, a boy.

This really was too much. Jibril Aziz was throwing security to the wind, as if preparing to die.

By then, the sun was flickering on and off against the horizon, and when it disappeared they saw a yellow Toyota pickup stopped up ahead on the opposite lane. Around it stood five men, all of them toting rifles, with green bandannas around their skulls. Green. As John slowed the Peugeot, the men wandered into their lane, raising rifles high. John stopped less than a hundred yards away.

"What do you think?" Jibril asked.

"I told you not to take this road."

"Shit."

Two of the men stepped forward, waving them closer, smiling to show how friendly they were. One was shouting something. "What's he saying?" John asked.

"Oil for Libyans."

"Can't they see our Egyptian plates?"

"Yeah. I think they can."

John scanned the desert, not liking what he saw. The patch of sand around them wasn't solid enough to trust with the car, and if they got stuck they were finished. It was an ideal spot to corner someone. "We have to go forward, or back."

"Can we plow through them?"

It was a shockingly naive thing for an Agency man to say, but John controlled his surprise as, up ahead, the man who'd been shouting placed his rifle on the road and started walking toward them. "We can't risk it," John explained slowly. "If they blow a tire, we're dead."

"Don't tell me we have to go back."

"You've got the Kalashnikov."

Jibril raised it from between his legs.

"Can you shoot well?" John asked.

"Well enough."

"I trained as a sniper," he said, letting his own security slip. But Jibril did nothing—he simply held on to the Kalashnikov. "Well, then," said John. "Go to it."

The man in the green bandanna was close enough that they could read his eyes, which were full of smiles and welcome. His skin was tough and prune-dark. Jibril got out of the car and stood behind the open door for protection and translated for John: "He says they ran out of gas."

"Tell him we don't have enough. Tell him we'll send someone for them."

"He'll just ask for a lift."

"Then kill him."

The man raised his hands to show how empty they were, then continued talking. Jibril spoke briefly, and the man smiled, pointing at their car as he talked. John understood enough—he wanted a ride.

"What I said, Jibril. Shoot him now."

Jibril lifted the rifle to his hip, pointing it around the side of the door at the stranger, and said something John could barely hear over the rising wind whistling through the car. The man stopped, his smile faltering. A little more conversation, then the man shrugged elaborately, turned around, and walked back to his friends. Jibril got back into the car and closed the door.

"Well?"

"He says he understands. Lawless roads and all that. He thanks us for sending someone back to help them."

"And you believe him?"

Jibril hesitated. "If I'd shot him, we'd be in a war. We've only got one gun."

Just before reaching his friends, the man turned toward them again and raised a fist in the air, shouting proudly.

"Tell me," John said, though he recognized the slogan.

"He says, *God, Muammar, Libya—nothing but!*"

"Give me that rifle, will you?"

Jibril stared a moment, then shifted his knees to pass over the Kalashnikov. John took it and got out, the chill wind buffeting him. One of the other men shouted something, waving his own rifle like an old Hollywood Comanche. Again, John didn't need a translation. He walked around the back of the car and climbed onto the hot, filthy trunk. He lay so that his stomach was pressed against the rear windshield and his elbows were on the roof. As he took aim, trying to gauge wind resistance, he saw how fast the darkness was falling, which didn't make him feel any better.

Someone shouted something, and the men scattered. Two to the right, two to the left, jumping behind their truck. John fired once, knocking down the man who had come to talk to them as he bent to retrieve his gun. The man rolled into the sandy road and didn't get up again.

Bursts of automatic gunfire filled the whistling air, and he took aim at the Toyota and waited. Two bullets pinged off the Peugeot. One of the men stood up from behind the truck to fire. Though John aimed for the head, the shot entered the man's chest before he disappeared behind the truck.

John saw sparks of muzzle-flash beneath the truck, then heard the Peugeot's windshield crack, but couldn't get a bead on the shooter. So he swiveled his sight to the other side of the road, where a gunman had settled in a ditch. He waited. This time he hit the head he aimed for, a flash of red and pink.

He took a moment to refocus in the fading light. There were only two of them now. One under the truck, the other hiding behind a lump in the sand. "Jibril," he called as calmly as he could manage, for his nerves were shot through, and he had to hold back screaming everything that came out of him. "Jibril, tell them to walk out into the desert and we won't kill them." Jibril didn't answer. "Hey!" John called. "You hear me?"

There was a flash in the desert, then another ping against the car. He aimed at the spot. One more muzzle-flash, but the man didn't rise to aim. He was just there to distract. John turned back to the truck where, beside the rear wheel, there was movement in the shadows—a rifle, then a body snaking out to get a better shot. A head wrapped in green fabric appeared, and he shot twice. The movement ceased. John turned back to the lump of sand and shouted, "Do you speak English?"

He got two shots in reply.

"English?"

"Fuck you English!"

"Everyone is dead!" John shouted, trying to enunciate clearly. "If you want to live, drop your gun and walk away! Do you understand?"

The man made no sign that he understood a thing, but he didn't fire, either. John slid off the car on the passenger's side, opened the door for protection, and saw that Jibril was still in his seat, eyes open above a black pit where his nose should have been. His shirt was soaked through and his lap was full of blood. He was staring at the blood-speckled windshield, directly at the small hole in the glass that had materialized an instant before his death.

John closed the passenger door, walked around the rear of the car to his door, then sat behind the wheel. Despite a couple of holes in the hood, the car started without trouble. He put it in reverse and backed away until the Toyota was only a twinkle in the darkness, then turned the car around. He lugged Jibril's body to the trunk, wrapped in some old blankets. Settling him in that small space, folding his knees to his chin, John wasn't sure he was going to be able to do it. He thought he might be sick. But he managed the chore, aching arms trembling, slammed the trunk, then drove back to where they had come from.

He got no phone signal in Al ʿAdam, so he continued north toward the coast, the only lights coming from drivers heading back out into the desert. It was well after ten when he reached the low, dry outskirts of Tubruq, and he pulled onto the cracked earth on the side of the road and called Washington. While his direct superiors, Stan and Harry, were in Cairo, Cy Gallagher in the D.C. headquarters of Global Security outranked everyone because he had hired John, he signed his checks, and he was the only person John could assume was looking out for his interests. "You let him go through the desert?" Cy asked.

"I didn't have a choice."

"Jesus, we don't need these kinds of fuckups. Do you know how many contracts are up for review?"

"Just tell me what to do with the body."

"You've still got it?"

"Won't they want it?"

Cy paused. "Let me ask. I'll get back to you. In the meantime, get yourself back to Cairo."

"With a corpse."

"Right. Okay. I'll call you back."

John closed his eyes, and as the cold quickly seeped into the car he tried to put the afternoon out of his mind, but that was impossible. He'd known people who could do that, could silence their heads and zero out, find Zen in the middle of war zones, but he was stuck with the endless internal chatter, most of it not worth listening to, and from the jumble of words came lines of verse half-forgotten:

> In depraved May, dogwood and chestnut, flowering judas,
> To be eaten, to be divided, to be drunk
> Among whispers

He pressed his dirty fingers into his eye sockets, but couldn't remember what that was from. So familiar, yet his mind had gone blank. Some long-dead poet.

After ten minutes, Cy called to ask his coordinates and told him to wait. John waited for a while, then got out and walked to the trunk. He held his breath as he searched Jibril's pockets, coming up with a passport, phone, and wallet, but no keys. His clothes, John noticed, had no tags on them. He brought the items back to the front and switched on the interior lamp. The wallet was filled with cash in a variety of denominations, but empty of credit cards or anything that used a name. The passport, as he had seen at the border, was Libyan, and the name inside it was Akram Haddad. It was full of stamps and visas, a long record of travels through North Africa and the Middle East up to 2005, and then one more stamp from today. John pocketed the cash, took the battery out of the cell phone, then placed the wallet and passport and phone in the glove compartment. That was when he noticed the leather book that Jibril had picked up in Al`Adam.

He took it out and opened it. Names, just as Jibril had said, but they were all in Arabic script, handwritten. Names with addresses and phone numbers and notations that he couldn't decipher, many of the pages X'd over—these, perhaps, were contacts who hadn't survived Jibril's mistake six years ago. He extinguished the interior lamp and gazed off to the right, where the nighttime desert lay. Just a matter of walking out there and setting it on fire, and a part of him wanted to do this for the dead man. Another part didn't want to, and this was the part that said, *How are you going to light a fire?* For he didn't smoke, and he had stupidly brought no lighter with him into the desert.

So he put it back and closed the glove compartment, thinking that he would burn it in Cairo, while the disloyal part of him knew that he wouldn't.

Nearly an hour later, a filthy, tarp-covered truck parked in front of his Peugeot, and a small man with a fat mustache got out, asking in English after Akram Haddad. "Well, you can see for yourself," John told him as he walked to the trunk and opened it. The man sighed loudly. Together, they moved the body to the truck, where a large Persian rug was waiting. They rolled him up. Then the man smiled and opened his hand. John reached to shake it, but the man waved an index finger. "Payment, yes?"

"No one told me about that."

"They tell me you pay three hundred euros."

That came to about five hundred Libyan dinar, and he paid in a mix of currencies from Jibril's stash—dinar, dollar, and euro. Only after the payment was completed did the man shake his hand.

"Congratulations on the new Libya," John told him, but the man was already walking away.

3

It was a little before ten on Friday morning when he parked in Heliopolis, in the northeast of the city. He considered himself lucky to have gotten the car, with its holes and the bloodstains he'd wiped at and covered with a towel, all the way to Cairo, but he didn't imagine his luck would hold out forever, so he found a spot free of police on a narrow side street northwest of Othman Ibn Afan. He took a photo of the Arabic street sign with his phone and brought Jibril's things on the epic bus trip down to the Nile Road, a hot ride that grew more cramped and rancid as the buildings closed in, a weary urban claustrophobia taking hold. Cities the world over share a tendency toward chaos, and Cairo was no different, the bus surprised at every turn by traffic jams and collisions and surly street vendors who didn't want to push their carts out of the way. The bus driver spent half his time hanging out of the window, waving and shouting at people who wouldn't conform to his rules of the road.

A boy standing too close to his hip stared up at him, smiling. A pair of women, one in a hijab, the other's face hidden in a niqab, sat behind two men loudly arguing with hands and flexed fingers. He knew he smelled bad, and whenever women passed, glancing his way, he averted his eyes, ashamed.

Finally, they made it to the Nile Road, and John walked the rest of the way, muscles stiff and brain preparing to shut down from fatigue. From the arid desert he'd returned to the land of smells: roasting meats, car exhaust, spices, and sweat. He finally reached the quay, where the claustrophobia evaporated along the banks of the great river. He hurried past the stone lions, speckled with graffiti, that flanked the entrance to the low Qasr Al Nile Bridge that stretched across the Nile to Gezira Island. This had been one of the flash points of the revolution—black-uniformed Central Security conscripts had gradually lost a battle against the press of thousands trying to reach Tahrir Square, and, once the protesters had broken through, the security forces had scattered, running for their lives. While there were still burn marks on the sidewalk from flaming vehicles, the bridge was calm, lined with old men propped against the green steel railings with fishing poles. Once he reached Gezira Island he caught a bus north, deeper into Zamalek. It was nearly one o'clock by the time he made it to his third-story walkup on Ismail Mohamed, a leafy street of terraced apartments, cafés, and small hotels. Climbing the stairs, he felt as if he, too, had been killed in the desert.

It was a small apartment, partly because he lived alone and partly because he couldn't afford anything bigger in upscale Zamalek. And he was in Zamalek because, beyond a few phrases for waiters and taxi drivers, his Arabic was a joke, and Zamalek was where the illiterate expats could hide safely away from the realities of North Africa.

The first thing he did was put away Jibril's things. The passport and wallet went into a large Saiidi tea tin in his awkwardly narrow kitchen. The leather-bound book wouldn't fit, but he managed to squeeze it into an unused cookie jar on top of the refrigerator. He was too exhausted to brew up coffee, so instead he opened a bottle of Glenlivet and poured three fingers into a dusty glass. He brought it to the couch, took a sip, then dialed the familiar number on his cell. After two rings, Nancy, the pool secretary, told him that Harry Wolcott was unavailable. "But Stan's around," she said.

"Please."

Stan Bertolli picked up with a "John, you back already?"

"Yeah."

"We'll see you today?"

"No."

"So you're just checking in?"

"That's right," he said, then gulped down more whisky.

"Everything okay?"

"No," he said. "But I'll need to sleep it off. Just tell Harry that it didn't work. Please."

"It," Stan said with a touch of mystery. Harry had assured John that all Stan knew was that he would be out of town for a few days.

"I'll file my report for him Monday. If he wants it sooner, I can come in tomorrow."

"I'll let him know," Stan said, "but he's a little backed up today. We got some shit news from Budapest."

"Budapest?"

"Emmett Kohl was shot dead in a restaurant. He used to work out of here, from the consul's office. We're all looking into it."

"My condolences."

After hanging up, he refilled his glass. He considered checking the news for this Kohl character, but couldn't quite manage it. What he needed was a shower, but that felt so unlikely that he brought the bottle back to the sofa and kept drinking, then woke six hours later to darkness and the sound of banging.

Before waking, he was in Alexandria, climbing out of a car that he'd pulled to the side of El Geish Road, running alongside the Mediterranean. The car, a twenty-year-old Toyota Tercel, was painted black, and in the trunk, he knew, was Jibril. Parked in front of him was a white Egyptian police van with flashing lights. Two cops were getting out, holding their batons in front of themselves, smiling at John. To his right, the water was choppy from heavy wind, and the air was wet with surf. The police spoke to him in Arabic, and when he answered in English one of them struck his shoulder with a baton; it hurt. "Okay," he told them, gripping the shoulder, "I'll show you." He walked ahead of them to the trunk and opened it, but instead of Jibril he found Ray and Kelli, aged six and eight, folded tight into the small space. This wasn't right. He slammed the trunk shut as the policemen arrived, then waved them away. "Not here," he said. The one who'd struck him pushed John back so that he nearly stumbled into the road as a car sped past, while the other opened the trunk and shouted angrily. He thought that he should run, then realized he'd never make it across the busy road, so he approached their hunched backs as they reached inside and took a long, manicured hand that was connected to his ex-wife, Danisha. She was smiling as she climbed out, looking much like she had when Ray and Kelli had been babies; she looked stunning. She said, "John, I'm so tired," but she said it as if it meant something wonderful.

"Come on," said another voice, and John turned to find a clean and still-breathing Jibril behind him, reaching for his hand, beckoning him into the traffic. "First one across gets to go."

"Go where?"

Jibril, with a smile on his face, was already running.

He sat up, trying to orient himself in the stuffy darkness. It was evening. His cheek and the arm of the sofa were wet from saliva. His stomach cramped, gushing acid into his throat. When the banging started again, he heard a voice, too: "Wake the fuck up, John."

He got to his feet and with his first step kicked the whisky bottle across the room. It clattered against the legs of the TV stand but didn't break. He reached the far wall and slapped until he found the switch, filling the room with light.

"Hurry up, John." Three more sharp bangs against the door.

He wiped at his face, then wiped his hands on his jeans, wishing he had at least changed clothes. He could now see that there was a dark streak of blood down the side of his thigh, though it wasn't his blood. He unlocked the door and stepped back, calling, "Come in," as he continued to the bathroom, where he sat on the toilet and urinated, watching Harold Wolcott walk in warily, look around, and finally catch sight of him.

"Is this smell coming from you?"

"Maybe."

"Can't you take a shower?"

"I wasn't expecting guests."

Harry spotted the Glenlivet on the floor. He stooped to pick it up, then placed it on the coffee table. John flushed and washed his hands and face and neck in the cracked mirror. He looked as bad as he smelled. Harry's voice: "You're going to talk to me?"

"In a minute."

He toweled off and went to the kitchen, where he found a large bottle of water in the fridge. He gulped at it, took a breath, then drank more with a handful of aspirin. Glancing through the doorway, he saw Harry standing at the low bookshelves, reading spines—Stevens, Pound, Moore, Cummings, Eliot, and a translation of Fernando Pessoa's *The Book of Disquiet*. John lowered the bottle. "I hope you're not going to express your surprise," he said.

Harry looked over his shoulder, frowning. "That a mercenary reads poetry? Never even crossed my mind."

"It gets old, people being shocked by your literacy."

Harry grunted, turning back to the books.

Food, John thought as he returned to the kitchen shelves. He hadn't eaten since Marsa Matrouh, a day and a half before. He grabbed some old bread and stuffed slices into his mouth.

Harry wandered into the kitchen, holding a collected Cummings. He was a tall, very white man, early fifties, with a permanently sunburned neck. He was known for his addiction to mint-flavored gums that snapped when he chewed in the embassy, since smoking was not allowed. He was also the Cairo station chief, and he had never visited John at home before. Unlike some Agency employees, he was too professional to broadcast his disdain for contractors, but John could smell it on him in the way he could catch the whiff of bigotry or religious intolerance in others.

Harry said, "I hear from Stan that it didn't work."

"No, sir, it didn't," John answered through a mouthful of bread, then opened a cabinet and pulled out the Saiidi tea tin.

Harry set the Cummings on the refrigerator, right next to the cookie jar, before accepting the items. He flipped absently through the passport and glanced into the wallet. "Empty?"

"Right." John took out his own wallet and handed over what was left of Jibril's money. "It's about three hundred euros shy."

He looked at John, but not worried about the cash. He was just waiting for more. "Well?"

John raised a finger, swallowed, and said, "To the bathroom?"

Harry sighed. Despite his position, he'd never made a secret of his impatience with security procedures. Harry Wolcott was an oxymoron.

John went first, squeezing past him and turning on the bathroom fan, then the shower. He sat on the edge of the tub, a fresh slice of bread in his hand, and kept to a whisper: "We took the desert road from Tubruq. He met someone in Al `Adam."

"Who?"

John shrugged. "Dressed like a Bedouin. Acted like an old friend," he said, careful to avoid mention of the hand-off—for while he still wasn't sure he would burn it, he couldn't shake Jibril's conviction that *no one* should get the names of his contacts. "We headed across the desert and after about an hour ran into a crew of five Gadhafi supporters who wanted our fuel. They may have just been bandits, I don't know. It became a firefight. Aziz was shot in the face. So I turned around and called Cy. He checked with Langley, and they, I assume, sent the guy who showed up to collect the body. He has those three hundred euros. I crossed back into Egypt alone and left the car in Heliopolis. Might want to send someone to pick it up. I've got the street on my phone."

Harry rubbed his eyes and looked, briefly, as if he were going to slap John. Then the look was gone. "What about those bandits?"

"I think I killed four of them."

Harry inhaled loudly. "Sounds like a mess."

"It was, sir."

"Why that road?"

"Aziz claimed the coastal road was gridlocked, and maybe it was, but he obviously wanted to make his meet in Al `Adam."

"What did they talk about?"

"Well, they didn't talk in front of me."

"And you say we took the body?"

"The undertaker and I didn't discuss our employers. Langley didn't call you about this?"

If Langley wasn't telling him things, John was the last person Harry would share this with. "How are you feeling?"

"Some more sleep would help, and some food."

"And a bath?"

"And a bath. But if you'd like, I'll write up the report tomorrow."

Harry considered that, finally nodding. "Direct to me. I don't want Stan seeing this—he wasn't part of the operation."

"Of course."

Harry seemed pleased by his acquiescence. He said, "How long have you been with us, John?"

"Three months, give or take. Got a month left."

"You took over from Amir Najafi. Finishing his contract."

"Yes."

"How's it working for you?"

Were he an honest man, John would have admitted that he didn't know. The pros and cons of his job seemed nearly balanced. But he had little interest in being honest at the moment, so he said, "It works for me. Just don't keep sending me into the desert."

Harry nodded. "You're from Virginia, right?"

"Richmond."

"My son's studying at William and Mary. Loves it."

John wasn't sure what to say.

"Must've been hard," said Harry.

"Excuse me?"

"Libya."

"Well, I think it was harder for Jibril Aziz."

Harry raised an eyebrow.

"Where was he coming from?" John asked.

The question seemed to confuse the station chief.

"Look, he hadn't been in Libya for six years. He told me that. He wasn't even sure who would still be around. Was he retired? Based somewhere else?"

"Sounds like he told you a lot."

Harry said that with an edge, perhaps irritated that Jibril had shared anything with a contractor. He had shared a lot, but John wasn't going to admit it. "Other than telling me he hadn't been back in six years, he was a cypher."

"Truth is," Harry said after a moment, "I don't know anything about him. All I know is that Langley trusted us to send him over, and it didn't work out. The other thing I know is that it doesn't matter who he was."

"Of course it doesn't. But I was supposed to take care of him. I'd just like to know a little more about the man I let down."

Harry sniffed, then rubbed at his nose. "John, once you've been in the business a while the number of people you've let down will add up to something terrible. It's not a sign of your incompetence, or even your agency's incompetence, but a sign of how slipshod the entire business is. Intelligence is a pseudoscience, like astrology. Sometimes the outcome seems to prove that your methods and techniques are infallible. Other times, it proves the exact opposite. Don't beat yourself up over it. And trust me: The last thing you want is to get to know the corpses you've left behind."

Again, John didn't know what to say, or if any words were required of him. If Harry had meant to make him feel better, he had failed, and if he thought he was teaching John something he didn't already know, then he was wrong. There wasn't much John didn't know about letting people down.

Finally, he motioned at the shower. When John turned it off they could hear the hypnotic call to Isha prayers broadcasting from the nearby Al Zamalek Mosque, which meant it was after seven. He followed Harry into the living room and handed over the keys to the Peugeot. Rather than head for the door, though, Harry walked to the far wall and pulled back a bit of curtain that covered the glass doors to the terrace. With his other hand he crooked his finger to beckon John over, then pointed through the trees down to Ismail Mohamed, its cobbled sidewalk lit by the Hotel Longchamps across the street, where occasional pedestrians passed. But Harry was pointing at two

Egyptian men standing beside a newspaper kiosk, one smoking; the other, who was mustached, had nothing in his hands. Unlike everyone else on the street, they weren't going anywhere; unlike many Egyptians, they weren't supplicating themselves in prayer.

"Who?" John asked.

Harry shrugged and said, "Watch your back," then patted his shoulder and left.

4

As he toweled off after his shower they were marching, demonstrating for or against something. He couldn't see them, but he could hear them farther down Gezira Island, perhaps by the stadium, chanting something that rose over the rooftops and filtered down through the trees as he ate a dinner of scrambled eggs and toast, finishing it beside the terrace doors, watching his shadow (one of them remained) waiting indifferently for orders, or for him.

With a corpse—no, *five*—on his conscience and a shadow waiting on the street, he wondered how he'd ended up here, but he knew the answer well enough to know the question was pointless. You cruise through life, knocking against obstacles and decisions along the way until, eventually, you've got blood on your pants and paranoia digging into your shoulders.

As he washed the dishes he remembered a young John Calhoun growing up in Jackson Ward—single mother, hardscrabble friends— with an interest in verse. Though he enjoyed the flow and beat his friends would break out on the sidewalk, listening to Melle Mel and Run-D.M.C., he found himself more entranced by the words cobbled together in the distant past: Cummings, Pound, Yeats. Once he even tried, with disastrous results, to put some of William Carlos Williams's *Paterson* poems to hip-hop. Humiliation grew into withdrawal, and those long-dead white men became his private vice.

He'd loved the caress of the words and how they could make him feel, if for only a moment, that something important hid just behind the flat facade of his black-and-white world.

He'd brought those sometimes puzzling yet inspiring verses with him to the army, and to the ranges at the Fort Benning sniper school. He'd even brought them across the ocean to the Hohenfels Combat Maneuver Training Center in Germany, but their cryptic wisdom hadn't been enough to make him wise: In 1995, late into a whisky-soaked evening, he beat a Bavarian to a pulp. He still barely remembered the fight, which had put the fat, virulently racist Bavarian into the hospital for nearly a month, one arm broken, four ribs cracked, and one lung punctured. He was lucky to be sent home with a dishonorable discharge, his CO told him, for the locals wanted his "black ass taken to the butcher's."

As he toweled off his hands he remembered the Langston Hughes his mother used to recite like a mantra:

> *God in His infinite wisdom*
> *Did not make me very wise—*
> *So when my actions are stupid*
> *They hardly take God by surprise*

Lines like that could help a man through his day.

By the time he dressed it was nearly eleven. The headache he'd brought with him from Libya still lingered, but it had cleared enough to convince him that he could handle whatever the man downstairs wanted to give him. Or perhaps this was a sign that he hadn't recovered, and he was still crippled by Danisha's prognosis. Did he really not have the sense to flee from danger? Maybe, but the army had taught him a thing or two about preparedness, so he returned to the kitchen and dug through the pots in the low cabinets until he'd unearthed another tin box, one that had once been used to hold nougat bars and now held an old Glock, filled to capacity with seventeen rounds. It was, as had been explained to him his first day in Cairo, against Agency rules to keep firearms in one's own house—to do so would have required permits from the Egyptian Interior Ministry, helping it to ID Agency employees—but once they were outside the confines of the embassy Stan had given him the name of a supplier in New Cairo who continued a long tradition of supplying nervous embassy employees with peace of mind. He slipped the pistol into a beaten shoulder holster, stretched into his jacket, and headed downstairs.

At Global Security's training facility, a decommissioned army base about thirty miles north of Tuscaloosa, Alabama, he'd been told, *They're going to watch, so let them watch.* During their trips into town to spend an afternoon trailing random locals through their daily routines, it had seemed possible to live without anxiety while under surveillance. But that had been a game; Tuscaloosa was not the rest of the world.

He'd been followed before. During a six-month stretch in Nairobi, thin young men with bashful smiles used to circulate through crowds as he made his way through the markets. In Lisbon they'd been lazy, sitting whenever possible in café chairs, on the rims of stone fountains, on front stoops. During a brief tour in Afghanistan, children had kept tabs on him and other Global Security grunts as they made their rounds through villages. The kids would shout up and down the streets to the next checkpoint, and though this steady procession of underaged surveillance operatives frayed their nerves, the fact that it was out in the open and so obvious had helped them. It made things predictable; it taught them when to keep their eyes open for IEDs and irregular roadblocks.

In Cairo, things were different. It was a crowded city, the most populous in the Arab world, and it defied predictability in the best of times. Before the revolution, John had gotten used to the constant intrusion of security personnel hanging around, whatever path he took. During the revolution, though, they'd had bigger things to deal with than a low-level embassy hand, and now, with sections of the hated security apparatus in disarray, when a shadow came he was one of the awkward, fumbling rookies who knew the neighborhood but wouldn't know tradecraft if it slapped him in the face. So when John headed out and almost immediately lost track of his shadow, he was worried. The man tracked him for one block before fading into the crowd, and when John took a couple of detours between apartment buildings he wondered if he'd lost him. But no—a block short of Deals he spotted the mustached one again, which suggested he wasn't alone. What had John done to deserve these man-hours? He hoped that it had to do with something innocuous, like one of the numerous meets he'd observed, but with the headache still scratching at him he knew it was not.

Yet he moved on. Though a part of him wanted to, he didn't take evasive maneuvers and double back to find out how many there were. Nor did he sit in wait to snatch one off the street, because there was the other part of him, the stronger part, the same part that told him not to burn Jibril's secret list, and now it was telling him that his shadows could be taken care of tomorrow. It told him that tonight all that mattered was to get everything out of his aching head as quickly as possible.

So he walked ahead, feeling their breaths on his collar, and reached Said el-Bakri Street without any taps on the shoulder or throat clearings or excuse-me-Mr.-Calhouns. He trotted down the stairs and opened the door to the bar and didn't even look back as he lowered his head to avoid hitting the overhang.

It was eighties night at Deals, and "Tainted Love" was playing to a full, smoky house—so smoky that he had to squint to see the far walls of the pub, checkered with framed pictures. With watery-eyed effort, he spotted a familiar face. Maribeth, who worked in the visa section, was at a table by the wall, drinking with a tall Egyptian man he didn't know. She was wearing a shorter hairstyle and a new sleeveless dress that showed off her admirable biceps.

He stared for too long, and she met his eyes, smiling, waving him over. He skirted through the crowd, nodding at faces he knew, shaking the hand of someone he didn't remember at all, and when he reached the table Maribeth kissed his cheeks. She was from Tennessee, and cheek-kisses were her favorite part of living outside the United States. They had also slept together twice in the last month, so the kisses lingered a little longer. Then she pushed him away and motioned at her friend. "Meet David Malek."

John shook his hand. The Egyptian was maybe forty, weary eyes but youthful cheeks, and had a strong grip. He worked out.

Maribeth said, "David is a *novelist.*"

"Really? You don't look like one."

David grinned with overt modesty, as if being a novelist were something to be proud of. "First one comes out in the fall." John had been wrong—that accent was All-American.

He sat next to Maribeth. "What kind?"

David cupped his ear.

"Genre?" John said.

"Thriller. Called *Desperate Intentions.*" When he saw the look on John's face, he added, "Publisher's idea. That wasn't my title."

"What was your title?"

David hesitated, a faint smile flickering around his lips, and said, "*Stumbler.*"

"I'm not sure I like that one any better."

Maribeth poked him in the ribs. "Don't be an ass." To David: "John's an anachronism. He reads *poetry.*"

"You must be the last one," said David, smiling, unconcerned by John's assessment of his title, maybe even pleased by it.

"You researching a new one?" John asked.

"About the revolution," David said.

As John offered good luck, Maribeth's hand settled on his thigh. He leaned back and stretched an arm across the back of her chair. Was that a flash of disappointment in David Malek's face? John said, "What's your main character going to be? Egyptian?"

David scratched at his ear, grimacing. "Don't know if I could pull that off. An American, probably."

"A novelist?"

"Ha!" David said, slapping the table, fully recovered now. "No, that's best avoided, too. Maybe someone at the embassy? Maribeth tells me you work there, too."

John wondered what else Maribeth had told him. He'd never

admitted to his real function, but she'd certainly noticed, the last time he slept over, the work-related call he'd received in the middle of the night before rushing off. "I hope it's someone more interesting than me," John told him. "I just schedule travel for the important people."

"Know any CIA?"

Maribeth turned to listen to this.

John opened his free hand to the ceiling. "Never one that would admit to it."

Instead of deflating him, David seemed to take this as a challenge. He leaned closer. "But you know people who *don't* admit to it."

"Tell it from an Egyptian's perspective," John said. "Much more interesting."

Maribeth let out a disagreeable grunt. "He wants to *sell* the book."

John got up and ordered a round of drinks from the bar. He wasn't particularly interested in the conversation, nor was he all that interested in Maribeth's hand sliding along his upper thigh once he'd returned with three beers. Yet here he was, trying to forget about blood in the desert as he drank his beer in great gulps and nodded at David Malek's unself-conscious praise of the revolutions trembling through this part of the world. His optimism, John realized, wasn't naive. Like Jibril's, it was merely American, the belief that all anyone in the world wanted was to live in their own little America. Finally, John cut in. "You know, don't you, that they're going to vote in Islamist parties who have no time for the United States. Look at the history here: Nasser, Sadat, Mubarak. Failed wars, failed culture, and failed social policies enforced by a secret police. The Muslim Brotherhood has been taking care of the people for decades, far better than their governments ever have, and now it's time for their reward."

Innocently, David said, "And why not? It's called democracy. You sound like Gadhafi."

John frowned. "What?"

"The first volume of his magnum opus, *The Green Book*, is called 'The Solution of the Problem of Democracy.'"

Green, thought John.

David said, "You think democracy is problematic. It is, of course, but that's the way it goes. Either they're democratic or they're not."

"Yeah," said Maribeth. "We can't give them only half democracy."

"We're not *giving* them anything," said John, leaning forward. He was a big man, and he knew it. He also knew that a little physical intimidation tended to help his arguments. "If we've given them anything, we've given them thirty-odd years of authoritarianism by supporting their oppressors. Now, we act as if we've given them a new world because they're using Twitter to talk to each other."

"Look who's the wet blanket," Maribeth said. David was grinning wildly at his outburst. No one here was intimidated by him.

He looked away, scanning the crowd again, but his shadows hadn't bothered following him inside. As he took another drink he had a flashback to his dream, opening up the trunk of that Tercel and finding his son and daughter inside. Danisha climbing out and telling him how tired she was. Jibril beckoning him into the street.

He knew, of course. A man who knows poetry knows how to read his own dreams. He had populated this one with people he'd let down, just as he knew he would eventually let down Maribeth, who was now squeezing his inner thigh. *God sure didn't make me very wise.* He'd let down a lot of people during his time on earth—women, friends, and employers—and as Maribeth's nails dug through his jeans he hoped that no one would be too surprised the next time he failed.

She squeezed harder, nails pinching. He nearly yelped.

5

When he woke around noon on Saturday, his head throbbing to the anguished melody of a call to prayer wafting in through an open window, he briefly had no idea where he was, nor where he had come from. He was not in his own bed. His pillow was damp, and there was a stink of acid that made him think that he'd vomited, but when he sat up, gripping his head, he found no traces. Then he recognized the disorganized room, the pastel colors, and the Mickey Mouse clock. From another room, he heard CNN playing on a television.

Maribeth appeared with a cup of coffee, wearing a long T-shirt, disheveled hair, a smile, and nothing else. "You look *bad*, John." She handed over the cup. "You need this more than I do."

"How much did I drink?"

"Everything they had. I'm starting to think maybe you have a problem."

He did, but he didn't think drinking was it. With his first sip of hot coffee he was overcome by the desire to urinate, and when he got up he noticed he was still wearing underwear. "Did we . . . ?"

A short laugh, then she shook her head. "You couldn't have raised your voice by the time we got back here, much less that."

He gave her a weary grin, handed back the coffee, and went to the bathroom. From where he sat on the toilet he could see his face in her low mirror. He was pale, his eyes shot through with red. "Mind if I take a shower?" he called through the closed door.

"I think I'm going to insist," she called back.

It took a while for the hot water to reach her fourth-floor apartment, and once it did it burned. He stood under the steaming downpour, thinking through the previous night. The memories were disturbingly slow in coming, but they did come, and he remembered laughter and loud voices—mostly his—and the novelist David Malek and later on some friends. He remembered an argument with a Slav, but couldn't remember what it had been about. Then he had a quick flash of panic—where was the pistol? He hurried through his shower, toweled off, and squatted naked at the foot of the bed, hunting through his pile of clothes. "Looking for your gun?" Maribeth asked from behind. She had dressed in a long white skirt and an open-collared mauve blouse.

"Uh, yeah."

"Only travel agent I know of who carries heat," she said. "It's in the living room. Why don't you get dressed and have some breakfast?"

He did as she suggested, then found the pistol in its holster on the coffee table. There were still seventeen rounds in the clip, and none in the breech.

Maribeth had cooked up Swiss cheese omelets, ham, and buttered toast, and they ate in her modest dining room—an extension of the kitchen—while through the window came the noise of downtown traffic. The coffee and food began to temper his hangover.

Maribeth spent her work hours approving and more often rejecting visa requests, and each week she collected a handful of stories of colorful characters who believed that simply scrawling marks on a form entitled them to an entry visa. "They always get it wrong," she said. "We start with the assumption that everyone wants to jump ship and set up a new life in America, and it's up to them to prove otherwise. But when you tell them this, they act as if you've just insulted them. On Wednesday a woman spat at me."

"She spat on you?" he said, a slice of toast halfway to his mouth.

"*At* me. Splattered across the divider window. There's a reason we have those things, you know. She said, *But we're democratic now, just like you! Why would I want to leave?*"

"I'm not sure I'd call a military government democracy."

"People believe what they want," she said, then nodded at the television behind him. "You hear about that?"

He turned to find a talking head on CNN relating the story of Emmett Kohl, deputy consul in Hungary, who had been shot in a Budapest restaurant. There were, apparently, few clues, and only an unidentified security photo to guide the investigations: a wide face, hairless, with a cut on one cheek. A real bruiser.

"You knew Kohl?" he asked.

"As well as most, I suppose. He thought he was hilarious."

John was struck by the cynicism in her voice. "You didn't like him?"

"He was just . . . you know. One of those bosses who slaps your back and makes a joke and says that we're all in this together. But when the shit hits the fan you never know where he is. I've worked for worse."

"I'll bet I have, too."

She smiled over the rim of her coffee cup and said, "Where *have* you worked, John? Where did you come from before you magically appeared here?" She took a sip, and when he didn't answer she said, "Look, I'm not trying to pry, but it's obvious you don't schedule flights for people. Jennifer tells me you spend most of your time on the fifth floor, with the spooks."

"Spooks?"

She reddened. "You *know* what I mean."

He did, and so he told her a little about himself. She already knew of the ex-wife and children, so he brushed over his time in the army, skipping mention of his dishonorable discharge. "I kicked around for a while, got married, had some kids. That didn't work out."

"Whose fault?"

"What?"

"You heard me."

He thought about it, but he needn't have—the question had haunted him for years. "Both of ours."

"*Both?* Is that the answer she'd give, too?"

"Spoken like a real bachelorette."

"I prefer the word spinster."

"My point," he said, trying to ignore her mocking grin, "is that we share the blame, just like we share the kids." It was a diplomatic answer, which was another way of saying it was untrue. John would always blame himself, for he had been the one who couldn't hold down a job, who chose to reach for the car keys whenever a fight erupted, who began to feel like his own absent father even though he lived in the same house as his kids. He said, "I remembered how good I'd had it in the army. Lots of order in that kind of life. You know when you're waking and when you're going to sleep. You know what you're supposed to do, and when. The rules are clear—there's never any ambiguity."

"Unlike in a family," she said, her eyes locked on him, no longer taunting.

"Right," he said, then paused before going on. The lies about his job hadn't been required—he'd just been asked to avoid advertising his real position at the embassy. She was waiting. "So I applied with Global Security, and a few years later I was sent here."

"Global *Security*?" Maribeth placed the coffee cup on the table, her eyes slitted. "You're a *contractor*? Like that—that guy in Pakistan?"

He nodded.

"Well, damn," she said, almost a whisper.

Before she could go on, there was a knock at the door, and as she went to get it John finished his toast, wondering how to escape. He had no idea how this revelation was affecting her, and, given the way he was feeling, he wasn't sure he wanted to find out right now. Then he heard the newcomer's voice: "My *love!*" It was Geert Rutte, a Dutch media consultant, another Deals regular. John didn't feel he had much choice in the matter—he got up and went out to say hello.

Despite being near fifty, Geert dressed like a hipster, with thick-framed black glasses and bowling shoes, and was full of overabundant, meaningless smiles. He also maintained an absolute indifference to the feelings of others—empathy had never been part of his upbringing. "John! What a surprise!"

"Morning, Geert."

"Is it still morning? Maribeth, is it still morning?"

"I think it's early afternoon," she said, smiling at John.

"Yet this is a wonderful coincidence, John, for I have two propositions for you!"

"Do you see my face?" John asked him.

"Yes, John. I do."

"How does it look?"

"Pale. Well, paler than usual. It's hard to tell with you people."

"I'm hungover. So please talk quietly."

Geert's eyebrows rose. "Ahh," he said before lowering to a whisper. "I have two propositions for you, John." He wandered in, sniffing the air. "Is that coffee?"

"Would you like some?" asked Maribeth.

"Of course."

They all went to the kitchen, and as she poured another cup, Geert sat in Maribeth's chair and bit into a slice of her toast. "My propositions."

"Perhaps you could just spit them out," said John.

"The first one is an investment opportunity."

"Do I look like I have money?"

Geert paused, staring in shock. "You don't?"

"Well, not enough to invest in anything."

"But you have a job. With the American embassy."

"I also have an ex-wife and two children."

"That's criminal."

"It is what it is. What's the second proposition?"

"Don't you want to know what kind of investment?"

"What's the point?"

Maribeth placed a fresh coffee in front of Geert. "Doesn't anyone want to offer me an investment?"

"Do *you* have money?" Geert asked her.

"Not really."

Geert shrugged elaborately, then came out with one of his ubiquitous smiles.

"What's the second proposition?" asked John.

Geert finally looked at his coffee. "Milk?"

"It's next to the plate," Maribeth said, giving John a quick grin.

As he poured the milk, Geert said, "Now that I know you're poor, the second proposition might be more interesting. A part-time job making conversation with pretty Egyptian girls."

"You're kidding me."

"Conversational English. That's all they want. Thirty euros an hour, and they pay for the tea."

"Who are these Egyptian girls?"

"And why am I being passed over again?" Maribeth demanded.

"Because," Geert told her, "you are a woman. And no," he added, holding up a finger, "I'm not ashamed I said that. John," he continued, turning away from her, "they're *women,* not girls. Married, as well. To members of the protest movement. They know their husbands' stars are rising, so they're desperate to look good and speak well when faced with foreign diplomats. With English, they will be prepared for most situations."

John shook his head. After Libya, this felt ridiculous. He imagined sitting in the Marriott or Arabica or Starbucks with an Egyptian housewife discussing beaches and servants and diplomats' wives, then being asked, "And what do *you* do for a living, Mr. Calhoun?"

"I'm not sure," he said as Geert took another bite of Maribeth's toast.

"It's the easiest job in the world, John. And they want you."

"There are thousands of native English speakers in town."

"Me, for example," said Maribeth.

Geert shrugged. "But most of them are not American blacks."

Maribeth looked at John, who said, "Neither are most English-speaking diplomats, Geert."

"Maybe they want to speak the jive to your president," Geert said, and when neither of them gave him a smile of encouragement he shrugged again. "I can't explain the inner workings of the Egyptian female mind. I never will be able to. All I know is that when I described you to Mrs. Abusir, she perked up as if I had shocked her toe. She told me—in confidence, mind—that she was sure the other wives would *love* to meet you. But don't tell her I told you this."

"Tell her thanks, but I'm not interested."

"Really?" Geert looked surprised. He believed he had sold it well. "Maybe when you feel better, you'll change your mind. How many tequilas did you have?"

"I need to go to the embassy," John said, rising to his feet. He thanked Maribeth for the breakfast, then slipped on his holster in the bedroom. As he was pulling on his jacket, Geert appeared in the doorway.

"You should watch it," the Dutchman told him. "Too much tequila and you'll end up in jail. You don't want to see the inside of an Egyptian prison."

"Maybe you're right, Geert."

"You'll end up like Raymond Davis."

Raymond Davis was the contractor Maribeth had been thinking about. A month before, he had been arrested for shooting two Pakistanis in Lahore, and it had blown up into large-scale protests all over that country, demanding his execution. Raymond Davis's situation had terrified everyone in the contractor community.

"And if you're in jail," Geert said, "what will poor Mrs. Abusir do?"

6

From Maribeth's building on Hussein Basha Al Meamari, he walked to Talaat Harb Square, a large yet elegant intersection of six streets circling the statue of Talaat Harb, economist and banker. He kept an eye out for shadows but saw nothing, worrying that his roughshod brain wasn't up to the challenge. Yet as he continued down the street toward Tahrir Square, it occurred to him that perhaps he'd had it wrong. Perhaps—and he briefly felt a sense of warm relief at the prospect—the two men outside his place had been watching someone else in the building. He didn't talk to his neighbors, but he wasn't the only foreigner on that leafy Zamalek street. By the time he'd made it through Tahrir and was entering Garden City, the charm of this thought had gone a ways toward relieving his headache.

The air—fresher on the weekend—was also doing him a world of good. He reached the embassy on Tawfik Diab Street and gave his passport to one of the local guards, a conscript with the Central Security Forces, which was responsible for, among other things, guarding embassies. The Egyptian glanced at the passport, then took a good look at John's face. "You are in bad shape, no?"

"Not as bad as I look," he answered unconvincingly.

There were a few extra marines posted on the grounds, looking hard yet serene. They didn't bother asking his condition.

Another guard stopped him just inside the door, and once he'd stated his intention John removed his Glock and handed it over. The guard didn't seem surprised by the pistol, just took it over to a steel cabinet and put it into a locked drawer. Then John handed over his keys, phone, and change, stepped through the metal detector, collected everything again, and went to the far window, where he told the doorman, Eric, where he would be. Eric was maybe twenty-five, from Wyoming, and was losing a battle with psoriasis. He had a remarkable memory for the hundreds of faces that passed him each day. "Haven't seen you since Wednesday, Mr. Calhoun."

"Even wage slaves get a day off now and then."

"So I've been told."

"They've got you on weekend shift?"

"Anything and everything for the Man."

He took an elevator to the fifth floor, which was officially part of the U.S. & Foreign Commercial Section, but in reality the primary offices for CIA in Egypt. While Stan Bertolli, his direct boss, controlled five primary agents, he was still just a submanager. John knew of three others—Jennifer Cary, Dennis Schwarzkopf, and Terry Alderman—but he didn't know the sizes of their staffs. Add in the agents who never actually came to the embassy, living instead as foreign businessmen in the city, as well as the local assets, paid and coerced, and Harry Wolcott's little empire likely numbered more than a hundred souls. Today John saw half a dozen faces he'd never been introduced to. They gave him gruff nods on their ways to the communal coffee machines before heading back to their cubicles to keep track of whatever they kept track of. John supposed they were looking into the death of the deputy consul in Hungary, but he wasn't about to ask. He knew his place.

Stan's office was locked, but there was an open anteroom beside it with an old desktop computer, solely for reports. A sticker on the monitor informed him that it could be used for information up to SECRET. In fact, the machine wiped itself clean whenever anyone logged out, and so each time John logged in he was faced with a gutted computer. It wasn't connected to the Internet, but reports were sent to other computers via Ethernet lines after logging out. That is, he would write his report, list the recipients, and press SEND, but only once he had logged out would the computer send the report on before erasing it locally. This, he had been assured, represented the highest achievement in data security.

His identifier was LAX942, which was automatically used in place of his name on the report. The date, "March 05 2011," and location, "Embassy, Cairo," were also filled in by the computer, so the first space for him to type in was labeled "Operational classification."

He thought about that a moment. In other reports, the subject had been self-explanatory: Agent Meet, Surveillance, Courier. He decided on Transport.

Security Classification: Secret.

Subject: Jibril Aziz.

Below was a blank space without the aid of directions. Here, then, was where he was to explain a failure that had cost the life of an American agent. He began with the particulars of the operation, the orders he'd received, and the pickup at the Semiramis. He described the route they'd taken and the stop in Marsa Matrouh, including the meeting with the man in the red-checked ghutra, their movement through the border, and Jibril's purchase of the Kalashnikov.

He spent some time on their disagreement over the road they were to take, even admitting to having believed Jibril's traffic excuse. "However," he wrote, "once Mr. Aziz met a contact in Al `Adam, it became obvious that his reasons were not limited to our narrow timeframe. Traffic was less a reason than an excuse."

"Hey, John," he heard. Stan Bertolli was approaching, a laptop bag hanging from his shoulder.

John gave him a nod.

Stan frowned at his face. "Harry putting you through the ringer?"

A ripple of worry passed through him—Harry had told him to keep his Libyan trip quiet, yet all Stan had to do was take three steps forward and peer over his shoulder to get a good idea of what had been going on. John considered replying, but feared that anything he said would be an invitation to approach, so he just shrugged.

"That the report?"

John tensed, then nodded.

After a moment's uncomfortable silence, Stan unlocked his office and went inside. John exhaled and, after staring blankly at the screen for a few seconds, gathered his wits enough to get back to it.

He described the contact, but realized that the description was too wordy and deleted it in favor of "a tall man, dark-skinned, in traditional Bedouin dress." Though he nearly put it into words, he avoided mention of the leather book that he had promised to burn.

By then the sentences were flowing and, as if he had been taken again by the anxiety of the events he was remembering, his fingers flew over the keyboard as he described that last stretch of road that led to the bandits. He brought up the conversation about their families and even Jibril's explanation of his obsession, via his father's tragic murder, before remembering that he had lied to Harry about what Jibril had shared. So he deleted that paragraph. Then they were at the Toyota truck. He paused, closed his eyes, and tried to see it all again. He slowed it down, smelled the dry, cool wind, saw the bright green bandannas on their sunbaked heads, squinted into the darkening sky, and heard *Fuck you English!* Then he typed.

Stan

———◆———

1

They shared the same bed, but he did not consume her. It was too soon for that, he knew, though it was a struggle to convince his hand on her hip to remain where it lay. She was there with him, but a part of her was still with Emmett and would be for a very long time. Hadn't that always been true? Yes—but now, Emmett Kohl had graduated from cuckoldry to sainthood, and that would not blow over quickly. She fell quickly to sleep, proving that they were not really strangers, or perhaps it only proved how exhausted she was. Either way, he was left staring at the smooth curve of her shoulder rising out of the sheet, asking himself if just one small bite would wake her.

He wondered how many nights his father had lain in Italian beds, unable to sleep for all the clashing thoughts in his head. Though he had shared some things with his son, Paolo Bertolli had preferred to avoid discussions of dirty reality, detailing only his moments of glory—the afternoon in early 1978 when he wore a wire to a meeting to plan the kidnapping of Aldo Moro, the intelligence he passed on about the location of the kidnapped Brigadier General James Dozier in 1981, and the 1983 arrest of Vanni Mulinaris. Nothing about how he had learned to sleep when the fear was eating him up, leading to a midlife of chronic ulcers that had required three separate surgeries. His mother, when she had chosen to speak of his father at all, told

Stan that he wept in his sleep. Unforgivingly, she would say, "And what kind of a man does that?"

A man with things on his mind.

He knew too little, and as he dwelled on the few facts in front of him he remembered Harry's expression from the day before, when he'd asked about John's under-the-table job: the forehead suddenly full of wrinkles, as if it had been slapped. He remembered it because it was the same expression he had seen when he'd brought evidence of Emmett's crimes to Harry the previous year, asking that it be passed on to Langley. That expression had shrunk Harry's face, and after a long moment of reflection he'd said, "I'm not giving those smart boys back home an excuse to reshuffle my station. We take care of this on our own." Taking care of it on their own, it turned out, had simply meant sending a bad apple to another orchard.

Zora Balašević had told Dragan Milić that Emmett hadn't leaked information. Dragan was right to doubt this—for why else would the Egyptians have hired her? But what if she'd been telling the truth, and she had found another embassy source? Harry? Could Harry have been the leak, using Emmett to cover his tracks? *We take care of this on our own.*

Or was Stan growing paranoid? By then it was after two in the morning, and he was lying beside a woman who filled him with cannibalistic desires. How could he think of trusting himself?

He remembered a single piece of advice his father had given him toward the end of his life, when he was confined to a hospital bed, tubes poking out of every orifice: *Stan, when you live in a house of mirrors, the only way to stay alive is to believe that every reflection is real. The downside is that this can cost you your sanity.*

Then it was Saturday morning. Coffee, fresh orange juice, and bagels that the embassy shipped in from America. With cream cheese on her lip, Sophie tapped at the surface of her iPad, checking mail over his Wi-Fi. "Thirty-two messages," she groaned.

"Ignore them."

"His parents want to know why I'm not with his body."

"Ignore them," he repeated. "Or tell them you're fine but don't give details. In fact, don't tell anybody you're here."

She frowned at him. "I'm here now—no one stopped me. So it doesn't matter."

"I'm not going to tell anyone," he said, "and we might as well not contradict each other."

Briefly, a look of understanding flashed across her face, but just as quickly it faded away. "Why am I a secret?"

"I told you before: Harry will want to handle you. If he knows you're in town, he'll figure out you're staying with me, and he won't be as open with me he would otherwise. I'm just trying to buy us some time."

"You think he knows?"

"What?"

"About us."

Stan smiled. "If he didn't before, he'll figure it out once he knows where you're staying."

"And that would be a problem for you."

"I suppose," he said, as if he hadn't thought of that already. The fear of exposure had ruled his life last year, and now that she was back in his life the fear had returned. "It's not like you coming here is a secret—your passport left Hungary and entered Egypt. The Budapest embassy should know where you are. Soon enough, they'll call Harry just to let him know you're around. They'll probably say you're unstable. Let's give ourselves the weekend before going to Harry."

She nodded, finally understanding. "Do you think I am?"

"What?"

"Unstable."

He walked to the sofa, leaned close, and kissed her forehead. "You just want to understand. There's nothing unstable about that."

She looked up at him and, after a moment, nodded imperceptibly. Then she reached into her pocket and removed a folded sheet of paper that was crumpled and misshapen, as if it had been read and refolded many times. She held it out for him, and he took it.

"What's this?" he asked as he saw what it was—a classified cable. She said, "Tell me about Stumbler."

He knew he was reddening, but he played along, reading the message and seeing, right there, Jibril Aziz's name. Stan knew about Stumbler, but he'd never known that it had originated with Aziz.

She stared at him, waiting, and so he sat across from her and began to explain.

Stumbler had been one of twenty or so ideas that crossed their desks in 2009. Young, creative, sometimes brilliant analysts at Langley's Office of Collection Strategies and Analysis sat around wondering how to make the world a safer place for American enterprise, and when they had their eureka moments they spent a few weeks researching the plausibility and real-world applications of their plans, the repercussions and risks and rewards. But the Agency had long ago learned that a plan half-baked is worse than no plan at all, and so eventually the plans were taken from the analysts and sent around to regional experts to further assess risks and rewards and, additionally, to spread the responsibility. If ten different regional experts agreed that a plan was solid, when it later fell apart their signatures could be used as references. "But in the real world, it means that everyone's covering their asses, and very few plans get past the assessment stage."

"And Stumbler?" she asked.

"You can read it right here," he said, holding up the cable. By then he'd seen the address line at the bottom of the printout and knew she'd gotten it from WikiLeaks. This wasn't the first headache that site had caused, and it wouldn't be the last. "No one in the Cairo embassy wanted to sign off on it, and Harry passed on our assessment."

"But what was it?"

"Regime change in Libya," he told her, for it was a dead plan, and there was little risk in sharing. "This analyst—"

"Jibril Aziz."

"Apparently, yes. He had cobbled together a network of Libya-based groups and tribes that he thought we could bring together. That was the first thing we doubted. Getting various factions in a place like Libya to work toward a common goal is damned near impossible, and it's one of the reasons Gadhafi has remained in power so long—it's why he's still holding on to power right now. Aziz saw signs of the regime's instability wherever he looked, but he chose not to look at anything that contradicted his vision. That was obvious from his report."

"Are you saying he was delusional?"

Stan rocked his head. "No. Maybe. I don't know. Let's just say he didn't seem perfectly reliable. Also, Stumbler required—if I remember right—a couple hundred of our own troops to act as the axle around which the tribes would roll. That's what killed it. If something like this were to become known, that we'd had an active hand in regime change there, the political fallout would be immediate. I'm talking about riots throughout the Middle East, worse than what's actually going on now. Leaders we support would suddenly be branded American puppets. Our business interests in the region would be open to attack. That scared the shit out of us, but Aziz considered it a minor issue. *That* was delusional. So we nixed it. You can see it right here, Harry's words. We suggested continuing our present line: funding the groups we were already funding, perhaps increasing their share a little, but essentially doing nothing." He paused, reflecting on what was going on now in Libya. "Of course, time has proven Aziz right in many ways, but two years ago there was no way for us to know any better."

He hadn't told her much that she couldn't have gleaned from reading between the lines of the cable. She sipped at her coffee, thinking about this, and said, "What about Emmett? Was he part of the assessment group?"

Stan shrugged. "Harry might have pulled him aside for a question or two—part of the argument for regime change was economic, and that was Emmett's specialty. I'd be surprised if he told Emmett the full plan."

"Then why was Aziz meeting with him?"

"If I knew, Sophie, I would tell you."

"We have to find Aziz."

"I'll go in and see what this leads to."

"Does he have a phone number?"

"Who?"

"Jibril Aziz."

"I'll find one," he said, straightening and pocketing the cable. "I should have most of the floor to myself today. I'll call you—is your phone on?"

"No."

"Good. Take this," he said, stepping into the kitchen. From a drawer full of batteries and twine he took an old cell phone and charger. He plugged it in on the counter and then powered it up. "I'll call you on this, and if you run into something you call me and I'll follow up on the Agency database. I'll try to meet with Harry, too, and this afternoon we'll compare notes." He gave her his serious look. "Sound good?"

She thought about it a few seconds, then shrugged. "It's better than nothing."

"It's certainly that."

He gave her a kiss before leaving, and the desire for consumption returned. He packed up his laptop and went downstairs, pausing briefly to check the empty sidewalk. Dragan's boys were nowhere to be seen. He got into his car, but before starting up he called Harry, who was at home over in Zamalek, helping his wife with preparations for an embassy event that apparently required an enormous number of lilies. He appreciated the interruption. "Can we meet?" Stan asked.

"When?"

"Now."

"You've obviously never been married, Stan. Be reasonable with your demands."

"An hour?"

"Four o'clock," Harry said. "The Promenade."

2

When he reached the fifth floor of the embassy, he was surprised to find, at the computer terminal outside his office, a large black man hunched over the keyboard, typing rapidly with two fingers. "John," he said, and the man looked up, blinking.

"Hey, Stan," said John Calhoun.

He was enormous, the kind of man one could easily misjudge as a stupid brute, but Stan had read his reports—John's English was better than any of his agents'. Today, though, he looked exhausted, his dark skin splotchy and both eyes bloodshot. "Harry putting you through the ringer?"

A shrug.

"That the report?"

John nodded but said nothing, so Stan continued to his office, closing the door behind himself. Soon John was getting up and leaving, his report finished and sent, and he gave Stan a mock salute as he lumbered toward the elevators.

Stan logged on to the secure server and retrieved the file on Jibril Aziz. He learned of a wife, Inaya Aziz, and found an Alexandria, Virginia, phone number, which he wrote down. There was some background on his family—Libyans who immigrated in the nineties, with a father killed by the Gadhafi regime in 1993. Then he followed Aziz's career from the National Clandestine Service (Regional and

Transnational Issues), where for four years, from 2001 to 2005, he had been based in North Africa, presumably focused on Libya, to the Office of Collection Strategies and Analysis. A few pages in, Stan found a chronological listing of trips he'd taken in the last five years on the Company dime for Collection Strategies. There was no mention of Budapest, or even Cairo. That didn't mean he hadn't made those trips, just that he hadn't arranged them through the Agency's travel office.

Considering that Aziz was only thirty-three years old, it was a packed CV, yet it told him little that might connect to Emmett's murder.

There were two e-mail addresses listed for Aziz, and he sent off brief messages asking him to get in touch. Then, around three o'clock, eight in the morning in Virginia, he tried Aziz's home number. The answer was immediate, an excited female voice. "Hello? Jibril?" Inaya Aziz, he assumed.

"I'm sorry, no," he said. "I was actually looking for him. I'm from the office."

He could hear the deflation in her voice. "No, I—I'm . . . no. He's not here."

"Do you know when he'll be back?"

She paused, as if his question were out of line. Then, suspiciously: "What's your name again?"

He didn't like her tone, so he hung up. She was on edge and—a little more digging told him—seven months pregnant. He pulled at his nose, thinking. She'd said little, but enough to tell him that she had no idea where her husband was.

At three thirty, he packed his laptop and powered down his desktop, then left, nodding at the on-duty marine and saying farewell to Eric at the front desk, as well as the Egyptian guard at the gate. Life in administration had taught him to be a little more congenial than he naturally was.

He drove west, crossing into Zamalek on the 15th of May Bridge, then parked a block away from the monstrous Cairo Marriott before finding his way to the Garden Promenade restaurant, one of Harry's regular haunts. The station chief was already at a back table, drinking what Stan knew was gin and tonic from a Collins glass. He caught a passing waiter and ordered the same. "You're running around on a Saturday?" Harry asked.

"Just pulling at some loose threads."

"You need a wife, Stan. She'll give you balance."

In recent months Harry had started using words like "balance" and "equilibrium" as if they were concepts he'd only just stumbled across.

Before Stan could begin, Harry scratched at his cheek and said, "Have you talked to Sophie Kohl since that phone call?"

Like the mention of Zora Balašević, it seemed to come out of nowhere. Instead of lying directly, he said, "Why?"

"Seems she's gone missing." There was no sign of guile in Harry's face, just curiosity.

"Missing?"

"Damnedest thing," Harry said, reaching for his glass. "Stepped out of her life yesterday, before her flight home. Not answering her phone. Just gone."

What, Stan thought, would an innocent man say in this situation? "She wasn't kidnapped, was she?"

"No, no. She was spotted at the airport. Flew somewhere, but the Hungarians aren't sharing that information with us."

"Why not?"

"Have you dealt with the Hungarians lately? They demand payback for everything. This new administration is a real ball-cruncher."

"I didn't realize," Stan said.

Harry took a sip. "Well, if she *does* get in touch with you again, let me know. Budapest station is starting to get frantic."

"Will do."

Harry set down his glass. "What do you need?"

There were many possible questions he could pose, but he had decided to begin with the fresh piece that Sophie had brought to the table. He said, "I need to know about Jibril Aziz."

Like it had the day before, Harry's forehead contracted as if Stan had slapped it; then he leaned back in his chair. "Who's Jibril Aziz?"

He was lying, but Stan didn't know why. "CIA, Harry. You know his name already because he was the architect of that plan we nixed a couple years ago—Stumbler. He also met twice with Emmett a week before the murder."

"Well, *that's* interesting."

"Yes, it is. And if we're going to investigate, then I need to know about him."

Harry took a long breath, gazing into his glass. "I'll make some calls, then."

There wasn't anything to do, so Stan just nodded. It wasn't the first time Harry had lied to him, but repetition made it no easier to accept. "Would you like to hear about Zora Balašević?"

"You tell me, Stan—would I?"

"She lived over in Islamic Cairo last year, and—"

Harry cut in: "And now?"

"Back home in Serbia."

"*Not* in Hungary."

A crowd of youngish Westerners, seven or eight in leather jackets, spilled noisily into the restaurant, laughing. At a glance, Stan suspected they were members of a film crew. He said, "Dragan Milić claims he never received anything from Emmett. Balašević told him Emmett wouldn't play ball."

"You believe this?"

"Dragan doesn't. Nor do I. The important point is that by then she was working for the Egyptians."

Stan couldn't see Harry's forehead, for he'd covered his entire face with his large hand, thumb and pinkie rubbing at his temples. Finally, he took down his hand and gazed at the Hollywood types gathering around a long table with seats for twice as many.

Stan said, "There's always the chance that she wasn't lying, you know. Maybe we were wrong, and Emmett didn't share. In that case, the embassy sprang a different leak."

Harry blinked a few times. His hair wasn't as pristine as usual; a few errant white strands had fallen across his high forehead.

Stan said, "Ideas?"

Still looking at the far table, Harry shook his head, and there was something so bleak in that movement that Stan's suspicions rose again, all at once. The Paolo Bertolli in him was thinking, *Of course it's him. And here you are, spilling everything to the man you should've caught last year.* Now *tell me how the Agency keeps people quiet.*

"Come on, Harry. Speak to me."

In reply, Harry lifted his glass and drained it completely. He set it down again and said, "How're your secret-keeping skills?"

"I'm a model employee."

"Then let's take a walk."

Harry paid for the drinks, and together they left the hotel through the front, headed past busy porters and taxis crowding the entrance ramp, then found a convenient spot to cross Mohammed Abd El-Wahab to reach the Nile, where narrow piers shot out into the water, harboring small boats. Instinctively, they sped up and slowed, sometimes stopping, in order to lose anyone who remained near them for more than a few seconds. Harry said, "First of all, let's get one thing out of the way—you can forget about Jibril Aziz."

"Why?"

"You're right—I know the name, but that doesn't matter now, because he's dead. And no," he said, raising a hand, "I'm not going to tell you how or where or when, because that's not for you to know. Just don't waste your time trying to find him."

Dead? Stan took a second to catch his breath. "Then how about why?"

"I'm just a station head. Don't ask me things above my pay grade. Langley tells me what to do, and I huff and I puff and I do it."

How, Stan wondered, was he to connect a dead Jibril Aziz to everything else? How was he ever going to put any of this together? "What's the second thing?"

Harry rubbed the side of his neck as they reached a gangplank that led to a long restaurant boat. A sign in English called it the Veranda Restaurant and Lounge. Stan thought he was going to take them down the ramp for another drink, but Harry just stopped, reached into his jacket pocket, and took out a pack of Marlboro

Lights. Cupping his hands, he lit one with a Zippo and inhaled deeply. A fresh breeze rose, bringing the rot-stink of the Nile along with voices from the restaurant boat, staff members complaining to one another as they set up for the evening's business. Harry was stalling, and Stan's anticipation brought out a layer of sweat beneath his shirt.

Eventually, Harry said, "Do you really think that you were the only one Langley came to last year? Those were some serious leaks."

"What are you talking about?"

"Langley gave you a portion of the story and sent you off. After a while, you came back with Emmett."

"What do you mean, a portion of the story?"

"I mean what I say, Stan. How many pieces of compromised intel did they share with you before you tracked them to Emmett?"

"Four."

"There were at least *nine* pieces, Stan. At least, that's how many pieces they gave me when they sent me off to find out who the leak was."

"Why didn't you tell me?"

"Don't get self-righteous, Stan. You don't have that right."

Stan wasn't sure what he meant, but the tone in Harry's voice was clear. It was as close to a slap as Harold Wolcott ever came, and Stan felt the chill of his shirt sticking to him. The station chief placed a hand on a post beside the gangplank to steady himself. There were more voices from the boat, and he saw two waiters on deck, shouting fiercely at one another about something, and that was when Stan finally got it. Stupid, stupid Stan finally understood that, despite what their emissary had said, Langley hadn't trusted him at all. He felt flushed. Aloud, he said, "They were testing me."

"They were testing us both, Stan. Why do you think I didn't throw Emmett at Langley? I saw you walk in like you'd been hand-picked by God to dig for a mole, and I knew you had only been given a few cards to deal with. You were starting with limited intelligence."

"And who did your evidence point toward?"

Harry exhaled smoke. "Emmett, too. But the difference between us is that I believed him."

Stan swallowed hard. "Which is another way of saying you weren't sure you could trust me."

"Who trusts anyone these days?" Harry said, then put a heavy hand on Stan's shoulder. "Don't take it personally. In a situation like this, everything should be examined, and if you're missing some crucial piece of information it's best to assume you don't know *anything*. I do know how those planners in Virginia think, though. Sometimes they're like string theorists—what's real is not real. Hell, it's possible that there was no compromised intel in the first place."

"You believe that?" Stan asked, thinking of the mutilated undercover agent outside Homs. *That* was real.

Harry didn't bother answering, but he said, "If the evidence we got pointed at Emmett, yet it now turns out that Emmett wasn't giving away anything, then one possibility would be that Langley wanted to get rid of Emmett. It's not unprecedented."

A way to keep him quiet, Stan thought—Omar Halawi's warning. He was gradually recovering from his humiliation, considering this new idea. "Emmett talked to Jibril Aziz. Did he know about Stumbler?"

Harry nodded. "I needed his help on the economics. He asked to see the whole plan, so I sent him a copy. But that doesn't mean they were talking about Stumbler."

"Is there any other subject you can imagine them discussing?"

Harry flicked away his cigarette. It arced down toward the murky water. On the boat, the two waiters were fighting now, fists held up close to their chins, like boxers from another century. "Let's not assume we know anything, because we still don't."

"So what do we do now?"

Harry grinned. "Ask yourself what your father would do."

"Sometimes, Harry, you're a real dick."

3

Sophie called from the spare cell phone as he was driving, and without preface she asked what he'd found. "Not much," he said, then promised to be home soon.

He had begun the day full of good intentions, still regretting his lie about Balašević, but he realized that he couldn't open up to her yet. Not until he had a better idea of what was going on. Harry was right—to assume that they really knew anything was folly, and he was terrified of saddling her with half-truths and rumors that would eat away at her. He believed he understood to some degree what she was going through, and he knew how, in the absence of verifiable truths, guilt and paranoia could ruin a person. Her last moments with her husband had been spent admitting to an affair—how could she not be broken by this?

He stopped by a restaurant for takeout, and when he got home Sophie was at her iPad, sitting exactly where he had left her. Her skin was pink, though—she must have gotten some sun on the terrace, perhaps gazing at those pyramids. She looked serious. "Something?" he asked as he gave her a kiss, but she shook her head. She was looking at Yahoo! News.

He presented grilled chicken, and though she played along well he felt in his bones that she was keeping something from him. She said, "Did you find out about Jibril Aziz?"

He covered his hesitation by walking into the kitchen to plate the food. "Not much," he called to her. "Just his position in the Office of Collection Strategies. I sent him an e-mail—maybe he'll get back to me."

"No phone number?"

"None," he lied.

"Why not?"

Because he's a corpse, Stan wanted to say, but he'd thought through this on his drive home. Aziz was Sophie's only solid lead, and if she knew he was dead there would be no reason for her to stay. "Sometimes they don't list numbers," he said, muddling his way through some semblance of bureaucratic logic. "Either they're changing offices or the section head wants them undisturbed because of a project."

"How about a wife? A family?"

"None," he lied again, remembering the panicky woman on the phone.

He could hear the frustration in her silence. He said, "I've got a few leads I can follow up on tomorrow."

"Like what?"

"Well, he's Libyan by birth, and I've sent out feelers to some of the exile groups mentioned in the Stumbler memos." He was surprised by the fluidity of his own invention. "If he's moving in their circles, we should be able to track him down easily."

"Okay," he heard her mutter.

How much did they lie to one another? he wondered as he collected utensils. How often had they lied? He flashed suddenly on his own parents—a father who lived by lies, and a mother who allowed her husband's lies to drive her to alcoholism. Though divorce had not been a part of their worldview, by the time his father died they were only a washed-out facsimile of a married couple.

Maybe this was why he decided, despite his fears, to be a little more open with Sophie. He wanted something lasting with her, something more permanent in his life of transience—and that required a measure of risk. Not much, but some. Over dinner, he said, "I need to tell you a few things about Emmett."

He told her that, last year, he had discovered Emmett was leaking information. He paused, searching for a reaction in her stony gaze. He found nothing, so he said, "Emmett was reporting to Zora Balašević."

She blinked a few times, digesting this, then made the connection that he'd feared would be her first stop. "You pretended you'd never heard of her. You *lied* to me."

"You caught me off guard. I'm sorry, I won't do that again."

"You lied," she repeated.

He saw the hurt in her face and felt the desire to slam his own face against the edge of the table. Instead, he said, "You just appeared. Suddenly, back in my life. I was confused. I made a mistake, and I'm sorry. But I'm telling you now: I won't do it again." That, perhaps, was the biggest lie. "Do you believe me?"

The hurt was taking residence in her features. She nodded almost imperceptibly, but it was a nod, then she said, "Go on."

He cleared his throat and wiped his lips with a napkin. "When I discovered it, I confronted him. I told him to cut it out. Do that, and no one need ever know. But I think he was more scared of whatever Balašević was holding over his head. I could have just reported to Langley, but that would have ended in disaster. Instead, I brought it to Harry."

After a while of staring, she said, "He told me this. Before. It."

He frowned. "About me, too?"

She nodded again, and the understanding flooded into him. *This* was the secret she'd been carrying the previous night, the distance he'd felt between them. She'd known from the start that he was holding back, and she'd been waiting for this moment. He'd been right to open up to her. He watched her get up from the dining table and sit on the sofa, where she'd apparently spent most of the day. She said, "Where is Zora?"

He followed her and settled down beside her. "Serbia. She went back home in September. Since Emmett was gone there was no reason for her to stay."

Sophie blinked, taking this in. He waited for her to ask more, for the questions had to have been numerous, but she didn't push yet.

He said, "She told Emmett she was working for the Serbs. That was a lie."

She raised her head to look squarely at him, squinting. "What? Are you sure?"

"My Serb contact says that by then she was working for the Egyptians."

"Do you believe him?"

"I don't believe anybody." After a lengthy silence, he added, "But, yes, I suppose I do believe him."

Her gaze wandered around the room before returning to him, eyes moist. "He told me he was innocent. Emmett."

"He told me that, too."

"Why didn't you believe him?"

Stan sighed. "Because he met with her."

"How often?" she asked, interest now in her face.

"Just once that we verified. But we had a look at his computer—he took home the same files that were leaked."

She nodded at that, and while she looked as if she might cry, she also looked as if she believed him, so he didn't bother saying that Balašević also claimed that Emmett had been innocent. What was the point? Finally, she said, "What kind of disaster?"

"What?"

"You said that if you'd brought Emmett's crime to Langley, it would have ended in disaster."

"Right."

"Well?"

He paused. "They would have taken him out of Cairo. He'd have been ruined."

"But he was giving away secrets."

"The disaster is that you would have left, too."

She drank some wine, giving him no sign that she understood the sentimentality of his statement.

He said, "What did Balašević have on Emmett?"

She sighed loud and long, then leaned closer and laid her head against his chest. He raised an arm to hold on to her, wondering where this sudden tenderness was coming from. Exhaustion? Was the tenderness real, or did she feel she owed him? Did she believe she had a choice?

That was a question. What choices did Sophie Kohl have in Cairo, and who was in control when Stan kissed her neck and stroked her leg, making his desire clear? When she responded with a hand on his thigh, then raised her face so that he could reach her lips, what was motivating her? A widow fresh off her husband's murder wasn't expected to reciprocate like this—but what did he really know about widowhood? He suspected there was a whole world of complications and motives inside of Sophie that he would never get in touch with, so that it would always be impossible to say precisely what bent her to his will at that moment.

That night, though, he set aside these concerns. She was with him, finally, and his appetite rose. They were out of most of their clothes while still in the living room, and then she—she, not he—led him to the bedroom, where she allowed him to finally have her.

Afterward, he watched her drift into sleep, feeling possessive and eager and childlike. It was so much better than it had been before, and in that postcoital glow he resolved to put all his efforts into taking care of her. Clear up the mysteries around them and quell her fears and confusions. She was so still that he held a hand under her nose and waited to feel her warm exhale; then he rested a hand on her hip under the covers, and closed his eyes. He had no answers, but some things are better than answers.

4

On Sunday morning, he found it impossible to leave. He was tired, but after a shower they made love again on the sofa. It was different between them. Different from the standoffishness of the last couple of days, and different, too, from the illicit attraction of the previous year. It felt fresh and new, and not unlike empathy. Why would he walk out the door when this was in his home?

She felt otherwise. By eleven she said, "Don't you need to go track down Aziz?"

"Right."

He dressed and gave her a kiss that she returned with wrists linked behind his neck.

He said, "You can stay here, you know."

"Well, I wasn't planning on a hotel."

"I mean longer. As long as you want."

From her face he could tell she understood, but being perceptive didn't mean that he had the faintest notion of what was going on in her head, for her words at first baffled him: "They're burying him today."

He first thought of Jibril Aziz, but she was talking about Emmett. "Yes, of course. Boston?"

"Amherst."

"You wish you'd gone?"

She thought about that, then shook her head. "Funerals aren't much use."

He gave her another kiss, chaste, and headed out the door. It was the last time he would ever see Sophie Kohl.

Since he lived close to the embassy, he left his car behind and walked, buoyed by the change in his fortunes—smiling, even. When he got to his office and found an e-mail from Saul, fortune seemed to still be on his side. He didn't know what connections Saul was using, but his results were swift. He had tracked down the September 4 footage from Frankfurt International, which he had uploaded to one of the Agency's secure servers. Six hours of Zora Balašević wandering the corridors of the airport, from a variety of angles, in a total of seventy-nine video files with time code embedded. He started to download them and, as soon as the first file was completed, began to watch.

Balašević was five-six, five-seven, and despite the wear on her face she moved like a healthy forty-year-old, though she was a decade and a half older. Her hair was tuned to a pitch black common to the Balkans, and there were signs that either she worked out or her lifestyle demanded a lot of her physically. She wore a knee-length skirt with high black heels. She walked with confidence. She didn't look around for watchers, nor did she hesitate when faced with gun-toting airport security. She carried a leather shoulder bag—large, with a vertical brown stripe as decoration, perhaps a laptop bag.

The footage began with her entrance into the airport around 9:00 A.M. in Terminal 1 and rolled along in files ranging from thirty seconds to twenty minutes. Stan watched her enter shots and shrink as she headed out of them, sometimes in the thick of a crowd, sometimes alone. She went first to a functional little café for some caffeine, then headed to the toilets. Inside, she used a stall briefly, then washed her hands and moved on, the bag always very close.

Though she didn't come across in the video as aimless—she headed to each rest stop as if to an important meeting—it soon became clear that she was just killing time. She would double back to a café she had been in an hour earlier, or sometimes sit at the same gates she had visited before, thumbing messages into her phone. But with her purposeful demeanor, no one in that airport would have thought that she was solely waiting around; everything she did absorbed her entirely.

Then, at 11:08, two hours into her wandering, she sat down at Gate 32 and pushed the bag under her seat. Then she straightened and used her left heel to push it deeper. She took out her phone and started fooling with it again.

At 11:16, a man crossed between the camera and Balašević, an identical bag on his shoulder, and took the seat behind Balašević, so that they were sitting back-to-back. After placing his bag on the floor beside his chair, he also took out a phone and worked at it. His mouth, though, was moving. So was Balašević's.

He was younger than Balašević, a light-skinned Arab in a pricey business suit. Long nose, thin lips. Just another traveling businessman in an airport full of men like him. At one point he glanced up at a passing security guard, his hard face full and well lit.

Their conversation took all of four minutes before Balašević checked her wristwatch and got up, taking the man's bag with her. Though he knew the man would also leave soon, reaching under the seat to retrieve Balašević's bag, Stan didn't see him do this because the video ended and picked up with Balašević heading to her next pointless destination.

There were nearly four hours of footage left, but he didn't bother watching any more. He replayed the video of the meeting, a file called 93-040911-394294-P.mov, and returned to that man looking at the security guard, at 11:18:23. He zoomed in and froze it, then exported the frame as an image.

He mailed the image and a link to the video file back to Saul and asked him to track down the identity of the man meeting with Balašević. This was simply a matter of following the man to his own departure flight and checking the airline's ID scan at the instant his passport went through it. With that name, he might be able to untangle a few threads.

For the moment, though, he was stuck. Ali Busiri had not answered his request for a meet, and the dead Aziz had no means of answering his mail. He sent an e-mail to Jake Copeland, Aziz's direct supervisor, asking where his analyst was, and, thinking of his lie the previous night, he queried a Libya watcher based in Langley, asking for any chatter among the exile community about Aziz. He returned to the database, thinking of Aziz's four-year tenure in North Africa, from 2001 to 2005, and searched agent reports on Libya. During that period, most agent communiqués dealing with the region had come not from Tripoli but from Cairo station, and as he went through reports he followed a hunch, cross-referencing them with Harry Wolcott's name. This was how he came upon reports of an agent known by two names, the cryptonym ASHA and the legend Akram Haddad.

Though heavily redacted, there was enough here for Stan to put together a narrative that matched Jibril Aziz's resume almost perfectly. A young agent who arrived in Cairo in 2001, taking a small apartment in New Cairo, from where he traveled with increasing frequency across the border into Libya to connect with locals, garner intelligence, and build networks until, in 2005, he was blown and barely escaped Libya with his life. Each and every ASHA report was forwarded to Langley by Harry Wolcott, Cairo station chief, who met ASHA in his apartment after each Libyan visit in order to debrief him and collect his reports.

Stan rubbed at his eye sockets until they hurt. Harry hadn't just read and turned down a proposal by Jibril Aziz—he had *run* Aziz for four years. Why hadn't he admitted this? What was he hiding?

His inbox dinged for his attention. Two sentences from Jake Copeland: "Mr. Aziz is on personal leave. I'm afraid I couldn't tell you were he is."

As he was considering a reply, some diplomatic way to push Copeland for more, his phone buzzed. When he recognized the number, he cursed. She was calling from her Hungarian phone. "Hey," he said.

"Stan." For an instant, he thought that a stranger had taken her phone. It was in her voice, a coldness. As if she had become someone else.

"What's up?"

"You've been lying to me, Stan."

How could he reply to that? He said, "About what?"

"Jibril Aziz, Stan." He didn't like the way she was repeating his name.

"What about him?"

"His wife, Stan. You told me very definitely that he didn't have a wife."

"It didn't seem important," he said, suddenly confused.

"Didn't it?"

"You're right, Sophie. I've been holding back."

"You've been lying."

"I've been trying to protect you."

"Oh, Jesus," she said. "Do men really think that the only thing women want is protection?"

"I'll be home in fifteen minutes," he told her, using his commanding voice. "Wait for me. I'll tell you everything you want to know."

"Everything?"

"Yes," he said, because he was tired of lying. Perhaps she would walk out on Cairo, but the rules of espionage ought not apply to those we love. He needed at least one relationship in his life that was clear and clean.

"I don't know, Stan."

What didn't she know? "Just wait. I'll be there as soon as I can."

He waved at Eric as he burst out the front doors and ran across the grounds, out the gate, and through Garden City's winding streets. It took him only seven minutes to get home, so it was more than a shock when he found the apartment empty—it was devastating. He felt it in his legs, which had once brought on his desire, and were now bringing on cramps. Unself-consciously, he held on to himself, arms around his stomach, and moved from room to room, finding only empty spaces. He was confused, angry, and in love, but he didn't really know what pain was until he reached the bathroom, with its marble sink and large, unframed mirror where, scrawled across the glass in Sophie's burgundy lipstick, was a single word, underlined.

<u>LIAR</u>

5

———

Though he would never see her again, Stan never considered this possibility. She might have walked out on him, but she was in *his* town. He was, at heart, an optimist, and he believed—he *knew*—that within hours or days they would be together again. Ragged, perhaps, a little scarred, but together.

By ten that evening, through a call to a contact in Egyptian security, he learned that she had checked into the Semiramis InterContinental, just around the corner from the embassy. While his first impulse was to follow her there, crash through her door, and smother her, he knew that she needed space. Once her anger had passed she would come around, for who else did she have in Cairo? He was the only one who truly wanted to help her.

Patience, his father once told him with typical exaggeration, *is the only worthwhile tool in an agent's arsenal.*

His one concession to his desire was to ask Paul to sit in the Semiramis lobby to watch out for her.

"Sophie Kohl?" Paul asked over the line, incredulous. "What's she doing here?"

"That's what I'm trying to figure out," Stan said as coolly as he could manage. "Don't make any approach. Just make sure she doesn't get hurt, and if she leaves, you call me and keep track of her. Once we have some answers, I'll take it to Harry. In the meantime it's between us. Got it?"

Afterward, he lay down but couldn't sleep. He was too disorganized, too muddled, his mind flickering over the tangled mess of things he knew and didn't know, so he got up again, swallowed two Tylenol with a glass of water, and tried to think back to Thursday, before Sophie had arrived to scramble his thinking. What had he learned?

From Dragan Milić: Zora Balašević had not been reporting embassy secrets back to him. She'd been reporting to Ali Busiri in the Central Security Forces. Whether the secrets had come from Emmett or someone else was another question entirely.

On Friday, Omar Halawi, or RAINMAN, had passed on a piece of advice through Paul: *If you want to find Emmett's murderer, you need to look at yourselves.* Someone in the Agency, Halawi was suggesting, had wanted to keep Emmett quiet.

Perhaps that was true, but Stan was still hesitant to trust an Egyptian's word.

Then there was what Sophie had brought to the table: Jibril Aziz, Emmett, and Stumbler.

Finally, there were the elusive facts that Harry had given up on Saturday. Aziz was dead, but he wouldn't say how or why. Was his death connected to John Calhoun's secret mission? Harry had also dredged up Stan's original investigation into the leak last year, throwing even the existence of a leak into doubt.

There was one more thing, but it was only a question: How did Sophie find out that Aziz had a family?

This was what he had, but the facts refused to gel into a comprehensive theory. Sleep remained distant. He stared into the darkness at the ceiling until, at 4:48 A.M., the call to Fajr prayers convinced him to give up. He showered, dressed, and ate, and was back at the embassy by six. Security. Elevator. Office. He didn't bother powering up his computer. Instead, he unlocked the old five-drawer file cabinet in the corner and opened the bottom drawer. Like all the other drawers, it was full of manila folders, labeled with names and locations, background information on paper that hadn't yet been transcribed into the databases, but he wasn't interested in old information. He reached into the file marked HOTELS ELEC and removed three stapled sheets of paper. On the first two was a list of Cairo-area hotels, and he found the Semiramis quickly. Beside it was a code, BRB-9. He reached into the rear of the drawer and took out a rubber-banded stack of twenty hotel keycards. BRB-9 was the last one.

He reached the Semiramis before six thirty, just as the sun was rising to cut through the cold, and waited on the Corniche El Nil that separated the hotel from the river. He called Paul. After a few minutes, the young man was jogging across the road to meet him. He looked tired, perhaps as tired as Stan was, but he put on a good show. "Quiet as the grave," Paul said.

"Nothing? No one in, no one out?"

"No one that I recognized. But the staff sure took an interest in me."

They both knew that this didn't matter. The hotel staff would inform Central Security that some Westerner was camping out in their lobby, and the Egyptians would use CCTV footage to identify Paul, but he was breaking no laws. And he probably wasn't the only foreign spy reading newspapers and drinking coffee on their sofas. "Go back inside," Stan said. "I'll relieve you later on."

As he watched Paul cross the street again and head back into the hotel, Stan took out his phone and called the front desk. He asked for room 306 and listened as it rang and rang. Six thirty in the morning, and she wasn't answering.

He hung up and crossed the street, pausing in front of the Semiramis's glass doors. A valet eyeballed him. What was she doing up there? Was she overcome by paranoia now, trembling in fear whenever the phone rang? Or was she simply cold and hard, shaped by tragedies like the murder of her husband and the deception of her lover? Eventually, she would have to call him. There was no other choice.

Or was there? He'd had the sense during their hours together that she was holding something back. He'd assumed it was that final conversation with Emmett about Zora Balašević—but what if it was something else? What if she wasn't alone in Cairo? Someone had told her about Aziz's family. What if . . .

Before he could think through the pros and cons, Stan entered the lobby and patted the air in reply to Paul's questioning look. He ignored the clerks and concierge as he headed toward the elevators. He was just another Caucasian face breezing through town on business, never getting to know the city, never tipping enough, and never learning a word of the local language.

On the third floor he found a young couple trying to reason with their three- or four-year-old boy, who was sitting in the corner beside a potted plant, refusing to go anywhere. When the father looked up, his face full of despair, Stan gave him a sympathetic grimace and then looked at the boy, who had an oddly adult face—narrow and long, eyes sunken and intense. Almost judgmental. The boy watched Stan as his parents pleaded with him, and Stan could feel his eyes boring into his back until he turned a corner and continued on.

Her room was halfway down a long corridor, and in front of it was a *Herald Tribune* Sophie hadn't bothered to pick up. He knocked and waited, listening. Nothing. He tried again and said, "Housekeeping." Still there was nothing, so he took out BRB-9 and stroked it twice against the magnetic pad; the door clicked. He opened it slowly.

The room was empty, the bed disorganized as if it had been quickly abandoned. The dresser drawers were empty, and so were the tables.

He settled on the bed, feeling heavy and sluggish. She was gone. He thought he might cry, but he didn't.

When he finally went downstairs nearly an hour later, he sat beside Paul on the lobby sofa. "Did you leave last night?"

Paul frowned and shook his head. "Of course not."

Stan sighed, thinking first of kidnapping and only afterward of escape. There were other exits from the hotel, but he hadn't imagined that Sophie Kohl would have the foresight to use them. Perhaps she had. Or perhaps her kidnappers had.

"What is it, boss?"

Stan looked at his hands in his lap; they were trembling. He took out BRB-9 and handed it to Paul. "Room 306. Stay in there and wait. If she returns, make sure she doesn't leave."

"Using force?"

"If necessary."

In the embassy, Stan nodded at his co-workers and shut himself in his office, thinking of organization. *Start at the beginning,* he thought. It was a method, he knew, a way of pushing away the terror he felt. Where was she? Who was protecting her? Why had she left him? His hands shook as he typed on his keyboard and clicked the mouse, finally tracking down the original Stumbler memos from 2009. He wiped at his eyes and began to read.

Jibril Aziz had been prescient. As justification for his plan, Aziz had cited growing unrest throughout the region almost two years before anybody else in the Agency had thought to tie them into a regional shift. Stan and others had viewed the sporadic demonstrations and crackdowns as brushfires—Jibril Aziz had seen them as portents.

It took a while to wade through the pages of Aziz's optimism, and, thinking of what Emmett would have been consulted on, he reread the section titled "Fallout," which dealt with the economic repercussions of regime change. Aziz had put forth the idea that, with Tripoli in its pocket, with the support of the Egyptian government (which, before Mubarak stepped down that month, they could have been assured of), and with the compliance of Tunisia (which, again, was a given before that chaotic year had begun), the United States would gain effective trade control of the entire North African coast—a third of the Mediterranean coastline. They could have done simple things, like negotiate reduced port fees for their own freighters, but more importantly it would have given America better access to the African market for anything from toilet brushes to nuclear power plants.

Even with the benefit of hindsight, this still felt like a stretch, and he imagined that when Harry had read it he'd thought the same thing. But neither he nor Harry was an economist. Emmett had been.

Stan went to his file cabinet, and from the middle drawer removed a slender folder in which he'd kept the documentation he'd collected to establish Emmett's guilt. Among the list of files from Emmett's computer was a ten-digit code that, he saw now, matched the Stumbler documents. Yes, Stumbler would have reached Zora Balašević as well.

As he was returning to his seat, John Calhoun tapped on his door. "I'm free if you need anything."

Stan blinked at him, still caught in the myopia that had taken control since visiting the Semiramis. He considered pulling in John for some legwork, or even to grill him on Jibril Aziz, but then changed his mind. The man didn't look well, and as soon as he started asking about Aziz John would go to Harry—that was a given. "Go get some lunch," he told the big man. "Take it easy."

Once he was alone again, he closed his eyes, shoving away his fears for Sophie, imagining instead the sequence of events. Emmett copied the Stumbler plans from his laptop onto a flash drive and passed them on to Zora Balašević, who sold them to Ali Busiri. Months later, Emmett discussed Stumbler with Aziz, and both he and Aziz soon perished. From these sketchy details, it certainly did look as if Omar Halawi was right in at least one way: Emmett, and presumably Aziz, had been killed to keep them quiet. Quiet about what? Emmett's treason? Stumbler? Or . . . the identity of the real leak?

And who really wanted them silenced? CIA? Egypt? Dragan Milić, covering up a plateful of lies he'd been feeding to Stan? Without knowing the answer to one question, the other could never be answered. Without knowing who was behind this, he would never find Sophie.

His computer dinged an incoming e-mail. It was from LogiThrust LLC about the wonderful world of penile enhancements. The codes were ridiculous but effective. He checked the text against a list of translations and learned that Ali Busiri would be waiting for him at al-Azhar Park at five thirty that evening. Finally.

He went back to the memo, but there was another tap at his door. It was Nancy. With a smile she told him a single word: "Harry's."

6

<hr/>

"Y̶ou know," Harry began once his guest had taken a seat, "a lot of people think of our station as a backwoods outpost, even now." There was a spot of red against his pale chin; he had nicked himself with a razor that morning. "We stumble into our intrigues, which from our perspective seem world-shattering and life-and-death. But from Langley's perspective our time is taken up by tempests in teacups."

Harry paused, as if this were something Stan needed a moment to comprehend.

"They're wrong, of course. They often are. What they forget is that Washington is not the center of the world, and it hasn't been for at least a decade."

That he was referring to 9/11 before his after-work cocktail wasn't a good sign.

"Don't get me wrong," Harry said. "They pay us lip service like it's going out of style. They throw money at us and pass on our reports to members of Congress. But don't ever fool yourself, Stan: Anytime one of us has an idea that contradicts one of Langley's starched collars, it ceases to be a battle of ideas; it becomes a battle of school ties."

He was getting at something, but he was taking the long way around to it. Like Stan's own father, he showed his anxieties by launching into overstatement and weak metaphor. "We're not the British, Harry."

"And how does that make any difference?"

Stan shrugged. "You really think it's that bad?"

"Worse," he said, finally engaging with his eyes. "It's why Cairo station has to be seen—from the outside, at least—as better than Langley. As more ironclad, more impeccable. More pristine. It's the only way to stand a chance against the old-boy network. You and me, we have to be more; we have to be better."

Stan nodded. Harry seemed to have woken in a mood of constructive self-criticism, or maybe he was misinterpreting.

"And then, Stan, there's you."

"Me?"

Harry rubbed his eyes and avoided Stan's for a second, saying, "A senior member of this station making calls to people he's not even supposed to know." Their eyes met. "You know what I mean?"

Stan went through the calls he'd made recently. Who was he not supposed to know? Sophie? Saul? "I'm not sure I do."

Harry took a breath, opened his desk drawer, and took out a single sheet of paper. "One Inaya Aziz, of Alexandria, Virginia."

"Right," Stan said, hesitant relief slipping into his shoulders. "That was Saturday, before you and I talked. Just a few seconds—I never identified myself."

Harry knitted his brow, forehead contracting, and spoke in a hard voice. "Don't lie to me, Stan." He looked down at the paper in his hand. "Twelve-oh-nine in the afternoon on Sunday, from your landline, twenty-eight minutes of conversation." He looked up at Stan, his expression pained. "*Land*line? Jesus, Stan. Are you working *for* the Egyptians? Because if you aren't, then you might as well ask them to pay you for all this volunteer work."

There it was, the trap opening up in front of him. Stan hadn't been at home at 12:09 P.M. yesterday. Sophie had. Stan had been in the office, running through Frankfurt surveillance footage. A glance at the front desk's entry/exit records would have told Harry this, but he apparently hadn't checked that yet.

Which was the worse crime? Calling the widow of a man he wasn't supposed to know about, or harboring the widow Sophie Kohl without telling anyone?

In this case, he wasn't sure.

How had Sophie gotten Inaya Aziz's number?

Harry said, "I believe I told you to forget about Aziz. Wasn't I clear?"

"I had to verify some things."

"You had to *verify* some things? What does that mean, Stan?"

He took a breath. "Look, Harry—if you're not going to be upfront with me, then I've got no choice but to follow up on my own. Jibril Aziz met with Emmett, and soon afterward both were dead. You're not telling me how or why Aziz was killed. So I kept digging, and it turned out that you used to run Aziz—you ran him for *four years*. You didn't think I should know this?"

"There's a reason it's called undercover," Harry told him, features stiff.

"Undercover. Okay. I'm sure you've got plenty of reasons to keep me stupid, but did you expect me to sit on my hands? So I called his wife to find out if she knew where he was."

Harry rubbed his left eye. "And what did she say?"

"That she didn't know where he was."

"And what did that *verify* for you, Stan?"

"The only thing it verified was that you know more than you're sharing, and it's time to stop playing games. Talk to me about Omar Halawi."

"Who?"

"RAINMAN. He works out of Ali Busiri's office."

Harry raised his head, squinting.

Stan said, "Omar Halawi says that we killed Emmett."

There it was—the slap, square in the forehead. "He says *what*?"

"He sent me this message through Paul. I haven't had a face-to-face with him yet. I want to talk to Busiri first."

Harry leaned back, fingers threaded together across his narrow chest, and said, "Why, pray tell, did we kill Emmett?"

"To keep him quiet."

"About what?"

Stan shrugged. "Stumbler? Or maybe the identity of another leak in the embassy."

Harry sighed and, with a loose left hand, pointed at the ceiling. "It's raining shit."

It was an unexpected thing for him to say, but Stan held his tongue.

Harry said, "I'd be careful about what Ali Busiri says. He's a sneaky bastard."

"I know."

"I don't think you do. About a month ago, when things fell apart for Mubarak, do you know what he did?"

Stan shook his head.

"He called me for a meeting. In a *hotel* room. He was pouring martinis. Made me wait forever before he got around to it—he wanted to come over to us."

Stan frowned, but waited.

"He was scared. Terrified. He thought he was going to end up with a bullet behind the ear, and so he made me an offer. We give him a nice house in California and new names for him and his wife, and he gives us everything."

"Everything?"

Harry nodded.

"But you didn't take him up on it."

Harry shook his head. "When you've been neck-deep in it for as long as I have, you learn to smell who's bullshitting you. I smelled it—that hotel room was lousy with it."

"Did you tell Langley?"

"How well can they smell from five thousand miles away?"

Despite his anxiety, Stan grinned. "But he survived the changes."

"So far he has," Harry said. "My only point is that you should take Ali Busiri's intel with a grain of salt. The same's true of his employees, like Omar Halawi."

They both thought about that a moment until Harry said, "Does Sophie have a theory?"

Stan blinked. "When she called me, she was in shock."

"But certainly she shared some kind of opinion with you. After all, you were lovers."

Stan said nothing.

Harry smiled softly, then waved at him. "Did you think I didn't know? You kept using the same hotel room—bad security."

Now Stan was the one rubbing his face. Yes, it had been bad security, and of course Harry had known. He was surprised that Harry had never brought him in for a talk, but now that it was out in the open he felt anxiety falling off his shoulders.

"This," Harry said, "would be the other reason I didn't haul Emmett off in chains. You can see the conflict of interest, can't you?"

Stan could see it very clearly.

Harry covered his mouth again and looked at the ceiling, as if it were turning brown from the rain. "So let me ask you again: Do you know where she is?"

Stan remembered her words: *Do men really think that the only thing women want is protection?* "I have no idea," he said, and that, at least, was true.

The desk phone buzzed. As Harry answered it, Stan considered asking for help tracking down Sophie. Harry knew, after all, about the affair—that obstacle had been taken away, yet Stan wasn't ready to ask for help. Why?

It was because of a single gesture, that forehead, which seemed to cover up a whole world of secrets that he could not even guess at. *If you're missing some crucial piece of information it's best to assume you don't know anything.* There was enough missing here that he couldn't even assume he could trust Harold Wolcott.

Stan waited as Harry listened on line one; Nancy was talking to him. Harry's face changed again. His mouth hung open, and unconsciously he touched the nick on his chin. "Okay," Harry said into the phone. Then he hung up and met Stan's gaze squarely with his own. "Look at the ceiling."

Stan did so, and it looked the same as it always had.

"When it shits, Stan, it pours. Sophie Kohl is in Cairo."

"Where?"

A heavy shrug. "The Hungarians finally told us where she went. The Egyptians haven't verified it for us yet, but I assume they will eventually." He frowned. "Question is: Why hasn't she gotten in touch with us?" He wiped at his nose. "You'd think she didn't trust us."

7

———

Stan returned to his office and called Paul, who had spent the whole day in room 306. "Nothing," he told Stan in the midst of a yawn. Hope was bleeding away. "You want me to leave?"

"No," Stan told him, then hung up. He settled back in his chair, again looking at the Stumbler memo, and rubbed at his eyes. He thought back to a year ago, to the dour Langley man telling him of intercepted communications from the Syrian, Libyan, and Pakistani embassies. Pretending to be giving him the whole story. Had Langley really not trusted him, or Harry? Had—

His desk phone rang, breaking his wandering thoughts. He picked up. "Stan Bertolli."

"My man," said Saul, his voice rough from a lingering cold. "I got your name."

Briefly, Stan didn't know what he was talking about, then it came to him—the video still from Frankfurt, Balašević with a man. "Tell me."

"Michael Khalil, American."

"American?"

"So his passport says."

"What do *you* say, Saul?"

"I say it's fake because his passport number matches a guy who died of a coronary in 1998. He can't use the passport to get into Fortress America, but he's used it to visit other countries. We're running his face through the recognition software, but God only knows how long that'll take."

"Where's he been recently?"

Saul hummed as he read through his information. "The Khalil passport spent a week in Tripoli last year, but the rest of that year it was in your town—except for that one-day visit to Frankfurt. Then last week he visited Germany. Munich."

"For how long?"

"Three days, March 1 to March 3. Then he flew to . . . well, why don't you take a guess?"

"Cairo," Stan said.

"I don't care what anyone around here says, Stan. You're one smart kid."

Stan closed his eyes, thinking about that flight in and out of Munich. After murdering Emmett, Gjergj Ahmeti had been tracked to a train heading from Budapest to Munich. Emmett was killed on March 2. Khalil could easily have flown in and out of Munich for a visit to Budapest to oversee the killing—what other way could he interpret it? Which meant that the man Zora Balašević had met in Frankfurt—her Egyptian or Serbian client—had been behind Emmett's murder. Not the United States of America.

Stan stared at the dead phone still in his hand, then checked with Nancy: Harry had stepped out again, destination unknown. He was overwhelmed by the feeling that he was playing catch-up, yet he didn't know what he was trying to catch up to. It was getting late.

He called Paul. "Close it down. Go home."

"Need me in the office?"

"Just get some sleep. I'll call you later if I need you."

"Yes, *sir*," Paul said, evidently pleased.

8

———

The low sun was hidden behind clouds as he drove to al-Azhar Park on the east side of town. He parked along a quiet section of the Passages Insaid al-Azhar Garden, near the main road, then locked up and headed into the vast, sculpted park. As he moved forward, he assessed (as Paolo Bertolli might) everything he saw: a long line of empty cars parked down the curb, a couple taking a relaxing stroll toward the enormous cafés on the man-made lake, two old men on a bench talking over a hand of cards, a woman in a hijab watching three children dance to a transistor radio playing Arabic pop. He followed a cobblestone path deeper into the park, where it opened up and palm trees were aligned geometrically and marble bridges crossed over little streams. It wasn't busy here—most families were preparing for dinner—and he saw a couple with a teenaged girl packing up a picnic and heading out. He settled on a bench, gazing across the lake with its fountains and restaurants and sunken garden on the other side, a spot of tranquility in the clogged mess of Cairo. As he waited, the clouds released a sprinkle of welcome rain that dimpled the lake and misted his hair, but only briefly.

He thought of these Egyptians whose world he passed through every day—how many friends had he made among them? None. He and most of his embassy co-workers were ghosts in this town, circulating only among themselves, as if the locals were there just to make sure their electricity and water flowed, and that they were well fed. He lived among Egyptians but not with them, which, on those rare days when he grew philosophical and criticial of his life, bothered him deeply.

Ali Busiri found him easily. They didn't know each other well; a couple of meetings in other parks were the sum of their personal relationship. There were no pass-phrases with a contact as high-ranking as Busiri.

He was plump and healthy-looking, and if Stan hadn't known Busiri's file he would've been tempted to use the word "jolly" to describe him. But he knew enough about Ali Busiri to know that he was far from jolly, and his expression that day, interrupted only by drags on a filtered Camel, did nothing to change his opinion. He sat down beside Stan, stinking of smoke. "This is about Emmett Kohl?"

Stan nodded.

"Otherwise I wouldn't have come. He was a good man."

"Maybe you didn't know him that well," Stan said in spite of himself.

Busiri turned to give him a look, something close to disgust. "You wanted to talk."

"First I have a question: Do you know where Sophie Kohl is?"

The older man blinked. "Emmett's widow? No. Is she missing?"

Stan very nearly answered the question before changing his mind. If Busiri didn't know where she was, then that part of the conversation was finished. "I'd like to talk about Zora Balašević."

Busiri smiled thinly; it did nothing to brighten his face. "The lady Serb. What about her?"

"She was working for you."

Busiri rocked his head from side to side, but he wasn't up to playing games today. "Yes."

"She passed you intelligence from the American embassy."

"Yes."

"And her source was Emmett Kohl."

This time the smile did brighten his face, just barely. "No," he said.

Stan took a breath. "Then who was it?"

Busiri turned away from him to look up the length of the path. Stan supposed he was looking for shadows, though there seemed little reason for it. Meetings between American diplomatic staff and Egyptian civil servants happened all the time. Some, Stan had heard, were even friends. Speaking in the direction of the rest of the park, so that Stan could only see his profile, he said, "Mr. Bertolli, what did you think of Omar Halawi's warning?"

"Who?"

Busiri turned back. "You think I don't know about Omar? You call him RAINMAN, as if he's some idiot savant, but he's not."

"You've been running him?"

Busiri looked surprised. "Of course. You didn't know?"

No, Stan hadn't known, though he'd had his suspicions. He felt stupid.

"But his message, Mr. Bertolli."

"That we should look at ourselves."

"Exactly."

"I don't know what to think. Particularly now that I know everything he told us was coming from you."

Busiri snorted softly, then shook his head. "Omar liked Emmett. Omar also has some problems that I believe will eventually require medication."

"Are you saying he's paranoid?"

"I am no doctor. However, for some people the layers upon layers of lies have a detrimental effect. One has to rewire the brain to do the kind of work we do. One crossed wire can throw everything off."

"What does he believe?"

Busiri took another drag and exhaled smoke. "Why don't we start with a simple question? The inverse of yours. Where is Jibril Aziz?"

"Tell me what Omar Halawi believes; then we can move to that."

"So you *do* know where Jibril is?" he asked, a trace of hope in his voice.

Stan nodded.

Busiri considered him for a moment, smoking, then tossed the unfinished cigarette into the damp grass, where it sizzled. "Omar and Jibril are friends. When Jibril drafted a plan to overthrow the mad despot in Tripoli, he brought it to Omar for consideration."

That was a surprise—Aziz had brought a top-secret plan to the Egyptians? Stan shook his head; it didn't matter now. "You know we rejected it, right? The Agency shelved the operation."

"Did you?" Busiri asked. "Perhaps *you* rejected it. Jibril was certainly *told* that it was rejected. But what was the reality? In some back room at your Langley, the planners were reconsidering. They reconsider everything, don't they? They put everything on *ice*."

"I couldn't tell you," Stan admitted.

"I'm not going to be coy with you, Mr. Bertolli," he said, opening his hands. "You see how open I'm being. However, you'll also notice that Omar has been reticent of late. This is his decision, not mine. He's appalled by what he believes the Agency is up to."

Stan shifted on the bench so that he could see Busiri's face better in the sudden darkness—sunset had occurred without him noticing, even though a distant prayer should have reminded him. "I don't have keys to secret back rooms, so you're going to have to be clearer with me. I'm just a cog."

"Just a cog?" Busiri grinned, then lit another Camel. "I'll tell you, Mr. Bertolli, because maybe you are just a cog, or maybe you're the man with his fingers on the controls. Either way, you should know what I know, for perhaps that will lead you to reconsider your actions."

Stan waited.

"Jibril called Omar a couple of weeks ago. February 22, five days after the Day of Revolt in Benghazi. He said, 'They're doing it, Omar. Stumbler is beginning.' That's all he had to say."

Though Stan knew the answer, he still wanted it spelled out. "What did *it* mean?"

Busiri brought the cigarette to his mouth, blinking, and took a drag. "It meant," he said, smoke coming out with his words, "that it was all set up. Once the Libyan people began to work for their own future, once they were dying in the streets, your people were prepared to take advantage of the historic moment. Take advantage of their courage and their martyrs. It meant that your world-renowned Agency was ready to steal the revolution from the bloodied hands of those in Libya who love freedom." He paused, took another drag, then said, "And because of this breach of basic human decency, I suggest you keep your distance from Omar. If placed in the same room with a representative of your Agency—with you, perhaps—I fear he may become violent. And we don't want that, do we?"

Stan thought about this a moment, briefly feeling Omar Halawi's anger, an anger Busiri seemed to share. Busiri wasn't talking about the CIA helping the revolution but taking it over, installing America's handpicked leaders in the presidential palace. He could understand the Egyptian's anger, but only to a degree. He thought again, then said, "I'm not going to take a lecture on basic human decency from a member of the Central Security Forces. We weren't gunning down protesters in Tahrir Square." Stan paused, but Busiri didn't react, so he went on. "What do you think the radicals are going to do once there's a vacuum in Tripoli? Do you think they're going to sit back and watch from their caves? No. They're going to threaten and sweet-talk the electorate until they get power, and then it'll be sharia law, women as chattel, and the export of teenagers with backpack bombs. Which would you prefer on your border—a Western-leaning government, or an Islamofascist state?"

Busiri scratched the edge of his lip, smiling. "You speak as if there's a world of difference when dealing with those two kinds of entities. There isn't, Mr. Bertolli. States are predictable, particularly when they have an extreme ideology. So are intelligence agencies."

"What about you?" Stan asked. "Should we be careful putting our representatives in the same room with you?"

Busiri raised his eyebrows. "Omar is passionate; I try not to be. I believe that things are very complicated. I *believe* that in the end this has little bearing on the security of Egypt, and so perhaps I shouldn't care."

Stan was hot, sweating inside his shirt, distracted by the wrong question: Was the Agency trying to hijack a popular revolution in

Libya? And if so, what would this mean? He was losing track of the smaller threads, the ones he had requested this meeting to discuss. Busiri's cigarette had gone out; the Egyptian noticed this and tossed it away, irritated, then stood.

Stan got to his feet as well. "Why did Aziz meet with Emmett Kohl a week before his murder in Budapest?"

"Do you want to know what Omar believes?"

"Yes."

"Use your imagination."

Busiri's eyes were weary. He wasn't goading Stan; he simply wanted him to do a little thinking for himself, so Stan spoke aloud as it came to him. "Aziz was going in to undermine Stumbler. Emmett was working with him."

With a look of scorn, Ali Busiri clapped silently, then glanced up at the clouded night sky. "Allah tells us it's time to go."

"Wait," Stan said as a new thought came to him.

The Egyptian frowned with impatience.

"Did you really try to defect?"

Busiri's eyes widened. "What?"

"I was told that you tried to come to our side."

Busiri sighed, then glanced at his watch, a Rolex. He glared at Stan. "Who told you this? It's ridiculous."

"So you're denying it."

"Absolutely."

Someone was lying, but Stan wasn't sure who.

Busiri stepped forward and, in an unexpected sign of kindness, put a hand on Stan's shoulder and squeezed. "You and me, we love our countries. My country may be different now, but do we lose our love for a woman because she has matured?"

"Are you going to tell me who Balašević's source was?"

Another pat on the shoulder, and this close he could see all the haggard lines in the old spy's face. "It's time for you to tell me where Jibril is."

Stan hesitated, but Ali Busiri was through sharing his information. "Dead. I don't know where, but he's dead."

Busiri withdrew his hand. "How?"

"I don't know. But I was told he was dead."

"By whom?"

"My station chief."

"Harold Wolcott."

Stan nodded.

"Do you believe him?"

"I think I do."

After a moment, the Egyptian said, "I suggest you put some thought into your career path, Mr. Bertolli. Remember: Love makes us blind." He raised a hand in farewell and, before turning to leave, added, "The answers are always in front of us."

As Stan walked back through the darkness toward his car, he still felt the weight of Busiri's hand on his shoulder. There had been times when, after reading some journalistic revelation or other, he had questioned his choice of employer, but those moments were rare. What he knew, because he'd been there, was that the people who clocked in each day at Langley were essentially decent. They tried, through whatever means necessary, to assure that their country remained safe. He'd never questioned that fact. The problems occurred when it came to the details, the *how*—that was when things became dirty. It was true of everything. Even so, the Agency tried to maintain a certain standard of morality—not for the sake of morality itself, but in order not to be caught with blood all over its hands.

Would Langley back a plan to put a friendly government into Tripoli in the middle of a popular revolution? Maybe. There were huge risks, but they weren't insurmountable. More likely, though, Langley would follow the path of least resistance: Wait until the dust had settled, take a look at the situation, and then make its decisions.

Someone like Omar Halawi believed otherwise. He was influenced by the same misinformation the Agency had done too little to combat, the failed operations and occasional misdeeds that painted the Agency as a monster that needed to be kept caged if the world wanted its sons and daughters to remain safe. To people like Omar Halawi—and, perhaps, Busiri—CIA was part of a vast conspiracy to turn the planet into drones friendly to American business.

He was near the entrance to the park when he paused beside a palm tree. Busiri's final words came to him. *The answers are always in front of us.* Before that: *Love makes us blind.* He closed his eyes and squeezed the dome of his forehead against another impending headache. Ali Busiri wasn't talking about the CIA. He was talking about . . .

He said "No" aloud. He held on to his stomach.

For a year he'd had all the facts in front of him, everything pointing in the same direction, yet he'd been blind to the obvious conclusion. He thought back, raising the puzzle pieces and refitting them, and . . . *there.* He saw with despair just how well the pieces meshed. Not all of them, no, but the mystery of the leaked information. It was right there. It had always been right there.

It took a few minutes for him to recover, but it was only a partial recovery. He straightened, fighting against the pounding in his head, and dialed her number. No surprise: She was unreachable. He stared at the phone in his hand. In an instant, she had become someone different. A stranger.

What would his father do?

His father would slink off in order to live another day, but Stan wasn't his father, and he never would be. He would find Sophie. He would withhold judgement until they had spoken, because Harry was right: Until he knew everything, he didn't know anything.

He jogged the rest of the way to the Passages Insaid al-Azhar Garden, along the line of dark cars until he reached his own. He unlocked the door and climbed inside, thinking alternately of Sophie Kohl and of revolutionaries fighting in Libyan streets. Dying, so that they, and no one else, would control their fate.

The inside of the windshield was foggy, and he wiped at it with his sleeve. It took a moment, him sliding the key into the ignition, before he noticed the smell in the car: garlic. A strong stink of roasted garlic. Then he thought: The glass is *fogged.* He looked up at the rearview mirror, and from the darkness of the backseat he saw a nose, eyes dark above them, and a bar of light shining across a large ear that—why?—had a tip of blue rubber sticking out of the canal. All of these details so close he could touch the face rising from the gloom. It was a face he'd seen before—a light-skinned Egyptian—and as the fear swelled (he now understood why the man wore earplugs) the recognition followed. On a computer screen, sitting down in Frankfurt Airport, glancing up at a passing security guard. Stan said, "Who the hell—"

John

1

Saturday night he stayed in. He poured himself only one glass of whisky and sat in front of the television. On BBC the news of the dead deputy consul in Budapest had been supplanted by more important events, and through their cameras John watched Libya erupting. He listened to talking heads pronounce the end of an era, and the ecstatic voices of revolutionaries proclaiming the beginning of something wonderful. But he remembered those protesters in Tahrir Square who, nearly a month ago, had attacked an American TV journalist, an angry tangle of men descending on one terrified woman, groping angrily at her breasts and groin, an assault that went on until a crowd of Egyptian women and soldiers broke it up. There were no saints in North Africa, because there were no saints anywhere. There could be no new world, John believed, because the people who filled it would be the same ones as yesterday.

Was that really cynicism? Jibril had thought so, and perhaps he was right.

In Libya, Zawiya was in rebel hands, while in nearby Tripoli Gadhafi was giving families four hundred dollars apiece and announcing to the world that the Libyan people had his back. His handsome, well-spoken son, Seif al-Islam, was doing interviews with Western news outlets, looking very in control as his country was torn apart, explaining that those fighting against the government had been given hallucinogenic drugs and were being controlled by al Qaeda.

Had he made it through, Jibril would probably have been in Zawiya by then, plotting his infiltration through government lines into Tripoli. Squinting at the television, clutching his empty glass, John thought that for all his foolishness Jibril had been a brave man, more so than he could ever hope to be.

No, bravery wasn't the point, and Jibril had tried to make that clear to him. The point was responsibility. As you knock around through your days you acquire other people, and with them come commitments. Eventually, as the weight of those responsibilities grows, you reach a point of no return, and a man could be measured by what he did at that moment. Either he faced his new commitments or he fled. John's father had fled before his first birthday. Jibril had been so tied to his commitments that he had abandoned the newer responsibilities of fatherhood in order to deal with the old ones. And John? Fatherhood had been his primary commitment, yet he'd gone to Cy Gallagher at Global Security, asking to be taken away from his broken family, which had grown too heavy to bear.

Which was why he woke on Sunday with the conviction—his first conviction in a while—that it was time to straighten a few things out. He hadn't called his kids in weeks, and he committed to doing so in the evening, once they were awake and had had their breakfast. In the meantime he would clean himself up. He shaved and showered and brushed his teeth, then made strong coffee and cooked scrambled eggs. After washing the dishes, he called Geert and told him that he would be happy to meet with some of his Egyptian clients looking to improve their English, because part of getting your life together is getting hold of your finances. Geert was ecstatic.

He went to work on the apartment, picking up bottles and bagging oily paper bags and takeout tins, then opened all the windows and got down to vacuuming. He even used damp paper towels to wipe the dust off of everything, amazed and disgusted by how much he picked up. He found books in the strangest places, and behind the hamper came across one in a Zip-loc bag—a collector's item, a 1920 printing of T. S. Eliot's *Ara Vos Prec*. It had been a gift from Maribeth when she discovered that the big black soldier she'd slept with was an avid reader of the old poets. John took it out of the bag gingerly, its heavy paper tinted and stiff, and opened it to a random page, reading:

> *Unnatural vices*
> *Are fathered by our heroism. Virtues*
> *Are forced upon us by our impudent crimes.*
> *These tears are shaken from the wrath-bearing tree.*
>
> *The tiger springs in the new year. Us he devours.*

He sat down and read through the whole poem slowly, realizing that "Gerontion" was the source of the verse that had come to him while waiting for the Libyan undertaker: *In depraved May, dogwood and chestnut, flowering judas . . .*

He slipped it back into the bag and onto the bookshelf. Then he collected the three heavy trash bags and carried them down to the Dumpster in the street. By then it was two in the afternoon. He was doing so well. He could see the rest of the day—reading, he thought, would be a proper way to spend his time. He wanted to get back to the Eliot, and since arriving in Cairo he'd set down three novels around the thirty-page mark; it was time to finish at least one of them. He would call Kelli and Ray, and then, once dark had fallen, he would get rid of Jibril Aziz's secret list, finally washing his hands of that mess. A gift for the Nile, and a clean break for him.

Talking to his kids was supposed to make him feel together, to pull him back into the world of human relations. He said all the right words, the ones that are written in the encyclopedia of civil society. He asked about their friends, their classes, and how good they were being. He asked what books they enjoyed, what movies, what they'd had for breakfast. He was unpracticed, but they were generous with him, and like always he wondered why he didn't call them every day.

Afterward, Danisha came on and asked when they should expect to see him next. "A month, give or take," he said, and she hummed quietly.

After the final, tumultuous year of watching, helpless, as their marriage fractured and crumbled, the divorce itself had been an amicable affair. There had been no getting away from the fact that they cared about each other, and the addition of children had meant that, no matter how bad it got between them, there would be two tethers mooring them to one another unto death. John's bank made the automated alimony payments to her account, and so their only issue of contention was his absence. "They need to know their father's around," she'd told him numerous times. "It's hard on them." To which he always pointed out that they had Owen. "It's not the same," she said of her new husband, and when she said this he always thought about the kids he'd seen in Nairobi and Lisbon and Kandahar who had lost both their parents and, in some cases, entire extended families. He always wanted to tell her about these children, but he'd never become unhinged enough to make that mistake.

Now, she said, "Try to call more often, okay? It gives them a glow."

Really? he wanted to ask. A call from a man they hadn't seen in more than half a year? A man they only saw on off-weekends even when he was in town? Did he really mean that much to them?

Were we all really that young once?

So he agreed, as he always did, to call more often.

Dusk was falling as he hung up, cooling off the city, and he stared at his newly cleaned home, wondering if it was all just a facade—or if (and this with hope) it was the facade that would eventually make his reality. Only one thing left to do, and he went to the kitchen to get Jibril's book. As he was reaching up to the cookie jar, someone buzzed from the street. He pressed the intercom button and heard Maribeth. "I was sitting around Deals wondering where I could find a good time."

2

In the morning Maribeth wandered in, sipping at a coffee, as he was brushing his teeth. She'd found one of his long shirts; she wore it well. "Want some culture tonight? Derek's showing some of his abstract messes."

Derek was a hippie acquaintance from New Jersey. "Not sure," John said as he rinsed off his toothbrush.

"Afraid of making this regular?"

He watched her in the hazy mirror, watched how she pulled back the corner of her lip in a sly smile. What was there *not* to like about Maribeth Winter, really? Attractive and intelligent, with a biting sense of humor. And while she'd been through enough troubled relationships to know better, for some inexplicable reason she liked *him*. But was all this enough to sustain something more than the occasional one-night fling?

Before the marriage and divorce he wouldn't have asked himself such questions: He would have allowed the pleasure of her company to dictate his actions. But he was older now, old enough to know better than to trust his romantic instincts. *God sure didn't make me very wise.* The idea of taking responsibility for yet another person was terrifying. "I'm here for another month," he said. "Then I'm gone. Starting something now just seems self-defeating."

He wasn't sure what he'd expected, but her easy smile surprised him. She took another sip of coffee. "Relationship? Don't be silly, John."

"Oh. Sorry."

She came closer, poking the nail of an index finger into his bare back. "When I want a relationship, you'll *know* it."

"And you don't."

"I like you, John. Don't get me wrong. But you're not really my type."

He thought about that as he washed toothpaste off his lips, then ran a brush through his short-cropped hair. "No?"

Again, she shook her head.

"What's your type?"

"Someone I think will survive the year," she said, her smile sliding away.

He put down the brush and turned to her, frowning. She was a full head shorter, but he had the sense that if she wanted to she could take him.

She said, "You've got to admit it, John. You're a little self-destructive. People who want to go on living don't drink like that."

Yes, he thought. She could take him easily.

"You've got some nasty nightmares, too. You woke me up five times last night."

"Sorry." He had no memory of any dreams. "Did I say anything?"

"*Yih-bill.* Something like that."

Jibril.

When they left, he took her around to the corner to Mohammed Thakeb and, like a gentleman, opened the passenger door to the dirty old Subaru he hadn't used for nearly a week. It coughed a few times before starting, and then they were following the traffic off the island and back into Garden City. On the way his phone rang—it was Ricky, one of Stan's agents. He wanted John to meet him at a café on Talaat Harb Square, not far from Maribeth's apartment. She had to get to work, though, so he dropped her off at the embassy. Before getting out, she paused a moment, then leaned over and kissed him firmly on the lips. "Gallery show tonight. Think about it." He said he would, then watched her walk down the sidewalk.

He drove farther inland, parked off the square, and found Ricky sitting at an outdoor table, hunched over some hot tea. When John began to sit down Ricky shook his head. "Give the place across from the Cosmopolitan a look-over, will you? I've got a meet there in half an hour."

John wandered two blocks up Kasr Al Nile, then turned right into the narrow streets that had been falling into disrepair since the 1950s. Across from the rounded corner of the Cosmopolitan Hotel was a café with cheap plastic tables and chairs on the sidewalk. It was relatively empty for nine in the morning. He sat just inside, where the accordion wall had been pulled back, and ordered coffee and a roll in his meager Arabic. As he waited for it three workmen wandered up, already powdery from a construction site, and sat outside with their legs stretched out in front of them as they smoked. Almost at the road, two young women with covered heads placed their cell phones on a table before sitting down. His roll came first, followed by the coffee, and as he nibbled he scanned the opposite side of the street—vendors hawking jewelry, the hotel entrance, and cars in all conditions. Eventually, a white box truck painted with an assortment of vegetables pulled up on the curb, almost hitting the women, and blocked his entire view. The driver got out and jogged down the street, into (John saw as he got up to look) a carpet store.

Watching, John had been told numerous times, is a kind of art. There are plenty of tells—eye movements, bulges in pockets, nervousness—but the truth he'd discovered on his own was that the world is like that; it's filled to overflowing with tells because that's what people are: collections of tells. Watchers pretend that they can spot the difference between the nervousness of a man down to his last penny and that of a man gearing up to shoot a state leader, but this is a pretense for the people who pay them. Were there a real, scientific method to watching, assassinations would never occur. John called Ricky to tell him that everything looked fine.

He left the restaurant briefly to check the other side of the truck, and when he returned Ricky was already sitting a couple of tables from the young women, one of whom was talking on her phone while the other laughed in amusement. The construction workers were drinking glasses of something clear—perhaps water, perhaps not. John avoided Ricky's eyes as he headed back to his seat inside. As he sat down, his phone rang. It was Geert. "Date number one," he said.

"So soon?"

"*Mistress* Abusir would like to give you a whirl tonight. Seven o'clock at Steaks?"

A restaurant in the Four Seasons. "Are you advertising me as a gigolo, Geert?"

High, forced laughter. "Feels like it, doesn't it? Just relax and enjoy it. Thirty dollars an hour, and she buys the tasties."

As he hung up, the anxiety scratched at him. A teacher now—more responsibility. The feeling was not unlike the anxiety he felt at the prospect of a short-lived relationship with Maribeth, the fear that he wasn't up to taking on so much, and that he would inevitably break—either break and run, or break the people who were depending on him.

Cut it out.

He rubbed his face and returned to the job at hand. One thing at a time.

Ricky, it turned out, was meeting with SLEDGEHAMMER, an informant John had watched over before. Though he knew little about the Egyptian, he'd noticed that at the end of every meeting he received an envelope under the table. Not all informers worked for pay, but SLEDGEHAMMER always did.

It was only a twenty-minute meeting, without incident, and before it ended the vegetable truck drove off, giving him a view of jewelry vendors, taxis pulling up to the hotel, and the height and breadth of one of the residential buildings. Two windows were open, and in one an old woman was gazing out at the street, and at them.

After a handshake, SLEDGEHAMMER left first. Ricky laid some coins on the table and walked off in the opposite direction while

John finished his second coffee. It was only then that he noticed something glint in the old woman's right hand: a small digital camera. As far as he could recall, she hadn't raised it to her face, though of course there was no need for her to do so if she wanted to take a picture.

This detail troubled him, but like most tells it could be explained away with a little imagination. A son's gift that she took to the window, trying to learn how to use. Better that than a government employee asked to sit inconspicuously in her window and take shots of a suspected traitor.

When he reached the embassy, he found Harry hovering outside the gates, smoking and waiting for him. "Let's take a walk, John."

He followed Harry slowly toward the high rise of the Hotel Semiramis, which blocked their view of the Nile. Harry said, "Any visits from those friends on the street?"

"No, sir. I think they followed me Friday night, but I can't be sure. Haven't seen them since."

"Good," Harry said, nodding. "Anyone asking about Libya?"

"Well, Stan seems pretty curious."

"Yes?"

"But I haven't said anything."

"Good."

They had reached the corner, but instead of heading west toward the river, Harry turned right, deeper inland. Locals passed them, thin men puffing on their own cigarettes. John said, "Is there a problem?"

"Problem?" Harry considered that. "Well, Langley's man is dead, and I'm not allowed to tell anyone about it. I don't like keeping secrets from my staff."

"Why can't you tell?"

"Ask Langley. No, forget it. *Don't.* Look." Harry stopped suddenly, and John nearly ran into him. He turned to peer into John's eyes, looking up slightly, as if measuring him. "You're a pretty solid guy, aren't you?"

"I like to think so."

"Can you keep an eye on Stan for me?"

John didn't like these little bubbles of secrecy that floated through the station, and he didn't like having to keep his immediate superior at arm's length. This wasn't the kind of thing they'd trained for in Tuscaloosa. "You mean follow him?"

Harry considered that. "Don't go out of your way. Not yet. In the course of the day, just be aware of what he's up to."

"What am I supposed to be watching for?"

"Anything," Harry said. "He's fishing around the Aziz situation like a hunting dog. I've got a pretty good idea he's hiding someone away from me. And I'm starting to worry that he smeared someone's name last year in order to cover up his own crimes."

John rubbed at his sore temples. "That sounds heavy."

"It is," Harry said, "but it's just speculation. His other boys are too loyal to do this for me. But you . . ."

"I don't know the meaning of the word 'loyal'?"

A grin passed over Harry's features; he waved it away. "You're not blinded by loyalty, John. That's your strength."

3

———

With a cup of scorched Maxwell House beside him, John sat at the terminal and wrote up his report on Ricky's meet. Since the fiasco in Pakistan with Raymond Davis, Harry had been demanding multiple-perspective reports on everything, including simple meets, and as he wrote he continually noticed movement in his periphery. The office was restless, uncomfortable and itchy, which he supposed was what diplomatic murders did to people.

Stan spent much of the afternoon on the computer, and when John checked in to find out what was needed, or if he could glean something to pass on to Harry, Stan told him to relax a little. "Go get some lunch. Take it easy." Was he trying to get him out of the office? Or was it simply that Stan could sense that John was still working at about fifty percent?

When he returned from lunch, Stan's office was empty, though after a while he emerged from Harry's, looking distracted. Stan sat at his desk and made a couple of calls, and as he talked Harry passed by, heading for the elevator, and gave John a knowing nod. Soon, though, Stan was grabbing his coat and heading out as well. Maribeth sent an SMS asking if he was coming to Derek's show. He texted back, "Gotta teach English," and she didn't bother replying.

It occurred to him, as he stared at the blank screen of his phone, that Maribeth Winter was the only person in Cairo he really felt comfortable with. It was her directness—unlike his co-workers, she never misled. To her, facts were facts, and they were there to be shared. She welcomed him into her bed, but that didn't stop her from telling him exactly what she thought of his self-destructive behavior. She was, he realized, the best thing about Cairo, and his stomach ached when he considered the ways in which he would surely ruin what they had.

Mrs. Abusir arrived late, leaving John to spend twenty minutes feeling less and less comfortable at Steaks, inside the Nile Plaza Four Seasons. The restaurant was overpriced, decorated with black-and-white photos of luxurious city scenes, and the Tuesday night crowd was choked with foreigners. Tonight was the steak-and-sushi buffet, and its aroma was making his stomach groan loudly enough that he feared others could hear it. His discomfort was useful for distracting him from other things, like Jibril Aziz, Stan Bertolli, and Harry Wolcott. Maribeth sent him a message: "These paintings are dreadful."

Then Mrs. Abusir arrived. She was a large woman in the sense that she was as tall as John, and a few years older. She was heavy as well, but given her height the weight gave her real presence when she walked into the restaurant, unaware of her tardiness. She wore a lavender hijab on her head, but her ankle-length skirt and long-sleeved blouse were entirely Western. She smiled and shook his hand with both of hers and said that she was excited by "the prospect of my English to sound American."

"That's wonderful," he said, "but here's a first lesson: It's 'the prospect of my English *sounding* American.' In this case, you don't use the 'to' form of the verb—it's called the infinitive—to say that. Usually, you use the infinitive only after another verb. 'I *want* it *to* sound American'—that sort of thing."

Her smile faded, and he wondered how she had imagined they would do this if he didn't correct her. She said, "Mr. Calhoun . . . thank you," as if the thanks were being ripped out of her.

Once this initial awkwardness was out of the way, things moved more smoothly. For the last decade she had been the wife of Samir

Hanafi, who had recently been tapped as a possible presidential candidate for the National Progressive Unionist Party in the planned November elections. He asked why she was interested in learning American-tinted English, and she had an answer ready: "I am wanting to stand proudly beside my husband."

"I want to stand proudly beside my husband."

"Yes, exactly."

She would go on to do that throughout their two-hour session, brushing off his corrections with "Yes, exactly," as if approving of his version of the English language without endorsing it enough to speak it herself.

Before marriage, Mrs. Abusir had been a cardiac surgeon at Dar Al Fouad—"the House of the Heart," she translated proudly—and met her husband when he came in for treatment for pericarditis, "when the pericardium—that is the sac around the heart—it is inflamed. I repair his heart and we fall in love."

She said all this with a smile, knowing that it was self-evidently romantic, and then explained that while her husband was fifteen years her senior, the divide had been bridged by their families, which had been friendly since the sixties. Samir Hanafi had been in politics for a long time, at first joining Mubarak's party, the National Democrats, in the mid-eighties. But that hadn't gone well—she avoided mentioning why—and soon he cast his lot with one of the marginalized opposition parties that, while they were technically legal, had no resources to assure any significant gains in the People's Assembly. Then, in 2004, he joined with Kefaya, a coalition of opposition groups that pressed hard against the regime. "Kefaya, it mean 'enough.'" Though the coalition had lost its way after 2005 due to internal conflicts, it had made its mark, and its members had quickly joined with the young Twitter generation that had taken to the streets. "Now," she said, "the National Democrats will be wash into the gutter, and real Egyptians will have a voice."

"It sounds very exciting," he said.

"It *is*." She leaned forward and clasped the hand he'd left beside his teacup. "A new year, a new world."

He withdrew his hand. "Is it really so important to have perfect English for the elections?"

She rocked her head from side to side, considering this. "We think about the future, Mr. Calhoun. That is what we all think about. We think about how a politician can take care of his country internally, but we know that how he looks to the outside world is of equal importance. If he has a wife who speaks gutter English, he will be judged a man who picks his women from the gutter. I am wanting no one think of me that way."

"Not a chance," he told her.

She seemed to like that.

"And it's *I don't want anyone to think of me that way,* or *I want no one to think of me that way.* Not *I am wanting.* The rest was terrific."

"Yes, exactly."

At nine o'clock a Mercedes pulled up in front of the restaurant to take Mrs. Abusir home. She thanked John for his help, and they made another date for Wednesday. As they headed for the door, a big man in a fitted suit emerged from the crowded tables and smoothly inserted himself between them without a word. He opened the door for Mrs. Abusir and walked her to the Mercedes. John followed from a distance; then the man came back to him and, without ceremony, handed over 350 Egyptian pounds, about sixty dollars, then returned to join her in the car. They were finished with him.

4

It took an hour to walk home. The streets were quiet, most Egyptians exhausted by the changes and the postchange protesting, but he couldn't help thinking of those shadows from Friday night. He continued past his building, eyeballing his living room window, which was dark, then the Longchamps Hotel across the street, which wasn't busy. He checked other windows and doorways before, at the end of the block, turning around, heading back, and climbing his stairs. He got to his door, the keys held tight in his hand, and that was when he noticed the door was cracked open. Without a word, he used a finger to push. It gently opened to reveal . . .

A mess.

All the work he'd put into cleaning the place, he saw, had been pointless. The cushions on the sofa were sliced open; the floor lamp had been smashed; the television was disassembled. Rugs had been tossed into corners, and the ceiling lamp had been ripped out. He stepped over refuse to the kitchen, where everything had been thrown from the cabinets—cups, glasses, plates, and bowls, as well as pots and pans. The nougat tin where he'd kept his gun lay on the floor, open and empty. Not far away, beneath the kitchen table, were the two broken halves of the cookie jar that had held Jibril's book of contacts. He didn't bother investigating further. There was no point.

That he soon found himself heading back to Deals was de rigueur.

What else was there to do? Clean up? Try to figure out who had turned the place over and stolen what he should have burned in the Libyan desert? He hated himself enough—no need to bother with more self-recrimination.

Besides, this was not his fight. This had to do with Jibril and Harry and maybe Stan, but not him. *You're not blinded by loyalty,* Harry had told him, and only now, as he opened the door to the bar, hands shaking, did he realize that the old man really had his number. But Harry was wrong about one thing—it wasn't strength. It was fear.

He found Geert and Shoshan by the bar. Shoshan was a thin, large-featured Egyptian woman who'd lived with Geert for nearly a year. Though she didn't touch alcohol, she for some reason tolerated her boyfriend's excesses. That night he was drinking margaritas, one after the other, and he bought one for John. "You are making the women of Cairo very happy, my friend," he said.

"What?"

Shoshan rolled her eyes.

"Mrs. Abusir is *delighted* with you."

"I only left her a couple hours ago."

"As your manager, I of course checked on your performance."

A woman's voice said, "Just the brute I was looking for," and he turned to find Maribeth smiling at him.

"Hey, pretty lady."

"Beauty and the beast," Geert proclaimed.

John looked past Maribeth—everyone, it seemed, was there, even the painter Derek, passed out in a corner.

He wasn't interested in conversation, but that was how his life had become. He hadn't wanted to break his promise to the late Jibril Aziz, but he had. Given the sudden wash of paranoia, he wasn't feeling a strong desire to sleep with Maribeth—not tonight, at least—but he was gearing up to do precisely that, if only to stay out of his apartment. Sometimes, John believed, you have to go with the flow. Fighting only ties you up in knots and gives you too many opportunities to discover your own limitations. Fighting can be the quickest route to despair.

So he drank and he smiled. As the glasses were replaced with new ones, he listened to Geert expound on his hopes and dreams for his career and his life in the new Cairo, and John tried not to smash those dreams too much. He encouraged Maribeth, too. He tried to be agreeable for everyone, which, like most things in life, is just a matter of showing up.

The next morning, when the alarm on his phone woke him at six, he got up and made coffee, and Maribeth finally asked what had been bothering him.

"What makes you think something's bothering me?"

"You were nice to me last night."

"I'm not usually nice?"

"Not that nice. I like you, John, but I know the limits of my power."

He handed her a cup and kissed her hair where it met her forehead. "Maybe I'm nicer than you think."

She seemed to like that, then she raised an eyebrow. "I hope you're going to change before you go in. You reek of Deals."

He sniffed the sleeve of his shirt—cigarette smoke—then called a taxi. Before he left, Maribeth straightened his lapels and said, "Are you really gone at the end of the month?"

"That's what my contract says," he told her, then hesitated as a new thought came to him. "But I suppose I could apply for an extension."

"Don't worry," she said as she patted his arms. "Just curiosity."

He wasn't sure how to take that, nor how it made him feel, and as he rode in the taxi back to Zamalek he tried to picture it: another six months in Cairo, another six months of these streets he didn't understand, another six months of the underlying contempt on the fifth floor. It could also mean another six months of Maribeth Winter. Did that balance the scale? Enough?

Yes, actually. It did.

That realization was enough to keep him in a state of mild shock until he reached his door at a quarter to seven. There, he paused. Again, it was cracked, though he had locked it last night. He felt naked without his gun.

With a finger, he pushed open the door. The same trashed home faced him. He paused, listening, then stepped inside. "Hello?" No answer. He closed the door, then slowly toured the house. Everything was the same—living room, kitchen, bathroom. In the bedroom, though, he found a man sitting on his bed with a Glock on his lap, staring hard at him. The shock of his feelings for Maribeth were overcome completely by the sight of this man. It was David Malek, her novelist friend. He was fingering his pistol, frowning at John.

"Where is she, John?"

"Maribeth?"

"No, you idiot. Sophie Kohl."

"Who's Sophie Kohl?"

Malek looked as if he'd been up for weeks. Was this how John had looked when he'd returned from the desert? If Malek had come to shoot him, John supposed, he would already be dead. That thought kept him from bolting. At the same time, though, it occurred to him that in this part of the world people usually carried guns with the intention of using them. It took effort, but he held himself still.

Malek scratched his jawline with his free hand, making a rasping sound. "The wife of Emmett Kohl."

The dead consul. Christ, this really did have nothing to do with him.

Malek said, "Did you kill Jibril Aziz?"

Or maybe not. John resisted the urge to take a step back. "No."

"You took him into the desert, though."

John nodded.

"Is he dead?"

John hesitated. "Do you mind telling me who you really are?"

"Answer my question first."

"Yes, he's dead. There were bandits. Why would I want to kill him?"

Malek considered this a moment, then nodded at the torn-apart room. "Who's your decorator?"

"Not you?"

Malek shook his head.

"It was like this when I came home last night."

Malek climbed to his feet, the pistol hanging heavy by his side. He reached into his jeans and handed over a badge wallet. John took it and opened it up to find an FBI badge, Malek's face, and the name Michael Khalil. Surprised, he handed it back. "What's your angle?"

Malek—no, Khalil—shrugged as he pocketed the badge. "Well, when an American citizen gets killed in Libya, we're interested. I don't care what agency he worked for." He waved the Glock. "Let's move to the living room, John. We've got some thinking to do."

Reluctantly, John did so. Thinking with this man was the last thing he wanted to do. What he wanted was to take a taxi back to Maribeth's, lie in her bed, and pull the sheets up over his head.

John rearranged the destroyed sofa cushions and settled down as Khalil righted an overturned chair. As he sat, he said, "Let me explain a few things to you."

"It's not necessary."

Khalil frowned. "You don't want to know?"

"Whatever's going on, it's not my problem. I like it that way."

"A contractor, right?"

"Right."

Khalil finally laid his pistol against one knee, fingers barely touching it. "Well, I need your help," he said, "so you've got no choice in the matter."

"I seldom do."

A brief smile, then Khalil told a story about a CIA operation called Stumbler, which had been concocted by Jibril Aziz. A plan to overthrow Muammar Gadhafi. He described Aziz's shock and anger when he realized, only a couple of weeks ago, that the CIA was preparing to use his plan to undermine the Libyan revolution.

"How do you mean, undermine?"

"I mean, send in its own people to turn a popular revolution into a CIA-backed coup. To give America complete control over the development of the country. Understand?"

John did, though he wished he didn't. He remembered Jibril: *What Langley thinks is a drop in the ocean of history.*

"So Jibril went into Libya, with your help, to make sure the Libyan people kept the fruits of their sacrifices," he said. "Now, I've been on this case a while. I've got nearly everything figured out. But there's one thing I'm missing."

This flood of information made his temples pound, but he managed a whisper: "What's that?"

"Did Aziz give you anything before he died? A list of names, perhaps?"

John nodded.

"I'd like to have it, please."

John shook his head. Khalil's eye twitched, the pistol shifting from one knee to the other. "It's not here anymore," John clarified. "My decorator took it."

Khalil leaned back and, with his free hand, pulled at the hair on his scalp. "Well, that's some bad news."

Silence followed, until John said in a hesitant voice, "He told me to burn it."

"Who?"

"Aziz. He told me the people on the list would end up dead."

"Maybe they will," Khalil said. "Which is why we need to get it back. Can I depend on your help?"

"As long as you're holding that gun."

Khalil looked down at it, smiled, and pulled open his jacket to reveal a shoulder holster. He slipped the pistol into it, latched it shut, and said, "How about now?"

John was ready to answer in the negative when a chirp-chirp birdcall filled the room. Eyes still on John, Khalil removed a cheap-looking phone from his pocket, checked the screen, and raised his brows. He answered with the word "Salaam," then went silent, his expression tightening. He spoke a sentence in Arabic and, briefly, John was impressed by how good his accent was. America was a land of immigrants, but he seldom met American civil servants who could speak Arabic like a native. Malek's long face was animated, tightening and then loosening—whatever he was listening to was trouble-some. He didn't say anything beyond the occasional *tayib*, which John knew meant "okay."

When Khalil was finished he didn't bother with good-bye; he just hung up, pocketed the phone, and stared at John—through him, really, for whatever he'd listened to had had little to do with John. Finally, he focused back on John's features and stood up. "Change in plans. We're going for a ride."

John didn't move. He looked up at Khalil. "You don't need me, do you?"

"I think I do, buddy. Come on." Then, to make himself clear, he opened his jacket and touched the butt of his Glock.

5

<hr/>

Khalil's spotless black Mercedes was so clean that John thought the evidence pointed to an obsessive personality. The FBI agent waited for him to get inside before opening the door and settling behind the wheel. "Music?" John shrugged. Khalil played a CD already in the stereo, and Arabic pop filled the car as they cruised slowly down the cool, early morning street. Slowly, for even at seven in the morning the traffic was thick.

It wasn't until they were crossing the 15th of May Bridge, getting the full impact of the gorgeous Cairo vista, the Nile still in shadow beneath them, that it occurred to John that there was something wrong with this FBI man. American agents often drove American makes from the embassy pool, but if they decided to buy their own cars they seldom chose one as flashy as a high-end Mercedes. Then there was the music—a woman's voice warbling over thin strings—and John said, "You're going native?"

"Huh?" said Khalil, distracted.

"The music."

He rocked his head from side to side as he left the bridge and turned right onto the Corniche El Nil, which followed the river south all the way through Cairo. "You don't like it?" Khalil asked.

"It's nice."

"Maybe I should play Bruce Springsteen? Jay-Z?"

"No, no. This is good," John said, turning to gaze out at the water. His unease grew. Khalil had shown him a badge, but when looked at from a certain angle, he didn't look like a Bureau man at all. How hard was it to fake a badge? Not hard at all, he suspected.

John's phone rang, and he took it out.

"Who is it?" asked Khalil.

"The office."

"Tell them you'll be late."

John hesitated, then turned back toward the water and answered. "Yeah?"

Ricky said, "John? John, where are you?"

"It's not even eight yet."

"All hands on deck, man."

"I'm running late," he said. "Sorry."

"Get it in gear. Things are falling apart here."

"What's up?"

"You didn't see the news?"

"What news?"

"Stan," said Ricky. "Stan's dead. Somebody shot him in his own car, over at al-Azhar Park. It's a fucking mess."

John's hand went cold. He felt Khalil's gaze on the back of his head. "I'll be there as soon as I can," he said and hung up.

"News?" Khalil asked.

"Stan Bertolli's dead."

Khalil continued driving in silence. They were past the center now, on the southern end of town, near the diplomatic enclave of Maadi. Finally, Khalil said, "They were together, you know."

John didn't bother asking for clarification. He was overcome by the feeling that he had made a tragic mistake entering this car. Stan was dead, his own apartment had been torn apart, and an armed man who claimed to be FBI was driving him to places unknown.

Khalil went on. "Stan and Sophie Kohl. Lovers. She came to Cairo a few days ago and stayed with him. They've been trying to figure out what happened to her husband." He paused, frowning at the road. "I guess Stan got too close to the truth."

If only to establish how much trouble he was in, John said, "What truth would that be?"

"That the Agency killed Emmett and Jibril Aziz. Once he got close enough to those facts, the Agency got rid of Stan, too."

"Bandits killed Aziz. I was there, remember?"

"Did you interrogate them? Were they carrying their Libyan Banditry Association cards?"

Though he didn't trust this man, he couldn't help but think about it. He hadn't tried to find out who those gunmen were, so what if Khalil was right? He thought of Harry, the white-haired Agency bureaucrat who had sent him out into the desert with Jibril. Had Harry chosen his most disposable employee, a simple contractor, to take Jibril to his death? Had Harry been surprised to find him alive on Friday?

At the same time, Harry had asked him to keep an eye on Stan, as if Stan were the suspect one. Suspected of what? Had Harry killed Stan?

Christ, he thought. That embassy was a mess, and he wanted no part of it. Yet here he was, stuck in a car with a man he didn't know at all: an FBI agent who drove the wrong car, listened to the wrong music, and spoke too much like a native.

> *Think now*
> *History has many cunning passages, contrived corridors*
> *And issues, deceives with whispering ambitions,*
> *Guides us by vanities.*

What good was Eliot now?

"What about Sophie Kohl?" John asked.

Eyes on the road, Khalil said, "What?"

"If Stan's dead, where is she?"

"It's a question."

Khalil said that almost flippantly, as if it no longer mattered. It had, back in his apartment, but now no. Not after the phone call he'd received, and the change in plans. John said, "Who called you? Back at my place."

Khalil considered this as the buildings around them thinned. He smirked and said, "Your decorator."

"Who's my decorator?"

"You'll find out soon enough."

They left Cairo to the south, veering inland from the Corniche El Nil to connect to the Autostrad-Al Nasr, following signs toward 15th of May City, just east of Helwan. The buildings had fallen away, and to their left the rolling desert spread out, whitewashed by the low eastern sun. He thought of the ride through the Libyan desert, but now he was the passenger, in the sacrificial seat, while Michael Khalil was running the show.

Could he stop this car without killing them both? He might be able to, for the Glock was hidden away in Khalil's holster, but the question was: *Should* he stop the car? Khalil might not be who he claimed to be, but did that mean he was working on the wrong side? What *was* the wrong side? Was Harry his enemy? Stan? This woman he'd never met—Sophie Kohl?

"Where are we going?" John asked.

Khalil gave him a sidelong glance as he accelerated around a slow-moving truck, gravel spilling out from under its tarp and pinging against the car. Khalil cursed under his breath, passed the truck, and said, "We're going to get our prize."

"Which is . . . ?"

"That book you lost."

They passed a large factory complex and took a left off of the highway, heading toward a loose collection of sand-colored buildings that looked like another factory, abandoned. As they drove, another Mercedes passed them heading back to the highway, and Khalil showed concern, slowing and trying to peer at the driver, but the tinted windows revealed nothing but bright reflected sun. Once it had passed, Khalil slowed to a stop and stared into the rearview until the Mercedes turned right onto the *autostrad,* heading north toward Cairo.

"What is it?" John asked.

Khalil began to drive again. "I suppose we'll find out."

"You're really not going to tell me anything, are you?"

"Just help me out, and I'll make sure you're taken care of."

Long before they reached the abandoned buildings, they took a right, and Khalil muttered "Fuck" under his breath as they headed deeper into the desert. Though this road was paved, rocks had blown into it, and he had to take it easy, swerving occasionally to get out of the way of stones big enough to damage his transmission. They drove south, parallel with the *autostrad* still visible on their right, and then took another left down a road that sank into a valley of low dunes. Soon they could see nothing behind them. Ahead, the road curved to the left until, eventually, it simply stopped. At the end was a scratched white BMW, empty, and farther ahead, beyond the road, a large tarp shelter with a post at each corner and a single post in the middle, so that the roof pointed at the hot sky.

Under the shelter, they could see the shadowy forms of three people. Thinking of Libya, John said, "I don't like this."

"You think I do?"

"We should call the embassy."

Khalil shook his head but didn't bother explaining himself. He opened his door, letting in a gust of hot, gritty wind, then took the Glock out of his shoulder holster. "Don't worry, okay?"

"You're not very reassuring."

"I'm not here to be reassuring."

"Why am I here?"

"Don't be a pussy. Come on."

Khalil got out, and after a moment John followed. His eyes hurt—he'd forgotten his sunglasses—and he held a flat hand against the side of his head for shade.

As they approached the shelter, the figures beneath it grew more distinct. Three men—two standing, and one sitting in a foldout chair. None of them was moving. They were just watching. Then one of them moved—a tall man in a white button-up shirt and brown slacks emerged from under the tarp, the light making him briefly glow. He was Egyptian, young, and had thick eyebrows. Like Khalil, he carried a gun. There was something familiar about him.

"Who's that?" John asked.

"It's all right. He's okay."

As the young Egyptian approached, the other standing man walked slowly from one side of the shelter to the other. The man in the chair didn't move at all.

"Salaam," said the Egyptian.

"Salaam," Khalil answered.

Frowning, the Egyptian asked a question in Arabic, and Khalil's answer contained the words "John Calhoun." John's presence, he saw in the Egyptian's face, wasn't welcome, but he was not ordered back to the car. He wanted to run, but two men with pistols weren't likely to miss a back as large as his.

Together, the three of them continued toward the shelter. Khalil asked questions, but the Egyptian seemed to be telling him to wait for his answers.

By then they were close enough to make out the other man pacing under the tarp. He was an old man, thin, his cheeks bristling with white hair. He stood at the edge of the shelter, watching them approach, and he wasn't smiling. Khalil hesitated and asked another question: something sharp—not anger, but fear. In reply, the younger Egyptian placed a hand on Khalil's shoulder and pushed him forward.

John said, "I shouldn't be here."

Khalil turned on him and snapped, "You just fucking follow, understand?"

John did, but more slowly. He was in no hurry to enter that shelter, for by then he'd noticed that the figure in the chair had not moved at all. Nothing.

The old man—Egyptian, too—didn't bother stepping into the light. He waited for Khalil to reach the edge of the shelter and spoke softly to him in Arabic. There was no "salaam," just a rattle of quiet words. The old man held out his hand, and Khalil handed over his Glock, grip first. The old man looked over Khalil's shoulder at John, his face twisting in a sudden spasm of annoyance, and said a few words to the younger Egyptian, who walked over to John. John stepped back, for he'd made the connection: This was one of the two shadows from outside his apartment on Friday night. This was the one who had followed him to Deals.

"Come on," the Egyptian said to him, accent heavy. "You don't need to be here."

John didn't doubt that, for by then he'd seen enough. He'd been able to make out the form in the foldout chair, a heavyset man with his head tilted back. His shirt was a tangle of red, and from the angle John could just barely see that there was no nose on whatever was left of the man's face. The sand all around the chair was brown but no longer wet. Sticky, he guessed. And while he couldn't see them, he could hear the angry buzzing of flies.

As the Egyptian walked him back to the car, John waited for things. He waited for a gunshot in the back of his head. He waited for more distant gunshots—Khalil, or the old man, being killed. If nothing else, he waited for the sounds of argument from the shelter. There was nothing.

Finally, they reached the scratched BMW, and the Egyptian let him into the rear seat. John slid inside, immediately sweating in the stuffy heat, but the Egyptian closed the door again. There was no way to roll down the window. He settled back and waited as, outside, the Egyptian took out his phone and made a call. John could hear none of it.

Who were these people? He was quite sure now that Khalil wasn't FBI. If he was, then he was on the take from the Egyptians. What did any of this mean? Was he ever going to make it out of here alive? Despite himself, he thought of Maribeth, who wanted someone who would survive the year. She'd been right to hesitate when it came to him.

Outside, the Egyptian finished his conversation, then made another call. As he spoke, he came to the car and opened the front door. He slid into the passenger seat, the phone still to his ear, and said to John, "What happened to Jibril Aziz in the desert?"

"He was killed by bandits."

The Egyptian spoke in Arabic a moment, translating his answer. Then, back to John: "How do you know they were bandits?"

"I don't know for sure. They wore green. If that helps."

The answer was relayed. The Egyptian got out of the car and slammed the door shut, then finished his conversation. As he hung up, he raised his head to look in the direction they had driven from. John turned around to peer through the dirty rear windshield at a Mercedes with tinted windows kicking up dust as it joined them. It was the same Mercedes that had passed them on the way here. A driver got out. Another Egyptian, but much larger, more menacing, and—*yes*. It was the second shadow, who Harry had pointed out from his window. John's Egyptian opened his door. "Come on."

John got out and followed him to the Mercedes. The big driver was heading away, toward the shelter, but from this distance John couldn't tell what was going on under there.

"You will drive her back to Cairo. Understand?"

"Who?"

"The keys are in the car," the Egyptian said, then jogged off to catch up with the other man, both of them heading toward the shelter, to Khalil and the old man and the corpse in the chair.

John opened the driver's door and peered inside. In the backseat was a woman—very pale, with straw-blond hair. She was somewhere around forty, he guessed, but it was hard to tell because she looked like she was in shock, rolled up on her side, fetal. Her eyes were closed, but he could hear her clotted breathing behind the tangled hair that hung over her features. Though he suspected the answer, he asked, "Who are you?" Then he opened the rear door and got in beside her. He checked her pulse—fast but not dangerous. There was blood on her forearm, but no sign of wounds. What had they done to her? In the well was a large purse. "Can you hear me?" he asked, placing a hand on her shoulder, gently shaking.

She opened her eyes, blinking, and used a hand to brush away hair. She didn't sit up. John noticed a red mark in the meat between the thumb and forefinger of her right hand, and he suspected that by tomorrow it would be a bruise. She peered at him, trying to focus. "Hi," she whispered.

"Do you need a doctor?"

Stiffly, she shook her head. "Just sleep."

"Who are you?"

She opened her mouth, then closed it. "Sofia."

"Sophie Kohl?"

She nodded.

He stared at her a moment more, then got out and closed her inside. Pausing beside the driver's door, he heard a distant sound on the warm desert breeze: two gunshots. He jumped into the Mercedes and started it up, turned the car around, and raced away as fast as he could.

SOURCE: Constitution Protection Office, Hungary
(*Alkotmányvédelmi Hivatal*)

"Transcript report of meeting between Emmett Kohl,
USA diplomatic staff, and Michael Khalil, American"

AUTHOR: Varga Tamas

4 March 2011

ADMINISTRATOR'S NOTE:

The following transcript records a conversation from the afternoon of Wednesday, 2 March. Later that evening, Emmett Kohl was assassinated in Chez Daniel, a restaurant in Pest (Szív utca 32). At the time of the recording there was no suggestion that Mr. Kohl's life was in danger, which is why the recording was not transcribed until after the event.

As background, Mr. Kohl's Audi A5 was wired on 26 February following concerns voiced by Kiraly Andras over Kohl's meeting with an American agent (see: Aziz, Jibril) who was later seen in suspicious company. I suggest that any complaints concerning the perceived delay in producing this document be directed at Mr. Kiraly, who was responsible for the operation.

TECHNIQUE:

The following consists of two sources: the above-mentioned microphone installed in Mr. Kohl's automobile, within the radio/ CD-player, and another microphone, shotgun, held by one of Mr. Kiraly's two agents, who witnessed the scene. The text has been marked to reflect the change in sources, observational notes in italics.

PRE-TRANSCRIPT:

Mr. Kohl was attending a scheduled lunch at Menza (Liszt Ferenc tér 2) with Linc Gabor, of Danubian Games Kft. Their subject: the export of Danubian Games products to the American market. Mr. Kohl was the first to leave, followed by a previously unnoticed stranger from another table, who had been drinking coffee. Description: approximately 180 cm, 80 kg. Well dressed. Dark hair and skin, brown eyes, Arabic characteristics. He identified himself as Michael Khalil, American.

Mr. Kohl crossed Liszt Ferenc tér, heading toward his automobile. Mr. Khalil hurried to catch up.

<u>Source: Shotgun microphone</u>

Michael Khalil (MK): Emmett?

Kohl glances back, not recognizing the man.

MK (smiling): Emmett Kohl. I *knew* it was you!

Kohl slows but does not stop. The man approaches and offers a hand; they shake.

Emmett Kohl (EK): I'm sorry, do I . . . ?

MK: Michael Khalil. We met at that party . . . (Pause.) How's Sophie? I always thought she was a stunner.

EK: Listen, Michael, nice to see you again, but I've got an appointment.

MK: Emmett, I just need a moment to talk. It's important.

EK: But I have to—

At this point Khalil reaches into his jacket and takes out out a small leather wallet, opening it for Kohl to read. From a distance we are able to make out large blue letters: "FBI."

(<u>NOTE</u>: Queries to the local FBI office have met with denials: They claim they have no local agent with Khalil's name or description. Kiraly Andras believes the identification is a forgery; we are undecided.)

EK: What's this about?

MK: Isn't everything about the security of Americans? (Pause.) Listen, Emmett, I'd prefer not to talk out in the open.

Khalil motions toward Kohl's gray Audi, two car-lengths away.

MK: I swear I'll just be five minutes.

Kohl takes out his car keys and walks around to the driver's side door, then pauses before opening it.

EK: We'll talk outside, or we won't talk at all.

MK: Emmett, this stuff is private. Some of it concerns your wife, Sophie.

EK: What about her?

MK: Not the kinds of things you want passers-by hearing.

After another pause, Kohl unlocks the car, and both men sit inside.

MK: First things first. I need to ask you about a meeting you had last week with one Jibril Aziz.

EK: Who?

MK: Let's not play around. This is serious business.

Pause.

EK: But he's one of us. (Pause.) He *is* CIA, isn't he?

MK: Yes, Mr. Kohl. He is.

An audible sigh, assumedly from Kohl.

MK: So?

EK: We discussed an old operation. A *theoretical* operation. From my time in Cairo.

MK: Stumbler.

EK: You know about Stumbler?

MK: Of course. The Bureau had a look at it as well.

EK: Well, I . . . (Pause.) It was never put into motion, only discussed.

MK: Then why did Mr. Aziz fly to Budapest to talk to you about it?

EK: Because he's delusional.

MK: Oh?

EK: He's convinced that the plan wasn't buried. He's convinced it's been started up again.

MK: What makes him think that?

EK: Disappearances, first of all. In New York, Mohammed el-Keib and Abdel Jalil of the FLO; and in London, Yousef al-Juwali of the ADLF. Other disappearances, too—Paris and Brussels. Names I don't remember.

Pause.

MK: Right—that was the initial phase of the operation, wasn't it? Leaders of these exile groups are plucked off the street. They convene in Marsa Matrouh and Medenine, set their watches, and cross into Libya to spark the uprising. (Pause.) Wait a minute—are you saying that Aziz believed *we* started what's going on in Libya?

EK: That's just the point. According to him, they disappeared days *after* the protests started in Benghazi. So, no. He doesn't believe we started it. What he believes is that we're trying to hijack the revolution now that it's already under way.

MK: Is he angry about this?

EK: He's livid.

MK: But he came to you. Why does he think a deputy consul in Hungary can help?

EK: Because I'm one of the people who rejected the plan in Cairo.

MK: So did Harold Wolcott. So did Stan Bertolli. And they're Agency.

A pause, and through the windshield we can see a large smile on Kohl's face. Pride?

EK: That's because I'm the only one, among the two dozen who looked at the plan, who made a moral argument against it. I sent my assessment separately, in a direct to the Office of Collection Strategies and Analysis. I said that our country had made the moral error of trying to unilaterally bring about regime change in Iraq, and that the new administration should learn from the mistakes of the previous one. I said that in my line of work I'm called upon to defend my country, and while I can cite economic and military reasons for people to support the United States, the moment I'm unable to fall back on our moral strength, my arguments will fall on deaf ears.

MK: So you were against Stumbler on moral grounds.

EK: Primarily, yes.

MK: And this convinced Aziz that his plan was wrong?

EK: Not at all. But he *respected* my position. He knew that I was the one person he could come to with a moral problem and expect an honest answer.

MK: And what did you tell him?

EK: I told him that if the American government was putting Stumbler in motion in order to thwart the popular revolution in Libya, then I would find a whistle and blow it.

MK: Is that true?

EK: Absolutely, but it's beside the point now. Because Jibril is wrong. I tried to tell him that. We simply wouldn't do it. Forget the moral reasons—the risks are too great. But I promised to look into it myself. Which is what I did. And, no, we're not running Stumbler. (Pause.) Someone else is.

MK: What?

EK: Jibril's partially right—someone *is* working off of the Stumbler blueprints, but it's not us. Yesterday, London ID'd the man who took away Yousef al-Juwali. His name is Mutassim Jallud. He's not an exile, and he's not one of us. He's a member of *Mukhabarat el-Jamahiriya*.

MK: Gadhafi's intelligence service?

Kohl nods.

MK: What do you think this means?

EK: Maybe you should talk to the embassy.

MK: I'm talking to you.

Kohl shakes his head.

EK: I've given you enough. You said you had information about my wife.

MK: I did.

EK: Well?

MK: Tell me what you suspect first.

EK: Don't be an ass.

MK: I'm just doing my job.

Pause.

EK: Look, okay? Stumbler isn't happening. What we've got is someone worried it's *going* to happen. And by someone, I mean Muammar Gadhafi. He's sending people to get rid of the central players in the plan. The real question is: How did he find out about Stumbler?

MK: Maybe he's just getting rid of exiles who hate him. It wouldn't be the first time.

EK: But these *exact* exiles? The ones listed in the original plan? No, Gadhafi's people have a copy of the Stumbler documents. The question is: How? Who gave it to him? It leaked—for a variety of reasons I won't go into, I'll lay odds it leaked from the Cairo embassy—but to whom? And how did it then make its way over the border to Tripoli? *That's* what we need to be worrying about.

MK: Have you taken a look at WikiLeaks lately?

EK: The cable from Cairo—yes, I saw it. But that's just an assessment of Stumbler, not the original plan. They only got hold of the introductory cable—no operational detail, no names. Gadhafi isn't using WikiLeaks to track down the exiles.

Pause.

MK: And this is what you're working on now? Figuring out the path the documents took?

EK: Would you go about it another way?

Another pause, then Michael Khalil opens his door.

EK: Where the hell are you going?

MK: I'm letting you get back to your appointments.

EK: No, you're not. You're going to tell me about Sophie.

MK: You don't want to know. Trust me on this.

EK: Actually, Michael Khalil, I do want to know.

<u>Source: Visual</u>

Khalil gets out of the car, followed soon by Kohl, who jogs up and grabs Khalil's arm. They speak, heads close to each other. The shotgun mic is unable to make out the conversation. Whatever Khalil shares, however, has a visible effect on Kohl. He shakes his head and shouts, "What?" Then he comes close to listen to more, still shaking his head no. Finally, Khalil places a hand on Kohl's shoulder, whispers a quiet word, then walks briskly away.

Kohl returns to his car and sits inside for a full five minutes before starting it and driving to the American embassy at Szabadság tér.

Khalil is followed. He speaks once on his telephone, then continues on foot to his destination: the Hotel Anna at Gyulai Pál utca 14.

PART III

———

WHAT THE REST
OF THE WORLD
LOOKS LIKE

Sophie

1

—◆—

Were she honest with herself, Sophie would admit that the most jarring moment of the previous week, not counting the murder, was when she realized that she had been second, an afterthought. Zora had gone to Emmett first—*he* was why she had come to Egypt—but Emmett had been too strong, or too upstanding, to be swayed by her threats. Sophie, on the other hand, had folded immediately.

They had been in Cairo nearly a month, still fresh from Paris, and Sophie had been relaxing at the Arkadia Mall. This was long before looters gutted and set fire to the building during the uprising. Back then, in 2009, it had been a cool, pleasant place for moneyed shoppers to spend afternoons away from the sweltering crowds, and it was there that Zora appeared, as if plucked from a dream, smiling and opening her arms, saying, "*Sofia,*" in her dripping accent. Everything from Zora Balašević's mouth was drenched. She was older now, older but still vital, crackling with enthusiasm and intensity. Once, that intensity would have frightened her, for she remembered how Zora could swing between lightness and the weight of history. But now things were different—weren't they? They were both older, both mellowed by the years, just two old friends in a strange land.

Over cups of tea at Groppi, Zora asked her about France and the life of a diplomat's wife, using a form of English so different from the strangled Zora-speak of 1991. Over the past two decades she had ironed out most of the mistakes, settling on a slightly formal foreigner's take on the language. She smiled a lot, too, but it was a smile of amusement—they both remembered how life had been in Yugoslavia, and the life Sophie was describing sounded as if it were part of a lunar existence.

"Tell me honestly, Sofia," she said, sticking to the Balkanized name she'd used in 1991. "You are bored, no?"

Sophie laughed aloud to cover up a bubbling anxiety. Was Zora switching again—lightness to weight? "Of course," she said. "But I'd be a fool to complain."

"I don't believe so," Zora said, her generous smile slipping away. "You're *not* a brainless puppet. You never were. Leisure is not enough to satisfy your soul."

Sophie reacted instinctively to people who threw around the word "soul," but from Zora's lips it didn't seem out of order. Zora thought differently; she thought Balkan. Sophie said, "I suppose you're right."

"Of course I am, *draga*. You need something more."

As if this were something entirely fresh and original, Sophie leaned back and stared into her sultry eyes. She put Vukovar out of her mind and focused instead on those days before Vukovar. She remembered warm nights in the countryside, beer and *rakija*, dancing to Yugorock bands—Električni Orgazam, Disciplina Kičme, Idoli, Haustor—as well as the Velvet Underground, then afterward feasting on platters of grilled meats. Carnivorous and pleasurable. Unlike Vienna, Prague, and Budapest, Novi Sad had embraced them, absorbing them into a different way of living, boisterous and celebratory. There was so much happy chatter about Adriatic vacations and house parties and *What do you think of Yugoslavia?* before the politics would rear its head and the bitter shouting matches began. Yet each evening ended with forgiveness and kisses and proclamations of undying love. *Existentially fatalistic,* Emmett had called it. Their endless parties were an answer to the question: Why am I here? Their answer was to crank up the hi-fi.

Then she was back, and Zora was watching her. Sophie said, "You're right. I do need something more."

"You need a little adventure."

Sophie shrugged.

"Don't forget that I know exactly how you look when you're having an adventure. I'll bet it's been twenty years since you looked like that."

Sophie stared, repulsed by her audacity yet at the same time wanting more, wanting something to cut through the leisurely haze that she sometimes feared was consuming her. Zora was tapping on a door that, soon after their return home from Yugoslavia, she and Emmett had simply shut and locked. They'd come to the conclusion that they couldn't change the past, and so to dwell on their mistakes would only cause more damage. Now, two decades later, the one person on earth who could pick that lock had arrived in Cairo.

But Zora was smiling radiantly as she said these things. "You were alive then, you know? I thought at the time that you were the most beautiful woman I had ever known."

"I doubt *that*."

She rubbed Sophie's knee, long red nails lightly scratching her thigh. "Believe me, Sofia. You were magnificent."

Did Zora know what kind of effect her words would have? Now that Emmett was dead, she wanted to think that Zora Balašević had known everything. She wanted to believe that this Serb woman had been a master of manipulation, targeting her from the moment she learned the Kohls were in town, or maybe from the moment she laid eyes on that twenty-two-year-old Sophie back in Novi Sad. What she *didn't* want to think was that Zora Balašević was no more omnipotent than anyone else, yet the evidence now suggested this. She had first tried Emmett, failed, and afterward gave the wife a try—she had probably been shocked by how easy Sophie was. A handful of nostalgia and a pinch of seduction, and she was hers.

When Sophie asked what Zora was doing in Cairo, her answers had been elusive. "Work, business. You know." What kind of business? A shrug. "Information. It's the information age, no?"

Sweet, naive Sophie: "You have a Web site?"

A Balkan laugh, throaty and rolling. "Oh, no. But maybe I should get one. What do you think?"

"If you don't have a Web site, you don't exist."

Zora stroked the back of Sophie's hand. "I think I'll forget about the Web site, then."

She had the uncanny ability of making elusive statements and giving Sophie a knowing look that suggested she was sharing a secret, so that the idea of asking for explanation never occurred to her. It was just so good to be part of Zora's secret world that she didn't want to break the illusion by asking foolish questions. Eventually, Zora said, "Maybe you'd like to work with me now and then. I think you would like it."

Sophie just shrugged, flattered that anyone thought her worthy of employment these days, and later, after she'd posed the idea two more times, Sophie finally said, "Of course, Zora. I'm yours."

When asking a woman to betray her husband and country, the question cannot be posed outright. It must be worked into. No matter how willing the traitor is, subtlety is still required. That first day they spent five hours together, moving from the mall to a bar in the Conrad Hilton. When Zora suggested the move, Sophie hesitated, but Zora cut the silence short with "Emmett is working late tonight— where do you have to be?"

"How did you know that?"

"Information, *draga*. Information is everywhere."

So they ended up in the Jayda Lounge, Zora drinking Ketel One neat, Sophie diluting hers with cranberry juice. "Remember that club in the fortress?" Zora asked.

"A world away from this."

"Look over there."

She nodded at a table by the window that overlooked the Nile and the Cairo cityscape, where three men and a smoldering blonde were gathered. The men were large under their expensive suits, the pristine fabric straining to contain them. Two were shaved bald. "Russians?" Sophie asked.

"You were always astute, Sofia. The girl—she's a friend of mine."

Not once had the girl looked over at their table.

"What do you mean?"

Lowering her voice, Zora said, "Do not stare, *draga*. I mean that she works for me."

Sophie looked again at the sexy young thing. With her curves and mascaraed eyes and the long slice down the side of her dress, exposing so much thigh, she looked like candy—that was the only word Sophie could think of to describe her. She didn't look like an employee of anything having to do with "information." There seemed to be only one industry to which she was suited. Then the simple girl in Sophie understood, and she took a drink. "But who do *you* work for, Zora?"

"For myself."

"But you sell to someone."

"Those are my clients, *draga*. Not my employers."

"Who are your clients?"

"There has to be some confidentiality, no?"

It was an answer of sorts, but Sophie was curious. "Just name one."

"Why don't you guess?"

"Serbia."

"You know how patriotic I am."

This didn't feel right, and it took a moment for Sophie to remember why. "You used to call governments the first sin of humanity. You hated them."

Zora smiled. "I grew up, Sofia. Countries, like corporations, are not people; they're not worthy of hatred. Nor are they worthy of love."

"And all that other nonsense?"

"What nonsense?"

"The nationalism. The propaganda. All that stuff about the Croats. I looked into it after I got home. You really took some liberties with the facts."

Zora rocked her head, considering this. "We all fall victim to enthusiasms now and then. If I remember right, you did, too."

This was a different woman from the one she'd known in Yugoslavia, the one who had preached a love of Serbian soil. Her logic was less Balkan and more in line with how Sophie thought: Love was wasted on nation-states, even if that nation-state was the United States of America. Too much enthusiasm was bound to get you in trouble.

Since early 2001, she and Emmett had lived outside of America, and she often wondered how they would feel once they finally returned to the country that Emmett represented to the rest of the world. How American could one be after so long away? Or did it work the other way—was distance making them more American? She'd seen both tendencies in expats. Some immersed themselves in another culture, speaking English only when there was no other option, and prattled on about the mistakes America made throughout the world. Others—like Emmett—became defenders and progressively more acute apologists against the wave of anti-American sentiment that existed everywhere on the planet. It was his job, she supposed, to defend questionable wars and extraordinary renditions and executions by drone attack, but he was often emotional about it, and the question she always wanted to ask him was: *Do you really know what it is you're defending anymore?*

When was the last time they had driven out to Wal-Mart to load up on the week's groceries? They'd never attended a PTA meeting or voted in municipal elections, and the recession had had little effect on them. They didn't really even know what it was like to live in a city where they could listen in on strangers' conversations and actually understand every word—she'd forgotten what it was like to swim in a sea of English. Maybe this was why, during the occasional political argument at this or that diplomat's residence, Sophie grew so easily tongue-tied and confused. Unlike Emmett, she didn't have a government-approved list of rebuttals filed away. Every anti-American complaint sounded perfectly reasonable to her, and all she ever wanted to do was agree. Why get upset? After all, they weren't complaining about her personally, and they weren't complaining about someone she loved.

One thing about Zora had not changed in twenty years: her confidence. Sitting in the Jayda Lounge, Sophie again felt overwhelmed by this Serbian woman's surety. Being with someone so convinced of the rightness of her actions was a little intoxicating, and she felt the buzz again. "Do you have other clients?"

Zora smiled and tapped a nail against the side of her glass. "*Information wants to be free*—that's what people are saying these days. I wouldn't go that far, though. I believe I should be paid well for it."

When she smiled again, Sophie found herself smiling as well. Then an involuntary laugh escaped her. "Who *are* you now, Zora?"

Her eyes widened, big and dark and full of glamour. "I am an angel come down to raise you from the dead."

2

By the time Stan left the apartment on Saturday morning, she was only able to sit on the sofa and stare into space. She'd been in town a single night, and she was already exhausted: It had been a while since she'd dealt with this level of anxiety. Budapest had been dull, but it had been a vacation from deceit, from the faces upon faces. In Budapest there had been no clandestine hours with Zora's flash drives, sucking out all of Emmett's precious information; there had been no more clandestine meetings in cafés and suburban squares where Zora praised her, no visits to parks and crumbling buildings to seek out dead drops. And the lies—so many lies for Emmett and Stan and whoever else she ran into, for Zora had told her that the investigators could come from anywhere. *They will suspect you eventually—make no mistake—but you're very good,* draga. *You know how to mix and circulate and present.* Thus the lies had been for everyone. In Budapest she had lied to Glenda and Mary and Tracey and Anita about little things, but often the lies were only to give herself little injections of adrenaline. Budapest, really, had made her soft.

Once she pried herself out of her lethargy she poured another coffee and did what she'd been waiting to do: She made the call again, using Stan's old cell phone. Again, the Arabic recording told her that Zora's number had been disconnected.

Did she really think this would work so easily, six months later?

A single phone call, and presto: Zora Balašević would be back in her life?

Yes, for Sophie had never fooled herself into thinking that she was the only reason Zora Balašević had moved to Cairo. She was a small fish, while that sexy blonde with all the leg was much bigger—she was the kind of fish who could rub and kiss intelligence out of big Russian mafiosi on command.

Then it occurred to her: Of *course* Zora was still in Cairo—she had just changed numbers. Sophie had become a security risk as soon as she'd left town. Therefore, Zora had gotten rid of the phone she had used with Sophie, so that they could both go on with their lives. She'd said as much once: *When spies say good-bye it's really good-bye. We wipe our memories clean. You understand? In movies they're always getting in touch with old comrades, but this is not reality. Instead, we build new lives that have nothing to do with each other. This is how we survive.*

Changing phone numbers was a simple matter, but changing homes was more difficult, so she found a city map on her iPad and began to chart her route from Garden City to Al-Muizz Street. Bus lines. No taxi, for now she was thinking like a spy, wanting to leave no paper trail. She showered and made herself presentable in yesterday's clothes, patting them flat, then grabbed Stan's spare keys and descended to the street.

She took a long walk north along Al Kasr Al Aini toward Tahrir Square, absorbing Cairo with each step. She'd gone from airport to car to apartment, but now she was a part of the city that had once made her feel so liberated, and she tried to breathe it all in. The smell of exhaust and roasting meats, of cigarettes and cologne. The broad avenue teemed with pedestrians, dark and loud and full of some quality she believed Westerners lacked. An appreciation of loitering, perhaps, or some truer love of life—she didn't know. She only knew that it made her feel as if she still had something to learn here.

When she reached Tahrir Square, she took a few minutes to orient herself in that vast circle that had not long ago overflowed with human bodies demanding change, a mass ruptured now and then by security service thugs riding in on horseback, swinging clubs, firing guns. Now, it was nearly as she remembered it—cleaned up, almost elegant, some storefronts still covered in cardboard but most with new glass and doors. Disruption. People here knew how easily life could be disrupted. A whole world could vanish in an instant. They had understood this in Prague. They had understood it in Yugoslavia, too, where they had fought the chaos by feasting.

In the shadow of the Headquarters of the Arab League, she joined a crowd at a bus stop, then climbed aboard a diesel monstrosity that brought them up to Talaat Harb Square, where she waited twenty minutes before climbing aboard another bus that carried her all the way to Al-Muizz Street. On the way, among the warm press of locals, sweat tickling her back, she felt the low hum of that old thrill: anonymity and secret purpose. She was a stranger on a foreign bus searching for her controller.

As they passed through Islamic Cairo, however, the feeling drained, for she was soon back to Emmett. The next day was his funeral, and she imagined in-laws dressed in Protestant black, weepy but not loud, for too much noise was abhorrent. Emmett had made wicked fun of such things, and it was a shame that she wouldn't be there to make fun of it for him. She wondered what they would be thinking about her absence. Would they be angry? Worried? Christ—was *anybody* worried about her? Were they searching at that moment, scouring satellite photos and listening for the signal from her phone? Was there an office somewhere in Langley where some young agent had been tasked with finding Sophie Kohl?

She hadn't even turned on the television that morning—was her disappearance on the news?

She disembarked on the southern end of the ancient, sun-drenched street, and as she walked north she sometimes caught glimpses between the low buildings, some recently renovated, of the ever-present Citadel. It was not a long walk—ten minutes, maybe—but the stares she received made it feel much longer—she'd forgotten how Egyptian eyes could bore into her, how sometimes men she passed would hiss and cluck their tongues at her. She wiped at her wet forehead, trudging up stone steps with crumbling, medieval buildings on either side—ornate, arched entryways and windows, walls tiger-striped by layers of dark bricks and light. She passed the aromatic spice and perfume markets, the mausoleum and madrasa of the Qalawun complex, and the Aqmar Mosque, before reaching the mud-colored, flat-faced building across from the house of Mustafa Ja'far, an eighteenth-century coffee trader. There was a narrow entrance with three stone steps, and as she mounted them the peeling front door opened and a tall, handsome Egyptian came out, smiling at her. "Good afternoon," he said, knowing from her face and blond hair what language to speak.

"Hi, can you let me in?" she asked, then wondered if greetings were the extent of his English.

They weren't. He unlocked the front door and held it open. "You live here?"

"Visiting a friend. Number five."

He looked her square in the face, eyes bruised and a little glassy. "A friend of Pili's?"

"How did you know?" she said, thinking, *Zora's cover name, Pili.*

"She's the only one who speaks English."

"Right," said Sophie. "Of course."

She lingered in the doorway, watching the Egyptian disappear into the crowds, then stepped inside and let the door fall shut behind her. She stood in the gloom of the entryway, smelling dust from some ongoing renovation. Someone, somewhere, was cooking something wonderful. She climbed the narrow stairs she remembered climbing only twice before in her life—each time, like now, with apprehension in her gut.

Their meetings had usually been in nondescript, public places, so the two times she'd come to this apartment had been exceptional. Her first visit was to celebrate their initial success. Sophie had delivered a flash drive full of information, and afterward Zora had wooed her with champagne and the details of a UBS Bank savings account, opened at the Albisriederplatz branch in Zurich, which had jumped from zero to twenty thousand euros overnight. *You're a natural,*

Sofia. That had been a wonderful night, just the two of them drunk and dreamy and open. Emmett had been on a trip to Alexandria, and so she stayed over, though in the morning when she let her out Zora reminded her that they were never to meet there again. *Tradecraft*, draga.

Of course.

Yet there had been a second visit, nearly a year later. Zora hadn't been answering her phone, so Sophie came to the apartment. She'd survived a liberating year of betrayal, while Emmett was succumbing to an onset of evil moods that she would only be able to fully understand moments before he was murdered. Their fights had been mounting, and at the time she'd begun to believe that she was the cause. Her affairs: the one with Stan, and the one with Zora. She was beginning to believe that he *knew* she was selling his work on to their Serbian friend, though she had never even told him that Zora was in town. And if he *didn't* know anything, then she was sure he would figure it out eventually. Her only option was to withdraw.

But Zora must have sensed her apprehension, for she dropped out of contact, and Sophie's only recourse was to seek her out.

That had been April of 2010. By then she'd been a traitor for a year and an adulteress for nearly five months, and she felt as if her fragile world were going to collapse on her. So she'd rung Zora's bell, and after a moment was in. Zora began with apologies—"I've been out of the country."

Over glasses of bourbon, Sophie told her. It had been a wonderful ride, but she couldn't take it anymore. It was time for them to shake hands and call it quits. She couldn't go on deceiving Emmett.

"Because he is such an innocent," Zora said.

Sophie wasn't going to take the bait. She shrugged. "It's got to end."

Zora made fresh drinks, and when she returned from the kitchen she was a different woman. A woman that Sophie had yet to meet—or, perhaps, a woman she hadn't met in twenty years. Gone were the smiles, the easy sisterhood of information professionals, and the understated flirtation that drew Sophie to her, promising an erotic relationship that, despite overtures, had never actually been consummated. "You can't stop," Zora said. "Not now."

"Of course I can."

"Your material is in demand. The value is rising."

"So is my blood pressure."

"Then take medication."

"You're not listening, Zora. I'm done."

"No, Sophie Kohl. You are *not* done. When you *are* done, I will tell you." No smiles, no warmth.

Sophie set down her glass and stood. "I'm sorry. I really am. But we both knew it couldn't go on forever."

Zora set down her own glass but didn't get up. "Do you want Emmett to learn about Stan?"

Sophie lost track of her feet, spread her hands for balance, and stared hard at her. "You would *do* that?"

"To protect my information, yes."

She imagined this, Emmett learning about Stan, and how it might crush him. She could feel herself weakening, so she pushed the image away. "Then do it," she said. She was stronger than she had been a year before. If her world had to snap, then let it snap.

As she walked to the door, she heard Zora say, "And Vukovar? How do you think the American government would react to that? What their diplomat and his wife used to get up to in war-ravaged third world countries?"

She was touching the door handle, and she kept her hand on it as she turned to look at Zora. "You would ruin Emmett's career simply to keep me?"

"Worse," she said. "I would ruin Emmett if I was *unable* to keep you. We're not talking about thousands of dollars, Sofia. We are talking about millions. I would do a lot more for that."

"You're a bitch."

"You finally understand," Zora said quietly.

Their relationship became something completely different that day, and now, nearly a year later, Sophie listened at the heavy door to number five. She thought of Emmett. As bad as his final minutes had been, they could have been worse. Instead of learning about Stan, he could have learned about Zora. That would've killed him before the actual murder.

Through the door, she heard a radio playing and a woman's voice speaking Arabic, either to herself or on a telephone. Sophie raised her hand in a small fist, then rapped on the door.

3

———◆———

By the time she returned to Stan's apartment in Garden City and placed herself back on the sofa, the iPad in her lap and a cold cup of the morning's coffee in one hand, she understood in a way she hadn't before just how alone she was. She'd seen it in the unfamiliar face of the teenaged girl who'd opened the door to apartment five, a cell phone pressed to her ear. A pretty girl with eyes the shade of teak, she raised her eyebrows at Sophie, saying something like *Aye khidma?*

"Zora Balašević?"

The girl frowned, then muttered into the phone before lowering it to her hip. "You're English?"

"Yes, sorry. I—I was looking for my friend who lives here. Zora Balašević."

The girl—Pili, she assumed—shook her head. "We've been here since November. I don't know who was here before."

Sophie nodded, only too late realizing her eyes were filling with tears. "Okay. Right. Thanks." She raised a hand in farewell, then fled.

On the bus ride back she'd spotted among the dark crowds a pay phone outside a convenience store. She got off at the next stop and trudged back to the spot, finding a layer of dust on an old phone box that advertised the RinGo phone card. Most Egyptians didn't go near these machines, preferring the mobile phones that had helped make their revolution possible. She headed into the convenience store and bought a phone card from a sniffing man, a victim of late-season flu, then went back to the machine and took out business cards. Strauss, Reardon, Kiraly.

A crowd of women passed along the sidewalk, heads covered, chatting merrily, laughing. She almost didn't hear the voice on the line when it said, "Kiraly Andras."

"Mr. Kiraly," she said, nearly shouting. "Hello? This is Sophie Kohl."

"You're still in Cairo, I see."

"Have you told the American embassy?"

Silence, then: "You sound different, Mrs. Kohl."

"Do I?"

"I almost thought you were someone else," he said. "Pretending to be you." Then, realizing the emptiness of his statement, he said, "No, we haven't told the American embassy, and we won't until we better understand why you're doing what you're doing."

"You know the reason," she said. "Jibril Aziz."

"He's in Cairo?"

"I don't know. You told me he flew here."

"Yes."

"So he should be here, somewhere. Unless . . ." She frowned into the handset as it occurred to her. Stumbler. Aziz had written Stumbler.

"Unless what, Mrs. Kohl?"

"Unless he's in Libya."

Silence.

She said, "Do you really not know where he is?"

"I do not. Perhaps you should ask his family."

"Family?"

He seemed amused by her surprise. "Most people have families, Mrs. Kohl. If you give me a phone number, I can call you with that information tomorrow. From the office."

"What do you know about Zora Balašević?"

"Excuse me?"

She repeated the name, then at his request spelled it, and as he wrote it down she said, "She's connected to my husband's murder, but I don't know how or why."

"How do you know this for sure?"

"Can I just say that I know it?"

Silence, then he said, "Mrs. Kohl, if it hasn't become clear to you yet, you are the one in control of what you do and do not say. Eventually, I would like for you to say more, but for the moment you're choosing reticence. I will have to accept this."

"Apologies, Mr. Kiraly."

"I will look into this woman, as well as Mr. Aziz's family. Would you like to give me a telephone number?"

"I'll call you."

"Of course," he said. "Tomorrow, then, Mrs. Kohl."

"Tomorrow, Mr. Kiraly."

Back on Stan's sofa, she remembered what Kiraly had said. Did she sound like a different person? Maybe. Someone new? Or had she again become last year's Sophie Kohl, Sofia, who had thrived under Zora's tutelage?

Yes, but the world was different now, too. She was alone. Zora had disappeared. Emmett was gone. She was in a city that had become even more foreign, for now Hosni Mubarak was holed up in faraway Sharm el-Sheikh. She had felt this on the bus, surrounded by the young and old who, for the first time in memory, were part of the construction of their own society. It didn't matter that the military was in control; they knew that all it took to change their country was a critical mass of humanity willing to stand in the street. While she could appreciate this, it also scared her, for their newfound power made them that much more menacing.

All she had was Stan. Stan, who had lied to her immediately after her arrival by pretending to know nothing about Zora—but hadn't he just been covering for himself? It was understandable, and beyond that mistake he seemed to be trying. He was committed.

No, she wasn't alone, not really, and she could sense his desire when they stood close. She would have to make sure she didn't lose him.

She had told Emmett the truth: For a week she had thought she might love Stan Bertolli, but that feeling had gone away. Yet she was fond of him, and he was the only thing left to her.

She used his old cell phone to call him. "What have you got?"

"Not much. How about you?"

"I . . ." she began, then changed tack. "I've been dozing in front of the television."

"Give me another hour, and we'll talk when I get home."

When he returned that evening with a takeout bag of grilled chicken, she thought of Zora's other girl, the one with the long legs who could convince Russian thugs and kleptocrats to give up secrets, but seduction had never been Sophie's forte. She tried, though, for now she was thinking in terms of practicality, of balances of power, of what Zora had called *the push and the pull of seduction.* Yet when she focused on Stan, using her eyes, stroking her hair, trying to look dreamy and enthralled, she felt ridiculous, knowing that it wasn't working.

As he prepared the food, she said, "Did you find out about Jibril Aziz?"

"Not much. Just his position in the Office of Collection Strategies. I sent him an e-mail—maybe he'll get back to me."

"No phone number?"

"None."

That made no sense. "Why not?"

"Sometimes they don't list numbers. Either they're changing offices or the section head wants them undisturbed because of a project."

"How about a wife?" she asked, thinking of what Kiraly had said. "A family?"

"None."

So not even her gloomy Hungarian spy knew what he was talking about.

As they ate, he told her about Zora—Zora and Emmett and the ways in which Stan had gotten everything so wrong last year, hounding poor Emmett until he had to flee to Budapest. She wanted to cry, knowing it was her fault, but instead she turned it around. *Misdirection,* Zora called it. "You pretended you'd never heard of her. You *lied* to me." *Put them on the defensive, always the defensive.*

It worked, but as he made excuses, she felt the distance between them growing, and another part of her grew frightened: *He's the only one you have, and you're scaring him away.* So she moved to the sofa, knowing he would follow, and he did.

"Where is Zora?" she asked.

"Serbia. She went back home in September."

Where else?

Then he told her the thing that she would not be able to shake for a very long time. "She told Emmett she was working for the Serbs. That was a lie."

"What? Are you sure?"

"My Serb contact says that by then she was working for the Egyptians."

A year, a full year, believing that, if nothing else, she was helping Zora's people. She hadn't even been doing that. She'd been feeding everything that Emmett brought home into Hosni's grand machine. God, she hated Zora. Briefly, she also hated Stan for holding up this cracked mirror.

He went on, though, explaining how he'd put together his fantasy of Emmett's guilt, then telling her why he hadn't sent Emmett home. "The disaster is that you would have left, too."

She didn't have to do this, she realized. She didn't have give herself to him tonight. But she had to give herself to someone, and with Zora gone who else was there?

He said, "What did Balašević have on Emmett?"

Misdirection. Now.

She leaned close and placed her head on the side of his chest; he wrapped an arm around her. In her head, she saw a flash of dirty leg, spastic, kicking at the damp earth of a musty basement floor. All desire fled her body; the only thing left was survival. When he kissed her neck, she knew it was accomplished.

The first orgasm surprised her. Entirely mechanical, but strong. She'd almost forgotten how good it could be, and the little, shattering explosions transported her elsewhere, to a hard bed in the Hotel Putnik, and a much younger Emmett praying between her legs.

4

1991

On September 20, Sophie and Emmett arrived in Novi Sad desperate for sex, for their rough, seven-hour train ride from Budapest had felt like their first true plunge into authenticity. They'd shared a filthy cabin with a pair of fat old women who ate cheese sandwiches and eyeballed them, and as they waited at the border wailing Gypsies swelled outside their window, reaching up to sell them T-shirts, cassettes, bottled water, and toys. The Hungarian border guards seemed to be waiting for bribes, shooting them looks of scorn as they rifled through their papers, so by the time they crossed into Yugoslavia they were expecting trouble. Yet they received none: The Yugoslav soldiers gathered around to hear their American voices, one telling of a cousin in Chicago, another sternly advising them to mix bad wine with Coca-Cola for a perfect evening drink. Toothy grins surrounded them as the young conscripts pushed in to get a glimpse of the West.

This was when the arousal flickered in them both, and by the time they reached the high marble-and-concrete lobby of the Novi Sad train station, bought dinars at official rates from a surly clerk, and haggled for a noisy taxi ride to the center of town, they were famished for it. They didn't notice the haughtiness of the desk clerk or the mustached secret policeman watching them from behind a copy of *Politika* or even the scratches on the inside of their door that, had they been in the mood to notice, would have made them think that someone had been imprisoned in the room for a very long time. They weren't in the mood to look around at anything in Milošević's Yugoslavia, not even checking the nighttime view from their window until afterward, when Emmett, naked and satisfied, pulled back the heavy, dusty curtains to look down on a tree-lined street full of sleepy taxis under the tungsten glare.

It was late when they finally dressed and walked around the corner to Trg Slobode—Liberty Square—to mix with dour-looking dark-headed couples peering into sparse shop windows. The city hall was lit up like a cathedral, and the pedestrian avenue was choked with sidewalk cafés. They sat at one and ordered strong Turkish coffees. "Turska kafa," Emmett read from the menu, and the waitress, a pretty yet bedraggled girl, giggled at his pronunciation. Heads turned to look at them. In that postcoital glow, neither was concerned. They had crossed into the Balkans. Anything could happen, and they were ready to welcome the unknown with open arms.

A tall man, one of a table of three, turned a leg toward them and leaned against his thigh. "American?" Dark eyes, a cigarette gushing smoke around his face.

"That's right," said Emmett, chin out, defiant.

"MC Hammer," the man said, smiling now. "Madonna. Michael Jackson. J. R. Ewing."

"Yes," Emmett said, trying to hold back a grin. "All American."

The man leaned back and waved at the waitress and ordered Lav beers for his new American friends. Soon they had joined the three dark-haired men who turned out to be great fans of America. Voislav had relatives in New York, while Steva had spent a university semester in Pennsylvania. They asked questions, often returning to the most important one: How do you like Yugoslavia? After ten hours, what could they say? So far, so good.

"Come," said the third, Borko. "We go to disco."

Sophie hesitated. It was one thing to chat with friendly strangers in an open-air café around the corner from your hotel, but a disco required taxis; it required giving yourself over to the care of strangers. Then she saw the glow in Emmett's face. This was it; *this* was what he'd meant when he'd said, *To go. To see. To experience.*

They were soon stuffed into a tiny taxi, laughing and listening to the men sing old, incomprehensible songs, crossing a long bridge to reach the Petrovaradin Fortress that, according to their hosts, had been built by the Romans. It had been rebuilt and reinforced over the centuries, developing into a winding labyrinth of cobblestone walkways and dark, hidden crevices that led them eventually to an enormous, crypt-like courtyard where, in one corner, a DJ was playing "Birthday" by the Sugarcubes, while in the other corner young people were lined up to buy beer. Crushed plastic cups littered the ground. Filling the center of the courtyard was a heaving mass of sweating young bodies, writhing in some vaguely synchronous dance.

Sophie needn't have worried about their guides. Voislav, Steva, and Borko were riding a high of exhilaration, having recently been decommissioned from the army and their tenure in the drab, muddy camps where nationalist discord was fermenting. "And then we come back to find out Vojvodina is no longer autonomous," Voislav told them.

"What?" asked Sophie.

"Vojvodina. Where you are right now. Fucking Milošević took away our political autonomy. Ours and Kosovo's. It *stinks*." Then he raised his hands, palms out, and pushed away everything he'd just said. "I give myself a headache."

They were in dire need of a breath of fresh air, and to these three young Serbs in the last days of Yugoslavia this meant dance, drink, and travel. It didn't take long before they'd found three pretty girls— one Serb, one Romanian, and one Hungarian—to share their escape, and by midnight all eight of them had formed a loose circle in the middle of the crowd, jumping and writhing and laughing as the DJ spun, his set list of eighties hits growing more manic as the hours wore on. By one, they were exhausted and drunk, slumped over one of the many picnic tables that lined the long courtyard wall, and it felt to Sophie as if they had accomplished their mission: They had become different people. They had, for one evening, forgotten their anxieties and petty worries. They had forgotten *themselves*. It was entirely new to her, and with Emmett she became a satisfied wallflower, watching the joy of all the young people around her.

"They look happy, no?" came a voice. A woman's. Late thirties or early forties, with dark, sultry features. She had taken the seat to the right of Sophie. To Sophie's left, Emmett had leaned his head back against the dirty courtyard wall, eyes closed.

"It's nice to see," she told the woman.

"It is hysteria," the woman told her, her accent so deep and rough that Sophie imagined it could cut wood. "One last dance before end."

Sophie laughed aloud. "You're getting more from it than I am."

"Because you cannot to understand," she said. "You are American."

"Then why don't you explain it to me?"

"You would not understand. You must to know history."

"I went to Harvard, lady. I think I can manage."

The woman arched a brow, nodded, and then began to speak. She spoke not of these people dancing in front of them, but of the Turks and the Field of Black Birds, of Roman history and medieval times. She talked of the Congress of Berlin in 1878, the mistakes of which would eventually lead to the First World War, and by this point Sophie lost track, treading in a sea of loose facts. Later, once they had returned to Boston and gained some perspective, she would see that this was part and parcel of extremist thought the world over: the heaping on of selective trivia that only a computer could fact-check in real time, the raw accumulation of unverifiable anecdote that could create a new reality. Sophie knew this, but in that open-air disco there was something hypnotic about this woman's unabashed conviction. Emmett had woken and was sitting up straight behind Sophie, listening intently. There was no cynicism in this woman's attitude, just the pure, untainted light of absolute knowledge. She understood everything, and nothing would ever get in the way of her worldview. It was seduction, pure and simple: This woman seduced them with her long fingernails, her two-pack-a-day voice, her wrecked grammar, her sultry eyes, and the feeling that she was the last woman on earth who knew everything.

She said, "Serbs been humiliated through history. Usually, by others, but sometimes by first sin of humanity, its own government. We been too bashful, you understand? Too forgiving. It's time for Serbs to take his place on historical stage. Tesla, greatest of scientists, was our genius. Tito was one of world's great leaders. We make most soulful music, and we know this world better than Americans. Forgive me, but this is true. We are brave and strong. We done with humiliation. This is our decade."

Her name, of course, was Zora. A name that sounded like something out of Buck Rogers.

History would later prove her wrong about nearly everything, but in 1991, drunk on their newfound authenticity, there was no way to know this. Zora was right about one thing, though: "The war just starting. In Vukovar you can to see it. It's small now, but will grow. We are happy—you see?—to get rid of Slovenes, but Croats want to steal our coast. Who pay for those beaches? Bosnia is next. There will be fire—believe me—and fire will purge Yugoslavia of everybody except most loyal."

She was mad, certainly, but it was a kind of madness Sophie had never been introduced to before. Zora was no longer dismissing these ignorant Americans—she seemed, instead, to be holding out a hand, inviting them to join her. "Sofia," she said, leaning close, hot breath on her ear and long red-tipped fingers squeezing her wrist, "you are beautiful. Beautiful girls understand better than beautiful men. It is in soul."

Sophie was shaking her head no. "I don't believe in the soul."

Zora pulled back in surprise. "That a woman with *as* much soul as you, you don't believe in it?" Then she leaned close and kissed Sophie heavily on the lips. Sophie didn't know how long it lasted, but she remembered the taste of cigarettes, the dampness of saliva.

From somewhere far away, Emmett was saying, "Well."

Then it was over, and Zora was licking her lips. "You believe. I taste it."

What had happened? Where had they ended up? It had all felt so innocent and simple and happily naive, and then Zora had stepped into their lives—both their lives, for now she was reaching across to clutch Emmett's forearm, pulling him close so that their three heads formed a small huddle. She noticed that Emmett's mouth had formed a twitching, longing smile, but Zora didn't give him the kiss he obviously expected. Instead, she spoke to them both.

"You want to see? You want to know?"

What was she talking about? Did it matter? Emmett said, "That's why we're here."

While Sophie didn't know what was on Emmett's mind—a ménage à trois, perhaps—she knew what was in her own head: a small boy on the Charles Bridge, throwing her Lenin into the river. Yes, she wanted to know what even the small boys in this part of the world knew, the thing that had escaped her all her sheltered life.

Eventually, Zora drifted off into the crowd and disappeared. They asked their new friends about her, and Borko said he'd heard about her. "Dangerous—you know, criminal friends. I don't know what she's about, but you want to watch out."

By the time they got back to the Hotel Putnik at three that morning, famished again, they made exhausted love in their uncomfortable bed. Afterward, they discussed their night, still dazzled by the intensity of it all. They didn't know what to make of Zora, but doubted they would ever see her again. They would stay the week, then they would take the long train ride to Vienna to catch their flight home. In fact, the joy of that night had tempered Emmett's urgent desire for the real world. The funland of throbbing bass drums and hot flashes on the dance floor had been so liberating that they both suspected they would need the entire week just to absorb it.

But plans are best left on the cutting room floor, for it was during their dismal hotel breakfast that Emmett looked up from his toast and, eyes widened, said, "Oh shit."

"What?"

There she was, pulling up a chair to sit with them. Zora looked clean and fresh and hungry enough to eat them both. "Sofia, Emmett,

I want you should meet my friends. I think you are not ordinary Americans. I think you can to appreciate our beautiful country."

Neither answered at first. Sophie was remembering Borko's warning: *Dangerous—you know, criminal friends.*

Zora said, "You look worried. Why? This is wonderful thing. I invite you *into* my country. This is not land of discos. It is land of families and friends and great love. And . . ." She paused as something occurred to her; then she smiled and held up a long-fingered hand. "And I promise not to be bore. No politics. You are my guests."

5

On Sunday morning Stan made his desire obvious, and after one more bout of sex a fresh wave of guilt threatened to drown her: Emmett was being buried in mere hours. It wasn't the burial itself, but the fact that the sex had given her a flash of amnesia. Once she got Stan out of the apartment, she rushed to shower his smell off of her skin.

She would go, she had decided during that long sleepless night. As quietly as she'd arrived in Cairo she would turn around and fly out again, complete her journey to Boston, and while she would miss the funeral she could at least don black and try to reclaim some of the relationships that had once made Sophie Kohl that most refreshing of words: *normal*.

Though many arguments could have swayed her, it was Stan who had inadvertently convinced her. In bed she'd felt the full and overbearing weight of his passion, and she could read his mind in the movement of his hands, the thrust of his hips, the flick of his tongue. What he saw in their future was precisely that: an act of lovemaking—lovemaking, not sex—repeated and repeated until it became common law. Until Stan became the new Emmett.

Did this thought disgust her? No, but what Stan would never understand was that nothing about their relationship had ever been clean and never would be. When he'd first made his feelings clear at the embassy Halloween party, she'd duly reported this to Zora. *I have a feeling that if I let him, he would eat me whole.*

Then let him was her answer. *Live a little.*

That's not me, Zora.

Take a look at yourself, draga. *Who is this* me *you speak of? Did you ever read Jean Genet?*

Sophie hadn't.

You should. He said, "Anyone who hasn't experienced the ecstasy of betrayal knows nothing about ecstasy at all."

Sophie didn't know what to make of this.

And you know, don't you, that if any suspicions arise in the embassy, you will need allies. Lay the groundwork now.

Had she only slept with him to protect herself? No, not really. She had always been attracted to Stan, but once the affair began she had never been able to find the point where attraction ended and self-preservation began, for when the guilt overcame her in that Dokki hotel she would steel herself with Zora's words: She was laying the groundwork for her future security.

Certainly their relationship had grown beyond the confines of an insurance policy, but she knew how it had begun, and nothing would ever change that.

She found an EgyptAir flight leaving at nine thirty the next morning with a stop in London, and placed a reservation with her credit card, knowing that anyone would be able to trace her this way, but trying not to worry too much. Soon enough, she would leave all this behind.

She poured another coffee and stood at the kitchen counter, staring at Stan's old cell phone, thinking. She dug out that cheap business card, then used Stan's phone to dial. Only two rings, then: "Kiraly Andras."

"Mr. Kiraly, it's me."

"Aha. I was expecting your call." He sounded genuinely pleased to hear from her, some of the reservation gone from his voice. "I found something of interest."

"What?"

"His wife's phone number."

"His . . . whose?"

"Mr. Jibril Aziz."

She frowned, wondering suddenly if Andras Kiraly was playing a game—that might explain his change in mood. "But he's not married."

"I believe our information is up-to-date. She is also with child. Seven months, it says."

Stan had told her that Aziz had no family; Kiraly was saying something else. "Please," she said, "may I have that number?"

"Mrs. Kohl," he said, his tone changing, dropping a half octave, "I am willing to give you this, but I think you will appreciate that our relationship needs to progress. I have been free with what information I have access to. I would appreciate some reciprocation."

"Of course, Mr. Kiraly. I understand. The number, please."

She scribbled it on a slip of paper, her hand trembling as the realization grew inside of her: Stan had been lying. Maybe about everything.

"A question," said Kiraly. "Do you know the name Michael Khalil?"

"No," she said, nearly a whisper, still stunned by how alone she was. "Should I know him?"

"Not necessarily. He claims to be an American FBI agent."

"Claims?"

"We have our doubts. He had a conversation with Emmett on the day he was murdered. An unofficial meeting on the street. Liszt Ferenc Square."

"I see," she whispered, though she didn't really see. All she could see was the phone number in front of her. Could this number give her all the answers she desired?

He said, "They were discussing something called Stumbler."

She jolted out of her trance. "Stumbler? They were talking about *Stumbler*?"

"You know of this?"

"Take a look at WikiLeaks," she said. "It's an American plan for . . . for regime change. In Libya. Jibril Aziz dreamed it up. I think it's why he met with Emmett."

"Anything else?"

"It's difficult, Mr. Kiraly. People here are not as helpful as I thought they would be."

"I understand," he said, then: "What if I send someone? I could have one of our people help you navigate the city."

"No, thank you," she said, because for the moment she had what she wanted: a phone number. With that, she might find an explanation for Emmett's murder, or a hint. Maybe she would even learn that she had not been responsible for . . . for *I here for you*. Then she could leave in the morning with a clearer conscience, if only a little. "Really," she said. "I'll call you as soon as I know more."

"Best of luck, Mrs. Kohl. And are we to remain silent about your location?"

"If you would be so kind, Mr. Kiraly."

At twelve, she made the call, but had to hang up because Stan's cell phone was out of credits, depleted by her call to Hungary. Or maybe it was just a gentle nudge from God, suggesting she take a moment to think about this.

God? What was she thinking?

She went to the kitchen and picked up Stan's landline and dialed.

6

———◆———

Hello?" said a woman's voice, sleepy.

"Mrs. Inaya Aziz?"

"This is she."

"Uh, hi. I'm trying to get in touch with your husband, Jibril."

Inaya Aziz paused. "Who is this?"

"Oh, sorry. My name is Sophie Kohl. Your husband doesn't actually know me, but he knew my husband. What time is it there?" Quickly, she did the math in her head. "Oh, five in the morning. I'm so sorry."

"Kohl?" said Inaya Aziz. She heard breaths. "You're not . . . from the news?"

"Yes. You might have seen me on the news, about my husband."

"He was killed?"

"I'm afraid so, Mrs. Aziz."

"Inaya."

"Inaya."

Another moment of silence followed, until Inaya said, "What did you want to talk to Jibril about?"

"About my husband."

"How does he know your husband?"

"They met a few times. Through work, I assume, but he might know something about what happened."

Her reply was swift and logical: "Shouldn't the police be calling him?"

"You'd think so, Inaya. But they don't seem to be. Can you tell me how to get in touch with him?"

"If I knew, I would tell you."

That was an answer Sophie hadn't expected. "What can you tell me?"

"I can tell you he's not here. I can tell you that he was supposed to call me two days ago, but he didn't. I can tell you that I'm worried out of my mind."

That was how it happened. Two women looking for the same man. One of them—Mrs. Inaya Aziz—seven months pregnant and unable to do a thing; the other woman in the ideal place to begin looking for him. "When he last called, he was still in Egypt," Inaya said. "He was traveling with a man from the embassy named John."

"John . . ." Sophie muttered, thinking. She didn't think she knew any John from the embassy.

"He'd just left Marsa Matrouh, on his way to the Libyan border. But he was supposed to call me once he got to Ajdabiya."

"Why was he going into Libya?"

"To help the revolution."

Sophie closed her eyes, the phone pressed hard to her sore ear. She remembered Emmett's obsession with the news from Libya. *Just a few well-placed bombs* . . . "How?"

"Excuse me?"

Sophie wasn't sure of her own question, so she paused to regroup. "How did Jibril expect to help the revolution? He's one man, after all."

"Jibril's not a soldier, Sophie. He's an organizer. A single organizer can make as much difference as fifty soldiers."

"He went in alone?"

"I told you. With a man from the embassy named John."

"I mean, are you saying that the embassy *knew* he was going in? Or was it just him and this guy John?"

"You're asking if he was authorized."

"I suppose I am."

Inaya paused, thinking through her answer. Was she wondering if this caller could be trusted? Finally, she said, "I think so. But he . . . he seemed to have something on them."

"Them?"

"CIA."

"Oh."

"I mean, he didn't *tell* me that, it was a suspicion I had. That he was holding something over their heads. When the protests began in Benghazi, he was very excited. His father was killed by Gadhafi—the man has been his obsession since childhood. He wanted to pack up and join the fight, but he couldn't just go. He's an analyst now. Then after a couple days he came home from work in a mood. Angry. I thought maybe he'd asked to go and was turned down. I was happy. But it turned out that he was already booked on a flight—bought with our own credit card. 'They approved this?' I asked. I couldn't believe it. He told me they didn't have a choice. I told him he was being stupid. We have a baby on the way, and I'm not working. We can't afford him getting fired—or, God forbid, killed. But he wasn't listening to me anymore—how can a wife and baby compare to the fate of an entire nation? He left two days later."

As she was speaking, Sophie remembered Zora's conviction that some of the best information came from uninformed people trapped in stressful situations—in this case, the wife of a missing husband. Sophie had spent the last day and a half in the home of a midlevel CIA officer, yet Stan had given her nothing approaching this. Then she realized that Stan was never going to give her anything of use. He had lied about knowing Zora, lied about Jibril having a family. How could he *not* have known that the embassy had taken Jibril into Libya? How deep did his lies go? She felt flushed, the full weight of her stupidity beginning to suffocate her. She said, "Did he tell you more?"

Inaya hummed quietly, then: "Those last few days, before he left, I hardly saw him at all. He came home late and passed out. In the morning he was gone before I got up. But the night before he flew out he squeezed me into his schedule. He was very caring that night, something like what he used to be. He wasn't going direct to Libya. He was going to Budapest—I guess that's where he met with your husband."

"Why did he meet Emmett?"

"I don't know, but he was going to talk to some contacts there. Then he flew to Cairo, and this John drove him across the border. That's the last I heard of him."

Sophie closed her eyes so she could better see them both—Jibril Aziz and Emmett, sharing secrets about Libya. About Stumbler. She said, "Did he say anything about Stumbler?"

"Stumbler?"

"Yes, Stumbler."

Silence, again. Then: "Yes, actually. That first night, when he was angry, he said that they were doing it already. He said, 'It's Stumbler.' I thought I misheard him, and I asked what that was, but he didn't tell me, and he didn't bring it up again. Neither did I." A pause. "What is it?"

"A plan for revolution in Libya," she said. "Jibril drafted it."

"*What?*" Sophie could feel her surprise through the line. "I don't understand."

"Neither do I, Inaya."

They said nothing for a moment, and through Stan's windows she could hear voices and cars, little dollops of chaos. Then Inaya said, "You think this has to do with your husband's murder."

"I think so."

"Where are you?" she asked.

"I'm in Cairo."

"Are you working with the embassy?"

Was she? "No."

"Then you need help."

"I think I do."

"I'm going to give you a phone number, okay? Jibril has a friend in Cairo. You should have a friend there, too."

"I would appreciate that very much, Inaya."

"But wait a little bit before calling. I need to warn him. I want to talk to him, too."

Afterward, holding the local phone number in her hand with the name Omar Halawi scribbled under it, she felt pressure in her ears. It was light at first, a tickle of pressure, then grew until it pressed hard against her eardrums, threatening to rupture them. She couldn't hear a thing. It was like after Emmett's murder, when she'd had a gunshot ringing in her ears. Now she was simply deaf. Everything had shifted. That was when the tears came again, but this time she wasn't crying for Emmett. She was weeping for herself. She had gone to great lengths to convince herself that she wasn't alone, but like Stan's words, that had been a deception.

For all she knew, Stan had gotten rid of Emmett in order to get her back for leaving him. Anything, no matter how ridiculous, seemed possible.

When her hearing returned, she called Jibril's friend Omar Halawi, and they made arrangements to meet at a café in the Semiramis InterContinental at eight. He told her he was out of town and would have to drive back. Seven hours to go. Outside, the sun was high, bright in the way that only North Africa can be. She smelled car exhaust, and somewhere, maybe on a rooftop, someone was grilling lamb. She heard prayers in the distance, buzzy with the static of overworked speakers. She had time. She went around the apartment, collecting what she thought she might need. She packed her few items into her bag. It occurred to her that she needed clothes, badly. Then she went to Stan's terrace but did not sit, for she wanted to look across the Nile and over the city to see the three pyramids over in Giza, but sun-baked pollution obscured the vista, leaving only a hazy outline of the Great Pyramid, built to house the bones of Pharaoh Khufu. She went back inside.

Before leaving, she checked herself in the mirror. Dabbed on some blush and fixed her eyes. She ran burgundy over her lips, then stared at herself in the mirror, thinking of Stan's lies. She held the lipstick in her hand, staring a full minute before deciding what to write.

It didn't take her long to reach the Semiramis, for it, like Stan's apartment and the embassy itself, was part of the winding nest of streets that comprised Garden City. She walked westward to the Nile before turning right to head up to that beautiful thumb of tower rising from, and being reflected by, the great river. She was breaking a sweat, but not from exertion—it was the adrenaline of her sudden rash decisions.

The lobby was busy, and she stood in line, feeling the anxiety slip away from her as she handed over her passport and asked for a room. It turned out that they had only one free—"Your lucky day"—on the third floor.

The room was small but clean, and she lay down for a while, eyes closed, feeling the depth of her loneliness. From out of that depth the anger grew again, focused on the man who had been lying to her ever since she had arrived in Egypt. She had been betraying him as well, had betrayed them all last year, and that only deepened her anger. After a long time she sat up and searched in her bag until she had found her phone. She powered it up and dialed and said, "You've been lying to me, Stan."

She could hear the pain in his voice as he tried to convince her of his innocence, of his desire to protect her, and the shift in tone when he commanded her to wait at his apartment. "I'll tell you everything you want to know."

What, of all the things that came from his lips, could she believe? And why should she have to second-guess everything? So she hung up, knowing as she did so that she had burned the only bridge she really had. When she turned off the phone the room felt colder. Outside her window, the sun was low over the busy capital.

Omar

1

———

Over the space of his sixty years, twelve spent in the foreign missions section of the Central Security Forces, Omar Halawi had learned that the quickest way to uncover hidden facts is to keep an eye out for things that do not belong. This particular sense had many times proven to be his primary asset, and it was how he came to learn of Jibril Aziz.

Given the wealth of nationalities that made up the United States, it had always amused him how many white men with English and Irish and German surnames the CIA flew into Egypt, and so when, in 2002, a casual report on Harry Wolcott noted a three-hour clandestine meeting with a young Libyan American, Omar took notice. Once they had his name, Omar followed the files backward to the 1993 coup attempt against Muammar Gadhafi and the execution of young Aziz's father. It wasn't long before they had a barebones story for him: Jibril Aziz was in Cairo under nonofficial cover, meeting only occasionally with Wolcott, always outside the embassy, though his primary work had him slipping with mounting frequency over the border into Libya.

At the time, Abdel Suyuti ran Omar's section, and so together they pored over the facts in front of them. Abdel, unlike his successor, had considered it his duty to protect the foreigners in his land, whether or not they were spies. They decided to leave Jibril Aziz alone for the time being, as there was no evidence he was spying on Egypt. Aziz was plainly gathering information on that madman of the western deserts—who, despite proclamations of solidarity between Egypt and Libya, was an embarrassment to all of North Africa.

When Abdel retired in 2004, there had been good reasons for Omar to believe that he would move up to lead the section, so he was surprised to find Ali Busiri, from the sometimes-competing State Security Investigations Service, sitting behind the desk that had been empty for only three days.

Fouada had told him to send in a letter of protest. "It's not done that way," he explained. She didn't care how it was done, she told him. There was a principle here. There was also, he suspected, a woman's desire to be married to an important man, a desire that had remained just beyond her reach for going on three decades, just as the desire for children had been denied them both.

He had not protested Ali Busiri's ascension, but he had asked questions. He'd been around long enough to have friends throughout Central Security, as well as a couple in the very well-informed General Intelligence Service. In a sly café off of Halaat Tarb one old hand explained that Ali Busiri was friendly with Mubarak's inner circle, particularly with Omar Suleiman, director of the General Intelligence Service and arguably the next in line to rule Egypt. Cronyism had given Ali Busiri Abdel's old chair, but what else had he expected? Omar, in the end, was a realist, a flaw that Fouada often pointed out to him. "But don't get down," one of his friends told him. "Busiri's no wilting flower. He did great things at the SSI."

"Like what?"

"Stopped a Japanese Red Army hijacking. This was 1992. They were going to take over a flight from Cairo to Tripoli and demand cash from Gadhafi."

Omar frowned, running a hand through his hair. "I never heard about this."

"Which shows how well he took care of it."

His friend, it turned out, had been right: Busiri seemed born for subterfuge. While on paper their section existed primarily for the protection of various foreign diplomatic corps in the capital, Busiri soon raised the bar, expanding their mandate by issuing new directives to turn diplomatic staff into Egyptian assets.

Before altering their basic purpose, however, Busiri spent weeks reviewing the work that had been done under Abdel Suyuti, and they often had to face Busiri's rage as he blustered on about the ridiculous state the section was in. They'd been sitting on their hands, he told them. Collecting dust. When he came across a file chronicling the activities of one Jibril Aziz, he called Omar into his office. "Am I to believe that you discovered an American spy and didn't do anything about it?" Omar wasn't sure if the question was rhetorical. "Do you want to explain this apparently treasonous behavior?"

Unlike others in the office, Omar was too old to be intimidated by this newcomer's rage. "His territory is Libya, not Egypt. There was no point letting him know that we knew about him. Better to watch from a distance."

"And what has watching for an entire year taught you?"

"He visits often enough to suggest he has a large network inside Libya. He's been building up something valuable."

"How often does he go in?"

"It's irregular."

"How irregular?"

This was all in the file, but he answered anyway. "One or two months between visits. Stays between a week and a month each time."

Busiri sniffed, a sign of irritation. "Can you at least tell me the next time he crosses over? Is that too much to ask?"

"Of course, sir."

When in December 2004 Omar reported that Aziz had crossed over again, his boss said, "Thank you. It's so nice to be trusted with sensitive information."

While Omar bristled at this treatment—he was, after all, ten years Busiri's senior—he couldn't help but recognize that their section was entering a renaissance phase. For the first time in his memory, intelligence was moving *out* of their office on the seventh floor of the Interior Ministry to other parts of Central Security, to SSI, and to

GIS. They were depending less and less on the kindness of other departments. "Independence," Busiri told them during one of their weekly meetings, "is the great reward of intelligence."

Even so, there were failures. In early 2005, a colleague in the office, Hisham Minyawi, recruited a high-ranking official in the Libyan embassy named Yousef Rahim, using a double ploy of bribe and blackmail. There was a night of celebration in the office—cookies and tea for everyone—but it turned sour when, three days later, Rahim was recalled to Tripoli and summarily executed.

A few weeks after that incident, while Ali Busiri and his personal assistant, Rashid el-Sawy, were on a trip to Damascus to discuss new cooperation initiatives, Omar received a call in the office. A young man had been picked up on the Libyan border, hungry and dehydrated, without documents. He'd spoken to the border guards in Libyan Arabic, calling himself Akram Haddad. No one believed it, but since he refused to say more they e-mailed a well-lit photograph to Cairo, and each of the section heads was contacted by the fifth floor to help identify the stranger. Omar gazed at the image from the internal server, and in the features of that vacant face he recognized Jibril Aziz.

He had Sayyid drive him nearly eight hours to the border, where the guards—Bedouins, mostly, for they were the only ones who could take the climate—cleared out a communal dining room for the conversation. Their prisoner sat at the center table, a bowl of soup in front of him. Omar took the seat opposite and laid his fingertips on the edge of the table. In English, he said, "Hello, Jibril."

To his credit, the young man didn't react, only stared into his untouched soup. Only twenty-seven, but he had the skill set of an older man. Or maybe he was just in shock.

Omar continued in English. "There is no need for you to play this game. I am not going to take you away in chains." He patted his pockets, coming up with cigarettes. Back then he never went anywhere without his Winstons. He offered the pack to Jibril, but the young man shook his head. Omar lit one and spoke quietly. "We have been watching your progress for over two years. You are really very talented—that it has taken this long for you to find serious trouble in the Brother Leader's kingdom is a great feat. I know of good men who lasted less than a week before being returned in body bags." He was stretching the truth, but it didn't matter. "Can you look at me?"

Jibril did so. He was thin and too pale, his eyes still bloodshot; the man needed sleep. The border guards had told him that Jibril had appeared with dried blood smeared across his neck, but by then it had been cleaned off, revealing vertical scratches from his ear down to his collarbone. He needed a shave.

Omar said, "If you didn't tell them anything, then your networks are safe. I will not be able to tell them anything because I am not going to ask about your networks. Of course, I would be happy to accept any intelligence you want to share, but I don't want you to think that this is a prerequisite. We are going to give you a shave, some food, and get you back to Harry Wolcott once you're clean and rested."

Silence followed, and Jibril's dark eyes bored into him. He had the eyes of a refugee, as full of mistrust as they were of desperate hope.

"Come," Omar said, standing and making his decision quickly. "I am going to take you home."

Had Busiri been in town, he would have called in for instructions, but this wasn't the case. If he brought Jibril into the office, he would have no choice but to admit everything to Busiri later, and he wanted to keep his options open.

Sayyid drove them back while Jibril dozed in the backseat, and they reached Cairo by early morning. Sayyid helped their American guest to the door of Omar's building in Giza. Omar took the stairs first, climbing to the fifth floor and letting himself in and telling Fouada that they had a guest. "Why didn't you call me?" she demanded, suddenly in a panic, looking around their roomy home for things out of order.

"Because he won't be here. You'll never tell anyone that he was here. Do you understand?"

She did, though she didn't like it, least of all when she saw the squalid condition of the man Sayyid was helping through the door.

They gave him the guest room, the blinds closed, and the planned twenty-four-hour stay turned into three days. By the first evening Fouada had warmed to him. It wasn't so much Jibril she had warmed to, but the sudden presence of someone who, unlike her husband, was in dire need of her care. She washed him with wet towels and fed him soup the way a mother would feed a baby, or at least the way she imagined mothers fed their babies. On the second evening, Omar found her in the guest room singing a lullaby as Jibril slept.

In between these ministrations, Omar would sit with Jibril and talk, but never about work. He admitted to knowing of Jibril's father, the great general Mustafa Aziz. "His death, and the deaths of the others, was an abomination. One of these days, Libya will be free of that man, and it will be because of men like your father, who sowed the seeds of change."

Jibril looked at him, as if judging his honesty. "I'm not sure that's true," he said finally. "I don't think anyone's having an effect."

"That's because you have just had a grand failure. To you, all is destruction and woe. Give it a week, a month, a year. You will be optimistic again, and you will see that your work, as well as your father's, is chipping away at the foundations."

It turned out that Jibril's employers saw it differently. After Jibril had been quietly returned to Harold Wolcott, orders came through from Langley. Jibril was blown, and therefore he was being recalled to Virginia. Before leaving, however, he stopped by and had tea with Fouada until Omar returned home from work. The two men went to the guest room and talked in English in case Fouada was listening, Omar smoking his Winstons. Jibril was less dejected than he had been before, but he had bad news. "Half my network is still in place," he told Omar. "I got word from one of my Bedouins."

"The other half?"

He shook his head. "I don't know how I lost them."

"It happens," Omar said. "Even to the best. How many?"

"Eleven," said Jibril.

After a moment of silence to mourn the losses, Jibril said, "What would you think of working with me?"

"With Harry Wolcott, you mean."

"I mean me. I'm being moved to operation planning. Sometimes I may need help with details. We're not as all-knowing as we want people to think."

Omar grinned.

"It's not volunteer work," Jibril said quickly. "I'm talking about exchanges of information."

"Could you get clearance for such a thing?"

Jibril shrugged. "Asking for clearance might be a mistake."

"I see what you mean," Omar said, warming to the idea. "But I would be under no obligations, you understand? If I am uncomfortable—"

"Then it's silence," Jibril finished.

Though their business was taken care of, Jibril stayed for dinner at Fouada's insistence, and over a platter of grilled lamb Omar watched how his wife fawned with the attentiveness of an adoring mother over this skinny little Libyan American.

2

The section blossomed under Ali Busiri's firm hand. Largely ignored before, they now had a reputation in the ministry, for Busiri had become the go-to man for embassy intrigue. Visitors from the Military Intelligence Services appeared in his office with begging cups in hand. Most Thursdays, GIS chief Omar Suleiman could be found laughing with Busiri over tea. Busiri's greatest pride came when he heard the timid knocks on the door from officers of the SSI—his onetime bosses had come to sit at his knee.

Before the discovery of Zora Balašević, their section was already running twenty-six sources; Busiri was tapped into thirteen percent of the nearly two hundred diplomatic missions in Cairo. Among the larger nations represented, Russia, France, and Australia fed them a regular diet of national and allied intelligence. Intelligence bred more intelligence, for Busiri gave little away for free. Visitors with requests always came with a pocket full of intel, ready to share with the Oracle.

In January 2009, Busiri came to Omar with a special job. "You will create a line of communication with the Americans."

"I thought you already had that. You meet with Harry Wolcott, don't you?"

Busiri smiled, turning his hands palm up. "Occasionally, yes, but I'm thinking of something different. Harry and I have a congenial relationship. I share, he shares, but we have our limits. I'm not sure I believe everything the man says, and he certainly doesn't believe me, but that's the nature of such relationships. What I'd like from you is something different. You will offer yourself to them."

Omar felt a tingle creep over his scalp. "I don't understand."

"Of course you understand. You're being bashful." Busiri winked. "We haven't been able to acquire anyone at their embassy, but there are other ways to deal with them. Our primary goal will be to make them believe certain things. If I tell Harry something, he may or may not believe it. But if I tell him something and he verifies it with someone else in our office, someone he trusts, then he'll pass it on to Langley. You understand?"

Omar did. "What's our secondary goal?"

"Whatever we like," he said. "You won't be a volunteer. You'll demand payment. Not in silver, but concessions. You and I both know plenty of fine businessmen who would be happy to get into the American market. Perhaps we can help them out. Perhaps they will want to show us their appreciation."

Omar made his approach through the most unlikely route, the better to be believed. He stood on a crowded bus beside the embassy's newest employee, Amir Najafi, a contractor with Global Security. He leaned close to the young man's long ear and whispered in Arabic, "Omar Halawi wants to talk. Tell them that." Najafi just stared at him, gape-mouthed, as he quietly disembarked.

The ruse was easier to set up than he would have imagined. Through Najafi he was passed on to Stanley Bertolli, who during their conversation in a small hotel room in Dokki quizzed him on the *why* of his offer. Omar's explanation was as pedestrian as it was believable: He'd been passed over for promotion one time too many, and was ready to start working for himself. Did Omar have a preferred contact? Indeed, he did: the green Najafi. "He's not Agency," Bertolli protested, but Omar insisted.

As the relationship developed, Omar handing Najafi information given to him by Busiri, it occurred to him that he wasn't just doing a service for their section—some items he passed on dealt with other departments. Military and interparliamentary relations were discussed. Trade and commerce were detailed. Analyses of internal dissent were passed on. Busiri had turned Omar into a tool for the entire Egyptian government. Omar couldn't even imagine what his boss was getting in return.

Yet the stress of this heightened deception quickly wore on Omar. In early February 2009, at fifty-eight years of age, he suffered a minor heart attack, and while he was laid up at Dar Al Fouad his doctor put him on drugs and told him to cut down on the stress in his life and quit smoking. He quit smoking.

Later that month, Omar returned home to find Jibril Aziz sitting with Fouada, drinking tea and eating cake. They hadn't spoken since 2005, and he was shocked by the sight of a well-fed, almost cherubic Jibril. Fouada was beside herself with pleasure. "Jibril is *married* now. Can you believe it? I'm telling him why he has to have a child immediately, no hesitation. Tell him I know what I'm talking about."

"She knows what she's talking about," Omar said as he gave the younger man a hug.

Fouada wanted to go out to El Kebabgy for dinner, but seeing Jibril's hesitation Omar suggested they have their meal delivered. She didn't seem to care either way—her little boy had returned.

After eating, the men withdrew to the living room, where Omar had pulled the curtains closed. "You are looking good," Omar told Jibril in English, his fingers twitching as he fingered an imaginary cigarette. "She loves you, you know. Sometimes three days of nursing is all it takes."

"You're a lucky man," Jibril said, and Omar was struck by how diplomatic that sentiment sounded. He wondered how much four years in the Office of Collection Strategies and Analysis had changed the shivering wreck he'd met at the Libyan border.

"This call is not social, yes?"

Jibril shrugged. "Half and half. I was wondering if I could bounce a few ideas off of you."

"Depends on the ideas, does it not?"

Omar settled back in his chair and listened to the castles Jibril had been building out of air—for that was how he understood Jibril's job. Dreamers sitting at their desks, transcribing their fantasies into reality. *What a life,* he thought as he listened to Jibril's dream of a Libya rid of the man who had murdered his father. He had done his homework, analyzing the various exile groups, their strengths and great weaknesses, as well as the conditions that might bring them together. At the time, there was no evidence that a spontaneous uprising could occur in Libya, so it was up to a third party to light the fuse. America, apparently.

Initially, this did not sit well with Omar. He argued that any more American incursions into Muslim lands would break the camel's back. It would give final justification to groups like the Muslim Brotherhood, which plagued Egypt, potentially triggering Islamic coups throughout the Arab world.

"If it's done correctly," Jibril explained, "no one need find out. The story will be that the exile groups, united by their desire for democracy, returned to overthrow the tyrant."

"Democracy?"

Jibril thought a moment. "Freedom."

That word was at least more palatable. "What is it you think you need from me?"

"Some insight," Jibril said. "We'd have to use Egypt and Tunisia as launching points. Tell me how Mubarak would react. Tell me how Ben Ali would react."

"Depends on what they knew."

"I don't think anything could be held back."

Omar considered this. While he suspected the two autocrats would be happy to get rid of the Brother Leader, it occurred to him that they would be too terrified to support a regime change. "Have you thought about the repercussions? Mubarak knows the kind of trouble he has here. The public watched him support your country's invasion of Iraq—in their eyes, an unforgivable mistake. The economy is in very bad shape, and we have been forced to take orders from the International Monetary Fund. Food prices have skyrocketed, and we have started to cut back on public services. We are sick with corruption—this is an illness we had long before Mubarak arrived in 1981, but with the economy in shambles it has gotten worse. And now the people are marching in the streets. More than half our population—sixty percent—is younger than thirty, and they are out of work. The Kefaya movement has given them courage, and we are expecting trouble from some kids on Facebook, calling themselves the April 6 Movement—they have gained seventy thousand members. Imagine, for a moment, what all these young, angry men would do if they saw the Libyans tossing Muammar into the street. How safe would Mubarak be? More importantly, how safe would Mubarak *feel*?"

"But it's different here."

"Yes, but Mubarak and Ben Ali would certainly view it with trepidation."

Jibril's expression changed, as if he'd been drenched in cold water.

"Yet I suppose it *could* be accomplished," Omar mused. "Libya's borders are porous. If the exiles can get in on their own and gain control of one or two ports along the coast, then there would be no need for American troops to set foot in Tunisia or Egypt—the exiles can simply let them in themselves."

"They would have to gather somewhere," Jibril said, nodding as he considered this. "Marsa Matrouh, maybe."

"It would take careful planning," Omar said. "Preparation. The groundwork would have to be laid. But it may be possible."

Jibril brightened.

"Muammar's people will not be sitting still. Remember this. Remember how they caught you. Only four years ago. They are not amateurs."

Jibril didn't need to be reminded of anything.

"Did you ever find out how you were discovered?"

Jibril shook his head. "Never."

They hammered at it until late in the evening, and, knowing that it was only a draft proposal, Omar felt no compunction about helping construct this castle. He soon realized that he was enjoying it. Finally, as they were getting ready for bed, Omar asked for the name of this plan.

For the first time, Jibril hesitated.

"Remember our agreement?"

Jibril smiled, almost embarrassed. "Stumbler."

He laughed, for it sounded ridiculous. "Your idea?"

"A random name pulled off the computer."

"Computers," Omar said. "They will be the death of us all."

By the time he next heard from Jibril, two years later, he and Fouada had almost forgotten about the young man, for their country had been turned upside down. Hosni Mubarak was under house arrest in Sharm el-Sheikh, and the nation was being ruled by Field Marshal Mohamed Hussein Tantawi, chairman of the Supreme Council of the Armed Forces.

The legions of Central Security foot soldiers, most of them uneducated country folk, had splintered, leaving real security to the army as the demonstrators continued, even after Mubarak's ouster, to rip up asphalt and build barricades, demanding more. Busiri's old employers, the SSI, were the protesters' primary target, and everyone knew it was just a matter of time before the State Security Investigations Service was dissolved completely, its administrators jailed and placed on trial. No one believed the protesters would stop with the SSI, and the Central Security Forces, whose disheveled conscripts had become the black-clad enemy of those heady revolutionary days, was certainly going to be next. Everyone would be out, and many would be forced to mount vain defenses in kangaroo courts.

In the corridors you could hear the hum of paper shredders, and the officers had trouble looking each other in the eye. Some whispered hastily hatched ideas of flight, though only a few—notably Hassan Ghali and Rifaat Pasha from Special Operations Command—had actually disappeared. Then there were the unspoken ideas, the plans to build small fortunes before the purges, perhaps by selling secrets. To combat any sudden loss of patriotism, security was beefed up at all the exits, and by then entering or leaving the Interior Ministry building had become worse than boarding an international flight. The day after Jibril's call, on February 23, former policemen demanding their jobs back set fire to cars and one of the buildings inside the Interior Ministry complex.

The chaos, coupled with a suddenly enormous workload, served only to exhaust Omar, who kept checking and rechecking his blood pressure. Home was hardly a relief, for a tight paranoia had taken hold of Fouada.

"See those men? Under that streetlamp. They've been there for *three hours,* Omar! Look how long their hair is! They're taking revenge. Where's your gun?"

Though her words flowed from a wellspring of paranoia, she was right to be worried. His trips to and from the office were often stalled by impromptu checkpoints set up by angry revolutionaries.

With all this going on, how could he even think of Jibril Aziz? He might have been reminded of him when the Day of Revolt occurred on February 17 next door in Libya, but that unprecedented demonstration of popular dissent had given him no more than a passing feeling for the young man who had slept in his guest bedroom and been loved by his wife. So when his phone rang a little before midnight on February 22 and he reached over, his pillow damp from the sweat of a nightmare he couldn't remember, it took a moment for him to realize who he was talking to. "Omar, it's me. Jibril."

Omar got out of bed, padding out of the room in bare feet, whispering, "Jibril?"

"It's me."

"Where are you?" he asked as he continued to the kitchen and turned on the light. He was dressed in underwear, feeling the chill, but he didn't want to go back to get his robe; he didn't want to wake Fouada. "Are you here?"

"No," Jibril told him, then hesitated. A transatlantic gap followed, then Jibril said, "They're doing it, Omar."

"What?"

"Stumbler. They're doing it."

It took another moment for him to reel back his memories to two years ago, that late-night conversation. At first, he didn't quite understand Jibril's anxiety. "Thank you for the information."

"Omar, *listen*. What time is it there?"

"Midnight."

"Right, right. Sorry. But pay attention. They're doing it *now*, not five days ago. Are you following?"

Then, like a light being turned on, he saw it. *Now*, meaning five days after the Day of Revolt. Meaning: Libyan corpses in the street. Meaning: a swift overthrow of a regime being softened by the bodies of Libyan citizens. "I find this hard to believe," Omar said finally. "As far as I know they have said nothing to us. They have not laid the groundwork."

"They don't have to, Omar. Ben Ali is gone. Mubarak is gone. No one's going to stop a band of exiles from crossing the border. If the Benghazi ports aren't open yet, they soon will be."

He closed his eyes, trying to envision all of this, and it was frightening how easily it came to him. He opened his eyes, seeing 12:09 on the microwave. "What are you going to do?"

"I'm going to look into it," Jibril said with a young man's conviction. "There's a man in Budapest who might be able to find out more. I think he'll help."

"Who?" Omar asked, a tingle already tickling his scalp.

"Emmett Kohl. He's a deputy consul, used to work in Cairo."

"Right," Omar said, thinking of that man's wayward wife. What a small world it was.

"I've gotten word to some exiles who can meet me in Budapest. Then I'll fly to Cairo."

Recovered now, Omar said, "Fouada will be happy."

"Don't tell her," Jibril said quickly. "Don't tell anyone. I don't know who to trust yet."

Though he promised to remain silent, it was a midnight promise made only half awake. So in the morning, after laboring over the issue as he suffered the indignities of front-door security, he knocked on Ali Busiri's door and sat down to explain the situation. Busiri seemed angered by it, but said, "We know about Stumbler already."

"How?"

"How do you think? Sophie Kohl passed it on to Zora Balašević."

"Well, Jibril is going to meet with Emmett Kohl."

Busiri frowned. "Why?"

"He thinks Kohl is trustworthy. Of course, he knows nothing about the wife."

This seemed to trouble Busiri. He looked at some papers spread across his desk. "What do you think, Omar? Are the Americans really stupid enough to do this?"

Omar didn't think so, but . . . "After the Bay of Pigs, who knows?"

Burisi stretched out and pulled at his ear. "Maybe the Libyans will welcome them with open arms."

"At first."

"At first, it's always sunshine and flowers, isn't it?" Busiri said, grinning; then he got hold of himself. "Thank you for sharing this, Omar. If he gets in touch again, let me know."

Jibril called again on Saturday the twenty-sixth. He was in town, and Omar went to his room on the sixth floor of the Semiramis. He had told Fouada that there was an evening meeting, an emergency, and at first she had blocked his exit. "It's *dark* out there, Omar. You won't be able to see them until they're right on you." Riding the hotel elevator skyward, he could still feel where her fingers had clawed at his arm.

Jibril looked haggard and unshaven, but he was still the same boy they had welcomed into their home. He kissed Omar's cheeks and asked after Fouada. "All this hasn't been too hard on her?"

"She's strong," Omar lied. "How is marriage?"

Jibril blushed. "I'm going to be a father."

Omar clapped his hands and gave him a congratulatory hug. "Tell Inaya that we are wishing her all good things. Does she even know about us?"

Jibril nodded, smiling. "I left her your phone number. In case."

"Should we expect a call?"

Jibril shook his head. "She just wanted a number. Any number. She's worried about me."

"That is because she loves you."

The moment passed, and Jibril's smile faded as he went to the clock radio by the bed and turned it on. It was tuned to 92.7 "Mega FM," a pop music station. Jibril raised the volume to an uncomfortable level, then sat on the edge of the bed, waving Omar to the chair he'd positioned close to him. Omar settled down as Jibril leaned close and spoke softly. "I'm going in. On Thursday."

Omar had expected this. "You need help?"

Jibril shook his head.

"What did Emmett Kohl say?"

Another shake of the head. "He's more deluded than I thought. He doesn't believe it."

"What does he believe?"

"He doesn't think anyone's doing it. He thinks that, if anything, someone's trying to shut down Stumbler before it starts."

"But you do not believe this."

"I believe the data, Omar. I believe what I can see." Again, Jibril described the abductions. "They haven't been seen since. Nowhere. They're either in Egypt or Tunisia, or they've already crossed the border."

"So what can you do?"

"My networks weren't entirely destroyed—you know that. They're part of the uprising, I'm sure. I need to meet them face-to-face and tell them to defend their rear. The last I heard, a few were sighted in Ajdabiya. I'll get the updated list from my Bedouin in Al `Adam, and then track them down."

"How are you getting in?"

Jibril seemed to blush. "The Agency's giving me someone from the embassy."

Omar hesitated, not sure he'd heard right. "The CIA is giving you a guide?"

Jibril nodded stiffly. The radio cut to an old Britney Spears hit.

"Does this not suggest," Omar said slowly, "that they are *not* behind Stumbler?"

"What it suggests," Jibril said, for he'd dealt with this contradiction already, "is that they want to make it appear as if they aren't behind it."

Omar held up a hand. "Wait. You are talking to your employers. They're helping you go in. What is their story?"

"That they don't know. But they've seen the data, too, and they're worried someone else has gotten hold of Stumbler. Their worry, they claim, is that al Qaeda is going to use it to take over Libya."

Thinking of the Stumbler plans moving from Sophie Kohl to Zora Balašević to his office, Omar said, "Maybe not al Qaeda, but someone could have gotten hold of the plans. Information leaks. You know that."

"Is Egypt running Stumbler?"

Omar gave it a moment's thought. Busiri had probably passed the plan up the ladder, but what were the odds that their new military leaders would attempt to manipulate the Libyan revolution? They could hardly maintain control of their own country. "No," he said.

"Right," Jibril agreed. "And Tunisia doesn't have the resources to pull this off."

"So you are convinced America is doing it."

"I don't see any other options."

"Yet you put yourself into their hands," Omar said. "They are going to kill you."

"They won't," Jibril said, shaking his head. "Not before they get my network."

"You didn't give it to them?"

"Why do you think I was sent back to Virginia?"

"You were blown."

"Maybe, but what Langley really wanted was the network, so someone else could take it over."

"Why . . ." Omar began, shocked by this insubordination. "Why didn't you give it to them?"

"Eleven of my people were killed. I still don't know how they were discovered, and I wasn't about to share the names of the survivors with a bureaucracy as big as the Agency's. I wanted to give those people a rest."

"You took a rest as well. Six years later, you're coming back."

Locating the events in time seemed to put them in perspective.

Both men were silent a moment. Omar said, "Did you promise them the network?"

He smiled. "Of course, but I'm not handing it over. I kept their names in a book that I left with my Bedouin. Only I can get hold of it. As long as Langley doesn't have that book, I'm safe."

"Let us hope they don't get it."

"Agreed."

"And let us hope that your Libyan friends welcome you with open arms."

The radio sang, *Oops! I did it again.*

"The most important hope," Omar continued, "is that this is a quick and safe trip, and that you are home soon with your wife and child."

Jibril nodded. "God willing," he said, then got up to turn off the radio.

3

After the Semiramis, he called Busiri and drove over to his opulent villa in Maadi, an upscale neighborhood full of embassies and foreigners and affluent Egyptians. Quiet, unlike Omar's place in the twisting cacophony of Giza. It was nearly ten when he parked outside the gate. He didn't get out. Five minutes passed; then Busiri stepped out the front door and crossed the dry lawn, wearing the same suit he'd worn to the office that day, but no tie. He opened the passenger door and got inside. "It's late, Omar," he said with a hint of impatience.

In great detail, Omar told him of Jibril's plans.

"So he really does believe America is doing this?"

"He does, but Emmett Kohl doesn't."

"What does Kohl believe?"

"The opposite. He thinks someone is shutting it down."

"CIA?"

"The Libyans. If so, then the question is: Who told the Libyans?"

Busiri frowned, considering this. "You say the embassy has given him a guide?"

"I don't know who, but I can have Mahmoud keep an eye on him."

"No," Busiri said, shaking his head. "We'll need Mahmoud for other things. Sayyid, too. This is going to be another busy week. It doesn't matter who's taking Aziz in—it just matters that he's going in."

"You're not going to pursue this?" Omar asked.

"I'll go upstairs and talk with our masters. But I don't think they'll believe it. Other than a few public statements about the will of the people, the Americans resisted the temptation to meddle here."

"Mubarak was their friend. Gadhafi isn't."

"Friends?" Busiri asked with a wry smile. "In international diplomacy?"

"Well, someone who gave them what they wanted more often than he didn't."

Busiri rocked his head, as if this were a marginally better description. "Well, we'll see what our masters think." He patted Omar's knee. "I appreciate this."

"It's my job," Omar pointed out.

Busiri sniffed. "Maybe, but you needn't have been such an excellent co-worker. After all, you did expect to be sitting at my desk when Abdel retired."

The subject had never come up between them. "Decisions were made. I'm not complaining."

"It's a thankless job, you know. The pay is atrocious, and those friends you see filing in and out of my office? Wolves, every one."

Omar nodded at the walls surrounding Busiri's villa. "The pay seems to be sufficient."

"Marry rich," he advised, smiling. As he opened the door he added a quick "Salaam" and left.

Despite Busiri's conviction that this wasn't important, on Thursday Omar left home before sunrise and parked behind a taxi outside the Semiramis Hotel, waiting in the dark. Just after the 4:00 A.M. Fajr prayers, Jibril emerged from the lobby and climbed into an old Peugeot. The driver, a large black man, chilled his blood. If the Americans wanted to kill Jibril, then a man that size would be an ideal vessel. As he drove behind them, he called and left a message with the office that he would be out sick.

Since he knew their destination, there was no need to remain in sight of the Peugeot, so he lagged far behind, only occasionally speeding up to be sure he hadn't lost them along the desert road leading to

El Alamein on the coast. Halfway to the border, Ali Busiri called to check on his condition, and he forced a nasal sound into his voice as he complained of sinus troubles. "It sounds like you're in a car, Omar."

"I'm on my way to the doctor's."

When, at around ten, the Peugeot turned off at Marsa Matrouh, he had a moment's panic. *This* was where they were going to get rid of Jibril. But a glance at his own fuel gauge showed him the truth, and after the Peugeot refueled he did the same thing himself.

They stopped in the city center, and he was surprised to see the men split up. Jibril headed to a small, ramshackle café, his phone to his ear, while the black man took off in the opposite direction and began to window shop among hawkers gesturing at open crates, walking in the direction of the white sand beach. What was going on?

Soon, Jibril was joined by a man in a red-checked ghutra, and they began to talk. While Omar didn't know the man, he suspected this was another of Jibril's Libyans, perhaps a splinter from his core network, who could add to Jibril's knowledge. The meeting was brief, and then Jibril and the black man were driving again.

He considered following them across the border, but he'd reached the limits of his authority and responsibility. He'd made sure Jibril made it through Egyptian territory unscathed, and now it was time to return home.

He didn't reach Cairo until after nine that night, and by then, with the little sleep he'd had the previous night, he really did feel sick. He was too old for road trips, and perhaps too old for intrigues, and his body was finally starting to protest. Fouada asked where he'd been. When he gave her a tired shrug, she raised her voice to a shrill pitch. Fear was taking its toll on her as well, and he was the only person she could take it out on. In the midst of her tirade, she said, "What could I tell Ali? A woman who doesn't know where her husband is is no wife. He knows that as well as anyone."

He raised his hands. "Busiri?"

"Of course. He called here to check on you."

Why hadn't he called Omar's cell phone?

Because, Omar realized with despair, he hadn't believed his feigned sickness. In the morning, Omar would have to mend that bridge. Then he heard something on the television. He left Fouada standing in the kitchen as he wandered into the living room, and that was when he learned of Emmett Kohl's murder the previous night.

Again, that chill went through him. If they were willing to kill their own diplomats, then what was Jibril to them? Nothing. Get him into the lawless deserts of Libya and leave the body to be swallowed by the sands. He went for his cell phone and called Busiri.

"Omar," Busiri said. "How are you feeling?"

"Tired, Ali. What's this about Emmett Kohl?"

"It seems he was killed."

"What leads?"

"They're pinning it on an Albanian. Gjergj Ahmeti."

Omar didn't know the name, but Busiri's quick description of Ahmeti fleshed out a simple enough picture. He was the kind of man the Agency might hire if it wanted to remain at arm's length from a murder. He was the kind of man any government would be happy to use. "I'm told the American embassy is working furiously on it," Busiri told him.

"Or pretending to."

"No, I think it's in earnest. I called Harry Wolcott to give condolences. He's a mess. He's hoping Stanley Bertolli can come up with something. Did you know of Bertolli's relationship with Mrs. Kohl?"

"Zora told me."

"We should watch him," Busiri said. "Information has a way of collecting like dust mites, and it would be preferable if he didn't learn that Mrs. Kohl was ours."

"I understand."

"In fact," Busiri went on, "we might want to help him out. Perhaps you'd like to warn him that he needs to be looking over his shoulder."

"It's not a bad idea," Omar admitted.

After a pause, Busiri said, "Did he make it over the border all right?"

"What?"

"Jibril Aziz. You were waiting outside his hotel."

There was no point arguing with the facts, so he simply said, "You had me watched?"

"You thought I wouldn't verify your information?"

"He made it all right."

"Glad to hear it," Busiri said. "Maybe next time you'll tell me this without me having to ask."

"Apologies, Ali."

Before heading into the office in the morning, Omar sent a coded message to Paul Johnson, who had become his embassy contact after Amir Najafi's death in November. They met in a Zamalek café not far from Paul's apartment, the young, bleary-eyed American clutching desperately at his coffee. "You are looking in the wrong direction," he told Paul.

"What?" Paul turned to look behind himself. "Where?"

"I am talking about the murder of Emmett Kohl. Tell Stanley Bertolli that you need to look at yourselves."

Paul frowned, slowly absorbing his words. He leaned close, a high whisper. "What does that mean? Are you saying someone in the *embassy* killed him?"

Omar shook his head. "I don't know. I am talking about your agency. Here, or back in America—I don't know."

"But . . . but *why*?"

"To keep Emmett quiet."

"Quiet about what?"

He considered telling the young man the whole story. Stumbler, Jibril Aziz, the co-opting of the civil war raging next door . . . but, no. Stanley Bertolli would be sharp enough to ask the logical next question: How did the Egyptians know about Stumbler? Then the connections leading back to Sophie Kohl would be child's play.

"Just tell him," Omar said. "Tell Stanley Bertolli to be careful." Then he got up and walked out, leaving the puzzled American to his steaming cup.

4

Afterward, once he'd made his way through the meticulous entry procedure to reach the seventh floor, he found Rashid el-Sawy walking the ministry corridors, looking for Busiri. "Rashid," Omar said, waving him over. "A word, please."

El-Sawy joined him in his office and closed the door. While he had been part of their section since the start of Busiri's tenure seven years ago, coming with Busiri from the SSI, Omar had seldom spoken to el-Sawy one-on-one. The younger man had a way of entering and exiting the building without anyone noticing, and during meetings could maintain an unnatural silence as the men around him shouted and cajoled. Sometimes Omar suspected this was due to embarrassment over his flat American accent; other times he suspected that el-Sawy was calculating how best to dispose of everyone in the room. Over the years he had performed a variety of undercover jobs for the section, often using his American childhood to great advantage; his most common alias was Michael Khalil, Federal Bureau of Investigation. He was one of those loyal dogs who tie their entire future to the fate of another man, rather than to the fate of an office—which, in light of the imminent dissolution of the SSI, had clearly been the wiser choice.

"How are things?" Omar asked.

El-Sawy shrugged. He was a tall man, easily six feet, and he seemed to be aware of this, always preferring to stand rather than sit. "You've heard about the SSI raids?"

Omar shook his head.

"The protesters. They've started breaking into SSI buildings around town, and of course the guards are just letting them in. They're collecting files. They say they want evidence of the SSI's crimes. They're going to start building guillotines soon."

Omar hadn't known this—he'd been too distracted by Jibril. He thought of el-Sawy's long tenure in the SSI and wondered how many of those files chronicled his visits to torture cells. He imagined el-Sawy was worried out of his mind, but there was no sign of this in his face. "Have you heard anything from Libya?" Omar asked.

El-Sawy frowned. "Why would I have heard anything?"

"Because you tracked me yesterday. I assume it was you. You followed me all the way to the border. No?"

"No," el-Sawy said.

"I've talked to Ali," Omar went on, despite the denial. "I should have reported in, but Jibril Aziz is a friend. I wasn't sure I'd get permission to keep an eye on him."

El-Sawy nodded again, a sharp movement that suggested the subject was finished. "Is that it?"

"Well, yes," Omar said, feeling vaguely insulted. "I want you to understand that I'm not complaining. You were doing your job."

"I *was* doing my job," el-Sawy said, "but not here. I wasn't even in Cairo. I only just got back. Is that it?" He stepped back to the door.

Did it even matter who had been watching him yesterday? Not really. "Wait," Omar said. "I want to look at some of the material we received from Sophie Kohl. The Stumbler file."

"I'll have to ask Ali."

"I'll ask him. Is he around?"

"Who do you think I've been looking for?" el-Sawy said before leaving.

It turned out that Busiri was not in the building, and so in lieu of the Stumbler documents he retrieved a file stocked with employees of the American embassy and looked through it until he'd found the big black man who'd driven Jibril to the border. He called Mahmoud and Sayyid to his office and explained that he wanted them to begin surveillance on an American, John Calhoun, who was living in Zamalek. "He may not be around yet, but either later today or tomorrow he'll get home, and I want to know what he's up to."

When Busiri arrived in the afternoon, Omar asked to take a look at the Stumbler file.

Busiri leaned back, the heels of his hands resting on the desk. "Why?"

"Because I've never seen it. Jibril described it to me, but I never read the final draft."

"I'm not sure you need to," Busiri said. "Jibril Aziz wrote it, and now the Americans are running it."

"Jibril certainly believes that, but he's emotional. He's young."

Busiri shrugged. "I'll have it sent over."

Mahmoud called when John Calhoun got home on foot. "The man's a mess. Filthy. Barely able to walk. Should we collect him?"

"No, no. Just watch."

He received the Stumbler file at four and stayed late to read it. He was near the end when Mahmoud called again. "Harry Wolcott just visited him. I think they know we're here."

"They're in a foreign country. They should expect it. Just stick to him."

When he got home, he found Fouada napping in front of the television. There was a plate of dinner in the kitchen, and he ate quietly, trying not to wake her. His phone, however, rang loudly, and as he answered it he heard her saying, "What! What?"

"He's at a bar now," said Mahmoud. "Deals. Expatriate place. Sayyid just went in to take a look. Oh—he's coming back. What?"

"You're here," Fouada said, stumbling into the kitchen. Her hair looked like a bird's nest.

He smiled at her and said into the phone, "What is it?"

"Sayyid tells me John Calhoun is talking with Rashid el-Sawy."

"What?"

Fouada opened the refrigerator, saying, "We're almost out of water."

Sayyid took the phone. "He's talking as if they're friends. They're with a woman—a friend of Calhoun's, I think. The three of them at a table. What should we do?"

Fouada took out a half-full bottle of Evian and, seeing what was on Omar's plate, said, "Don't tell me you're eating that chicken cold."

Why was el-Sawy meeting with the man who had taken Aziz over the border? Was he following his own investigation? "Don't approach," he told Sayyid. "Did he see you?"

"I stopped at the door. No, he didn't see me."

"Then pull back. Both of you. Let me find out what's going on."

He hung up and submitted to Fouada's mothering, waiting as she microwaved the remaining chicken and steamed some couscous for him. He listened to her stories of the day. Her paranoia, he was happy to hear, had ebbed. Her husband had not been ripped apart by angry mobs. Their place had not been ransacked. She had not been raped. She was beginning to realize that when the world changes, most of it remains the same.

After dinner, he withdrew to the guest room and called Busiri to ask about el-Sawy's interest in Calhoun. Busiri paused before answering. "Don't take this badly, Omar, but I'd like you to pull back from the Aziz situation. It's too personal for you. Rashid is better equipped to deal with it. He's used to working undercover—he's nearly American, after all. He'll find out what happened to Jibril, and then I'll tell you."

It was a brush-off, but Omar accepted it. Busiri was right—he *was* getting emotional over this, though no one outside of his skin could have really suspected it. Certainly Fouada couldn't tell; she just fed him and prepared for bed talking about the lack of water, and how could she have been so distracted to have forgotten about it?

He wasn't thinking of water, though, and as she drifted to sleep beside him, he remembered Stumbler.

Stage 1: Collect exiles right off the street. London, Paris, Brussels, New York. They disappear in the middle of their lives, no one the wiser.

Stage 2: Reassemble them just outside the Libyan border with a contingency of approximately a hundred American troops—Special Forces, each of North African descent, dressed in civilian clothes—as well as volunteers previously collected from the exile population. Half sit in wait in Medenine, Tunisia, while the other half hole up in Marsa Matrouh. The plan even listed the addresses of two ideal locations, one in each town—houses owned by sympathetic Libyans. They await the signal.

Stage 3: The signal. Networks within Libya rise up in three cities: Zuwarah, Ajdabiya, Benghazi.

Stage 4: Entry. The exile forces cross into Libya, surprising the Libyan armed forces, while the networks move their focus to the ports. Undercover ships begin supplying arms.

Jibril's predictions for success ranged from two to six months, but the primary objective of Stumbler was less a quick end to Gadhafi's regime than the post-Gadhafi political landscape. Having been viewed as early saviors of the revolution, the exiles would naturally form the new power elite who owed their sudden good fortunes to one country, and one country alone.

There was a time when this plan would have been less cynical than it now appeared. Now, the only moral course was to arm the rebels and let them take care of their own future.

Omar felt the weight of guilt. He could have squelched the operation during the planning stages, simply by insisting to Jibril that Mubarak and Ben Ali would treat any such incursion on their territories as acts of war. Jibril would have been dejected, but he very likely would have accepted his opinion and tossed Stumbler into the wastebasket.

He imagined Jibril at that very moment, over in Ajdabiya, making harried contact with his network, telling them that America, the country they had once risked their lives for, was now preparing to take advantage of their sacrifices. How would he put it? How could he break such news to them? Would they believe him? Yes, for they would be able to read the conviction in his face. Such an earnest young man.

5

On Saturday he resolved to stay out of it. He took Fouada to El Kebabgy for lunch, on the southern tip of Gezira Island, and from the rooftop terrace of the Sofitel they could see the filthy Nile flowing past and hear the noise of a demonstration in the direction of Tahrir. Feeling reflective, he told her about how naive they'd been—everyone in the security forces—before January 25. "This group of kids, they were on Facebook, calling people out to demonstrate. A joke, of course, having their demonstration on Police Day."

"Not a joke," Fouada said quietly. "A point."

He nodded, conceding this. "In the office, the other men laughed about it. 'They think they're going to pull another Tunis,' they said. So narrow-minded. These kids had been posting videos online of police torturing people with broom handles, evil things. The protesters had even been trained in peaceful resistance by Serbs—Otpor, the student group that took down Slobodan Milošević. Peaceful resistance?" He shook his head. "You can imagine what kind of jokes those boneheads in the office came up with. They understood it finally, shutting off the cell phones and Internet, but it was too late. The kids had modeled their flag on Otpor's—a fist. Peaceful resistance turned out to be tougher than anyone thought."

Fouada let him speak for a while, though he knew it wasn't the kind of conversation she'd been hoping for, and afterward they drove back to Giza, away from the demonstrations. At home, he avoided the news by fielding calls from a cousin in Port Said who wanted to worry with someone about his daughter's upcoming wedding. His plan went well until four in the afternoon, when Fouada began dressing to go out. "Where are we going?" he asked.

"Not we. Me," she said. "Don't you remember?"

He didn't.

"Junah's having her birthday party tonight. I promised I'd go. And I told you it was only women—not that I thought you'd want to come."

He smiled, saying, "Of course I remember," but not remembering at all. With everything else, this was just one more thing that had slipped his mind. Maybe, he mused, he should spend the evening planning his retirement.

Yet after calling her a taxi, walking her downstairs, and then coming back up to sit in the silent living room, his mind returned inevitably to Stumbler, to Jibril, and to John Calhoun and Rashid el-Sawy. Then he remembered the plan. Stage 2: Half the exiles collect in Marsa Matrouh. There was more to it, more detail—a building in the neighborhood around the old soccer field. He couldn't remember the address.

He drove back to the office and suffered through another body check before heading up to the empty seventh floor. He found the Stumbler file still locked in his desk and went through the pages until he had the Marsa Matrouh location: the corner of Tanta Street and Al Hekma.

That night, he told Fouada his plans, and she looked troubled. She didn't understand why he had to leave at four o'clock the next morning to drive to Marsa Matrouh. "I thought we could visit friends," she said. "A Sunday out. Today you seemed so . . . so social."

"You visit," he said, kissing her. "But I'll be gone all day. You'll be safe?"

"In that case," she said, some of the old fear creeping into her face, "I'll stay in."

They had been married more than thirty years now, and while

she suffered bouts of a fear that could shake the foundations of their relationship, he had long ago learned to respect this woman. Love, also, but love was too sandy a foundation to build a life on. He didn't like the idea of her sitting fearfully all day in this living room. "Would you like to come?"

She was shocked. "What?"

"It'll be long and uncomfortable, but maybe it'll be more interesting than that television."

This was, it turned out, an inspired suggestion. Fouada helped pry him out of bed in those predawn hours and get breakfast into his stomach. On the road, her conversation kept him pleasantly distracted from the things he would otherwise have glowered over—his aching back, for example, and the feeling that he was far, far too old to be driving a car six hours in one direction. She was so thrilled by their unexpected trip together that she never thought to complain about the discomfort, becoming instead an ideal travel companion, and the six-hour trip felt more like three—or, say, four. Not once did she ask why they were driving to a distant port town—she was just happy to have been brought along. He would have to do this more often.

By ten thirty, though, when they pulled into Marsa Matrouh, they were both flagging. Omar parked on Al Hekma, just off of the main road, around the corner from the dilapidated café where Jibril had met his contact. As they got out, a fresh burst of salty Mediterranean air enveloping them, it occurred to him that the café was only five or six blocks from the intersection of Al Hekma and Tanta. Jibril's contact had come *from* that address. So he took Fouada to the sidewalk café, where they ordered tea and sandwiches, and then he said, "I'm going to have to step away. A half hour, no longer. Will you be all right?"

She smiled, patting his hand. "I've always been all right, Omar."

He kissed the knuckles of her hand and left, the sun beating down on him the whole way. He'd forgotten to bring a hat.

Though the Stumbler plans didn't list a house number, it didn't take him long to figure out the building he was looking for. It was two doors west of the intersection, the only one that could be used to lodge a large number of fighters. An old, unassuming building, concrete, two stories high. With half its high windows boarded up, it appeared to be abandoned. The front door, though, was clean, as were the front steps, and he heard a radio playing classical music—something by Hasan Rashid, he thought. He pressed the buzzer and waited. A minute later, the door opened, and he immediately recognized the man who had worn a red-checked ghutra when he met with Jibril. Now his head was uncovered, and his graying hair shot out at all angles. He was skinny—not frail, but wiry—with sun-cured skin. Omar introduced himself, then stated his employer, flashing an ID card. He was friendly about it, but maintained an air of command as he asked the man's name—"Qasim"—and then asked if they could speak inside, out of the heat. Hesitant, Qasim let him inside.

The building was in the early stages of destruction. While a door to the right led to a functioning apartment, from which the music drifted, as he looked toward the back of the building he saw that walls had been smashed out, creating a rough cavernous space. "Redecorating?" Omar asked.

Qasim laughed nervously. "I just live in the apartment. I don't know what they're doing with the rest of it."

"But it's a big space," Omar pointed out.

"Yes, it is."

"Big enough for a hundred men. Big enough, too, for their weapons."

Silence. He turned to see Qasim's mouth clamp shut, eyes big.

"Come," Omar said to him, touching his shoulder. "Let's sit down."

They went into the small, dirty apartment and settled on chairs coated in concrete dust. The man was shaking. Omar walked over to the old transistor radio and switched it off. He said, "Where are they?"

Qasim shook his head, almost frantic.

"Where," Omar said, "are Yousef al-Juwali, Waled Belhadj, Abdel Jalil, Mohammed el-Keib, and Abdurrahim Zargoun?"

The man's mouth was hanging open, his head swiveling back and forth, but slowly now, a quiet *no*.

"If they're not here," Omar said, "then where would they be? Was the collection point changed?"

"No," Qasim finally got out, a whisper. "It wasn't changed. But I've seen no one."

"What did Jibril talk to you about?"

The man blinked, confused.

"The man you met in that café down the street. Three days ago. Thursday."

"Haddad," the man said. "Akram Haddad. He asked the same thing. He asked where they were. I said I didn't know. No one's spoken to me for years. I've heard *nothing*."

Omar nodded, accepting this. The poor man was terrified. He got up, ready to leave, then noticed an old electric clock on the wall. "Is that time right?"

Qasim looked at it. "Yes."

"Would you like to pray together?"

The man blinked rapidly, then shrugged. "Okay," he said and went to find a large mat he kept rolled up beside the refrigerator. It had been a long time since Omar had prayed, but he thought he could remember it well enough.

Later, once he'd returned to Fouada and they were drinking tea under an umbrella, he puzzled over Qasim's story. If Stumbler was in motion, then why hadn't the exiles arrived? Had they switched the entry point to Tunisia? That made no sense, for the Egyptian side of Libya was almost entirely in rebel hands.

Fouada smiled at him. "Did you ever think of retiring here?"

He blinked, suddenly ripped from his thoughts. "Retire?" Though he'd thought of retiring last night, it had been a passing idea. What did a man do when he retired?

"You can swim here," she told him. "The water's clean, nothing like the Nile."

He opened his mouth, unsure what to say, and was surprised by his own words: "I just prayed with a man I've never met before."

His wife's face creased; she was struck as much by the non sequitur as by the act he had admitted to. "I'm happy to hear it. You should pray more often."

"I think you're right."

"What's changed?"

He frowned, considering this. "What hasn't changed?"

She smiled at that wisdom; then they were both startled by the ringing of his phone. He looked at the number—he didn't know it, but he did recognize the country code. Who would be calling from America? Unsure, he answered it, watching Fouada turn to gaze up the quaint, sun-cracked street, imagining a new life in Marsa Matrouh.

A woman's voice: "Omar Halawi?"

"Yes."

She continued in English: "My name is Inaya Aziz. We've never met, but you know my husband, Jibril."

As he listened with trembling hands to this woman's story, he gradually felt that he was being cornered by wives. Fouada was in front of him, asking him to change his entire life, and in his ear the wife of Jibril Aziz was asking if he had any news of Jibril's health. Omar gave Fouada an apologetic smile, then rose, bringing the phone with him to the edge of the street, where the sun caught him again as old cars rattled by, spewing smoke.

He told Inaya Aziz that, as of Thursday, Jibril was in excellent health. "Then why hasn't he called?" she asked, and he tried to reassure her. He doubted his success, but she let it go and asked if he would please help a friend of hers named Sophie Kohl, whose husband had recently been killed. "I believe her, Mr. Halawi. She needs the help of people who care about Jibril. From what he's told me, I believe you care for Jibril."

"This is true, Mrs. Aziz, but I'm not sure you understand my position here. There's not much I can do. Not much I'm *allowed* to do."

"Talk to her. Just talk to her. How would you feel if your wife was killed in a restaurant, and no one would give you any answers?"

As she said those words, he swiveled to get a look at Fouada at their table, smiling at him. He gave her a little wave.

"Listen, Mr. Halawi. It's up to you. I've already given her your number, and she's going to call soon. You can answer it or not. As a favor to Jibril, and to me, I ask that you help her."

She hung up on him, and he stared a moment at the dead phone, then returned to his chair. Fouada stared questioningly at him. She looked so curious that he couldn't help himself. He said, "I just had the strangest conversation."

"Really? Who was it? That bastard Busiri?"

He waved that away—she'd never forgiven Ali for taking the job that had rightfully been her husband's. "It was Jibril Aziz's wife, Inaya."

Her face brightened. "Inaya! I've dreamed of that girl! How does she sound? Very clever? I'll bet—it's Jibril's woman, after all."

"She sounds very intelligent. She—"

He stopped as, on the table, his phone began to ring again. It was a Cairo number.

"Is that her calling back?"

He just stared at the phone.

"Well, if you're not going to answer it I will."

She reached out a hand, and he snapped up the phone. On the fifth ring, he answered it.

Sophie

1

1991

Zora's friends were numerous and varied, and none of them, as far as Sophie could tell, were criminals. They were artists and writers and students of various disciplines, intelligent people who wore their intelligence loosely, never afraid to slip off of their high chairs and laugh at themselves. After the self-conscious intellectuals of Harvard, this impressed her deeply. They seemed attracted to Sophie and Emmett's exoticism, but they had also been presented with a challenge the moment Zora introduced them: *These my educated friends from America, who have come for to learn everything.* Her friends took this seriously.

On that first day a gaunt medical student named Viktor gave them a lecture on the geography of socialist Yugoslavia: the plains of Vojvodina (of which Novi Sad was the capital), the genteel mountains of Slovenia, the great valleys of Macedonia, the Adriatic beaches of Croatia, and the wild crags of Bosnia and Montenegro and Kosovo—the birthplace of Serbian Orthodoxy. "What you have to understand is that, since the end of the Second World War, we've had every natural advantage right here in our borders. Lakes, mountains, sea—everything except deserts, as you have in America. We've always been able to travel, but going to other countries is a little depressing because of what we have at home. Everyone here has their own reasons for wanting to keep Yugoslavia together, but this is mine—I want to be able to see everything without having to leave my home." He turned to Zora. "Did that make sense?"

Emmett answered: "Absolutely."

Viktor held forth at the same central café as the day before, around the corner from their hotel, and after him a bobbed sculptor cum linguist named Nada talked them through the political development of Serbo-Croatian, the official language of Yugoslavia—"a cross-lingual compromise." Afterward, they piled into Zora's rickety Yugo to reach the Strand, a length of sandy beach along the Danube where they drank beer and bought oily paper bags of fried sardines to eat off of toothpicks. They found more of Zora's friends lounging on beach chairs under the shadow of *Most slobode,* Liberty Bridge. Eight years later, NATO planes would destroy that bridge, but in 1991 there was no sign that anyone was worried about war. They just wanted to show their new American friends a good time.

When they weren't lecturing about the many facets of Yugoslav history and culture, they asked questions about America.

Was Thomas Jefferson in favor of slavery?

Why do Indians live in squalor?

How hard is it to get a residence permit?

As the sun began to set, Nada broke out a foil-wrapped chunk of hashish and rolled it with tobacco squeezed from one of Zora's cigarettes. Sophie hesitated, but Emmett didn't, and so she followed his lead. Resistance was just a passing thought. The stew of alcohol and hash helped her relax fully into the experience. She was, she believed at certain moments, happy: She had friendly acquaintances, her husband was close by, and she was intoxicated enough to let her numerous inhibitions slip away.

It was dark when Milorad, a painter Zora described as a genius, suggested they move on to the *Tribina Mladih*—Youth Tribune—a multi-use space with a cinema, disco, art gallery, and bar, where they wandered, stoned, through the gallery, looking at violent conceptual paintings from a Belgrade artist before moving on to the bar and later sliding on to the disco. As on the previous night in the fortress, Sophie and Emmett found themselves drawn into the pulsing rhythm that seemed to lie just beneath the surface of everything they saw, yet while their first night had felt innocent and pure, the mood now was different. They could sense that Zora was neither innocent nor pure, and this knowledge colored the night. Still, the festivities were no less enjoyable—perhaps more so, because these people weren't strangers anymore. As she packed them into a taxi back to the hotel, Zora said, "Tomorrow is prison break." Sophie began to ask what she meant, but Zora slammed the door and called in Serbo-Croatian for the driver to get moving.

The explanation came in the morning, when Zora again found them hunched over their Hotel Putnik breakfasts, foggy and hung over. She, however, looked perfectly rested. "My friends," she said in a high whisper, "we get you out of this hellhole. It is time for prison break."

She had decided that it would not do for her American friends to stay in the dismal Putnik, and so she waited for them in the lobby, eyeballing the man who was still reading *Politika*.

Upstairs, as they packed, Sophie and Emmett discussed the change in plans. "What do you think?" she asked.

Emmett folded a shirt over his forearm. "I think she's pretty generous."

"Too generous?"

He grinned. "She's got a crush on you. Who wouldn't?"

So they climbed into Zora's Yugo, giving themselves over to her care. They crossed the Danube along the Liberty Bridge, chatting about their day on the Strand until the buildings fell away, replaced by countryside. This was farther out than they'd expected, and there was an edge to Emmett's voice when he said, "Where, uh, are we going?"

Zora pointed through the filthy windshield. "Fruška Gora," she said, naming the low mountain ahead of them. "My uncle has summerhouse up there. It is big and has electricity and hot water. You love it," she said, almost a command.

Viktor and two other young men were already at Zora's uncle's home, a three-bedroom cabin off a winding mountain road, perched on a hillside that gave them an idyllic view across the flat Vojvodina countryside of farms and villages. After dropping their bags in a dusty guest bedroom, Sophie and Emmett joined the men in the backyard, where chairs and a couple of tables had been set up in the high grass. Together they relaxed and drank bottles of Lav and uncorked red wine from Sremski Karlovci. Only up in the clean, clear mountains did they realize how dirty the air had been in town.

One of the new friends, a heavyset, balding anthropologist, began relating news items. The Slovenes were already talking to Western Europe, while the Croats were taking advantage of their newly proclaimed independence to begin ridding their land of Serbs and Bosnians. The anthropologist was already a little drunk, and when he talked of the fighting in villages across Croatia spittle collected in the corners of his mouth. Viktor told him to shut up, because a beautiful day shouldn't be wasted on nationalist bullshit, and it grew into a Serbo-Croatian shouting match. Sophie worried the two men would come to blows, but as quickly as it flared up the conflict waned, and soon they were embracing, kissing cheeks, laughing. Zora went inside and turned on a stereo, positioning the speakers in the windows so they could all listen to a New Wave band called Električni Orgazam.

Lying in the grass with a beer balanced on his stomach, Emmett asked, "How much does a house cost here?"

Sophie looked at him, but he was squinting at the sun, lost in his own thoughts.

"For an American, lunch money," said the third man, whose career they never learned. The others laughed.

Emmet got up on his elbows. "I'm serious. This is gorgeous. Isn't it gorgeous, Sophie?"

"It is," she said, because it was. For a moment, she allowed herself to consider this alternate life: a mountain cabin in Yugoslavia. For vacations, or as their primary home? What would life be like in a place where you couldn't understand the people around you? In a place where simple statements of opinion grew into fights that ended in kisses? Where, she asked herself, was this marriage really headed?

Zora called Sophie inside to help her prepare lunch. It was a small kitchen, and Zora's smoking soon made the atmosphere lethal. Sophie banged on the windows to get them open, then helped Zora clean chicken thighs, shape ground meat into patties, season pork chops, and skin potatoes. Outside, the men had fired up an age-old grill and were lighting charcoal. Zora said, "You think you like to live here?"

"Maybe," Sophie said. "Maybe later, after I've got my career going."

"That means never," Zora said with finality.

They drank and gorged themselves on meat, and when the sun went down the anthropologist produced an acoustic guitar. They sang "American Pie." Afterward, Zora brought out a bottle of plum brandy they called *rakija* and began to speak.

As with their first meeting in the Fortress, she still knew everything, but with the leisure of hours spreading out around them on that slanted field Zora was able to talk more lucidly about the things that were important to her. Art, music, literature, and, yes, politics. This Zora, whose arms were wrapped around her knees as she rocked back and forth, struck Sophie as thoughtful and smart, a different woman from that first night. Rational, yet utterly unafraid of conviction—this, Sophie realized, was her most attractive quality.

She thought of the lecture halls she'd lived in those previous four years, of the refrain that persisted in her liberal education: question, question, question. With enough questioning, the very ground could evaporate into conjecture. What she realized, sitting comfortably with Zora in the backyard of that house, her bare feet drawn up beneath herself as she sipped the fiery *rakija* and Zora chain-smoked, was that the act of questioning had been getting in her way for years. When asked what she believed, it was always easier for Sophie to turn the question around rather than answer it, and when forced into an opinion she would immediately qualify it.

Of course there's no God . . . but how can I know that for sure?

Communism is a failed ideology . . . but has real communism ever been practiced? Certainly not in the Soviet Union.

The world is round . . . but I'm basing that on other people's evidence, not my own.

Where did her beliefs lie? Did she even *have* any? Her parents did, but once she'd gotten out from under them she'd decided that their beliefs would not be hers, and so she'd started from scratch, entering Harvard looking for an educated way to construct her world. Education, though, had only confused the issue, and she had left as hollow as when she'd entered. If everything could be argued, then nothing could be believed.

That night, in Zora's uncle's narrow guest bed, she pinned her husband's wrists down against the pillow, lowered her head, and bit his nipple. He yelped, but when she looked at his face his eyes were closed, his expression dreamy.

For three days they lived this way. Late breakfasts with Zora, laughing about the previous night, and in the afternoons friends arrived with bags of groceries and drink, with guitars and a battery-powered Casio keyboard. On the third day a loud woman brought a stack of canvases and acrylics, and in the yard they fingerpainted as they passed around a paint-spattered bong. Halcyon afternoons stretched into dinnertime, when the men controlled the grill, the women preparing food in the kitchen.

Over a dinner of pickled red peppers and grilled pork chops Emmett asked about Vukovar, as if only now remembering why he'd wanted to come to Yugoslavia. "What's going on with the war?"

Zora was gnawing meat off of a long, sharp bone. She paused, the bone hanging from her greasy fingers. "You interested for that?"

"It's sort of why I wanted to come here."

She wiped hair off her cheek with her wrist. "You want to *know* about it?"

Emmett nodded, but Zora hadn't been looking at him when she asked that; she'd been looking at Sophie. Sophie also nodded.

"It is not war," Zora began, dropping the bone onto her plate. "Not yet. But will be. Soon. A war, you know, is agreement between two countries for to fight. Right now, only neighbors agree. They make paramilitaries like old partisans and defend homes. The army's there, but it try just to settle those little battles. Soon, though, Belgrade and Zagreb make agreement, and then real war start. As it must."

"Must it?" Sophie asked.

"Of course," Zora told her. "Tito, he force us together for half century. He move everyone around so Croats and Serbs and Macedonians and Bosnians share same land, but he no could make us to like each other. If he lets everyone stay where they are, okay, separation is easy. Borders easy to mark. But now there is Croats deep in Serbian land, and Serbs in Croat land. You think Serb farmers want to live in nation run by Ustaše?"

Sophie considered not asking, but knew she couldn't wing it without explanation. "Run by who?"

Zora looked at her a moment, blinking, perhaps puzzled by her ignorance. "Croatian fascists," she said after a moment. "Great murderers from Second War—they put SS to shame. And now . . ." Suddenly, she raised both hands in an expression of surrender, her palms slick with grease. "I promise no politics. I no get started." She lowered her hands again, smiling now. "But you interested in coming war," she said, nodding. "Maybe we can to do something about that." Seeing the expression on Sophie's face, she leaned forward and touched her thigh with a clean knuckle. "Don't worry, *draga*. I keep you safe."

Despite her greasy-palmed vow, later that night Zora told them about the Jasenovac concentration camp, which had been the largest "place of extermination" in fascist Croatia during the Second World War. "No one know exact number, but some say a million murdered there. They killing Jews and Gypsies, but most was Serbs. You can imagine?" she said, shaking her head, as if she'd spent decades trying to imagine just this. She sipped at her wine, then went on. "Jasenovac for men, the women shipped to Stara Gradiška. Twelve thousand, at least, murdered there. In Sisak they collect children. Serbs, Jews, and Gypsies. Just children. The guards . . . they pick up children by feet and swing them against walls until they dead. For fun, you understand? Thousands killed."

Neither of them had an easy reply to this. Frowns, nods, sips from glasses. Emmett looked as if he were gearing up to say something wise, but nothing came out. Sophie wondered if any of this was true—or, if it was, just *how* true was it? What details were being twisted in order to condemn an entire population? Finally, she said, "That was a long time ago, Zora."

"Yes, Sofia," she said as she thoughtfully lit a fresh cigarette, slowing down. "But it is not easy to forget such things." She told them that, after the war, once the major criminals had been executed, Tito told everyone to make up and be friends. "But what about that young soldier, who swing a child by ankles? Men like him, they go back to farms. They make more boys, who impregnate Croat women. Those sons and grandsons—those are ones on front line now."

"Enough," said Viktor, rising and stretching. "You get her going and there's no end to it."

Bitterly, Zora snapped at him in Serbo-Croatian, and another incomprehensible fight ensued, ending only when Zora marched inside. Viktor settled into a chair and finished his beer thoughtfully. "She's good," he told Sophie and Emmett. "I'll fight with her, but I know she's right about everything. I love that woman." Then he got up and followed her inside.

"It's true," Emmett whispered after a moment. "A lot of what she said. Some of it, at least. I didn't know the names of the camps, but I learned about the Ustaše in a seminar. They weren't very nice."

Sophie looked at him. After what she'd heard from Zora, Emmett's casual assessment—*they weren't very nice*—seemed unbearably diplomatic. They'd listened to the same stories, and while they had provoked a banal statement from Emmett, Sophie felt like finding a long knife and carving her initials into the faces of those Croatian fascists. The desire was refreshing, as if it were the first real conviction she'd felt in her life. She'd certainly never felt so strongly at Harvard, where she'd been indoctrinated in the constitutional separation of head and heart.

When they made their way back to the guest room, they saw Zora and Viktor tangled and naked, dozing in Zora's bed. They made love, too, but afterward Sophie dreamed of children, gripped by their ankles and swung like baseball bats.

In the morning, Zora spent some time on the phone in her bedroom while Viktor dressed and left for home. Sophie boiled eggs, and when Zora came out looking disheveled she sliced bread and cheese. They settled down to their meal. Zora said, "Sofia, Emmett, I take something to my friend. He live in small town, in west, and I think you like to see something more. Something authentic."

"Where?" Emmett asked.

"Little village. You never hear of it. Close to Vukovar. You like my friend, I'm sure, but he no speak English. He is musician. You *must* come," she said, her mood rising with each new word. Her all-knowing smile was radiant.

2

Where was she? Where had her decisions brought her? Clutching the iPad, she passed anxious tourists and drowsy businessmen in the lobby of the Semiramis as she found her way to Café Corniche, a cramped gathering of marble-topped tables and elegant straight-backed chairs. She had to work her way around an old Australian couple and a young family camped, with bags, at a table, before settling near the glass cases full of sweets. She ordered espresso from a white-clad waiter, and as her heartbeat gradually settled she wondered if she could go back to her life. She had reserved the plane home, after all—in the morning she would be heading to Boston. With the optimism that is an American's birthright, she believed for a moment that everything could be left as it was. Just go.

After finishing the coffee, she opened the cover on her iPad and began for the first time to read the backlog of e-mails she'd been too anxiety-ridden to look at before. Sixty-two: friends, family, the Budapest embassy, journalists. Glenda was terrified; Ray was official. Her parents simply wondered why she hadn't gotten in touch yet, and asked what was wrong with her phone. No word from Emmett's parents, and she wondered if their silence was a kind of recrimination. Droves of people, some of whom she couldn't recall, wanted to give their condolences. And a short note from Reardon—whose first name was George: "Ms. Kohl, please contact me at your earliest convenience for some follow-up questions."

So many questions to answer. There wasn't really any choice—was there? She had to fly home and assure everyone by her presence that she was all right. Then, later, she could return and work to uncover the mystery of Emmett's murder. That was the proper way of going about it. Anything else, she felt all at once, was patently unbalanced.

She even put the iPad to sleep and looked around for her waiter, prepared to abandon the meeting, but that was when her contact arrived, squeezing past the family with all the bags, looking sternly at her.

He was older than she had expected. Elderly, even, though she had trouble discerning the ages of Egyptian men. Tall, lanky, with at least a couple days' worth of white hair on his cheeks and chin, yet well dressed in a mud-colored suit. He was walking heavily, as if his bones hurt. He didn't offer a hand, but came close, leaning over the table, and whispered "Mrs. Kohl?" in a heavy accent that turned *Kohl* into *Kowuhl.* She nodded. "And you are?"

"Halawi. Omar Halawi."

She gave a smile of welcome and opened her hand to the free chair. "Please."

Before sitting, he looked around, as if worried someone might catch him joining a Western woman, or perhaps he was worried about more sinister things. Once he was seated, he said, "I will be honest with you, Mrs. Kohl. I do not like this."

"This?"

"*This,*" he repeated, then placed ten fingertips on the surface of the table. "If Inaya did not call me herself, I would not be here." He cleared his throat. "We may be watched."

She looked around, suddenly worried, suddenly *knowing* that this had been a mistake. How quickly could she get back to Stan's place? "Who's following us?"

His lips pressed tightly together as if in preparation for an elaborate explanation, but all he did was shrug.

"You're confusing me, Mr. Halawi. You're saying that someone may be following us, but you don't know who they are?"

"I don't know."

She didn't like the sound of this. "I have a room," she said. "Upstairs, number 306. We can talk in private."

When a look of terror crossed his face, she understood that she'd stepped over a line. He wasn't some halfhearted Muslim who would head up to a woman's hotel room unchaperoned.

Enough.

"Look, Mr. Halawi. Inaya told me I could trust you. She said you could help me. If that's not the case, then fine. You go, and I'll return to where I came from." This statement came out of her quickly, and once it was out in the air she felt as if a weight had lifted. *Give up. There you go.* She saw a boy on a bridge sticking his tongue out at her. *Stop pretending you're anything but a scared little woman.*

It could have happened, and much later she would wish that it had. He could have accepted her suggestion, given her another little nod, and simply left. Instead, he stared at her empty espresso cup, weighing options, then pursed his lips again. "Yes," he said finally, then looked into her eyes. "For Jibril."

And that was that. Her course was now determined. "For Jibril," she agreed, though she was thinking of Emmett.

With this settled, he relaxed, but when a waiter drifted by and looked at him he tensed again, shaking his head angrily. To Sophie, he said, "Inaya told me some things, but I am not sure I entirely understand your position. Your husband spoke to Jibril before he was killed. Yes?"

Killed—it was a word no one around her had wanted to say. "Yes."

"You learned of this, and so you came to Cairo to find Jibril."

"Yes." He was staring at her, waiting, so she went on. "Jibril came up with a plan for the embassy. For regime change in Libya."

"Stumbler," he said, waving it away. "I know of this. Go on."

Who *was* this guy?

She said, "Emmett used to work at the Cairo embassy. I know people there. I thought they could help."

"Have they?"

"Not yet, no."

"Yes," he said, but was shaking his head no. "They would not. Do you think that they know about Jibril?"

"He's a government employee—I suppose they know plenty about him."

Again, he shook his head, this time with impatience. "The book—do they know about his *book*?"

"I don't know what you mean."

"The *names*. Do they know about the *network*?"

"Maybe . . ." she began, then stopped. "Look, I really don't know what you're talking about."

Halawi leaned back and scratched at the hair on his cheek with the fingers of his right hand, again considering her. He said, "Who else were you seeking in Cairo?"

Wasn't she supposed to be asking the questions? "Stan Bertolli. I thought he could help."

Voice lowered, Halawi said, "I don't mean your lover, Mrs. Kohl."

He said that with a touch of disdain, and her impulse was to throw coffee into his face, but her cup was empty. "Then who *do* you mean, Mr. Halawi?"

There was little movement in his features as he said, "Your controller, Zora Balašević. Were you also looking for her?"

Her anger was quickly replaced by a deep-in-the-gut sickness; her head tingled. "I . . . don't . . ."

He tipped his head closer. "She controlled you; we controlled her. At least, we tried to control her. I don't think she was that easy to control."

It was as Stan had said. Zora had been reporting directly to the Egyptians. They knew everything about her affair, for Zora had told them about it. They knew each megabyte of information she'd vacuumed off of Emmett's laptop, because Zora had given it to them. Not *they*, necessarily, but he—this stoic, old Egyptian in front of her. He knew everything. For the first time in a long while, she was in the presence of someone from whom she had no secrets. It was terrifying.

"I wanted to get that into the open," he said after a moment, the fingertips of one hand now touching the fingertips of the other.

She tried to control the pitch of her voice. "Yes, I was looking for her as well, but she's not here."

"She returned home. There was no reason for her to stay after you left. Her only advantage was her friendship with you and Mr. Kohl. We were lucky, you understand—she knew that we could pay her more than her own countrymen."

Zora had abandoned her ideology—those convictions she had so admired—and given herself to the Egyptians for mere money. But hadn't Zora said as much herself? *Information wants to be free . . . I believe I should be paid for it.* How much about Zora had she believed simply because she wanted to believe it? She felt as if she knew nothing. "But she wasn't here just because of me. She had other people," Sophie said, thinking of the blonde with the Russians. "She pointed one out to me."

"Did she?" he asked, raising a brow. "Did you talk to these other sources?"

She shook her head.

"We watched Zora Balašević. If she had other sources, I think we would have known."

The gall. Of course Zora had no one else—Sophie was the only one. Easy Sophie. Gullible girl. She inhaled loudly through her nose, trying to keep herself steady. "Is Zora connected? To Emmett. To his murder?"

Halawi rocked his head from side to side, then said, "I cannot be sure, but I think not. Not to your husband's murder. Since she's been gone, I have heard nothing from her. I believe she is happily living in Serbia with the money she earned here. She has no financial reason to get back into things, and she has no ethical stake in what happens in this part of the world. Jibril, however, does."

She nodded, trying to rebuild her world, brick by brick. "You were talking about some names."

He nodded, then stared a moment, eyes bleakly searching for something in her face. Finally, he said, "When he went into Libya, Jibril was to receive a book with the names and contact information of everyone in the old networks."

"In what old networks?"

"Jibril's. From before. When he ran his own network in Libya."

She stared at his shaggy chin. "I thought he worked in an office."

"You know nothing about him, yes?"

"No," she said, impatience creeping up again. "So maybe you should tell me."

She read hesitation in his face, but he had already made his decision. He had already dropped his bombshells. He took another look around to be sure no one was listening, then began to describe a beautiful young man, a family man, "a man who wants nothing more than for his people to live in peace, and to live well." Jibril was young, yet he had witnessed "things you must usually be as old as me to see."

That Halawi had respect for Aziz wasn't in question, but as he spoke it became clear that he idolized the younger man, and this began to scare her. When he said, "Jibril, he is a moral force," she cut in.

"Right. I get it. He's wonderful. But I'm trying to find out who killed my husband. Do you know?"

"Of course," Halawi said matter-of-factly. "Jibril's employers."

"CIA?"

"Yes."

Sophie rubbed her eyes, hard. "*Why* did they kill Emmett?"

"Because of Stumbler. Because he was talking to Jibril about Stumbler."

She was starting to feel as if the conversation were just spinning in place. "*Why* was he talking to my husband, of all people, about Stumbler?"

Halawi scratched at his long nose. "He knew about your husband. He knew your husband was . . . like-minded. Both good men interested in what was right. Your husband was a moral force as well."

Emmett? A moral force? "Specifics, Mr. Halawi. Please be specific, because if you aren't I think I'm going to walk out of here."

When anger flickered through his features, she had the sense that women didn't talk to him in this way, but he recovered gracefully and placed both hands flat on the table. "Mrs. Kohl, this is about an American plan to steal the revolution from the hands of the Libyan people. Jibril created Stumbler years ago, when the aim was to rid the world of Muammar Gadhafi. A *moral* aim. But now the world is different. Now, the Libyan people have begun their own Stumbler, and when they succeed *they* will run their own country. It would be wrong for America to take over that fight and place its puppets in Tripoli. Do you understand now?"

She nodded.

"*That* is why Jibril spoke with your husband. He realized that the Americans were going to steal the revolution. He only knew one diplomat who would agree that this was a crime—Mr. Emmett Kohl. He spoke with your husband in Budapest, one week before his murder, and then went into Libya to warn the people in his book that they would have to fight off the Americans as well."

For a while, she just stared at him, trying to absorb all this. "Was Emmett a party to Jibril's plans?"

He shook his head. "Your husband was not a *part* of this, no. Jibril went to your husband to verify what he had discovered. Your husband was not CIA—he was objective."

"Emmett verified that America was going to steal the revolution from the Libyans?"

Another look crossed Halawi's face, but it was neither shock nor anger—it was embarrassment.

"Well?" she asked.

He shook his head. "Mr. Kohl said that he did not believe it. He believed America was doing nothing of the sort."

Sophie thought a moment. "Wait a minute. You're telling me that the CIA killed my husband. Yes?"

He nodded.

"Because they wanted to cover up Stumbler. Correct?"

"Yes. That is correct."

"But Emmett didn't believe we were behind it."

"Correct."

"Then why did they kill him?"

Halawi rubbed his eyes, maybe tired of spelling out the world to this woman. "Because Langley did not know for sure, Mrs. Kohl. It did not look deeply enough into the circumstances of their meeting." He paused. "Mistakes were made. They often are."

"And Jibril?"

"Yes?"

"You don't know where he is, do you?"

"He is in Libya."

"But you don't know where in Libya."

There was no point answering that, so he didn't.

"What makes you think he's still alive?"

Another smile, this one bordering on angelic. He placed a hand on his heart: "Because I *believe*, Mrs. Kohl."

She wanted to laugh at him, but she didn't. She wanted to cry as well, because for all the information he was willing to share, she was starting to believe he was as much in the dark as she was.

He sighed loudly. "Mrs. Kohl, this is not your fight. You know who murdered your husband. You can go home without shame."

"You don't know me very well, Mr. Halawi."

He smiled, as if he really did know her, and said, "What do you plan to do that others cannot do better? You should be honest with yourself." He inhaled through his nose, and she thought she saw sympathy in his features, but maybe it was a mirage. "You do not belong here, Mrs. Kohl. You should never have come."

3

She lay on her bed in room 306 and stared at the ceiling, troubled by the fact that she was still unsure. She had her plane ticket, yet she kept asking herself questions. Was she really done here? Or was she going to try to find Jibril Aziz? What would she do once she found him? What answers did she expect from him? And if he gave her the same answer this Egyptian had given her—that the American government had killed Emmett—then what would she do with it? Would she call *The New York Times* and start shouting down the line?

She wasn't sure she trusted Omar Halawi. He had an air of madness about him, the kind that changes the faces of zealots and bigots. He was building his world on a foundation that was subtly different than her own, and therefore whatever he said was just beyond her own way of looking at things. It was a cultural difference, perhaps, but it also made him sound like a loony to her.

What if she did call *The New York Times*—what then? She tried to imagine the reaction of the American government, of the CIA. How long would it take for them to discredit her? How hard would it be for them to connect the dots and discover that, for over a year, she had been an agent of a foreign power? And how would she defend herself—with the story of Yugoslavia in 1991? That was no defense.

The real question, she suspected, wasn't what she would be able to accomplish, but what was *right*—and in this situation what did *right* mean?

Even though she knew better, she wished that Stan were beside her in bed. He might give her lies, but at least his mouth would distract her from her confusion for a little while.

There was a tap at her door. At first, wrapped in her thoughts, she didn't hear it, but then it came again, louder, and she sat up. It was after ten. She considered not answering, but then a voice said, "Sophie Kohl? My name is Michael Khalil. I used to work with your husband. May I have a word?"

She got up, went to the door, and touched the handle before hesitating. She used the spy hole and saw a man holding up a photo ID that said on one side, in blue letters, "FBI." On the right was a photo and "Michael Khalil."

"I'm FBI," he said unnecessarily.

She started to open the door, then remembered Andras Kiraly. The old Hungarian had asked about Michael Khalil, who claimed to be FBI. *We have our doubts.* Khalil had spoken to Emmett about Stumbler on the day that . . . on *that* day. "What do you want?" she asked, a sudden, deep fear tightening the muscles in her back.

Through the spy hole, he lowered the ID so she could see his face. A swarthy man, tall and thin, with a smile. Handsome, even. He looked Egyptian, but his voice was flat midwestern. "Sorry for the hour. I wondered if I might have a word."

"You couldn't have called first?"

Irritation sharpened his features. "Well, I'm coming here unofficially. And I'd appreciate it if you kept this conversation to yourself."

"We're not having a conversation yet."

"I hope you'll decide to talk to me."

"Why should I?"

He frowned, glancing up the corridor again, as if expecting—or fearing—someone. "I'm here because I don't want you to get killed."

It wasn't the answer she had expected, nor was it the answer she had desired. "Why do you think I'm in danger of getting killed?"

"May I come in?"

She stepped back, thought a moment, then secured the door latch up beside her head. She opened the door until the latch caught, leaving five inches through which Michael Khalil could see a slice of her. "You stay there."

Again, irritation. A tongue rummaged in his cheeks.

"Now tell me why you think I'm in danger of getting killed."

Another glance down the hall, and he lowered his voice to a high whisper. "Do I have to say it aloud?"

"I think you do, Mr. Khalil."

He tugged at the lapels of his jacket, straightening it. "You know by now who murdered your husband?"

"Why don't you tell me?"

"CIA." He paused. "Is this a surprise?"

"It doesn't matter how many times I hear it—it'll always be a surprise."

"Emmett was preparing to betray the Agency. He'd learned about an operation in Libya, and he was going to expose it. He told one colleague—direct quote—that he would find a whistle and blow it. Emmett didn't mince his words."

She leaned back a little, thinking of how good Emmett was, and how little she'd really known him. "Stumbler," she said, then shook her head. "But Emmett didn't believe that. Jibril Aziz believed it, but he didn't. He wasn't going to blow any whistle."

"Did Mr. Halawi tell you this?" he asked.

"How do you know about him?"

A half-shrug. "I just know him. He's a good man, but that doesn't make his word gospel. Consider your husband's position—he's got a young man, a man with a family, preparing to rush into Libya and get himself killed. What would a good man do? Let calmer minds prevail. Lie to Jibril, get him to go home to his wife, and then go about it the diplomatic way—memos to people who matter."

"Wait," she said, and he did just that, his face relaxing as he stared at her through the gap, waiting. She took a moment to think this through. She said, "Emmett's the one who wanted to write memos, not me. I still don't understand why I'm in danger."

Again, he looked back down the corridor. "Well, you didn't follow the script, did you?" he said as if to a child, full of patience for the nonprofessionals of the world. "You didn't bow down like a grief-stricken widow and go home. You've come to Cairo and started digging. You've gone to Stanley Bertolli, an officer of the Agency, for help. Why don't you figure out how long it took for the Agency to find out exactly where you were and what you were up to?"

"Stan didn't tell anyone," she said quickly.

"Do you really believe that?" He gave her a moment to come up with an answer, then said, "Listen, I'm not saying Stan Bertolli isn't decent, but he's first and foremost an Agency man. He may not even know what's going on, but he's certainly going to follow procedure. It's in his DNA. His father was CIA, too, you know."

She didn't know—he'd never talked about his family, which probably should have told her something. She stared into a space just to his left, a bit of wallpaper, wondering if she could believe this stranger. Stan had been so worried about discovery—and this man, who was he? Kiraly thought he wasn't who he claimed to be, but maybe the Hungarian was wrong. Weren't they all liars? "Did you talk to Emmett about this?"

"I didn't have a chance."

"You never talked to Emmett?"

He hesitated. "Your husband was dead before I could talk to him."

Who was lying? Why would Kiraly make it up? "And who are you?"

"I told you, I'm Bureau. We cooperate with our friends in the Agency, but we are quite separate."

"No," she said, shaking her head. "I mean, who are *you*? What's your stake in this?"

He blinked at her, as if stunned by her question. "Well, a man was murdered, Sophie. One of our people. And it turns out that another section of our government is responsible. It's sort of my job to be worried about this kind of thing."

She straightened now, feeling the anger bubble up inside her but trying to keep it under control. She was sick of people being vague and handing her outright lies. "Connect the dots for me," she told Michael Khalil. "Show me how this puts my life in danger."

"Connect the dots?" he said, opening his hands. Impatient again. "Okay, Sophie. It's this way. Your husband wanted to blow the whistle on Stumbler. If he'd done that, it would have been a major embarrassment for the Agency. A disaster. So they got rid of him. His wife—you, Sophie—has not disappeared like she's supposed to. She's slipped her handlers and run off to Cairo, presumably to uncover who killed her husband. Do you really think the Agency's going to sit around and wait for you to connect them to that Albanian thug?"

"Where *is* the connection?"

He opened his mouth, then closed it.

"Go ahead, then. If you've got all the damned answers, then hand them over."

Michael Khalil leaned forward, face close to the crack in the door, and she could smell garlic on his breath. His eyes were big and veined. "Someone like Gjergj Ahmeti, he's a ghost. You won't find his name in any records. He's hired for specific jobs, paid in cash, then sent on his way. So you won't find a paper trail—the best you can do is find a person who knows what the Agency is up to. The best you can do is track down Jibril Aziz."

"And how, pray tell, am I going to do that?"

"Let me in, and we'll discuss it."

"No," she said.

"You're being childish. You saw my badge. I just want to come to an arrangement, Sophie."

There was noise up the corridor, and he glanced back. She soon saw what he saw—a laughing couple, maybe a little drunk. Germans muttering in slurred accents to one another, his hand on her ass. They paused in their revelry to eyeball Khalil and the slice of Sophie they could see. They passed, but before he could speak again three men arrived in the corridor—Germans, again—singing "Hände zum Himmel." Khalil, clearly frustrated, turned back to her and whispered, "Let's meet in the morning. Okay? You're nervous—I understand that. So I'll meet you for breakfast downstairs. Agreed?"

She nodded.

"What time?"

She thought, *At nine thirty I get on a plane and leave all of this behind.* "Ten o'clock," she said, smiling the way Zora had taught her to do when she was lying. "I'm sleeping late tomorrow."

He hesitated again, brow furrowing, then nodded sharply. "I'll be waiting."

4

———

As she had done in Budapest, she was going to walk. She'd come here urged by an overwhelming sense of guilt, hoping to find anyone—Zora or Stan or Jibril—who could assure her that she was not responsible for Emmett's murder. No one was able to assure her of anything. Instead, everything was ballooning out of control. She had entered the realm of coups d'état, of deceit, of murder, of the desert. She wondered where Jibril really was now, maybe living some thrilling and terrifying existence among desperate men fighting for their lives, while back in Alexandria—the Virginian Alexandria—his pregnant wife worried herself sick about him.

That image, as much as anything else, convinced her that she was making the right decision. Emmett had gotten caught up in boys' games. She had, too, for more than a year, but she'd survived her childish phase and come out the other side. It was time to go home.

She set the alarm on her phone for seven and showered and climbed into bed wearing her last pair of clean underwear. By nine thirty, she would be on the plane. Then she would be in Boston. She turned off the light and closed her eyes. And saw:

A leg kick-kicking in the dirt.

Jackbooted soldiers throwing babies into the air.

Her own voice: *It's mercy. He'll starve.*

A man screaming behind a filthy gag.

The banging that woke her brought immediate terror, for the dream had followed her into the blackness of the hotel room, and the banging on her door had the ring of a boot heel kicking against one of those heavy Yugoslav front doors.

A familiar voice: "Mrs. Kohl? Mrs. Kohl, I must speak to you."

She clawed at the darkness until she found the switch for the bed-side lamp. She gasped for breath, assuring herself that she was the only person in the room.

Thump, thump, thump. "Mrs. Kohl?"

It was Omar Halawi—she would know that hesitant accent any-where. "A minute," she said, then wrapped herself in a hotel robe. He ceased his banging, and in the spy hole she saw him, fisheyed, standing rigid, hands behind his back. She opened the door, forget-ting the latch, and read the surprise in his face before understanding the reason. Why was he surprised? It was two in the morning—he was lucky she wasn't naked.

He said, "Mrs. Kohl—"

"Wait," she cut in, raising a hand. "You don't have to worry, okay? I'm out of here in the morning. I've had enough."

He opened his mouth, hesitated, then said, "I fear that may not be possible."

"And why not?"

Again, an open mouth, and she saw that he was missing at least two molars on one side. He lowered his voice, glancing up the empty corridor. "The man who spoke with you." He shook his head, voice now a whisper: "Do not trust him."

Christ, it was starting up again. She just wanted to get out of here. "He's FBI."

"No, he is not FBI. And his name is not Michael Khalil."

While Kiraly had told her this with that unsure deference that made her so comfortable, Halawi had said it with such stern convic-tion that her heart caught in her throat. "Then what is he?"

"He works for my superior, Mrs. Kohl. He is not FBI."

She stepped back, repulsed as much by the man as by his infor-mation. She, too, was whispering now: "It doesn't matter. I promised him I would meet him, but I'm leaving in the morning. I'll never see him again."

"You are on EgyptAir 777, leaving at nine thirty. Yes?"

She swallowed. "Yes."

"If I know this, then Mr. Khalil does as well. So, too, does my superior." He gave her a moment to comprehend that simple logical sequence. "Please, you must come with me."

She took another step back, and he stepped to the doorframe but did not enter.

He said, "I do not think he will let you leave."

"Of course he'll let me leave. I'm nobody."

"It's not who you are, Mrs. Kohl. It's what you know."

"But I don't *know* anything!"

He held up both hands to calm her, then glanced up the corridor again. He whispered, "I was wrong. Jibril was wrong. All of us were wrong."

"About what?"

"About everything. This is not about Stumbler. It's about . . ." He faded out a moment, frowning, as if unsure of the word. "It's about betrayal."

Betrayal. Finally, something Sophie Kohl understood. She said, "Tell me about betrayal."

He took a breath through his nose, and she heard the clotted sound of a cold coming on. He didn't look all that well, either. He sighed. "It would be a breach of security to share with you at this point."

"It would be a betrayal."

"Exactly."

"Wouldn't it be a betrayal to hide me from your superior?"

"Maybe not," he said, as if that explained anything at all. "Please," he said. "Gather your things. I can keep you safe."

She didn't want to go, but in less than five minutes she had dressed as he waited in the corridor. She lugged her bag, trying to keep up with him. They did not take the elevator, instead using the stairwell to reach the rear of the ground floor. Before they stepped out, he said,

"Don't go into the lobby. There's someone who will recognize us both."

"One of your people?"

"One of Stanley Bertolli's men," he said.

"Stan's not going to hurt me," she told him.

Lips tight, he shook his head. "I am more worried about who's watching Mr. Bertolli's man." Then he opened the door.

She let him lead her back through glass doors and across the courtyard with its pool and garden, then they reentered the building and squeezed around a soiled room-service cart to reach a service elevator. Silently, they took it down into the guts of the building, the doors opening onto an underground parking lot. A car was waiting, behind the wheel a young, tough-looking Egyptian with thick eyebrows. She caught the name Sayyid as they got into the back and Halawi ordered the driver to go. He drove quickly past rows of cars and up ramps until he flashed a badge at an old lot attendant and they finally pulled out into light traffic. While she was initially able to tell their direction—north and then west across Qasr Al Nile Bridge, all the way across the southern tip of Gezira Island and then into Dokki—she was soon lost in Cairo's tangle. That was when it occurred to her that she didn't really know these men at all. All she had was the word of a woman she'd never actually met. They could be kidnappers. They could be al Qaeda. They could be CIA.

As they were entering Dokki, she said, "What is it your boss thinks I know?"

Halawi hesitated only briefly. "The identity of your husband's murderer. Or, the person who ordered the murder."

She sat up. "*You* know?"

"Not yet."

"Do you think *he* did it? Your superior?"

"I cannot say for sure."

"You don't know much, do you?"

He didn't bother answering that.

"How long are you hiding me?"

He considered the question. "Maybe until this evening. Maybe

Tuesday. No later than Tuesday, I think." He was turning, looking out the rear windshield as they wove through traffic. "I am taking you to my home. I would like you to stay inside until this has been settled. My wife will take care of you."

"Wife?" she said, surprised, for she had assumed he was a bachelor.

Omar Halawi's home turned out to be a fifth-floor walkup on a narrow, treeless street. Graffiti marred one of the buildings. The three of them went up together, both men opening doors for her along the way. When they reached his apartment, Halawi knocked, and after a moment a woman in her sixties opened the door. She was pleasantly plump, black hair shot through with gray, and she had a wide mouth that formed a warm smile. "Salaam," she said, nodding at Sophie.

"Salaam," Sophie answered.

Halawi whispered, "She speaks no English."

It was a small apartment, smaller than she would have expected from a member of the Egyptian secret police—for that, she had gleaned from his insider knowledge and the way he had at least one young tough at his beck and call, was what he probably was. His home was claustrophobic the way old people's homes always seemed to be, stuffed with trinkets of a long life, things without function or, in many cases, much aesthetic beauty. They seemed to serve only as reminders that the resident had once lived life rather than just watch it go by.

The wife's name was Fouada, Halawi told her, and she brewed tea nervously while Halawi and Sayyid stepped outside for a talk. Sophie, feeling exhaustion returning all at once, said, "Fouada?"

The old woman turned to her, hesitant.

"Sleep?" Sophie said, placing two praying hands against the side of her tilted face. The rush of understanding seemed to give Fouada great pleasure, and she quickly ushered Sophie back to a guest bedroom that smelled of lavender. There were fresh folded towels on the dresser, and she was given a tour of the spotless bathroom. "Thank you," she told the woman. "*Shukran.*"

Fouada smiled, clapping her hands together, saying, "*Afwan,*" and then more words that breezed by. Still fully clothed, Sophie lay on the hard bed and closed her eyes. A brief rest before undressing, she thought, then wondered what Emmett would say if he could see her now. Would he be surprised? Might he even be impressed? She was soon asleep.

5

1991

Zora drove them down the mountain, north toward Novi Sad, and then headed west, occasionally skirting the Danube as they passed through towns that she named along the way—Sremska Kamenica and Ledinci and Rakovac and Beočin, whose cement factory was fed by an offshoot of the Danube. She pointed out historical tidbits: Sremska Kamenica had been the home of Jovan Jovanović Zmaj, "greatest Serbian children's author." Ledinci was a young town, built after World War II to house the inhabitants of Stari—Old—Ledinci, which had been burned down by the dreaded Ustaše. In Rakovac the Croatian fascists had killed ninety-one citizens. Beočin created the first Serb schools in the Vojvodina countryside. She then pointed out another town, Čerević, where the Ustaše had killed eighty-seven.

Sophie thought of the concentration camps, the one for men, the one for women, and the one for children. She thought of ankles and the sharp corners of brick buildings.

As they made their way through small towns in that tiny Yugo, they listened to Zora's roll call of atrocities. "They no rest until they exterminate every Serb. It is moral crime to let that to happen."

When they didn't answer, Zora looked at Sophie in the rearview. "You no believe me."

"I believe you," Sophie said, knowing it was the only thing to say. They were deep in the countryside, farms stretching as far as the eye could see, in a country where they couldn't speak the language. They were depending on Zora for everything. But that's what they'd been doing for the last four days, and hadn't she only given them kindness? She remembered Viktor's assessment: *I'll fight with her, but I know she's right about everything.*

From the passenger seat, Emmett winked. Nothing to worry about. All fine.

They were soon in a region Zora called the "Serb Autonomous Oblast of Eastern Slavonia, Baranja, and Western Syrmia," but was firmly inside the territory that Croatia was claiming for itself. As they passed a sign directing them toward Vukovar, she told them about Borovo Selo, a town just north of Vukovar. "They make big deal out of attack our boys do on Croat policemen, but that was retaliation. A Croat government minister—for fun, you know—use antitank missiles to blow up three Serb homes. *This* is what they think of us. Weekend sport. Since referendum on Croat independence, they do what they like. Eighty-six Serbs in Vukovar just *disappear*." She paused. "You know what that means. We all know."

Though they could hear the distant thumps of artillery and see smoke rising on the horizon, they were not able to go into Vukovar, where the Vuka and Danube rivers met, for it was surrounded by the JNA—the Jugoslav National Army. Instead, Zora drove them to a muddy village east of town that she never bothered to name. There were tired-looking horses standing amid the rusting Yugos, but the streets, lined with small old-style houses, were empty until they reached the center, where a single shop advertising ice cream had attracted a few disconsolate-looking young men in army uniforms clutching bottles of Lav. They watched Zora's Yugo drive by.

"It's dead here," Emmett said.

"Not behind doors," Zora said as she turned up a puddle-choked side road and stopped at a tiny house with smoke drifting from a chimney. Like the others, it looked a hundred years old, brick walls covered with cracked, sand-colored mortar, a clay-tiled roof. When she parked behind a mud-spattered pickup track, the front door opened and an enormous black-bearded man in battle fatigues limped outside, arms raised high.

"Draga moja, Zoro!" he shouted, and she climbed out and splashed through the mud to accept his embrace. He lifted her more than a foot off the ground. They kissed cheeks, and she brought him over to meet her Americans. His name was Bojan, and he spoke no English. While he seemed initially pleased by their unexpected appearance, he hesitated and lowered his voice and spoke to Zora. A look crossed her face; then she shrugged elaborately.

"Something wrong?" Sophie asked.

"Nothing, nothing," Zora said as she brought Bojan to the trunk of the car. She popped it open and let him look inside. A broad smile broke out on his hairy face as he reached into a ragged cardboard box and took out a military-green, pill-shaped metal canister, about the size of his hand, with a tube leading to three prongs opened like the flower petals. There were letters on the side, and Sophie could make out PROM-1.

"Bravo!" Bojan said.

"What's that?" asked Emmett.

"Land mines. Bojan is paramilitary, but the army no share its mines."

"We were driving with *explosives* in that car?" Sophie snapped.

Zora smiled and raised a finger. "And we live. Praise God! Come, we drink."

They crowded into Bojan's cramped, dirty kitchen. On the counter, beside the sink, were two old pistols with wooden handles and cylinders. Perhaps he'd been cleaning them, but now he ignored the guns and went to a cabinet, inside which were three large plastic bottles of homemade plum brandy.

"Does he have anything else?" Emmett asked, for the *rakija* they'd drunk the last days hadn't done his stomach any good.

Zora asked, and Bojan said, *"Samo pivo."*

"Just beer," she translated. "But first we toast successful trip."

The *rakija* burned and then warmed her, and when Emmett switched to Lav, she stuck with the brandy. It helped keep her calm. Though he couldn't talk to them directly, Bojan wanted to tell stories, but not war stories. He told them about his youth in Tito's Yugoslavia, of swimming on the beaches north of Dubrovnik, now part of the Republic of Croatia, and climbing the Slovenian mountains. He was full of the glory of the communist past, yet he was no communist. "Ideology," Zora explained, "is not his bag. He is simple man, and he like to remember good times. I think we all this way. In few years, after you make new life in America, you think of us nostalgically, too."

By then the room was spinning, and Sophie was ready to agree. They were here, *here*, in a war zone, drinking with a sentimental soldier who—tomorrow, perhaps—would be back on the front lines, fighting against the children of the Ustaše. They had come. They had seen.

Emmett said, "What was that?" He was cupping his ear.

"I hear nothing," Zora said, still smiling.

Sophie didn't hear anything, either, and then she did: thumping. Not the distant thump of artillery, but something closer, under their feet. It was faint, but it was there, and it was close, inside the house.

"Yeah," she said. "I hear it."

Zora looked at Bojan, her smile finally fading, and said something to him. Bojan shook his head, almost embarrassed, and rubbed his face with a big, hairy hand. He spoke to Zora for a few minutes, another story, his face twisting into shapes of agony and anger as he went on. Finally he waved his hands, pushing everything away.

"What?" said Emmett.

Zora turned to them, her face hard now, no trace of warmth in it. "It is a man. Down. In basement."

"Who?" Sophie asked.

"A monster."

Silence followed. Then Emmett said, "Maybe you want to be more specific."

"Ustaša," Zora said. She lit a fresh cigarette and leaned back. "I tell you about them, no? About what they do."

Emmett placed his hands on the edge of the table, as if he were going to push himself to his feet. "You're holding a man *prisoner* down there?"

He had directed that question at Bojan, but Zora didn't bother to translate. "Emmett," she said soothingly, "that monster—I can't even to call him a man. He is with Croat paramilitary. They move into Serb town not far away and kill everyone who does not run. There is woman who just give birth. It is difficult birth. She is bedridden. So they find her in her little house with baby in cradle. This man come in, say hello to her, pick up baby and toss it into air. Like a football. Soccer—that's right?"

Neither of them answered her.

"He catch baby and toss him again, like he playing. But the mother, she know what kind of man is this. She begs him please to put child down. So he says okay, holds out baby in front of him, like so, and counts backward from three. On *one*, he drops baby and kicks. Like soccer ball, you know? Kicks baby across room and against far wall. Killed." She snapped her fingers. "Instantly. The mother," she said, cocking her head to the side and breathing loudly through her nose. "Well, you can to imagine. She is hysterical. Screaming. So he walks over, puts hand over her mouth and nose, like so, and when she fights he takes out hard cock. And fucks her. As she is suffocated."

"You don't know this," Emmett said after a moment of not breathing. He shook his head. "You can't."

Zora shrugged. "I *can* know this, because later, when he drink with comrades, he tells it. He says he fucks this woman to death. He think this is funny. Bojan hears all this when they retake town. The Croats tell him."

Sophie thought she was going to vomit. During the story Bojan had gotten up and left the kitchen. Emmett swallowed loudly and spoke in a whisper. "I don't believe it."

"I no make it up," said Zora. "Bojan does not."

Another pause. Then Emmett said, "What's he going to do with him?"

"Starvation. It take maybe a week. Maybe more. He is down there two days."

"Give him to the police."

Zora shook her head, a quiet laugh escaping her lips. "The police in this area, they are Croats. Are you not been paying attention? You see what kind of world we live in. No. This man will die in basement. It is better than he deserve."

"Then he should just shoot him."

Zora shook her head. "Bojan sees too much to give mercy so easily."

"I want to see him," Sophie said.

"What?" Emmett looked as if he'd forgotten she was there.

Zora hardly reacted. She only watched Sophie.

"I mean it."

Zora nodded and stood up.

"No," said Emmett, reaching out to her.

"We have to," she told him, for a kind of plum brandy insight had come to her: *To go. To see. To experience.* If they left this house without looking, it would haunt them forever. "We *have* to," she repeated.

Zora took one of the pistols off the counter, checked that it was loaded, then called something to Bojan. He appeared in the doorway, looking bleary but hard, resolved, a key dangling from his pinkie. A few more words passed between them—he was perhaps asking if Zora was sure about this. Sophie was sure; she was casting aside her ambivalence tonight. They hadn't gotten close to a war zone. They were *in* a war zone. This was as far from Harvard Square as it was possible to be.

Bojan led the three of them through his dusty living room, where a silent television showed snowy images of an old movie, to a padlocked door at the end of a brief hallway. He unlocked and opened it. He flipped a switch, illuminating rickety wooden steps leading down into the earth. But he didn't go down. He handed the key to Zora and returned to the living room, where he sat down, lifted an acoustic guitar onto his lap, and stared at the television.

6

——

Then it was morning, and she felt as if she'd been in a dream. Not only of Yugoslavia, but of Egypt. A dream that was lingering still, for what was this cinnamon smell? That flowery, brown-tinted wallpaper? The green knitted blanket under her? Harsh daylight cut through venetian blinds. The ache in her back was enough to tell her this wasn't a dream, but she had to sit up, look around, and then hobble to the bathroom she'd been given a tour of the night before to really believe it. After she flushed the toilet and washed her face and hands and opened the door, she found the old woman—yes, Fouada—standing in the corridor, smiling at her, holding out a large cup of tea. Gratefully, Sophie accepted the steaming cup. She said, "Omar?"

Fouada shook her head and pointed toward the living room—toward the front door. On the mantel against the far wall was an ornate clock from another age: It was one in the afternoon. How long had she slept? She wasn't sure, but the mere smell of the tea began to revive her. She wasn't living in a dream, she told herself. She had never lived a dream, not even when it had seemed that way. Not in Yugoslavia, and not here, during those adrenaline moments with the flash drive and Emmett's computer, when she'd felt a distant echo of that Serbian basement. Zora hadn't been a dream, nor that tingling, electric attraction that had bound the two of them. Those afternoons with Stan hadn't been a dream, either. It had all been real, and her mistake had been to think of it as a dreamlife. It was why she was here without friends and at the mercy of people she could not even communicate with.

She took a long, hot shower. Through sign language and eager nods she got a pair of clean but oversized panties from Fouada. While the prospect of sharing her intimate garments clearly disturbed the older woman, she gave in, realizing that this poor girl hadn't packed properly. Sophie forced herself into her old clothes, which were getting stiff by now. So be it. She drank her tea, dark and strong, then went to the kitchen, where Fouada had laid out a plate of toast and cheese and olives. She took a few bites—it was delicious. But Fouada wouldn't let her eat for long. She took a severe look at Sophie, then disappeared into her bedroom, returning a while later with a long summer dress and a belt. She held it out with one hand, then used the other to point at the clothes Sophie was wearing and then pinch her nose. She handed over the dress and belt. All of this was done with a serene smile. While the dress—a mess of abstract patterns in yellow and brown—was too large, cinching the belt made it wearable. Only after getting her to model a bit did Fouada leave her to enjoy the olives.

Later, Sophie returned to the bedroom and closed the door and took out her phone. There wasn't much charge left, but there was enough. She checked the recent calls and selected Kiraly's number.

He answered after a single ring. "Mrs. Kohl," he said, his accent bringing on a rush of familiarity. She'd forgotten how much she liked that overly earnest Magyar pronunciation. "I am glad you called."

"I wanted to apologize," she said. "I think it's time to tell you what's going on. Someone needs to know."

There was no joy in his voice, only a kind of morose patience. "Thank you, Mrs. Kohl. I should tell you first that the American embassy knows where you are now. That you're in Cairo."

"That's fine," she said. "I want to make a confession to you. Will you listen to it?"

"I'm not a priest."

"You're the closest thing to a priest that I know."

"I take that as a compliment, Mrs. Kohl."

He waited, and she told him. She told him everything, answers to the questions he never would have thought to ask, as well as telling him stories that were far beyond his mandate. There were still so many things she didn't know, like how everything had ended in two bullets entering her husband, but someone else could put it together. All she knew was that her story had led, somehow, to that restaurant, and eventually her guilt would be uncovered. So she told it all to a man whose job it was to make connections. He asked no questions, only listened, and sometimes she had to say, "Mr. Kiraly?"

"I am here."

And she went on.

It took about fifteen minutes to get it all out, a brief time considering that the story spanned decades, and when she was finished she felt exhausted and empty. Free. Not really, but at least her shackles were lighter, easier to bear. In the tired silence that followed, she lay on the bed again and stared at the ornate ceiling lamp. Kiraly also sounded exhausted when he said, "Well. That is quite a lot."

"What are you going to do with it?"

Silence, as he considered his options. "I'm not sure there's anything to do about it. Not now, at least."

"Are you going to tell them?"

"Them?"

"The embassy."

"I don't see the point of that. Do you?"

"I suppose not," she admitted.

"Thank you for your openness," Kiraly said.

"Thank you for listening," Sophie said and hung up. A minute later, her phone bleeped to tell her that its battery was dead.

7

By the time Omar Halawi returned home, the sun was half hidden by the buildings around them. She'd rested on his terrace for a while, watching the sun make its way down, and between clay-colored towers she could see the pyramids. She'd forgotten about that—how from so many spots in Cairo you could just look out and find them sitting on the edge of the city. The ancient world watching over the modern one.

Halawi looked as if he had been through the wringer. She knew that he had been at his office, wherever that was, but she didn't bother asking what the trouble was. She had enough difficulty keeping track of everything on her side of the national divide to fret about his. He sat beside her on a wicker chair, both of them taking in the view.

Without looking at her, he said, "Mrs. Kohl, I asked you last night, and I will ask again. Why are you here? What is it you want to do?"

In the clarity that had followed her confession, she had her answer ready. "I'd like to face the man who killed Emmett. Find out why he did it."

"The man who killed your husband was Gjergj Ahmeti. We will probably never find him."

"The person who paid Ahmeti. That's who I want to talk to. And maybe," she said after a moment, "do something more than talk."

He nodded solemnly, as if none of this was a surprise, as if everything she'd said had been preordained.

"And then I want to go home."

"Of course."

She took a breath. "I should probably talk to Stan again before I leave. He deserves some answers."

"I will see if I can arrange that."

"Are you going to tell me?"

He raised his eyebrows, as if he didn't know.

"Who paid Gjergj Ahmeti to kill Emmett?" When he didn't answer immediately, she said, "Was it Michael Khalil?"

"I don't know."

"He spoke to Emmett," she said. "In Budapest. On the day he was killed."

The Egyptian's voice rose an octave. "*Spoke* to him?"

There was something gratifying about this. Sophie, for once, knew more than he did. "Khalil claims he didn't, but the Hungarians saw them speaking."

Omar blinked rapidly, hands moving in his lap; this, clearly, was a revelation. "What did they speak about?"

"Stumbler, of course."

He pursed his lips, nodding. "I will certainly find out about this," he said, then turned and said a few words in Arabic. She realized that Sayyid, his tough young man, was standing in the doorway. Sayyid said something back.

"It's time for dinner," Omar told Sophie, then stood. At that moment his phone rang, and he answered, listened briefly, said a few more words in Arabic, and then walked the phone back inside, muttering the whole way. She followed Sayyid to the kitchen and helped Fouada set the table for dinner. Sayyid made no move to help with anything; he settled on the sofa and scrolled through messages on his phone. Omar returned, rubbing his eyes hard enough that when he released them he had to blink in pain. "What is it?" she asked.

He shook his head. "Nothing." He was lying to her, she knew, but part of her postconfession clarity was the understanding that there were things she would never know, so she did not press.

Meals, she remembered as she picked at her falafel and salad, had been important in Yugoslavia. After Vukovar, they had stayed for three more days in Zora's uncle's house, for after Vukovar they couldn't be comfortable with anyone else. Their shared secret tied them to Zora. They ate and drank with her and her friends—more strong-willed young people who mixed politics and art and faith as if they were gin and tonic and lime. There had been plates piled high with grilled *čevap, sarma,* meats of all kinds, pickles, cheap beer all around. Eat, drink, and back to the war—which was where she felt like these Egyptian men were heading when, after eating, Sayyid and Omar prayed together. The ritual washing. Hands on either side of their heads, behind their ears, praising Allah, then the near-crouch of hands on knees. Supplication. They had prayed in Yugoslavia, too, but never so humbly. The Serbs' god stood as their soldiers' rear guard. These people's god was always far, far ahead.

Then the men were gone, and she helped Fouada clean up. But this was not Sophie's kitchen, and eventually Fouada shooed her away. She returned to the terrace, hearing voices and car engines and, more distantly, prayers. She remembered drinking Cosmos with Glenda and listening to her complaints about Hungarians. She wondered with despair how she could have ever hated that life.

Because, Zora once told her, *you want something better, something more than mere happiness.*

And where had that gotten her? What kind of arrogant bitch could claim that there was anything more important than happiness? What kind of a fool could believe such a twisted philosophy?

This fool, this one here, sitting huddled on a stranger's terrace, unable to speak a word to her hostess. This was how you ended up alone.

8

———

1991

Emmett and Zora were arguing.

"This is *criminal*," he said. "Jesus Christ—can't you *see* that? It's *sick*."

"What *he* do is sick. You don't see what is in front of your nose?"

"And this doesn't make it any better!"

"It is *justice*."

"*Starving*? It's medieval. Just shoot the guy if you have to, but this?"

Sophie had said nothing. They had descended into the musty basement, the distant thumps of shells still going off in the direction of the city, and under the harsh glare of an unshaded lightbulb they'd found him tied up and gagged in the corner. Pale and filthy, a blond beard growing out on his face, sunken eyes wild with terror and, briefly, a moment of hope that evaporated when he saw the old pistol in Zora's hand. That was when Emmett had broken, waving his hands around, sometimes striking the low beams that ran just over their heads, sawdust and dirt raining down on them.

Sophie just used her eyes. She looked at the Croat soldier's torn fatigues and saw crusted black blood on his sleeves and collar and thighs. She watched the heels of his filthy boots digging into the damp dirt, the bruised, glazed eyes rolling in their sockets, the sharp red marks in his cheeks where the gag pressed. Looking at him made her sick, but thinking of his crimes was worse. She imagined the jackbooted Ustaše rounding up bony villagers and driving them, packed in trucks, to extermination camps. She saw a laughing man holding a small girl's ankles, swinging her against a brick wall, long blond hair flying. She thought of this man—*this very one*—drunk on *rakija*, drop-kicking a newborn, raping a bedridden woman. Suffocating her. She imagined herself on that bed, unable to get any air, the pain between her legs.

On the train to Prague, Emmett had said, *This is what the rest of the world looks like.* She'd had no idea, not really. Books, she felt all at once, had taught her nothing. Those who want to know, do. Harvard Square was Disneyland.

"Give me the gun," she said quietly, but loud enough for them to hear, for they stopped in midargument to look at her. Again, Sophie said, "Give me the gun," and held out her hand.

Zora at first looked surprised; then her face filled with understanding.

Emmett said, "No, Sophie. This is *crazy*."

But Zora had already handed over the pistol, and Sophie felt the comfort of its weight. It was a dangerous world, so much more dangerous than she had imagined in Massachusetts. You needed something on your side.

Emmett stepped closer. "Give it to me. Sophie? Are you listening? *Give* it to me."

Sophie put voice to her reasoning, though when she said it aloud she knew it was an excuse: "It's mercy. He'll starve."

"It isn't our place," Emmett said, as if that meant anything. Hadn't they come here believing that this *was* their place—that they were responsible for what occurred in these Balkan homes?

She raised the pistol.

"*No,*" he said, holding up his hands and stepping between her and the groaning Croat.

"Move," she told him. Cold now. So cold.

"It is Sofia's choice," said Zora, approaching, "not yours."

Emmett pushed her away and focused on his wife. He looked hard into her eyes, trying to read intent in them. He saw her resolve—she was sure he could see it, for at that moment he changed as well. Wearing an expression Sophie had never seen before, he stepped up to her. One long, purposeful step. Lips pressed tight together, he grabbed the gun by its barrel and twisted. She let him take it from her hand. This was her husband, after all. He was thinking more clearly than she was—that was obvious.

Then Emmett turned the pistol around in his hand so that he was holding the grip. He turned his back on Sophie, raised his arm, and shot the Croat twice. Once in the stomach, then once in the chest. The Croat tried to scream and cough behind his gag, kicking hard, leg spastic, blood seeping through the gag. Though they could see his death shivers so clearly, they only heard the high ringing in their aching ears. Then Emmett dropped the gun into the dirt, shocked by himself. Eventually—who knew how long it took?—the leg ceased its kicking, and the man sank deeper into himself in a final gurgling sigh. Zora, mouth agape, could only stare.

Sophie was shaking uncontrollably, the tears starting, yet she was still together enough to be surprised by how still and hard Emmett's hand was when he put his arm around her and pulled her close.

They couldn't go home that night, for a skirmish had occurred along the road they'd come in on. Bojan, the guitar still on his lap, was listening to updates on television, and he told them to wait until morning. He didn't seem particularly upset that the Croat in his basement was dead. He just shrugged, as if someone had burned his dinner. Zora brought out the *rakija*.

Later, their ears still ringing faintly, she said, "I see it in you. In *both* of you. You are not tourists; you are not just passing through." When Emmett accused her of having manipulated them, she said, "You overestimate. I just bring something for Bojan. I think you want to see. The pig in the basement—I don't know nothing about him. How you feel?"

"Angry," said Emmett.

"Cold," said Sophie.

"You was ready," Zora told Sophie. "You see the problem, and you want to fix it." To Emmett, she said, "You are right—starvation is medieval. Sofia knows it, too. You watch out for her."

"You're delusional," said Emmett. "You *trapped* us, and she was just—"

"*No,*" Zora interjected, wagging a finger at them both. "Stop pretending. I show you something, that's it. And now it is our secret. Something between us. Our connection. No one will know."

"Bojan will," said Emmett.

Zora shook her head. "If Bojan survives winter, I eat my hat."

Suddenly finding words again, Sophie said, "You don't own a hat."

For two full seconds they stared at her in silence, and then both Emmett and Zora burst into hysterical laughter. A quick release of the anxiety rippling through them. Sophie couldn't laugh, not yet, for she understood that Zora was telling the truth: She hadn't manipulated them into anything. Sophie had done the manipulating. She wasn't even sure now that she believed the story of the Croat's crimes, and what was most troubling was that this didn't bother her. She thought of how she had felt on that bridge in Prague—vacant, naive, stupid—and wondered if she could ever become that way again.

They raised their glasses.

Zora said, "Our secret. What hold us together."

Everything was just beyond her understanding that night, but by the next day, when they returned to Zora's uncle's house, she understood it better. When Viktor came by, it took only an hour for him to accuse the Americans of having had a ménage à trois with Zora, and so they went with that story, Zora even kissing them both in public. There was a kind of pleasure in this deception, and Sophie soon wondered why she had wanted to be naive again. She was real now. She was authentic. Decades later, when Zora offered her a new path to authenticity, she leapt at it.

Back in Boston, the job applications and interviews Sophie went to felt so unimportant, and employers could read the lack of ambition in her face. No one called her back. Emmett, on the other hand, applied himself with new fervor, redirecting himself toward diplomacy. "We didn't understand anything there," he told her one night. "I don't want to be that ignorant ever again."

She smiled and kissed him. "And I will be your wife," she said, believing that this was enough. He had sacrificed himself for her, after all, and she would never be able to forget that. Much later, when she saw him looking handsome and strong in Chez Daniel, she would still think how lucky she was.

9

Very early on Tuesday morning, Sophie woke in the wicker chair on Omar Halawi's terrace, covered in a blanket, as Fouada shook her gently awake. The woman said something melodic yet urgent with the word "Omar" somewhere in it. It was dark and cold. Sophie blinked, straightened in the chair, and wiped at her eyes. She ached. Fouada left without another word, so she followed. In the living room, Sayyid was buttoning up a thin leather jacket, and Omar was clutching a cup of Fouada's ubiquitous tea, watching Sophie come in.

"Are you rested?" he asked.

She nodded, running a hand through her hair.

"You told me," he went on, his voice low and even, "that you wanted to face the man who ordered your husband killed. Is that still true?"

Again, she nodded.

"Okay," he said, then went to give his wife a kiss. As they whispered to each other, Sayyid took a woman's long coat from the back of a chair and held it open for Sophie. It was apparently Fouada's, for it, like the dress she still wore, was too big. Sayyid kissed Fouada's cheeks while Omar opened the front door. "We can go now."

She followed the two men down to their car, Sayyid again taking the role of chauffeur. They drove for a while through the empty, pre-dawn city, crossing the Nile and heading south through squares that she thought she recognized, but wasn't sure of because in the hours before morning they were so empty and dead. She'd never traveled through Cairo this early, and it felt like a parallel city that she'd never gotten to know.

Eventually, the buildings thinned and disappeared. Black desert spread out to their left, and occasionally between smaller buildings on their right she caught glimpses of water. They were following the Nile south. After a turn-off a sign told them they were heading toward 15th of May City. She'd never been out here, and she wished briefly that Stan was beside her to explain everything. Where was he? Had he given up hope of finding her? Maybe, but once she was back home she would call him and they could have a more honest conversation. How honest? That was still to be decided.

Eventually, they took a left turn and headed along unlit, sandy streets, turning again and again until the road had become rough gravel, winding through dunes. Up ahead, she saw a pinpoint of light that grew in definition. It was a lamp under a large tent with a roof but no walls, only poles, nestled between two dunes. They parked beside another car, a scratched BMW; Sayyid got out and used his telephone. Omar turned to her and said, "We have him there."

When she squinted she could make out two shapes under the tarp. The large silhouette of a man pacing, a hand to his ear, talking on a phone, maybe to Sayyid. The other silhouette was a man in a chair, his head moving as he talked and talked, unlistened to. Was it Michael Khalil? She couldn't tell.

"Did he tell you everything?" she asked.

"Enough. If you ask him who's to blame for your husband's death, he will say Muammar Gadhafi. Certainly there is some truth to that, but not enough. No, he is to blame for the deaths of eight people I know of. Among them are Jibril Aziz, your husband Emmett, and Stanley Bertolli."

A sharp pain shot through her, and she turned to get a good look at his weathered face. "Stan? What?"

"I am afraid so."

"He killed Stan? Emmett *and* Stan?"

"Yes."

"When? I mean, Stan is—" She inhaled deeply, then shook her head. "He can't be."

"His body was discovered last night, in his car. He'd been shot."

"Oh God."

"It is about information," Omar told her. "It's always been about information, and betrayal. That is the man who is responsible."

She was hardly hearing him. She was thinking of Stan telling her to stay, to wait for him. Would he have lived? Or had he been marked from the moment Zora approached her in the Arkadia Mall? Had they all been marked since 1991? She said, "I don't know you. Not really. Maybe you've been lying to me. Maybe *you* killed them."

"That is up to you," he said, undeterred. "Remember that Inaya sent you to me. And while you may doubt this man's particular crime, I can tell you that he is certainly guilty of another capital offense in Islamic law—*fasad fil-ardh,* spreading mischief in the land. He has been on the wrong side of truncheons and guns and fists for a very long time."

"And you haven't been?"

He shrugged. "Perhaps I have, and when I am in that chair you can consider the question. Until that time, this is the situation that exists."

She breathed through her nose. "What's his name?"

"It does not matter."

"Yes, it does."

Omar took a moment to think, then said, "It is my responsibility to safeguard my country. For that reason, I will not share his name. Yet I also feel it is my responsibility to help you. You performed a great service for my country last year. You made sacrifices, and you have been treated poorly for your efforts. Now, you have a decision to make. This man has killed the men in your life, yet you also blame yourself. You understand that the information you gave to Zora Balašević is connected to what has occurred. I cannot absolve you of this. Yet I may be able to help."

What was he *talking* about?

"Come," he said, and got out of the car. Sayyid, off the phone now, opened her door. Cold gusts of desert wind tugged at her, hissing, and sand tickled her nose. Her ears chilled immediately; then she sneezed. Omar approached her and pointed toward the tent and those two silhouettes. The second man hadn't gotten up, and it was then that she realized he hadn't raised his hands while he'd been talking, which in Egypt was a near impossibility. He was tied to the chair.

Omar said, "That is the man who ordered your husband's murder. I am a man of law, and I am trying to be a good Muslim as well—never an easy thing. According to Islamic law, there are two options. The murderer may be slain in the manner that he committed murder. This is called *qisas*. Then there is *diyya*: The victim's family may choose forgiveness and be compensated financially instead. Hold out your hand."

Dazed, she did so, expecting him to hand her a gun. Instead, he placed a single coin into her palm, one Egyptian pound.

"Put it in your pocket."

She did so, and he said, "That coin may be one of two things. It could be compensation, your *diyya*—an initial down payment, you understand. Or it can be your fee to kill him. As he has done, I would be engaging a third party to commit the murder."

She took a step back, horrified, and he said, "It is an offer of work, Mrs. Kohl. Not a command. I can engage either of these men to commit the act as well. I simply thought that you might want a chance at redemption."

She didn't know what to say. She was thinking, *Question, question, question.* She was thinking, *This is what the rest of the world looks like.* She thought, *Do I believe anything this man's saying?* Then: *Does it even matter?* Because the truth was that she wanted this, not for anyone but herself. She had also wanted it in Yugoslavia, though Emmett had taken it from her. *That* was the truth.

This man's guilt wasn't nearly as important as what she wanted to believe.

"You do not have to decide at this moment," said Omar. "Sit in the car and think. But I should like to have a decision before sunrise. We will need to clean up afterward."

Omar

1

In February 2009, still recovering from the heart attack he'd had at the beginning of the month, and a week before Jibril showed up to introduce him to a plan the computers called Stumbler, Omar discovered the existence of Zora Balašević in an agent report. As with Jibril seven years earlier, it was his eye for anomaly that guided him. She was an odd choice for Dragan Milić, whose staff in the Serbian embassy consisted entirely of men between the ages of twenty-four and thirty-seven. He brought this news to Ali Busiri, who suggested they assign some watchers to her.

Omar sent Sayyid and Mahmoud, and by their third day of surveillance they had taken photographs of this fifty-five-year-old Serb woman having drinks with an American diplomat named Emmett Kohl, who had arrived in town not long before she had. It was a brief lunch, but Sayyid moved close enough to overhear its climax. Emmett Kohl said in English, "I don't give a shit what you threaten me with, Zora. I'm not spying for you." Not loudly, but calmly and with the kind of self-control only diplomats and hired assassins can master.

Clearly there was something going on—if not from Kohl's blunt statement, then from the fact that Mahmoud recognized an American agent sitting at a table near the street, also snapping pictures. So with Busiri's blessings they picked up Zora Balašević the next day, and Omar spoke with her in English.

She was tougher than she looked, refusing to be turned by threats. She *was* a spy, after all—they knew that—and therefore it was within their rights to imprison her or kick her out of the country. Neither option seemed to concern her. So Omar turned it around. "Of course, the situation could be different. For spies who work for us, life in Cairo can be very comfortable. Profitable, even."

He'd gotten her attention.

She refused to be completely open with him, but she did reveal that she was preparing to tap a source in the American embassy. "We watched you try, Zora. We watched you fail."

She shook her head. "There are two ways to do this, and I've only tried one."

So Omar was on hand to watch the approach in the Arkadia Mall, and he listened to the wire Balašević was wearing in the Conrad Hilton. He marveled at her forwardness and the way she thought on her feet: Balašević motioned toward a blond woman with some Russians and claimed she was the woman's controller. Such marvelous invention! He was amazed and inspired.

It took two weeks of work before Sophie Kohl finally came around, and once that relationship had been established the rest of the infrastructure could be put into place. Balašević was paid through a front company called Beautiful Nile Enterprises, and in return she passed flash drives directly to Rashid el-Sawy.

The Serbian embassy soon realized that their agent was no longer loyal, and Dragan Milić attempted to have her sent out of the country. Ali Busiri met him for lunch to explain that Balašević was not to be touched, at least not within the borders of Egypt.

By April, once the quality of Sophie Kohl's intelligence had been established, Omar was taken off of the operation and moved to less demanding assignments. "You've had one heart attack," Busiri told him. "Why don't we let you survive to retirement?" It was left to el-Sawy and Busiri to collect and process the files before distributing selected intelligence to other departments. Again, Omar had been sidelined, but he chose not to dwell on this as he watched over the well-being of diplomats in their city and came to terms with the strong possibility that the acquisition of Zora Balašević would be the final accomplishment of his career.

A year later, in April 2010, Busiri asked him to meet with Balašević again. Why him? "Because she's getting angry with Rashid, and she doesn't know I exist. I'd prefer to keep it that way."

He visited her apartment on Al-Muizz Street and found her in a state. "What is the problem?"

Biting her nails and gulping Turkish coffee, Zora said, "Sophie is losing her taste for it. I am losing her."

"Has she told you she wants to quit?"

A quick shake of the head. "Not yet. But she will."

"This is normal enough," he told her. "You should threaten her. Can you use the threat you used against Mr. Kohl?"

She shrugged, unsure. "I don't want to."

"Then we can approach her ourselves. We have enough evidence of her cooperation—we threaten to make that public, and she will continue working."

"No," Zora said firmly. "She does not *know* about you. She thinks all this is for my people. You come in, and she will snap."

He wondered if this was true, or if Zora, with the greed that had brought her to Cairo in the first place, was afraid that she would be cut out of the chain and lose her considerable income. "Well, then," he said. "I suppose you have no choice."

She didn't seem convinced.

"What is the problem, Zora? Your work has been excellent."

Finally, she said, "I *like* her. I always have. She trusts me, but I also trust her. We have built something here, and this is going to destroy it."

He would have never thought Zora Balašević so sentimental.

"You know how much she has done," Zora continued. "All of it, for me."

Busiri had told him nothing, but he nodded.

She said, "She did not have to sleep with him. I don't think she wanted to. But I told her it could be important. I told her that if any suspicion came up, then it would be best to have him already attached to her."

"Who?"

She gave him a suspicious look. "Stanley Bertolli. Who else do you think?"

He tried to talk his way out of it, but his slip had been obvious. She said, "Who's running me?"

"Michael Khalil."

"I mean, who's running Khalil?"

"We are, Zora. That is all that matters."

Of course that wasn't all that mattered, for running agents is the closest of all relationships, closer sometimes than that between a husband and wife. Zora was shocked the way a wife would be if her husband had been sharing her intimate secrets with a stranger.

Once the Kohls left Cairo, he took it upon himself to visit Zora again as she prepared to leave the country. She was calmer now, more tired. A year and a half working for them had taken something from her. "Come to see me off?" she asked.

"You are heading home?"

"Indirectly."

"Yes?"

She measured him with her eyes a moment, then said, "They really don't tell you anything, do they?"

He settled on the sofa. "Why don't you tell me?"

She told him that by July she'd had enough. "It happens, you know. People tire." She had told Khalil that it was time to wrap things up. "I could see it in Sophie's eyes. She was dying. Her marriage was going to hell, and her relationship with Stan was killing her. And me—she did not even have me. Just as I predicted, she tried to pull out, and so I had to become the whip. When I was younger this would not have bothered me. But look at me. I am not young. I am tired. I want to live my life."

"What did Khalil say?"

"He told me that if I tried to walk away I would be arrested as a spy. Then he changed our arrangement. He told me that from that point on no money would be sent to my account. It would be collected, in escrow, until the time came for me to leave."

Omar cleared his throat, then wiped self-consciously at his nose. "I am sorry about that."

She shrugged. "So now we are down to passing packages in public places. I will meet him in Frankfurt, where he will give me the rest of my money." She laughed hoarsely. "I can't wait to get out of this shithole."

He wasn't sure what to say, so he got up and helped her latch a suitcase that was giving her trouble, then went to make two cups of coffee while she went to the bathroom. When she came out, she was smiling again, but the smile gave him no joy. "You just passed me on, didn't you?"

"I had no choice. It was not my decision."

She nodded at that and thanked him for the coffee. He followed her back to the living room. With the full boxes and empty walls it felt barren. He asked what she'd had on Sophie Kohl. After thinking about it a moment, she said, "I threatened to reveal to the world that she is wonderful, and that she has nothing to be ashamed of. I threatened to expose the fact that she is the kind of woman who can do anything, even if she cannot see it herself." She paused. "Do not ever make an enemy of Sophie Kohl."

Given this preparation, he expected something impressive from his first meeting with Sophie Kohl months later, but she was a disappointment. Perhaps Balašević had oversold her asset, but part of the problem was himself. By the time he arrived at the Semiramis, he felt as if his bones were going to splinter. Six hours in a bumping automobile to get back to Cairo from Marsa Matrouh—what had he been thinking?

The truth was that he had hoped he would never have to meet Sophie Kohl. His section had benefited from her information, but he had trouble feeling much appreciation for a woman who had given away her country's secrets so easily, and then began an affair with another man in order to protect herself.

He'd seen her picture plenty of times and had watched from a distance as she met with Zora, but he was unprepared for the woman he found in the Semiramis café. She was thin, her hair flat and unkempt—she displayed that inattention to her looks that naturally beautiful women slide into, assuming the shape of their faces will compensate for their laziness. Then he admonished himself: Her husband had been killed, and he should be kinder.

Despite appearances, she proved herself more astute than he imagined, catching the contradictions inherent in the facts. For example: Why would the CIA kill her husband if he didn't believe the Agency was behind Stumbler?

What could he say to such rational thought? This woman, like anyone outside of the intelligence services, believed that intelligence organizations worked by machine logic, and that this was their flaw. Their flaw was that they *didn't* work by machine logic. They worked by human logic, which was as frail and emotional as the people who filled the agencies of the world. The best he could offer was hardly an example of perfect logic: "Mistakes were made." Then he focused on his primary desire, which was to get Sophie Kohl out of Egypt. She was prying into sensitive things, and if she wasn't careful she was going to get hurt.

Did he care? Did it matter if an adultress and traitor was hurt or even murdered under his watch? Maybe; maybe not. But he was beginning to believe that the world really was a different place now that Mubarak was gone. The rules had been broken and tossed to the winds. A new beginning, the most important moment in any nation's history. This was the moment when new precedents were being set. If he let the CIA murder this woman in Egypt, then it would do so again. If she left unscathed, then hope remained that the country could become a place where even Fouada would feel safe.

After their meeting, still not knowing if she was going to follow his advice and leave, he waited in his car, which he'd parked in the same spot from which he'd watched Jibril leave with John Calhoun. It was nearly nine. He thought about how she looked, this Sophie Kohl, how tangled in body and mind, and he worried what she might get up to before finally leaving Egypt. So he put in a call to Sayyid, who showed up within twenty minutes, climbing into the passenger seat. "Mrs. Sophie Kohl, wife of the murdered American consul, is in room 306. I need you to keep an eye on her. If she receives any visitors, tell me."

Sayyid frowned. "What's she doing here?"

"She's trying to figure out who killed her husband."

"Are we helping?"

He wasn't sure how to answer, so he didn't.

2

———

Fouada was asleep when he got home, and after a half hour sitting on the sofa, feeling his sore bones and muscles creak, thinking over his conversation with Sophie Kohl, he was sure he wouldn't be able to sleep. Yet when his phone rang a little after midnight, it woke him. He snatched at it. "Yes?"

"A visitor," said Sayyid.

Omar blinked in the darkness, but nothing was coming into focus. "Who?"

"More than one, actually. Paul Johnson from the American embassy has been sitting in the lobby all night, but not long ago Rashid el-Sawy went to see her."

Omar sat up straight. "*What?*"

"He took the elevator, so I went up the stairs. He was standing outside her door."

"Did he go inside?"

"I think he wanted to, but she didn't let him."

"Do they know each other?"

"He introduced himself as Michael Khalil. After that, he talked too quietly."

El-Sawy talking to John Calhoun, and then Sophie Kohl. What was going on?

He told Sayyid to keep him updated, then hung up. A light came on in the bedroom, and he heard Fouada: "Omar? What are you do-ing out there?"

He went to the bedroom door, leaned against the frame, his back aching. The sheets were up to her chin, and she was smiling dream-ily. He said, "Work."

"No more trips to the coast, okay?" she said. "My bones."

He gave her a quiet laugh and came to sit on the edge of the bed, reaching out to hold her hand. "You're not alone."

"How did your meeting go?"

"Hard to say," he said, then hesitated.

"Yes?"

"I have the feeling that Ali Busiri is playing at something."

Her face darkened, her anger, years old by now, rising again. "Then you need to stop him."

Had a single trip into the field with her husband really changed Fouada so much? He stared at her, holding her hand, remembering how she'd been decades ago, when they were younger and poorer and, if not happier, then at least more energetic. Theirs had been an ar-ranged marriage, and so happiness had taken longer, but it had come.

Their bed was inviting, yet he really wouldn't be able to sleep now. Not yet. "I need to step out again."

She said, "Get the bastard, but don't break yourself in the process."

He kissed her high forehead, tasting her nightly creams.

On the drive to the office, Sayyid called to tell him that he had listened at Sophie Kohl's door. "She's getting ready for bed. Do you want me to make contact?"

"No," he said. "Just wait."

The night guards at the Interior Ministry were more lax than the day shift, and he was soon taking the elevator to the seventh floor, which was empty and dark. He powered up his computer, and once it was on he logged into the secure Web site, through which he found a database of flight manifests and a section marked "EXTERNAL TRAFFIC," dealing solely with flights that had entered or left Egyptian territory. He chose the "BY PASSENGER NAME" form and typed "Rashid el-Sawy." There were a few hits, but those were different el-Sawys. He tried "Michael Khalil," then read through the results. The earliest one, in April of last year, was to Tripoli. What was Khalil doing in Tripoli? He had no family there, and by and large his work should have kept him in Egypt. In September there was the flight to Frankfurt to pass on Zora's final payment, and on March 1—only five days ago—a trip to Munich, from which he had returned on the third. The ticket had been paid for in cash. Emmett Kohl had been killed on March 2.

He rubbed his eyes, wishing he'd picked up some tea on his way here. He let his mind drift back over what he'd learned during the last weeks. He thought of Emmett Kohl's conviction that the American government wasn't behind Stumbler, and Sophie Kohl's excellent question: *Then why did they kill him?* Was the difference between human and machine logic really the explanation? What if the CIA really hadn't killed Kohl? Then what followed?

Try the reverse, then: What if Emmett Kohl was killed because he *didn't* believe America was behind Stumbler? Did this mean that Jibril, believing the opposite, was safe?

And what about Marsa Matrouh? Qasim was there, waiting for the arrival of Stumbler's front line, yet he had heard nothing.

He went back to the computer and began searching the names of the men whose disappearances were to precede Stumbler, typing them one at a time. Yousef al-Juwali—still missing. Abdurrahim Zargoun—still missing. Waled Belhadj . . .

An article from *Le Monde,* which had just been posted online before its print appearance in the morning:

Last night, two workers discovered a body in a large sports bag at the lock in Soisy-sur-Seine.

The men called the police, who arrived at the scene at 18:54.

By morning, Sous-brigadier Bertrand Roux reported to journalists that the heavily decomposed corpse had been identified as

Waled Belhadj, Libyan national, 41 years old, who had been missing since 20 February. Evidence suggests that he was shot in the head before being placed in the sports bag and deposited in the Seine. It is believed that he has been dead for more than a week.

Waled Belhadj was previously a member of the Association of the Democratic Libyan Front, which advocates democratic change in Libya. He moved to Paris from London in August 2009 after a disagreement with fellow members of the Democratic Libyan Front and was rumored to be establishing a new organization.

According to sources, a current Democratic Libyan Front member, Yousef al-Juwali, went missing in London on 19 February. Police are not able to confirm a connection between the murder and the disappearance.

Exhaustion was one thing, but he was starting to feel nauseous. This made no sense. Why take the men if they were only to be shot in the head? Who would have wanted that? Who—

Within him, a spark struck. Great understandings were rare in Omar's experience, but when they came they did not come piecemeal. A spark was struck, and suddenly there was a whole furnace blazing. Such was the case now. The fire woke him up, burning away the nausea and the cobwebs. The puzzle pieces flew up in the air and settled back down in crystalline perfection. No, no sickness now. Just curiosity and the aesthetic pleasure of discovery. Then, as he examined the pieces, looking for anomalies that might rebut the entire theory, the curiosity twisted into a low, burning anger.

He called Sayyid. "Yes, boss?"

"She's still there?"

"Yes."

"If she tries to leave the room, stop her. Understand?"

"I . . . yes, I understand."

"I'll be there soon."

Before leaving, he checked the flight manifests again, and saw that Sophie Kohl had reserved a seat on a 9:30 A.M. flight back to America. If only she'd left yesterday. If only she'd skipped Cairo altogether. But she hadn't, and now it was too late.

3

He was impatient, but impatience would not serve him well. This had to be done right, or not at all.

When he brought Sophie Kohl home, he was reminded again of Jibril. He was too soft, he realized. Caring for strays was becoming his fate.

Fouada had never learned English, but she knew how to take care of someone without words. He told her, "She's been through a lot. She may become angry. If you like, I'll ask someone to stay here with you. Mahmoud could come."

Fouada waved that away. "This is about the bastard?"

"I believe it is."

"Then I will handle it. You do what you have to do." She kissed him on the cheek, then offered Sayyid some tea. A look from Omar convinced him to say no.

He and Sayyid spoke in the stairwell. "Are you going to tell me what's going on?" the young man asked.

"When it's verified, yes. Not before. But I need your trust. Do I have it?"

"Of course."

"We'll need Mahmoud as well. Can you see to that?"

A nod.

"Tomorrow, though, all three of us will be in the ministry like usual, as if nothing is amiss. By the end of the day it should be set-tled."

Sayyid ran his fingers through his thick hair, nodding.

"Go take a nap, and I'll see you in the office."

By the time he returned to the apartment, Sophie Kohl had fallen asleep on the guest bed, on top of the sheets, her clothes still on. Fouada said, "The girl is exhausted."

"So am I."

He was at his desk by nine, running through his mental list of items to look into. He went back into history, rechecking things he already knew, in particular Hisham Minyawi's disaster in 2005, when the source he'd gained in the Libyan embassy was executed. Omar walked over to Hisham's office on the opposite end of the building and knocked. Hisham was in his midforties, his thick mustache prema-turely gray, with a heavy paunch and bleak eyes. He was smoking a cigarette and wrapping up a phone call when Omar arrived. He waved the older man in. "Omar," he said, shaking his head. "Busy times, no?"

"Truly," Omar said, closing the door and taking a seat in the smoky room. "How's the family?"

"Very well. Fouada?"

"Excellent." Omar leaned closer. "I wanted to ask you about Yousef Rahim, from the Libyan embassy."

The bleakness in Hisham's eyes deepened. "Any reason you're revisiting my failures, Omar? That was six years ago."

Omar shook his head. "Don't misunderstand. I'm looking into other things, and wondering if this connects."

Hisham seemed to relax, just a little. Being reminded of that black spot on his record still made him sore. "What's to tell? It was an easy trick. Yousef was a queer. He'd been visiting boys over in Heliopolis, some dank little underground club. I offered him silence, as well as some compensation."

"So what happened?"

He lit another cigarette, frowning as he remembered the news of the quick execution in Tripoli. "I don't know, Omar. I ran it perfectly. No one could have known we were meeting. Full security procedures." He shrugged. "Maybe Yousef broke down and admitted it to the embassy."

"You believe that?"

Hisham shook his head.

"Then what other possibilities are there?"

Hisham opened his mouth, thought better of it, then shook his head again. "Ask Allah. You're the religious one, aren't you? Or you used to be."

Omar climbed to his feet. He had been a religious man a long time ago, but he'd lost track along the way. He'd ignored the mosque and, until recently, prayer—that most basic requirement of a Muslim had seemed beyond his means. Praying with that frightened man in Marsa Matrouh, to his surprise, had made him feel lighter. Yet as he walked back to his office even his faith slipped from his mind, for he was thinking about the words Hisham hadn't had the courage to speak aloud. The only possible way Yousef Rahim could have been uncovered was if someone in this office had leaked to Tripoli.

He had to wait until eleven for an audience with Busiri, whose morning had been full of meetings upstairs, discussing personnel changes. The revolution was trickling slowly down through the departments of the Interior Ministry, and Busiri had received a list of names whose continued employment in the Central Security Forces would be unpalatable to any new administration. He was collecting the files on these employees when Omar tapped on his door. "Omar! You look like hell."

He came in and settled in a chair. "Fouada's having sleepless nights," he said. "Which means I'm having them, too."

"I'm sure she's worth it," Busiri muttered, his eyes back on the files. "Did you know we have to say good-bye to seven people right in this office?"

He passed over the list of names, and Omar read it. He knew all these people, knew the ways in which they had, over the years, abused their position. He passed it back. "Nothing unexpected there."

"But still," Busiri said, and turned the paper facedown on his desk, finally giving him his full attention. "What news?"

Omar cleared his throat. "I'd like to know what Rashid el-Sawy is up to."

"Rashid? Why do you ask?"

"Because last night he met with Sophie Kohl. He tried to convince her to work with him to find Jibril Aziz."

Busiri looked around his wide desk until he'd spotted his Camels. He lit one. "Did Rashid tell you this?"

"Mrs. Kohl did."

He nodded, smoke wafting around his head, as if he already knew they had talked. Perhaps he did. "Any idea where she is now?"

"Isn't she in her hotel?" Omar asked, full of innocence.

"Apparently not."

"Then she's with Rashid."

Busiri shook his head.

"Why was Rashid meeting with her?"

"He's following leads on his own. I'll be sure to ask him. Why were *you* meeting with her?"

"I wanted to question her about her husband's murder."

"Anything interesting?"

Omar nodded slowly. "She told me she'd been staying with Stanley Bertolli. Did you know about that?"

"Of course."

"Apparently," he said, breathing steadily to make his lie come off more smoothly, "Mr. Bertolli believes the solution to the mystery of her husband's death lies not with the Americans, but with someone else. The Libyans, perhaps."

Busiri's eyebrows rose sharply. "Libya?"

Omar nodded, palms up, as if the proposition were just as ridiculous to him. "He thinks that the exiles who disappeared were taken by the Libyans, not by the Americans. Libya gets rid of the exiles, and Stumbler dies before it can start. The question is: How did the Libyans find out about Stumbler in the first place? This is the question Emmett Kohl wondered about. If Bertolli can figure that out, then he'll be able to find Kohl's murderer."

There was only a moment's pause before Busiri recovered. "But we know, don't we? Zora Balašević's ethical sense was about as lasting as Hosni's portraits are now. She sold to us. She sold to Libya."

It was an answer he had expected, for he'd gone through the various permutations of this conversation all night long. It was the only explanation he could have offered.

"Maybe I should get in touch with Paul Johnson, then," Omar suggested. "I could tell him to pass that on to Bertolli."

Busiri waved the proposition away. "I'm meeting with Bertolli this afternoon. I'll tell him myself."

"You're meeting him?"

"He requested it."

Omar nodded.

"Anything else?"

Omar shook his head and climbed to his feet. He took another walk down the corridor, and in the break room found Sayyid and Mahmoud talking on the sofa, a small television playing Al Jazeera. He nodded at the two men, then turned up the volume until it blared the gunfire of Libyan rebels into that small room. He sat close to Mahmoud while Sayyid pretended to be watching television. "I need you to watch someone today. Do not lose him."

Mahmoud nodded gruffly, then said, "Who?"

4

He left a half hour early and was home by five, where he found Fouada in the kitchen surrounded by the pungent aroma of freshly fried falafel. Sophie Kohl was resting on the terrace. "I'm beginning to find her dull," Fouada whispered to him. "Nothing like Jibril."

"You just like boys," he whispered back. Omar went to the bathroom in the rear of the apartment to wash up, then out to the terrace to sit beside Sophie. She was calmer now, rested, and as they spoke he remembered Zora Balašević's advice: *Don't ever make an enemy of Sophie Kohl.* Then she told him that Rashid el-Sawy had talked to her husband on the day he was killed.

He was shocked by this, then he wasn't. "What did they speak about?"

"Stumbler, of course."

Sayyid had arrived and was waiting in the terrace doorway. "We're going to be up all night," he told the young man in Arabic.

Sayyid shrugged. "This is the life I chose."

When they got up for dinner, Omar's phone rang—it was Mahmoud. "Yes?"

Mahmoud was breathing heavily. It sounded as if he'd been running. "Sir, it—he's dead."

"What? Who?" Omar walked inside, past Sayyid, heading for his bedroom.

"The American . . . Bertolli."

"Tell me."

Mahmoud took another breath. "I followed Ali to al-Azhar Park, and he met Stanley Bertolli. Ten, fifteen minutes. That was all. Ali started to walk back to his car, but after turning a corner he stopped and sat on a bench. Like he was waiting for something. After a short while, we both heard it. Quiet, but it was there. A gunshot. Ali got up again and walked to his car. I went back and found the American's car. Rashid. It was Rashid el-Sawy. He was getting out of the backseat, taking plugs out of his ears, walking away. I waited, then went to check. It . . . it's a mess."

By then, Omar was sitting heavily on the corner of his bed, all strength drained from him.

"What do you want me to do?"

Omar rubbed his face hard enough to make it hurt. He'd done this. He'd tried to provoke Ali, and his efforts had killed a man. He said, "The bastard probably went home. Verify this for me. Okay?"

It took about three minutes before Omar could find the strength to climb to his feet and join the others. Fouada had started placing food on the dining table, Sophie Kohl helping her. Sayyid put away his own phone and stood up. It was time to eat.

After dinner, Sayyid asked for the direction of Mecca, and Omar decided to join him. It felt good praying with the young man; it felt essential. Just because he had lost track of his faith didn't mean that it had left him. Afterward, he climbed to his feet and returned to the bedroom. Fouada followed to help him change into a fresh shirt. She said, "Are you getting any sleep tonight?"

"I don't think so."

"You need it," she said, placing a hand on his bony shoulder. "You don't look pretty."

"You do," he said, holding her hand, then kissed her cheeks. "Enough procrastination."

He and Sayyid left together, Omar driving them to a dark residential street corner in Maadi, where Mahmoud waited inside a BMW with scratches on the trunk—someone, Mahmoud explained sheepishly, had keyed his car last week. Omar spoke to Sayyid briefly. He was to go to John Calhoun's place and search for a book of names—it was, he had realized, the one missing piece, and if it was in Egypt it was either there or in the American embassy. Afterward, Sayyid should continue to a quarry that lay off the road leading to 15th of May City, south of Cairo. Omar admitted that he didn't know what the book of names looked like, or if it would even be there—but if it was there, then it should be in their possession, and no one else's. "And if Calhoun's there?" asked Sayyid.

"Maybe you should just ask him for it. Nicely, of course."

Sayyid smiled, then drove off in Mahmoud's BMW. Omar brought Mahmoud over to his car. "You'll be in the backseat," Omar told the big man.

"I'm being chauffeured?"

"Something like that."

They arrived at Ali Busiri's house, where the streetlights shone against the rain-damp road. Omar parked outside the gate and checked in the rearview—Mahmoud was down and out of sight. "Comfortable?"

"Does it matter?" came Mahmoud's muffled voice.

He took out his phone and called Busiri. "Omar?" his boss said cautiously.

"Sir, I need your advice on something."

"What is it?"

"It's not for the phone. I'm outside." He paused, then: "Apologies, but it's important."

He saw a curtain part, letting out light. It was one of the lower windows—the office, he knew. He rolled down his window and waved. A couple of minutes later, the door opened, and Ali Busiri came out wearing a smoking jacket over a clean shirt and pants, sandals on his feet. He looked as if he'd just come from a bath. After al-Azhar Park, he would have needed one.

He was in no hurry, and he looked very tired. Anxiety did that, Omar knew. It sucked you dry. Busiri came around to the passenger's side, opened the door, and climbed in, closing the door behind himself. "I hope you're not asking for love advice," he said breathily. "I'm a mess with that."

"No, sir. I wanted advice about the case."

Busiri nodded, a hesitant smile. "Go ahead."

Omar fingered the steering wheel, feeling his own anxiety bubble to the surface. "What if I had discovered that someone in our own section was responsible for much of what we've been seeing?"

"What? Who?"

"Rashid el-Sawy. He oversaw the murder of Emmett Kohl."

"What?" Busiri's hands began to flap around. "Why would he do that?"

"Because Emmett Kohl, like Stanley Bertolli, knew that the Americans were not behind Stumbler. He knew that the Libyans had been killing off the exiles who formed the first stage of Stumbler. To make sure it could never get off the ground. Gadhafi rightly fears the introduction of a second force in addition to the Benghazi rebels."

"You're saying those exiles were killed?"

"One of them was found dead last night. In Paris. Dead for over a week."

He let that sink in a moment, waiting until Busiri asked the obvious question: "This is all very interesting, Omar, but why would Rashid care about it? Why would he want to kill an American diplomat?"

"We received the plans through Emmett Kohl's wife. Maybe Kohl knew this, maybe he didn't, but either way the plans made a leap over our border at some point, to Libya, and he was preparing to focus on that."

"Are you saying that Rashid sold the plans to Tripoli?"

"Last April, he spent a week in Tripoli. I'm guessing he was transporting cash, as he did when he paid Zora Balašević in Frankfurt. In this case, though, he was receiving money—for intelligence he'd sold them."

"Well," said Busiri.

"This went on for years," Omar continued. "As far back as 2005 we were leaking to the Libyans. Remember Yousef Rahmin? That information moved fast. Of course, it would've had to—what if Yousef had identified Rashid as being in the pay of the Libyans? No, he had to get rid of Yousef Rahmin quickly.

"And then," Omar went on, "there was Stumbler. That must have been a surprise for Rashid. Who would have guessed that, armed with the Stumbler plans, the Libyans would kidnap and kill all the exiles? Who would have guessed that the architect of those plans, Jibril Aziz, would suddenly believe his plan was being put into action?" Omar shook his head. "Such bad luck, after years of perfect security. But how did Rashid learn of Jibril?" He paused, just briefly. "I asked myself that, and of course it was my fault. *Our* fault, really. Jibril talked to me, and so I talked to you. I told you everything I knew. And because you trusted him, you told Rashid. Am I correct?"

Silently, Busiri nodded. Like a man with enormous things on his mind.

"Rashid learned that Jibril had gone to talk with Emmett Kohl, and that Kohl suspected the Libyans rather than the Americans. Remember what I said to you? I said that, if this was true, the logical next question was: How did the Libyans get hold of Stumbler? Certainly you would have brought up that question to him. No?"

Another silent nod.

"Rashid was scared," Omar went on, "so he hired an Albanian murderer. They went to Budapest, Rashid traveling via Munich. He met with Emmett Kohl and spoke to him about Stumbler. I was surprised when I learned this, but it makes sense. He had to go himself, because even a fish as cold as Rashid would have wanted to verify that Kohl was a threat before giving the Albanian his orders."

Now Busiri was staring out the side window, across the street, so that Omar could not see his face. Quietly, he said, "But isn't this a lot of effort, just to cover up that he'd been selling some information?"

"I thought so, too," Omar admitted. "But think about it from his perspective. Think about it now. They're beginning to pick apart our offices. You're getting rid of seven people today—tomorrow, how many? Once the elections bring in these idealistic protesters, there will be no patience for anyone who has been selling intelligence to a dictator. Particularly intelligence that helps Gadhafi wipe out his own people. They wouldn't even have to put him in prison—just let the newspapers find out what he's done. He'd be dead within the week. The crowds are not very forgiving."

"No," Busiri said. "They're not."

"So he will do anything to protect his secret. He will murder an American in Budapest. He will murder an American in Cairo."

Busiri turned back, frowning. "An American in Cairo?"

"I'm afraid so," Omar said. "Rashid executed Stanley Bertolli. About an hour ago. That murder was witnessed." He paused. "You can see that he has to be stopped."

Busiri was scratching at his rough cheek. "Yes, I can see that."

"Do you know where Rashid is?"

Busiri opened his mouth, then shut it. "I'll call him. My phone's in the house."

"Wait," Omar said, placing a hand on his knee. "There's one thing I can't figure out."

Unsure, Busiri turned to face him. "What's that?"

"Where is Jibril?"

"He's in Libya. Isn't he?"

"He hasn't gotten in touch with anyone. I'm beginning to fear he's dead."

Busiri shook his head, as if this weren't to be believed, but said, "Stanley Bertolli believed this as well."

"He told you Jibril was dead?"

"Yes, but Rashid couldn't have killed Aziz, too."

Omar closed his eyes, absorbing this terrible news, then said, "If Jibril is dead, and it wasn't Rashid, then who? Was it the Americans? If so, then why would they have let him go into Libya in the first place?"

"You told me," Busiri said, his voice warbly now. "They wanted his contacts."

"Maybe," Omar said. "But what if they didn't care about them?

What if Rashid, panicking, made a final call to Tripoli? Told them someone was coming in to organize his old networks and whip the revolution into a frenzy? Told them, too, that if they got this man they would also get his whole network? All it would take was a phone call, or a meeting in a park to discuss it with someone from the Libyan embassy."

Busiri was chewing the inside of his cheek.

Omar said, "Gadhafi must be paying him a lot of money to be worth all these corpses."

Busiri didn't say anything.

Omar let the silence linger for a while, then turned to take in the broad expanse of his boss's home. "That's a very nice house. How much did it cost?"

Busiri reached for the door handle.

"Mahmoud," said Omar, and the big man emerged from the backseat, a leviathan rising from the shadows, his hands already fixing onto Busiri's shoulders.

If Omar expected surprise, he was disappointed. Busiri gave a single futile push, then dropped back into Mahmoud's embrace. The big man reached over to make sure the passenger door was locked, then brought out a Helwan 9 mm pistol and made sure their boss got a good look at it. Omar started the car.

"Where are we going?" Busiri asked.

"To a place of conversation," Omar said.

As they started to move, the door to Busiri's house opened. The tall silhouette of his wife watched them drive away. After a moment, a phone began to ring. "May I?" Busiri asked.

"I thought your phone was in the house," said Mahmoud.

Omar said, "Give it to Mahmoud."

Busiri did so, the light of the phone briefly basking them all in blue, and Omar said, "Get rid of it."

Mahmoud rolled down his window and tossed out the phone. It clattered against the irregular pavement, cracking down the middle, but continued to ring. Ten minutes later, the wheel of a moving truck pulverized it.

PART IV

—◆—

THE NEW YEAR

Wednesday, 9 March 2011

1:30 P.M. Eastern Standard Time (Boston)
8:30 P.M. Eastern European Time (Cairo)

1

She had been in America, beyond passport control, for thirty minutes, still wearing Fouada Halawi's dress, and she was overcome by the feeling that she'd entered a world of pale, oversized children. Pudgy white-haired men in T-shirts and padded, primary-color jackets wandered around poking at cell phones; wives and mothers in practical shoes and sneakers lounged at café tables, curbing their well-dressed children. The airport stores shone so brightly, drunk with colors, each storefront flashy and bold, something shiny to attract attention. Compared to Budapest and Cairo, Logan Airport felt like a candy-colored land of enterprise, the filtered air clean and smoke-free. *How*, she wondered, *can anyone be afraid of us?*

Then she stiffened inside as one of the children—a boy of seven, maybe, or eight—leaned back against a huge window overlooking the parked airplanes and watched her pass. His face looked so old, his expression so intense, that she hurried her pace, wanting to run from his accusing stare, but at the same time telling herself to calm down. That boy was American, not Czech.

She'd had enough of thinking about herself and what she'd done. She had dreamed about a gun and a wailing man who was at one moment Egyptian and the next Croatian, and when she woke up ten hours later in John Calhoun's wrecked apartment she had seen it all again in the twilight as yet another call to prayer filled the city. She'd been alone when she woke, and in that quiet time leafed through modernist poets until Calhoun returned from some errand and tried, once or twice, to speak to her, but she hadn't been up for it. He'd looked so uncomfortable. She told him she liked his books, and he seemed to blush. He answered a phone call and spoke quietly for a moment, then told her Harry was coming over. "Okay," she'd said, before going back to the mess of his bedroom.

Harry had been confused. "Look, I don't have it straight yet, but John has filled in some details, and tomorrow I'm meeting with the Egyptians to sort out the rest. Maybe you want to help me out in the meantime?"

"Is Stan really dead?"

He hesitated, then nodded.

"Are you meeting with Omar Halawi?"

Again, he nodded.

"He'll explain it," she said, for she didn't want to explain anything to anyone anymore. She was sick of the act of conversation, but primarily she was terrified that, were she to start speaking she would tell him everything, and he would not let her leave.

On the second plane, which left from Amsterdam, she'd sat beside a nervous woman who, twice during the flight, took out a prescription bottle and dry-swallowed a little blue pill with a K-shaped hole in the center. The second time, the woman—Irish, by her accent—self-consciously explained. "Klonopin. Modern pharmaceuticals are a godsend."

Now, as she lifted her shoulder bag higher and wandered through the crowd, following signs toward the exit, Sophie thought that she could use a godsend. Prayer had never been her bag, as Zora put it. A blue pill might do the trick. *To go. To see. To experience.* Enough of that. *Get thee to a nunnery,* she thought. To a cathedral of pharmaceutical revelation.

John Calhoun had driven her in silence to Cairo International at three that morning. He'd been quite the gentleman, carrying her bag for her and talking for her at the check-in desk, gathering the boarding pass and walking her all the way to security, where she was scanned. Appropriately, she set off an alarm, but it turned out to be only a hair clip left in a hidden pocket of Fouada Halawi's dress.

On the other side, she looked back to see John Calhoun, massive in the crowd, still watching, a phone to his ear, reporting her successful exit. Then, as she wandered to the gate, she saw Omar's young man, Sayyid, waiting at her gate, hanging up his phone. He smiled at her but didn't kiss her cheeks as he'd done with Fouada. After what they'd been through, this was a disappointment.

He asked how she was feeling and told her what her gates would be in Amsterdam. When she asked after Fouada, he shrugged. "She is good. She says you can keep the dress."

"Thank her for me."

"You must be looking forward to getting home," he said.

This confused her, though it shouldn't have, and she ended up using a cliché to express herself: "I don't know where home is anymore."

"It's with your family," Sayyid said matter-of-factly. It was so obvious. He frowned at her stupidity.

As she broke through the Boston crowd, it occurred to her that she might have dreamed the boy who had been watching her. That didn't seem out of order. She turned, scanning the crowd, but he wasn't there. Had he been, she might have marched over to him and told him that he wasn't real. No, he wasn't, but she was. She wanted to tell someone. Someone should know that Sophie Kohl was real now.

When she continued forward, though, she spotted three men in suits walking briskly in her direction. One still wore his sunglasses, while the other two—one young, one old, all three so white that they were pink—homed in on her. "Mrs. Kohl," said the older one. "I'm sorry—we were running late."

She stopped, the three men forming an arc around her, just in case she made a run for it. Were *they* real?

The one who spoke took out an FBI badge. It looked just like the one Michael Khalil had shown her. His name was Wallace Stevens, just like the poet. "When you're rested, we'd like to ask you some questions. Is that all right?"

Questions. They had questions for her, but standing in the desert, only yesterday morning, she hadn't had any at all. When she'd looked down at the heavy, sweating man tied to the chair, shaking his head yet *smiling,* so many questions had been blazing through her, but she'd only asked one: *This is him?* Omar said yes. Then, like Emmett twenty years ago, resolve took over, and she knew precisely what was required of her. Lips pressed tight together, she raised the gun and fired once. Her ears rang as the man screamed and shivered. She shot him once more and then let the pistol drop into the sand just before she dropped as well, weeping, all control gone. Sayyid helped carry her back to the car.

"Okay," she said to Wallace Stevens, no more than a whisper.

"We've got you a room at the Hyatt. I hope that's all right."

It occurred to her that she hadn't thought to reserve a room. Just getting back had felt like enough.

The one with the sunglasses offered to take her bag, and she let him. As she left the airport with her full contingent and they headed toward a Ford Explorer—black, of course—Wallace Stevens said, "I don't know if you've made plans, but tomorrow, after the interview, we can set you up with a lawyer."

"Lawyer?" she said. Christ, they already knew how real she was, and she'd just *given* herself to them! "Why do I need a lawyer?"

"Oh!" Wallace Stevens said, embarrassed. "Not that kind. I mean, an estate lawyer, to discuss your husband's finances, offer advice. That sort of thing."

She relaxed, but only a little, for he had to have noticed her panic, and the cop part of his brain must have gleaned that she was covering up something. By morning, she was suddenly sure, she would be in a jail cell.

Yet in the back of the Explorer, he only said, "I forget myself sometimes. You've been through a lot. I should have been clearer. I'm just trying to help."

He reminded her of Gerry Davis. Forward-looking, all about the future. All she wanted was to listen to his soothing voice tell her what tomorrow was going to be like.

Then they were riding down the highway and through busy

streets. It was overcast and beautiful in a way that Cairo never could be. It was Emmett's city, and in this town they had met at a keg party more than twenty years ago, him slender and intense and, almost from the start, completely in love with her. Then they saw the world together.

What else could anyone ask for?

Wallace Stevens noticed her smile. "Something funny?" He asked it in a way that suggested he could use a good joke.

She shook her head, but the smile wouldn't go away. "Just thinking about my husband."

"I heard he was a good man."

"Yes," she said. "No worse than most good men."

He rocked his head from side to side, and there was something childlike in that movement, something that made her realize that she could do this. She had murdered a man in the desert, but no one here knew about that. Or if they knew, they didn't care. They were taking care of a woman who had never stepped foot in America before, and her name was Sofia.

What would Emmett think of this new woman? Would he find her alluring? Would Stan still find her so appetizing? Her poor dead lovers.

She relaxed. Her back and shoulders tingled. Then she began to laugh involuntarily.

"Are you okay?" asked Wallace Stevens. "You need something to drink?"

She shook her head, covering her mouth, the full, sudden release of years of anxiety nearly gutting her, for what was left? Was anything left now that she had followed her life to its inevitable climax?

She looked at Wallace Stevens. He seemed very kind, but what did she know? She said, "The only emperor is the emperor of ice-cream."

He cracked a smile, bashful, but pleased by the recognition of his namesake.

What was left once it all ended?

Everything.

2

Omar immediately regretted having accepted Harold Wolcott's suggestion of a meeting in the Marriott's Garden Promenade restaurant. The busy dinner crowd was noisy, and to his right a big table full of laughing Americans made him long for a quiet rooftop dinner with Fouada. But such were the responsibilities of administration.

Wolcott was in the rear corner, drinking a gin and tonic—Omar knew from the file that it was the man's only drink—and when they shook hands he felt a thin, sticky layer of moisture on Wolcott's hand. He'd probably spilled some tonic. Omar ordered coffee.

It had been a day and a half since the execution of Ali Busiri, though in the office they were calling it a disappearance. Without a body, what else could they call it? Central Security agents were turning over stones throughout the city, and when he wasn't found, probably by Friday, Omar would lead an investigation. This was how it was done, for as the new section head it would be his responsibility to clean up any possible embarrassments from the previous administration. This was also why he had agreed to meet Wolcott.

"They're a film crew," Wolcott told him, nodding at the loud Americans. "Scouting locations for some kind of romantic comedy. Exotic location, some big stars, and you've got a hit."

"Good for them," said Omar.

"Sophie Kohl should be landing about now."

Omar nodded. Sayyid had helped her onto the plane and phoned in as soon as it took off. "And John Calhoun? How is he?"

"Good," said Wolcott. "Giving him a few days off, but he'll be back soon enough. Good guy. I like him."

Omar had no opinion of the man, but he filed away Wolcott's opinion; it was inside information. Just as he had filed away Jibril's precious notebook, though he had no intention of ever using it. This was how he would have to think from now on—collect everything, no matter how insignificant. He would be a hoarder of intelligence, just as Ali Busiri had been. Information was the only true currency, impervious to economic crashes, natural disasters, and even revolution. "Calhoun is a contractor, though. No?"

"Sure. But I think I'll ask to extend his contract. Not many guys around who know how to keep their mouths shut."

"It is a valuable talent."

"Indeed," Wolcott said. He reached for his cigarettes and offered one—Omar refused—before lighting up. "Are you going to tell me anything, or am I just buying you coffee?"

"Why don't you ask some questions?"

Wolcott took another drag, a hard one that made the end of his cigarette glow fiercely. "How about who killed Stan? That's something I'd damned well like to know."

"We are looking into it. We believe, however, that Ali Busiri ordered the killing, just as he ordered the murder of Emmett Kohl. The gunman, for all we know, was the same."

"Gjergj Ahmeti?"

Omar shrugged.

"He came to Cairo?"

"This is a guess. Does it matter who the gunman was?"

Wolcott's forehead creased. He wasn't particularly good at masking his emotions. "It does to me."

"As soon as I know," Omar promised.

There was a pause. Omar gave the Americans a look—a pretty blond girl was standing, holding up a glass of wine, making a toast.

Wolcott puffed at his cigarette, finally saying, "Look, Omar. I don't like these games. I want a little clarity. What I've got is a nasty stew of names. Emmett and Stan and old Ali. Sophie Kohl and Jibril Aziz are in the mix, too. Connect the dots for me."

He didn't have to tell this man anything. He could set down his cup and leave, and all Wolcott could do was file a complaint. With a military government in place, there was little chance of trouble. But he'd lived much of his life in Harold Wolcott's shoes, pushing around chess pieces without being able to see the other player's, living with only half-stories to shape his view of the universe. It could be maddening, and there was nothing more troublesome than a CIA station chief who'd gone over the edge.

"I can tell you this," Omar said, and watched Wolcott lower his cigarette, alert. "Ali Busiri was to blame for all of it. Sometimes directly, sometimes indirectly. But he was always behind the scenes. It's the oldest story. At first, money. Then survival. The things we all want, but Ali—he lost his moral compass."

And I would have killed more, Busiri had insisted under that wide, wind-rippled canvas. *Ten people. Twenty. Imagine what this new government would do with me if they found out I'd been selling intelligence to yet another North African dictator. Given the chance, though, anyone would have done the same thing. Even you, Omar.*

Wolcott was still grumbling. He wanted more, but Omar wasn't about to give him the rest. He wasn't going to tell Wolcott that Sophie Kohl had been their agent, and that so many of her husband's secrets had made it from Cairo to Tripoli.

If you want to blame someone, Busiri had said, *blame Muammar Gadhafi. When the troubles began in Benghazi, he remembered Stumbler, and so he sent his men to execute them all. Jibril got it backwards, of course—you told me that. You told me everything, Omar. Remember?*

So you warned Tripoli that he was coming.

My Libyan friends deserved some warning. That's only fair. Right?

They must have paid you well, Ali.

Oh, they did. And you're not going to find a single pound of it.

Ali Busiri had been working on another plane of existence, as if last year were still this year. But he had been wrong.

Using Sophie Kohl had been a rash decision, but in the new year, he had come to believe, wrongs should be righted in the correct way, according to a higher law. He'd had no idea how religious he could be. He had surprised himself. And she had surprised him when she climbed out of the car and accepted Mahmoud's pistol and walked with them to the tent. Ali Busiri, shaking his head and on the verge of laughing aloud, wriggled in the chair. A woman with a gun? he seemed to be saying. This is how you try to scare me?

This is him? Sophie had asked.

Yes.

Poor Ali hadn't seen it coming. He'd still been shaking his head, the disbelieving laughter bubbling before the explosion and the shot into his guts that rocked the chair back onto two feet, where it and Ali hovered, nearly falling, before dropping heavily back onto all four.

He'd screamed then. A pitiful, high-pitched scream, almost feminine, then blubbering moans. It hurt to see anyone in so much pain. Sophie Kohl was not a professional. She didn't know how to do this quickly. She just stood and stared, shocked by what she'd done, stunned by the noise of his misery. He'd been about to rip the gun from her hand and finish the job himself when she silently raised the gun and pointed it at the top of Ali's bald skull and pulled the trigger again, the pistol bouncing high. As the noise faded in their ears, she dropped the gun into sand that was muddy from all the spilled blood, then crumpled, weeping.

"I don't buy it," Wolcott said. "You're saying this was all about one guy's *greed*?"

"Yes."

"I mean . . ." Wolcott shook his head. "Where is he now?"

Omar shrugged. "Disappeared. In the desert, for all I know."

"What does his wife say?"

Omar shifted, but tried to show no other sign. Mrs. Busiri had been a problem, watching her husband head off in Omar's car. Had he known what he was going to do when he picked up Ali, he would have done differently. "She knows nothing. Like a lot of men, he kept his wife in the dark."

In fact, after this meeting he would visit her once again to settle his offer. He was lucky that she had despised her husband, but Mrs. Busiri's cooperation would still be expensive.

"Wait, wait," Wolcott said, patting the air with a hand. He really wasn't taking any of this well. "Busiri hires Ahmeti. But it's not like he's calling up the guy for a chat. It's not *done* that way. He had to have at least one accomplice. Another one of your men?"

"Nobody."

"Nobody, or *a* nobody?"

Add your bullets to his body, he had told Rashid. *You shoot this corpse, and we begin our relationship anew.* Omar hadn't wanted to lose someone so valuable, someone who could help to clean up what Ali had left behind. Rashid was that rarest of creatures—a loyal monster. He had stuck with Ali until the very end, and with this act of mercy Omar hoped to gain the beast's devotion.

He gave Wolcott a smile. "Harry, Egypt's friendship with the United States of America remains crucial. Once all the facts have come to light, I will give you a copy of the report. You will know all."

Harold Wolcott's face darkened. He looked past Omar at the film crew—the whole table was singing "Happy Birthday." Then he focused on Omar again. "You're not giving me shit, are you?"

Omar didn't answer.

Wolcott put out his cigarette, drained his glass, and stood up. "You can pay for the goddam drinks yourself," he said, then walked out.

3

—

Again, she was late. He had been waiting a full twenty minutes in Steaks, dressed better than before. He'd been given the week off, and he'd spent his first free day once again cleaning his apartment. He'd taken out a fine suit that he'd kept covered in thin plastic in the back of his closet. He had showered twice that day—once after taking Sophie Kohl to the airport in the morning, again before dressing to come here—and was by now in perfect shape. At least, in as perfect shape as John Calhoun would ever be. After class, he would meet Maribeth at Deals, and they would see how that went.

The aroma of grilling meats made him light-headed, so to quell his stomach he ordered a beer. As he took his first sip, he remembered what Harry had said yesterday, after he'd brought Sophie Kohl back to his home.

Don't jump to conclusions, John. You may think you understand what's happened, but you're just a bit player. So am I. Hell, maybe everyone is, and there is no lead in this play. Only the Egyptians can put it all together—that, I'm sure of. I doubt they'll give me the whole story, but they have to give us something. Stan's dead, for Christ's sake.

John had agreed with that—a bit player was all he wanted to be. It was how you stayed alive.

Or was it? How much had Stan known? How about Jibril? The

truth, which gnawed at him as he tried to enjoy his beer, was that it didn't matter how much he knew—what mattered was how much other people *thought* he knew.

He was halfway through his beer when Mrs. Abusir showed up, her long skirts fluttering as she approached. He put down his glass and stood to shake her hand. Her smile lit up the room.

She was in a delightful mood, though he began to despair of ever perfecting her English, yet he tried. When she said, "I seen a wonderful film on the Martin Luther King Jr.," he replied. "I have seen a wonderful film about Martin Luther King Jr. You don't put 'the' before someone's name."

A shade of her excitement slipped away. "Yes, exactly." Then it was back, for she believed that by watching the hardships suffered by midcentury African Americans in Selma, Birmingham, and Albany, she had gained new insights into her English teacher. John found this relentlessly charming, and let most of her awkward sentences slide by unnoticed. She gazed at him with eyes full of sorrow, as if he had been lynched by Klansmen only last week.

He was basking in this great wave of sympathy when, looking past her and through the large window, he saw a man loitering on the sidewalk. A tall man who looked Egyptian but spoke like an American. Who claimed to be FBI, but was not.

"What I have saw was terrible," Mrs. Abusir said, her English breaking down with her emotion. "How does your people cope?"

"What I saw was terrible," John corrected, though from the look on her face he knew that she hadn't understood his meaning. She nodded heavily, eyes so sad, and reached over to cover his hand with hers. John's hand was cold, and because hers was so warm he didn't bother setting her straight.